Harbored Secrets

Marie F Martin

4D Publishing

ACKNOWLEDGMENTS

I am grateful to my critique group: Debbie Burk, Cindy Dyson, Angela Townsend, Dixon Rice, Ann Coleman and Jake How for their encouragement and hours of reading with a red pencil in hand. From them, I learned how to put words on paper.

My gratitude also goes to Ron Glick for his technical support of uploading to Create Space and Kindle.

Also, I would like to thank Mary Jo Christiansen, Carol Connor, Marge Bakshas Gravelle and Sharon Stratton for their hours of proofreading. And, lastly, my thanks to my golfing buddies for listening to my plotlines over and over as we played.

Table of Contents

Chapter 1

To me, it was just my life. I never dreamed it was a tale of longings and betrayal, a legacy that unfolded with all the complexities of a Byzantine conspiracy. I should have known. Even as a small girl, I should have connected the whispers and snippets of intrigue, but didn't. Not until my father's second wife tossed a cache of poems on my lap and left me to read lonesome words that broke the heart. Why Alice chose to share them, I don't pretend to understand. A momentary weakness on her part? Perhaps. And yet, a puzzle still remains in an odd look, a dropped sentence, or a simple turn of her head; they all indicate something lurking in the past.

Years of working alongside her on my father's spread tempered me, and slowly I had accepted her secretive ways. So much so, that a barrier formed between my hurtful memories and living from day to day. Then quite suddenly, the urge to leave and build for myself grabbed hold and I couldn't shake the need. Why I finally reached that point of *enough* remains unanswerable.

Today, May 1, 1982, I parked my battered Ford pickup near a rise on the acres of Montana prairie I had purchased to build a home. I unloaded a bundle of survey stakes and a short-handled maul and carried them to the top of the rise.

The markers still in my arms, I eased down onto the solid prairie floor. I set the maul and stakes aside to make sure this was right -- the exact right spot. Too much depended on it. I crossed my ankles and pulled my feet close to my crotch, then removed my ratty old hat and nestled the brim under my thigh. I bent my face toward the dirt – sage, dust, sunburned grass and earth smell. Ants scurried out of reach. I scanned along the ground searching for their source of food. A gauzy web spun through the grass. A dead horse fly was caught in the filament and hung between the blades, a true sampling of prairie life. The kind I was seeking. This was it. The very place I'd sink the southwest corner of my foundation.

Wind played with my dangling hair in a peaceful sort of way. Some days the wind was a friend; others it drove the mind wild. I'd build strong walls to hold against those invisible currents, varmints and unwanted guests. I was alone, chose to be and demanded it, for this building would complete my cycle of life. The years to this moment stretched long, yet seemed short, sometimes cruel or kind, but never the way I wanted. This house would be me.

I bent deeper in supplication, slipping to the place where I dissolved nightmare images of fire, of my father's hands burned like spit-roasted pig, of my mother's face stretched in dead leather skin and of a bone that might be my baby brother's.

"Blanche! What are you doing?"

I jerked up, heart-pounding, cold sweat immediately on my brow. I glared at Alice, angry that she surprised me and disgusted I hadn't heard her arrive.

She glared back. "Don't look at me like that. I didn't sneak up on you, even honked the dang horn. Three times." She puffed out her chest, daring me to argue as she pointed back toward her pearl-white Lincoln Continental parked in the shade of my pickup. The car was a rancher's favorite, big and expensive. She wore a cotton house dress, nylons, riding boots and a quilted work jacket. White shoulder-length hair gleamed in the sun, and sunglasses were perched on her proud, angular nose.

"I figured you'd be here." She tried to sound pleasant. She didn't.

I stuffed my hat on my tangled hair, grabbed the maul and one of the stakes. "I need to build this," I said and knelt to set the first marker.

Alice stood over me and removed the sunglasses. Her cornflower blue eyes searched mine. "And I'm ready to help, but—"

"Don't have to," I cut in.

A pout touched her bottom lip. "But only if you want me to."

I rested back on my heels, knees digging into the dirt, the coarseness of the gritty surface bit even through my jeans. I couldn't remember her ever thinking of my wants, and doubted her. The offered help was just an excuse for coming. "Only if you will make peace with my decision." I meant it.

The depth in Alice's eyes changed, hard and maybe fearful. She was afraid.

A wind from the north strengthened, turned raw and shoved against us. I leaned into it. She drew her jacket tighter around her neck.

"Alice, I am being selfish. I know that, but can't you understand?"

Her eyebrows rose. "No. And you should know that."

I did, but had hoped she'd accept my leaving the ranch, hoped for a real truce between us instead of the guarded acceptance we had endured for decades. She snuffled from the chill, pulled out a lace-trimmed hankie and honked into it like an old rancher with blocked sinuses. After carefully folding the cloth, she stuffed it into the cuff of her sleeve.

"You're such a contradiction," I said.

Alice's eyes sparkled, proud at being contrary. "And you're an enigma." Haughtiness colored her words in the way I'd grown accustomed to. "Now set those blasted stakes before we freeze."

I carefully parted a clump of the gray-green grass and placed a survey marker into its center. Holding the stake straight,

I struck with a maul. The crust of prairie silt yielded, breaking apart enough to allow the pointed end to penetrate down through the roots. This parting was for my dream, a division between me and the past, my own personal place. The south corner of my house was set. I raised my fist and whooped. Tears smarted as I laughed.

I quickly marked off forty feet and set another stake. Alice huddled beside the first marker, arms crossed, and hands tucked into her sleeves.

"Aren't you going to tie the twine?" I asked, taken aback by her sad expression. I expected a fight about my leaving, or maybe a show of gladness – not this rarely seen emotion. Alice never showed sadness or regret.

She dropped the roll twice. Spouting choice words, she finally wrapped the string around the stake, knotted it and dusted off her hands. "That's it. It's too cold for my fingers. And you're too stubborn to be so happy. It's just marking a foundation you don't need any more than I need frozen joints." She reverted so quickly to nagging, it stiffened my spine.

"I never asked for your help," I said evenly.

Muttering something I couldn't hear, she unrolled the twine, letting it drop in a wavy line between the grasses and prickly pear as she walked toward me. She tossed the roll at my feet and tucked her red fingers into her pockets. "Buying this place was unnecessary. I told you I'd give you the west field. Even the cows know you've earned it."

"I want a fresh start on land I chose and paid for." I waited, hoping. The azure of her eyes sparked anger as bright as when we first tangled in childhood. For a moment, I thought she might finally accept my moving from the ranch.

She wiped her finger under her wind-raw nose. "Not that you'd care, but my back is killing me, and I've seen enough of your bent-over old butt in tight jeans." She stalked toward her car, ample hips swaying under her house dress, white hair blowing in the ever-present wind. She hiked up her hem and slid into her Lincoln.

"I'm in the prime of my life," I yelled. "And my bottom isn't any bigger than it used to be and my jeans are loose." I shook the denim at thigh level.

"From the angle I just witnessed, you're old and fat." She slammed the car door, fired the engine, looked back at me and cut the motor. She got out and leaned against the fender, chewing on the corner of her lip, and squinting against the sun. "I talked to Odette yesterday, she said.

So the real reason for the visit was out in the open – my younger sister again. "What did she want?"

"Not a thing. I phoned her, but you need to. She's depressed again. The shrink says she's still blocking out the past. Talk to her. Help her remember."

Alice got back into her car and finger waved as she drove down the gravel road. Dust blew up behind the car and drifted south. Both the dust and Alice headed toward the Didier Platt Ranch, the place where I had my beginnings in a tiny homestead shack. Now, forty-seven years later, my father's spread teemed with registered Black Angus, alfalfa and wheat fields, and solid, long-lasting buildings.

The dust of Alice's leaving dwindled and faded. Blast her. She nagged about what I had no control over and always left me worrying about things best forgotten; and she did it on purpose. Just like she withheld things. She did that the same way the prairie guards secrets in low-slung shadows, protecting, giving up only when sunrise seeps through the umbra. I'd like to search the dark recesses of her mind, illuminate them with a good shake, and see what my father had told her. He always refused to talk with me, but he trusted her in a way he never did my mother, my sister, or me. Why was the question? The bigger mystery was Alice's affection for him. I had watched for the answer to that, seeing mostly greed for land and wealth.

I took off my hat and ruffled my hair. The restless wind brushed through my curls. I faced the raw currents again, giving myself a chance to turn from worry. A gust blew sable strands into my eyes. As I pulled them from my face, I noticed more silver. I was becoming gray, and I wasn't ready. Energy and strength still pumped through me. I was tough and crusty, and liked it that way. It was time to build my house and not hassle about what Alice wanted.

I couldn't remember when the urge to have a house totally and completely mine first took hold, but it had. And now at long last, I held the deed to a half section of short grass prairie. I scooped up a handful of dirt and let the grains shift through my fingers. They spoke of fertility: simply plow, sow and reap, sink yourself into the terra firma and hold on against drought, blizzards, and loneliness, set your shoulder into the wind, brace against the constant force pouring down from the Rocky Mountains or sweeping in from the Canadian north, and adapt by growing a thick skin and a driven attitude.

And this is where I chose to build a house out of brick, the most permanent of building materials. Mortar and brick. Solid and long-lasting. It would overlook Sage Creek in a land so ample it encompassed thousands of ranches. Many descendants left the harsh plains, the loneliness, the extreme weather. But to me, the fertile fields of sun-ripened wheat, the broad flat lands where cattle wandered from one short grass clump to another, the vast skyline meeting the edge of nowhere held the beauty of life. It was the only place I desired to be after my forced exile, and then after my self-imposed exile.

Whispers of my past appeared out across the landscape in the constant motion of the living prairie. Honey bees droned near sweet clover, green grasshoppers nibbled on ankle-deep wheat, and barn swallows feasted on air-born insects. I breathed in the tang of sage until I almost saw my mother dancing with the waving grass, and I truly wished she could have found the peace that eluded her.

I dropped the maul handle, rubbed a faint scar on my index finger, gathered up the roll of jute twine and wandered over to the stack of cement bags to rest for a minute. My back hurt. I rolled my stiff shoulders and rotated my neck in an effort to relax them. Maybe I was too old to build this house.

The powdery clay inside the bag shifted under my weight. I settled into it with a sigh and slowly unrolled another forty-feet of twine, which fell at my feet in the same convoluted way the history of my family unfolded. Some truths came softly like dawn's rose blush. Others arrived brazen, piercing harshly like the molten rays of high noon. My thoughts slipped. I shook my head to stop a memory, then I gave in to the image, needing to remember how sharp and clear that day arrived, remember why we Platts broke, remember the reasons laid in a pile of ashes before the sun had set.

~~~~~

On September 2, 1935, the day of my eighth birthday, I ducked my eyes from the blinding arc of the coming sun and stole across the farmyard as quietly as could be. Holding my breath, I squinted at the weathered chicken coop. The Leghorn rooster still slept atop the slanted roof, guarding his flock of hens. Any second he would rise up, puff out his proud breast, and crow to wake up Sadie, the meanest hen ever to lay eggs. He stretched up onto his feet. Oh no. Once again, I had dawdled too long. His call sailed throughout the Platt homestead. I checked back toward our whitewashed house. *Maman* wasn't watching. Relieved, I held the egg basket high, scurried the last few yards to the coop, and eased open the door, still trying to be quiet, still hoping to sneak up on Sadie.

The stink of chicken droppings thickened the air, but not a feather on a hen ruffled. These old biddies needed more than one crowing to loosen their feathered breasts from freshly laid eggs. I tiptoed to the first roost and inched my hand toward the soft underbelly. Please let this be the morning that Sadie would give up her egg with a simple raising of her drumstick.

The vicious hen's eyelid popped open and the haughty eye dared me to try. I glared back and snatched for the egg. Sadie struck. I jerked back. Pain shot through my index finger and blood welled near the quick of my fingernail.

"Double *dang* you, Sadie!" I quickly poked my finger in my mouth and gagged. The metallic taste of blood clung to the back of my throat even after I spat on the floor. Blood pooled around the edge of my fingernail again. Dangling my hand away from the front of my only dress that still fit, I plopped the egg basket down on the straw-covered floor and shoved open the coop's loose door. Rusty hinges rasped. I purposely worked the door a couple of times to send Sadie into a frenzy of squawks and flutters.

The cock charged. I dodged him and ran for the house that *Maman* always called the *Shanty*. When I asked her why she never called it home, she murmured in a bittersweet way, "A person can only have one true home." My mother's heart belonged a half continent and an ocean away in my *grandmère's* French vineyard. I couldn't remember the French Alps or the vineyards. Faint sensations of crossing an ocean might only be reminders from talk between my parents about their homeland. Sometimes I felt vague listings under my feet, like a ship at sea, but wasn't sure. Father's holdings, the mercantile in Goldstone, and the one-room schoolhouse on the Bromwell's front section were what I knew.

I was about halfway to the coop when *Papa* called though the wide barn door, "Haven't you collected the eggs yet?" He set down a feed bucket inside the barn door, grabbed his gloves from a hip pocket and walked across the barnyard. My little sister scampered by his long leg. He was tall, rail thin and wore overalls with a plaid cotton shirt stained with yesterday's sweat and field grime. Brown hair hung over his ears, face narrow and scratchy; he wouldn't shave until after supper. He claimed old men shave in the morning and young men shave in the evening, then he'd hug *Maman* and rub his smooth chin on her neck. She used to laugh. Not anymore. Not since the new baby.

Four people spent my affections: *Papa*, *Maman*, Odette, and *Bébé* Larry. Most of all I looked up to my father, even though he never had much to say except about chores. He knew how to raise crops.

I held up my bloody finger. "I got pecked bad."

"The west field is ripe, and I need you to drive the tractor. Your mother says she can't do it."

Terror and eagerness rose in me like twin corn stalks breaking the ground to breathe air. Ever since the big John Deere tractor had been delivered, I secretly wished to work the harvest instead of staying indoors to tend three-year-old Odette and the baby. Wind tugging at my straw hat and the sun warming my toes was far better than dirty diapers and playing dolls. This was my chance to pull the odd-looking combine with the strange name of McCormick-Deering painted on it, and my chance to prove I was big enough for farming.

Now that I finally had the chance, I was flat *dang* scared.

Papa frowned. "Did you hear me?"

"I don't know if I can."

"There's no choice. Hired help takes money. Boy or not, harvest is a hard time for your mother to have a baby."

I gasped, hoping *Maman* never heard *Papa* say such a thing. Bad enough that Odette had overheard. She always tagged after him, sticking closer than a kitten to its milk plate and she had understood his meaning. She stared at him, appearing fairylike, with pale skin, wild black hair and questioning violet eyes.

Papa ignored her and stuffed a hand into a glove. "Listen Blinny. Crops won't wait. It's time you broke into doing real chores. Now, go have your mother bandage your finger, then get your hat and boots." He turned quickly and tangled up with Odette. She fell to the ground. Whimpering, she reached up her arms, wanting him to draw her up into his.

"Damn it, I don't have time for this. Go pester your mother." With a look between anger and remorse, he sidestepped Odette and strode toward the old farm truck.

I lifted Odette onto her feet. "Wipe your tears. *Papa*'s just worried. Come on, Maman's lonesome."

Her eyebrows drew together. She wanted to stomp and scream, but she spun and ran toward the safety of the house.

I barged into the kitchen, blood spilling from the end of my finger. "Sadie really got me this time."

My mother rocked in her squeaky chair beside the window with the good light, nudging a burp from *Bébé* Larry. "Wash it out with the lye soap." A French accent covered her English before she slid into the French she preferred. "I'll wrap it *dans une minute.*" For the first time since the baby's arrival, she appeared less haggard. A look of delicate peacefulness softened the lines around her mouth and eyes. "Blinny, when we're alone, let's speak only French. I don't care what your father says. I refuse to watch you lose your heritage in this God-forsaken land."

My worried spirits rose and matched the same secret defiance as hers. *Maman* instead of Mother was definitely better. *Papa*, my special secret name for him, was far more lyrical than Dad.

"*Papa* wants me to drive the tractor and he's in a hurry."

Maman sighed. "He always is." She tucked *Bébé* Larry into the wooden cradle next to her feet, stood, and brushed back frizzy strands of raven hair. Her flour-sack dress hung so loosely the pattern of faded yellow roses drooped. Her apron was tied extra tight, and her arms were too thin. If only she could get enough rest to put meat back on her bones and bring back her laughter. Since the baby's birth gradual changes in my mother concerned me in a way that walked around the edges of thought. A prick here, a nudge there, nothing to help me figure out why her smiles lessened, then vanished. The strain of birthing my brother? No, even before that. Somehow, as the baby swelled inside, she had grown more moody, talking mostly of her homeland, complaining that my father had taken her from a land ripe with grapes and filled with wine.

I couldn't help asking, "Are you done having babies now?"

"Would you deny your father another son?"

How could I answer? The hours of pain and blood I saw at the birthing still flowed and stank in my dreams, an image far worse than when *Aimèe* had her kittens, or when one of the cows dropped a calf.

"Blinny, I pushed you into the world eight years ago today. Are you sorry about that?" *Maman* had a way of piling on guilt, but soothed it by remembering my birthday. She touched my cheek; fingers cool against my skin. She always pressed hard enough to leave the memory of the touch, yet soft enough to show her love. "Don't forget, Blinny Platt, you were born a *petite-fille* to a vintner in the gentle valley of Lorraine. The French Alps know how to cradle a farm. Just like your *grandpapa* knew how to care for his grapevines and children. He understood the time it takes to grow."

Maman's words soaked into me like water into the parched prairie, but I needed to hurry. "*Papa*'s waiting." I hated rushing her. She was always busy. The baby came first, and any of her leftover moments belonged to Odette. Reassurance was the excuse, but Odette was her favorite. They mirrored each other -- delicate, wispy, sensitive. Something I'd never be. My character tended to question most things and my true feelings lay hidden behind a blunt tongue. I wondered which of my ancestors I would reflect.

Maman nudged my shoulder. "Go help our father, and I'm sorry you have a sore finger."

"I hate that mean old hen."

"You're smarter than a *poule*. Now run along."

I knew better than to fuss any more about Sadie and let the screen door bang shut. I grabbed my straw hat from a row of penny nails by the back door and my brogans from the stoop. Holding my hat on my head with one hand and clutching the shoes with the other, I ran from the porch.

Maman called, "I'll cook anything we have for your birthday supper. What's your pick?"

I turned back. "Sadie stew."

"*Papa* would have a *crise de colère*."

Picturing his fit, I dared to say, "You said anything."

"I don't have time for your *toupet*."

I shut my sassy mouth as *Papa* honked the horn. I dashed for the dented farm truck, scrambled up into the cab and slid onto the cracked leather seat. The inside smelled of gasoline and *Papa*'s sweat. Dust caked the dashboard. The gearshift vibrated with the engine's chugs. The door slammed shut on the second try, and I sat up tall.

I wiggled with excitement. "Old enough to drive is a *bonne* birthday present."

"Watch your English!"

My cheeks warmed. Why couldn't I stop my French around *Papa*? I stuffed my feet into the tight brogan, toes pinching as I drew up the laces and tied a knot. *Papa* promised to buy new ones after the harvest. I needed them, so did Odette. *Maman* said hers would last one more year. I doubted that.

The truck rumbled and bounced down narrow twin ruts that cut through a pasture. Wild aster, lupine, and sunflower blooms hung faded under the blistering sun. Prickly-pear cacti grew near clumps of Russian-thistle. The cacti full and thorny held on in the heat, but the thistle dried and tumbled into barbed wire fences and remained captured until a ground blizzard tore them free to run at the whim of the air currents. The Montana land was harsh. Mule deer stole hay, mice invaded granaries, and horseflies clustered on anything warm-blooded.

And my father was proud to own these sections. He told me time and again, "Blinny, we aren't beholden to a living soul and never will be again." Last year, he had pulled out one of his wheat plants in the west field and had shown me the roots. "This plant grew because it had the good sense to sink itself deep into rich soil. Our soil. Don't forget it."

I hadn't. His same pride lived in my character, alongside my sharp tongue and nosy curiosity. I added to my pride that day when I sat on the big tractor and drove it in the heat and dust.

The farm truck rumbled and bounced down narrow twin ruts that cut through a pasture. The truck groaned to a stop at the west field, and I hopped out to open the wire-and-post gate. I tried shoving the wire loop over the top of the gatepost, but didn't have the strength to squeeze the two posts together. And *Papa* was watching. I stepped back and took a look. There had to be more than one way to open a gate. I finally shoved up hard on the post. It just cleared the lower wire, and I let the awkward snaky gate drop free. I yanked it out of the way.

Papa shifted gears. They grated loudly. No matter how far he pushed the clutch in or if he doubled-clutched, the worn-out gearbox still squealed. The truck bounced through the opening, and I fought the gate back into position and hooked the wire back up over the post.

Ripe durum wheat stretched across twenty acres. The fat bearded heads waved proudly against a westerly breeze, as if they knew they made the finest spaghetti and macaroni in the world. Or so *Papa* claimed. I didn't doubt him.

Fear squeezed my shoulders like a cold snake coiling around a warm rock. I shivered. What if I couldn't drive the tractor? Selling the golden wheat was all the money we'd earn for a whole year, except for calves. If I failed, *Papa* would have to make *Maman* leave the house and work the harvest. He'd have to. *Maman* couldn't take staying out in the sun all day. Her milk would dry up. She was already feeding Larry thin cereal so he wouldn't cry so much.

Across four swaths of sharp wheat stubble sat the massive tractor with the huge combine already coupled by drawbar and pulley. The day it had been delivered, *Papa* gave me one trip around the barnyard. I gloried in riding high, looking down at Odette, proud that the Platts owned such a machine. How could I drive it through *Papa*'s wheat in straight swaths like he did?

I swallowed my fear and strode forward. The dry stubble poked and cracked under the soles of my boots. The sharp spears would've shredded my bare feet. Thankful for the too tight boots, I walked right up to the tractor as if I wasn't one bit scared.

The upright exhaust stack and skeletal back wheels with deep-gripping steel cleats towered above me. I was big for my age, bigger than both my classmates, big enough to be teased about it until I whacked one of them, but I felt very small standing in the shadow of this monster.

Papa helped me climb aboard, showed me how to turn it on, and disappeared in front of the tractor's long nose. I hoisted myself up onto the sun-hot metal seat and immediately jumped off. Holding the skirt of my dress in place, I gingerly sat down and squirmed until the heat eased. I scooted forward, pushed in the clutch and grabbed the steering wheel of Queen Mab's dragon.

Metal banged against metal, *Papa* grunted, then cursed. "Turn 'er on!" he yelled.

I quickly pushed the starter. The engine choked once and died. Seven hiccups and one belch later, the pistons struggled, missed a beat, then chugged into uncertain life, working a combination of steel parts to produce an awesome power. The tractor vibrated, and the flap on the tall exhaust stack rapped a cadence like a tin drum.

I licked sweat from my upper lip and prayed the engine wouldn't die when I let out the clutch.

Papa hurried to the combine and climbed onto the seat. He jammed a lever forward. "Now!" he yelled.

I tugged my hat down, grabbed the steering wheel with both hands, eased up on the clutch, and pushed the gas pedal. The cleated wheels dug into the soil. The nose was already pointed toward the end of the field. Holding the steering wheel steady, I fed just enough gas to keep moving. The tractor dug its way through the disk-rutted field.

"Faster," yelled *Papa*. Dust flew up and carried on the wind along with the gray smoke from the stack.

The sun beat down. Sweat tickled under my hat. I needed to drink, to pee, to relax my knuckles, none of which mattered. *Papa*'s wheat was getting cut. Pride crept into my thoughts. I fought it back. Pride came before a fall and I sure didn't want to fall. This was the one thing I could do for *Maman*.

Bull snakes slithered out of the way. A rattler coiled and struck at the front of the tractor. A cleat caught it, pulled it under and crushed it under the wheel. A gray-backed jackrabbit dodged and disappeared in an instant. I was glad the poisonous snake had met his maker, but gladder yet that the rabbit had escaped.

My hands and arms numbed from the constant vibration, and my sore finger throbbed. The hard seat dug into my legs, but I didn't dare slide back from the edge. At the end of the row, I forced the steering wheel to the right and managed not to tip the tractor over. Pridefully relieved, I dared to glance behind.

Papa worked the combine. The swather swished and sucked up the wheat in a constant *swoop, boom, swoop, boom*. The thresher pounded the wheat kernels from the stalks, then a conveyor belt carried the grain to an overhead hopper. The straw dropped to the ground, to be raked later into high golden stacks. The *clang, humph, gnash* and *chug-a-lug* throbbed across the prairie, covering the rasp of a cricket and the melody of a meadowlark.

The steering wheel jerked. I hung on. The front wheels straightened. I breathed again and dared to wipe one hand and then the other down the front of my dress. They were instantly wet again. Row after slow long row faded into a fog of heat, dry mouth, and full bladder. I couldn't imagine getting the whole field harvested and simply held on until *Papa* called, "We're full!"

I shoved the brake and the big machine stopped with a shudder.

"Blinny, you did fine," *Papa* said. "Get yourself a drink and stretch your legs. We should be able to cut four or five more loads before milking time."

The good feeling from his unexpected praise evaporated as the day stretched into more noise, choking dust, and endless rows. By the end of that endless day, I had cut a million golden stalks of grain, learned in every fiber of my body the vibration of the tractor, and felt the undulation of the land, moving like a vast antelope herd before the wind. I had seen each strip of field bared to the stubble; the soil grayed from summer drought. This field was mine.

Late that afternoon, the truck made it more than halfway home before the radiator boiled over, spewing steam from under the hood. *Papa* cursed and slammed his door hard. He lifted the hood. I stayed in the truck and leaned back, almost dozing off, but the sounds of his tinkering and cursing kept me alert until he yanked open the door.

"There's a busted hose I can't splice," he said. "We have to walk."

Papa was already entering the barn when I trudged, all dusty, dirty, and blistered through the barnyard toward the house.

He called to me, "Your mother wants a bucket of beans to snap this evening. You pick 'em. I'll grain the cows and do the milking."

I wanted to scream *no* and curl up anywhere and go to sleep, but didn't dare disobey and was too exhausted to figure a way out of it. I shed my boots, uncurled my toes, and grabbed the bucket from the back porch.

Maman stepped outside. A pleased smile played on her lips. "You look like you've been playing in a coal pile. Wash up before picking the beans."

I turned toward the pump, too tuckered out to even tell her about driving the tractor. It'd have to wait for the quiet bedtime moments when *Maman* snuggled the covers under my chin. I'd tell about the hot seat, vibrating wheel, dust, smoke, noise, flies, and thirst. I would also tell her that any mother who had just pushed a baby into the world should never drive a tractor in the fields.

"By the way," *Maman* called from the porch, "I'm simmering that tough old hen in a pot on the propane burner. It's too hot to fire up the cook stove."

"*Papa* will have a fit about wasting propane."

"He's had fits before."   My mother disappeared back inside the hot kitchen.

My tired limbs sprang to life. I hurried to the garden, knowing *Maman* would pay a price for the gift, and I sure wasn't going to add to the cost by taking too long picking the beans.

Chapter 2

Still perched on the sack of cement, I fiddled with the twine and stared at the markers for my house, knowing I needed to move; but I sat with a cold wind buffeting my back, remembering my mother's garden.

It lay north behind the shanty and far enough away to keep the soil fresh. Even the evening sun couldn't hide how baked plants had become after the hot summer months. The peas, radishes and lettuce long gone. Only corn stalks, potato vines and carrot tops remained, except for the string bean bushes. *Maman* had babied them with buckets of water hauled from the well. Still, the leaves rustled as I picked the last of the pods.

They plunked on the bottom of a galvanized bucket. The sound dulled to bean against bean by the time the first horsefly pestered around my face and buzzed by my ear. It didn't give up. I swatted, wouldn't be so bad if it were a honey bee, but a horse fly bites for no-good reason. I ran to the far end of the row to pick.

The fly buzzed behind and tried to light on the brim of my hat – the hat that had cost *Maman* two dozen eggs, two quarts of cream, and one story about her homeland. Mr. Galloway, who owned the mercantile, listened to her yarn in her heavily-accented English sprinkled with French. He chuckled and handed her the hat when she was finished.

I suppose the hat was considered plain, just a work hat; but the way the brim dipped toward my eyes and the sides curled up suited me. Who cared if it was too big? It was the only thing I owned that moved around comfy.

I still couldn't believe I owned a hat so fine and no dirty fly was going to soil it. Checking the slight upturn of the brim for fly specks, I discovered a thick coat of field dust. The tractor

"Blast," I muttered and flapped the hat against my leg. Dust flew. I kept flapping until the natural straw color gleamed again in the late sun. I brushed the black *faille* ribbon on the sleeve of my dress until it too was free of grime, then I rubbed my hand inside the crown to reshape it.

To the west, past miles of empty prairie, the sun slanted close to the tops of the Sweet Grass Hills. Blast. I had dawdled again. I grabbed a handful of beans from under the leaves and tossed them into the bucket.

The beans came only half way to the top. Was my bucket half full or half empty? If the harvest was good, *Papa* would say full. *Maman* would whisper empty, but don't tell *Papa*. Sadie Chicken couldn't say anything. She was stewing in a pot with creamy dumplings. I'd bite into her drumstick, just like she pecked my finger. Pleasure fairly bubbled. *Maman* had fulfilled her promise. Stewed chicken was the best present ever.

I tossed fistful after fistful of string beans into the bucket until one bounced out and fell to the ground. The bucket brimmed with enough beans to satisfy even *Papa*.

Bent against the weight of the pail, I hurried toward the lower garden gate, purposely slapping my bare soles deep into the hot soil. If any snakes curled along the mounds of corn, my thumping would send them wriggling away. Baby bull snakes and garter snakes weren't a bother, but rattlers and me didn't get along. *Papa* said the only good rattler was a dead one. I agreed.

I closed the garden gate and lugged the bucket up the path. A blackish cloud plumed above the house. Wisps of it broke away and floated south. Then I saw flames flicking in the single kitchen window.

Our house was burning!

"Fire!" I screamed. The bucket clattered to the ground and beans scattered. I dashed forward, dodging clumps of Buffalo grass; my hat flew from my head. Flames shot higher and licked around eaves like the forked tongue of a rattler. Fat red sparks flew with the black smoke. I skirted the house to dash down the swell. Odette stood at the bottom looking back.

I skidded to stop beside her. "Where's *Maman* and the baby?"

Fear rounded her violet eyes. She stuck her thumb into her mouth, sucking it hard.

I yanked her hand away; her lips smacked as the thumb popped out. "Where?"

"In the barn with *Papa*," she croaked.

"Come with me!" I sprinted past the corral and rounded the corner of the rough barn. I charged inside, blinking a couple of times to adjust to murky darkness. *Maman*'s soft laughter floated down from the loft. They were in the hay again. I raced boldly to the ladder and climbed to the forbidden place.

Papa looked up, eyes wide with confusion. "What?"

Words caught in my throat. I pointed frantically toward the house until I gasped, "Fire!"

Papa shot a look at *Maman*. "You left something on the stove?"

"I–"

He jumped up and ran for the ladder, fastening his overalls as he came. He grabbed my wrist and hauled me up out of his way. He was down the ladder before *Maman* straightened her skirt and staggered after him, screaming, "*Sauves mon Bébé!*"

I gaped at my mother. "He's with you. Odette said so."

"You should've checked!"

Below us, *Papa*'s feet hit the floor. I reached for *Maman*. She shoved my hand away and scrambled from the loft. I quickly followed and we dashed out the door.

Papa was halfway up the swell, running toward the prairie-dry house. He kicked the door inward. A horrible sucking roared and the kitchen burst into a raging inferno. Tar-reeking smoke and flames blasted outward. He ducked and jumped inside as soon as the fire shot upward.

Maman staggered forward.

I caught the hem of her skirt and yanked backwards. "It's too hot! Come away! I tugged and managed to lead her away a few of feet.

She collapsed to the ground, shrieking, "*Bébé* Larry! *Bébé* Larry!"

Where was Odette? Maybe she could distract *Maman.* My little sister stood crying about halfway up the swell. "Come here," I yelled. "Help me."

Odette plopped on the ground and sat kicking and screaming, "*Papa! Papa!*"

I grabbed my mother's face and turned it toward Odette. "She's scared. You have to go to her." It was as though I had not spoken. *Maman* twisted from my grip. She saw only the burning house, her hands clenched, her body rigid. I hurried to Odette and scooped her up. She braced her palms into my chest, twisting and fighting, but I held her trembling body tight and carried her to *Maman.* I sat down, clutching both Odette and the edge of *Maman*'s skirt.

Then I screamed, too. I screamed for *Papa.*

Finally, he burst from the door, hair and clothes smoking. He rolled in the dirt. His hands were cracked like pit-roasted pork. A down draft blew choking smoke over us as he crawled to *Maman* and pulled her into his arms. He buried his face in her hair.

"Essie Faye, listen to me," he said. "The cradle was already burned. I couldn't save him."

Maman flailed at him as if she was in water too deep. "How could I leave him alone? Go to the barn? Cook that stupid chicken?" She beat at his chest with each word.

The roof crashed down, sending a whirlwind of cinders into the air. They swarmed back to earth, surrounding us in a cloud of biting, burning embers. I jumped up and brushed at flames flickering on my dress.

Papa grabbed Odette and tore her dress free. He dumped me over and rolled me in the powder dust of the yard. It caked on my face and smeared into my eyes. He tried to clean the silt away with a corner of his shirt tail. "Cry, dammit. It'll wash out your eyes." He thumped my head hard and tears rolled.

Maman grew still, not even a whimper. She curled up on the ground, knees tight to her chest. Odette clutched a strand of our mother's hair, put it in her mouth, and sucked it. She watched *Papa*'s every move, looking for any sign he would let her into the comfort of his arms.

My eyes smarted, but the grit washed away. I wiped the tears and huddled closer to *Maman*, not knowing what to do or say. The baby I helped *Maman* push into the world was burned up. I couldn't imagine how she could ever laugh again. How could I? He should've had the chance to grow big, turn into a brother I could really like. It was hard to love a baby that drained my mother dry and left her melancholy for France and the vineyard.

Maman's last words echoed in my mind. *Cooked that stupid chicken.* I gasped. My selfish request could never be taken back. My poor, poor *Bébé* brother. More tears spilled and rolled down my cheeks, dripping onto the only dress I now owned, and it was riddled with burned spots. I cried for the dress, for *Bébé* Larry, for *Maman*, for *Papa*'s burnt hands, and for myself because I was the one who wanted Sadie cooked. What a dumb thing to ask for on such a hot day. The preacher said revenge belonged to the Lord. Why hadn't I waited? I should've been smarter than a *poule*.

Papa knelt close to *Maman* and brushed her raven curls from her pale cheek. "Oh, *ma belle marée*. We'll rebuild, have more sons." Even with his hands raw and blistered, he stroked her eyebrows with his fingertips, massaged her temple. "Rest now my love. I'll go make us a place in the hay loft. We'll be warm there. We'll manage."

He stared down at her unmoving face so intensely I thought his dark eyes might pierce my mother. The sound of sorrow as deep as a break in a limestone cliff released from his chest; the jaggedness in his breath scared me. Then he did an odd thing. He pulled away from *Maman* as though she had rebuffed him. He stood and faced what was left of the home he had built. Timbers smoldered in red embers, and flames tasted what they hadn't yet destroyed. Fire spread out in an irregular blackened line, singeing the dry grass and stopping as if satiated after consuming the Platts' homestead and son.

I scrunched closer to *Maman* and smoothed the tangled hair from her blank face. Soot smeared across the pale nose and chin. I wiped away the streaks as best I could. "*Maman? Maman?*" I patted the cold cheeks. "You can have another baby. Another son."

Maman neither moved nor made a sound. She seemed gone. To where, I didn't know. The only thing to do was lie on top of the still body to keep her here, not let her go to that place the tent preacher talked about. *Bébé* Larry was in Heaven that was for sure, but *Maman* had been sinning. Fornication the preacher called it. Would she go to hellfire and brimstone? That preacher had to be wrong. Nobody was nicer than *Maman*. God would be lucky to have her. But He'd better leave her here.

"*Maman*, you are scaring Odette," I pleaded, but she remained cut off as if I didn't exist.

Odette pushed at me. "Get off," she cried. She sounded so angry I rose and tried to calm her, but she yanked from me and fell on *Maman*, nuzzling against the still breast, like she was seeking nourishment.

I tried to pull her away.

"Blinny, leave her be," *Papa* said.

I reached for his hand. I tugged at his sleeve instead. He didn't even look down at me. "What's wrong with *Maman*?" I pestered, but he remained far away. "*Papa*, we gotta get the wagon. Go to the Bromwells." I hated the thought of that big noisy family, but they lived the closest. Mrs. Bromwell must know how to help *Maman*. She took good care of all her children, and they seemed healthy enough – anyway, the ones at the school were.

"Blinny, the crops."

I shoved at his arm. "We'll come back. I'll help, but we gotta go now."

Papa focused on me like I was the only sane thing within his reach. He grabbed my shoulders. "Watch over your mother. I'll harness the team."

"Hurry. We have to help *Maman*."

"Your mother will be all right. She just needs some time." He stumbled down the swell toward the slab barn. "She has to be," He mumbled over and over as he walked away. His words carried in the stillness like a prayer said without faith.

Papa was just as worried as I was. *Maman* might not stay with us. I'd seen enough injured or slaughtered animals to know once movement stopped, death followed.

I couldn't keep from staring at the ruins of the house. Poor *Bébé* Larry dead inside the smoking timbers. Had he died before the flames touched his fair skin and scorched his blond hair? I hoped so.

My sister still hunkered near our mother. She looked so lost and alone. "Odette, come sit beside me. *Papa* will be back in a minute."

"No."

She didn't want to sit by me? She had always run to me for comfort. Now she turned away and refused to look my way.

Cinders popped and flashes of fire shot upward. The barnyard was quiet except for the crackle of burned wood and the wind moaning against the blackened chimney rocks. Not a single hen pecked around the coop, the pigs lay like mounds in the muck inside their pen, and the milkers hadn't wandered in from the pasture. It was as though the whole farm mourned for *Bébé* Larry.

Papa still hadn't come back. What was taking so long? I was at the point of leaving *Maman* and checking on him when the team of Belgian horses clopped from the far side of the barn, the buckboard rattling behind them. I wanted to run down and spank them good with the reins, get them moving like they did when they galloped ahead of a fast-moving storm. Instead, they plodded proudly matching purposeful steps until finally they stood before us like regal kings. Joey nickered as if to ask what was wrong.

Papa hopped down and lifted *Maman* from the ground, gingerly placing her into the wagon bed on top of straw he had thrown in for a cushion. He straightened her skirt, smoothing it down over her ankles. He spread a horse blanket over her, and then piled on straw until only *Maman*'s stark white face showed.

Odette hadn't moved when *Papa* picked up *Maman*, and she still sat in the dirt, knees curled to her chest, face buried against them. She was trembling like cold had seeped to her very bone. He lifted her up beside *Maman*.

"Hush your crying, little girl," he said.

Odette sniveled and glared at him through tangled dark bangs. Poor shy mite. She'll be scared to death of all the boys at the Bromwells.

Papa leaned his hip against the wagon as if it was the only thing that could keep him upright. He seemed to understand we needed to leave but couldn't bring himself to stop staring off across the fields. I nudged him. He reeked of tar smoke and burnt flesh. "We have to go," I said.

He grabbed a burlap sack from the wagon bed, and we climbed up onto the wooden seat. Slowly, deliberately, he tore strips of sacking and wrapped his blistered hands until they were padded. He gripped the leather reins and flipped them gently on Joey's rump. The horses stepped forward. The wagon groaned and rolled, bumping across the barnyard to the two track road that led to the county road several miles ahead.

Lingering flames flickered on charred cottonwood slabs. The iron cook stove stood alone. Everything else was consumed. I tried to see *Bébé* Larry's cradle. "It's all Sadie's fault. The mean old hen burned us out and killed our *Bébé*."

"It isn't Sadie's fault." His words cut deep.

Chapter 3

The dust cloud from my stepmother's Lincoln approached like a whirlwind. Alice always mashed the accelerator to the floorboard. The classy auto bounced into sight, shot past the last power pole and slid to a halt just short of my construction site.

Alice slid from the vehicle and high-stepped in her clogs across the rough grading. "So the co-op finally ran your electric lines." Hands on hips, she scanned the home site. "Is that all the farther you've gotten on the foundation?"

The straw boss quality in her words worked against my preference for quiet, solitary hours. I leaned on the spade, breathing deep, letting the air in my lungs catch up with my need.

Alice's fine hair hung limply, her cheeks were rosy and her proud shoulders drooped. "It's hotter out than a snake in heat," she said.

"I've never thought of snakes as sexual creatures. They're cold-blooded."

"I don't believe everything written in science books. And you don't either, or you wouldn't be out in this blast furnace building this stupid house at your age."

I wiped the sweat running into my eyes. "How old do you think I am?"

"Sunstroke is deadly after fifty. And you're well past that."

"Did you get that fact out of *Popular Science* or *Good Housekeeping*?"

A smile touched her pouty lips. "*Touché.*" She walked over and peered into the cement mixer. "You should've flushed this out right away."

She annoyed me. I couldn't help it. I should be used to her goading, but I didn't want to be. "Hose is turned on if you're worried about it."

"Aha. Asking for help, huh?" Looking as pleased as that cold-blooded snake, she grabbed up the black rubber hose and twisted the nozzle. Water gushed and sprayed against the well house, drenching her shoulder and up onto her chin. "Sheesh, you've got plenty of pressure."

Satisfaction rose. I ignored it. "Alice, why are you here? I'm busy."

"'Course you are." She washed out the inside of the mixer and pulled up the handle to dump it. Water splashed into the mud surrounding the legs of the machine. Splatters hit her bare ankles. She disregarded that. "Are you ready for another batch?"

"You're not dressed for working. And I have to set this last form first."

She pulled off her dress and hooked it on a nail pounded into the side of the tool shed. "Are the extra gloves in here?" She shoved open the door.

"You're going to fry yourself wearing only that slip."

She stepped inside. *Clang.* Something was tossed aside. *Rattle.* That was the toolbox. *Blue word.* That was Alice. She came back out with a pair of leather gloves and a greasy old towel torn in the middle and pulled over her head to cover her shoulders. Even in that get-up, she was what Uncle Lanny would've called a looker.

I chuckled. "If you're wearing that to impress the men on this place, there aren't any."

She looked at me like I should be working instead of leaning on the shovel.

I smoothed the last eight feet of excavated dirt, readying it for the wooden braces that would hold the wet cement in place. Two-feet deep were the recommended dimensions. I needed a solid base for my house to rest upon.

Alice helped me set the plywood forms. We worked silently, like we always had on my father's ranch, giving each other room to move, not really caring if the other helped or not, but used to one another. She told me once that we weren't friends, and we weren't. We weren't enemies either.

We braced the forms with studs, laid rebar and were ready to pour the last side of my forty-foot square foundation. The support for my house was almost complete. Pleasure settled through me like a hard-fought question finally answered.

Morning ran into afternoon. The unbearable temperature rose as Alice mixed batch after batch of concrete. She'd dump a third of the ninety-four-pound bag of Portland cement into the mixer, top it with shovelfuls of sand and coarse gravel, and then add well water. She jumped every time she flipped the switch and the generator barked. The vat churned, the muck slapped, and the machine shook.

I shoveled and leveled each backbreaking batch into the forms.

We had maybe one more load of concrete to mix, haul in the wheelbarrow, and scoop into the trench when I stopped to stretch my back.

A meadowlark darted from the roof of my pump house and lit on the electric line running to my tool shed. I would gladly share my house with pretty, flighty birds, maybe a few chickens and a couple of horses, but nothing more. I'd waited too long to build this house; and if I was selfish about it, so be it.

"This batch is mixed," Alice called. Gray muck had splattered her arms and legs. The white cotton slip stuck to plump flesh that sagged little even at age sixty.

She grabbed the handles of the wheelbarrow and rolled it forward, fast-stepping to keep the weight moving. The load tipped as she rounded the corner.

I dropped the shovel and sprang forward to steady the front and caught it just in time.

Alice yanked the gloves from her hands and inspected her palms. The soft spots were pink but not blistered. She gazed at them for a moment as though lost in thought. "I expected them to look worse than your father's after the fire. Remember how awful they were?"

How could I forget? I didn't bother to answer and shoveled the wet concrete into the forms quickly. Blast her hide. I didn't have the time to think about the fire and its aftermath.

Alice hovered over me like a hen with chicks, while I sliced through the cement with a rod to make sure there weren't any bubbles or division in the foundation. She'd never been the mothering kind, and she was making me nervous.

I gave up and asked, "What is on your mind?"

"Did you talk to Odette?"

"I called but she wouldn't come to the phone." I eyed Alice with a mind-your-own-business look.

She tossed her hair back. The white gleamed in the sun. "Evil looks don't become you. If you ever want to catch another man, you'd better do something about your disposition."

There was no talking with her. I shoved the wheelbarrow to the hose and cleaned it and the mixer, the whole while keeping an eye on Alice. What was bothering her? Had my leaving the Platt ranch insulted her?

I was on the verge of apologizing when she demanded, "How long does it take for that muck to harden enough to build on?"

"Couple of weeks." I sprayed the soles of my boots with the hose.

"You'll never get the roof on and the windows in before the snow flies."

What possible difference did it make to her? "It's only the middle of May."

Alice rubbed her forehead. "I know I'm bugging you."

"There's never been a day when you didn't expect me to solve some disaster."

Her eyes suddenly gleamed. "You remember the first winter after you came home to help with Didier? We had a blizzard so bad snow drifted over every fencepost, and then froze hard as rock. The weight pulled out brads making the barbed wire droop."

I grinned. "Didier was so mad that his cattle were smart enough to figure out they could climb across and wander for miles."

"He bellowed like a bull all winter. Liked to drive us nuts."

"My father loved his cattle."

"Your fa–," Alice paused as if she was finding the right words. "Didier was a pain in the keister, but it gave him something to think about besides the pain in his bowels." Her brow furled. "Have you ordered your bricks?"

Her offhand question caught me by surprise. My bricks were none of her business. "Your legs and arms are going to have a rash from those cement splatters. Probably should rinse them off before you put your dress back on. Or are you going to parade around looking like that?" I couldn't resist the jab.

"Well, don't get all huffy." She kicked her clogs off and I aimed the nozzle at her legs and feet.

Alice jumped. "That's damned cold and that's high enough!"

I doused her good. She bent to scoop up mud. I pointed the water straight at her butt. She jumped like a wildcat, turned and threw the mud. I dodged it easily and burst out laughing.

Her blue eyes danced. "I heard about gals that do mud wrestling. Want to try?" She rocked on her feet, knees bent, arms askew like a wrestler. She looked more like a drenched rat. "I'd like to hold you down in the muck until you promise to go see your sister."

"I will deal with my sister when I'm ready and without your meddling."

Alice dried off with the work towel, slipped on her dress, and stuffed her feet into her clogs, acting the whole time as if I'd offended her to the umpth degree. "I'm not coming back here to help you."

"Good."

She marched to her Lincoln and drove off. The setting sun glinted off the chrome.

I turned my eyes away from the glare and clearly saw a stark image of my tiny sister curled against *Maman* in the bed of the wagon −*Maman* without movement and Odette shivering. I banned the memories years ago as too painful to think about. Now I let them come. Then, maybe I could erase them, once and for all.

What would it be like to live with absolution?

Nothing to feel guilty about?

A clean slate?

~~~~~

The Platt wagon rolled across the prairie toward the intense setting sun. I ducked my head forward and downward, protecting eyes that still smarted from fumes and smoke. The sunset lasted longer than it took our house to burn.

Beside me, *Papa* hunched forward, forearms leaning on his legs, reins slack in his charred hands.

The team of draft horses, Johnny and Joey strayed neither right nor left as they plodded down the dirt road at a slow, nerve-grinding pace.

I silently willed my father to whip the team into a hard-run lather. I was mad at him for not forcing at least a trot. I was mad at Joey for not understanding the need to hurry; how could Johnny just follow Joey's lead? I was mad at *Maman* for not taking care of us and mad at Odette for no good reason. I was also mad at the tent preacher for the things he had said about eternal damnation, and I was mad at our worthless old truck, leaving us at the mercy of the team's pace.

I fidgeted on the seat, tempted to grab the reins.

"Blinny, sit still. The horses know we're in trouble and will get us to the Bromwells. Hurrying won't do your mother any good. She just needs time to adjust. We all do."

That was more words than *Papa* had said since we first climbed into the wagon, and further pestering wouldn't help. I stared ahead into the darkening prairie, listening to the rasp in Odette's shallow breath; too many tears from such a tiny body.

I tried to calm my pressing urge to rush. Eyes closed, I drifted with the sway of the wagon and picked out evening sounds. A thatch of dry thistle rattled, possibly a jack rabbit on his way home. The sad, lonesome yowl of a coyote echoed deep in a coulee. Was he young and calling for his mother? I wanted to wail like him, let my fear carry upwards and across the plains. Instead, I choked down dread for *Maman* and focused on the rolling wagon wheel, willing it to turn faster.

When I jerked awake, the evening prairie had settled into a starlit night. I rubbed my eyes. I had dozed? How could I?

Maman still lay deathly quiet, needing something I didn't know how to give. The straw covering her had moved only where Odette stuck her hand through to hold onto *Maman*. Satisfied that they were all right, I looked ahead, trying to make out the road.

"How much longer?" I asked.

"I've been able to see the lights from the Bromwell's windows for a while."

Pinpricks of light twinkled, then were lost as the ground swelled. At the knoll's top, they flickered back into view. This off-again, on-again pattern lasted for another mile until we left the county road and entered the Bromwells' spread.

We followed a lane rich with pasture smells. Ebony outlines of ranch buildings appeared, one by one. Barking dogs charged out of the night, staying just clear of the horses' hooves as *Papa* pulled the team to a halt near the ranch house.

"Who?" a stern voice asked from the reaches of the inky porch.

"Didier Platt."

Short and wide, Mr. Bromwell stepped into the light from a front window. Three of his wiry, rifle-toting sons hopped from the porch and drew close to the wagon.

My father straightened and cleared his throat. "We're burned out. Everything's gone. Baby boy dead. Essie Faye's in a bad way."

"Can't help ya, Frenchman, if ya don't come inside. Mother, we got staying guests."

Papa hopped down as Marvel Bromwell hurried from the house followed by her brood of younger Bromwells. Her round, concerned face showed a hardworking ranch wife, one with pride in her bright eyes and bouncy step. Her nine sons and two daughters were good enough for any rancher. If anyone could call *Maman* back, she could.

"Monty," Marvel said in a take-charge voice. "Hand me that poor little Odette."

Monty gently lifted Odette from the bed of straw and carried her to Marvel. He was too old for the country school so I didn't know him or his older brother.

Marvel gathered my sister into her arms, and Odette snuggled against the wide shoulder.

I shied away from Monty's helping hand and scrambled down the wagon wheel.

"Blanche," Marvel said. "Come up here out of the way."

It took a second to register who Blanche was. I scurried up the steps. "You've got to hurry. My mother is like she's dead."

Marvel looked down at me, eyebrows knit with concern. "Hush, child. What do you know about such things?"

My cheeks warmed, but I sure wasn't going to let a bunch of staring people make me tongue-tied. I straightened to my tallest and looked Marvel right in the eyes. "Nothing, but *Maman*'s in trouble and I think you can help. When she's better, we're going to need some of your boys to help us build a new house."

Papa pushed me out of his way, brushed the straw from *Maman* and lifted her into his arms. Her head bobbed loosely, and he tipped her expressionless face against his torn, burnt shirt. Holding her gently, he said to Marvel, "She hasn't spoken or moved since I told her the boy was gone."

"Takes time for the shock to lessen. It's God's way of sparing her from too much pain."

I wanted to ask Mrs. Bromwell who made the pain in the first place, but figured I'd hear about watching my tongue.

Marvel turned to open the door and bumped into the smallest boy. "Eddy, will you get back?"

He dodged a swat and held the door open.

Marvel shooed the smaller children with a wave of her hand and led us through a long room lit by hanging lamps, their glow leaving the corners murky. Three lumpy couches lined the walls. Above them photographs of ancient Bromwells stared down. Deer heads were mounted over the mantel; rifles rested on racks below them.

I had never been in a room so fine. I caught my breath when I saw six calendars hung in the pattern of a cross. Each was turned to a seasonal landscape, as if a constant prayer for the crops was sent upward each day from the heart of the Bromwell ranch.

"Say one for *Maman*," I whispered as I passed by.

Marvel hurried to a door near the back, her sturdy black shoes tapping rapidly against hardwood floors. Someone finally knew enough to hurry.

"We'll put the poor soul in the girls' room," she said.

I hustled to keep up and squeezed through the narrow door beside *Papa*.

"Blinny, stay back," he muttered as he laid *Maman* in the middle of a squeaky, quilt-covered bed.

Marvel handed Odette to him. "Go on back to the menfolk. We'll clean up Blanche and Odette later." She lit a kerosene lamp and turned her back as if we were no longer a concern. She removed *Maman*'s soiled, singed blouse.

Papa nudged me out of the room and closed the door behind us. He lowered Odette to the floor and leaned limp as a wilted plant against the wall between the door and the calendar cross.

I stayed beside him, clutching Odette's hand.

Bromwell boys of various sizes filled the sofas. The age of the children determined the place they got to sit. The smallest children sat cross-legged on faded homemade rugs. Tom, the oldest son sat on the couch nearest the fireplace. Monty, the boy who had tried to help me from the wagon, sat next to him. He was slighter in size and maybe two years younger than his brother, probably about fifteen. His brown eyes met mine and I quickly looked away.

Mr. Bromwell filled the man-sized rocker near the unlit fireplace. His belly covered most of his lap, and his hands rested high on the bulge as if taking comfort from the fact that he grew enough food to expand his girth. His feet splayed out in run-over boots with the heels drumming lightly with each rock.

"Didier," he said. "Don't just stand there looking like the tail end of a nightmare. Mother's chair will hold ya."

Papa eased into the low pine rocker as if unsure whether he'd fit. His boney knees stuck up almost to his chest and arms hung down over the armrests. I thought he looked like an overgrown gangly hound sitting in a hen's nest. As he wiggled to get comfortable, he glanced back at us huddled by the wall.

"Take Odette and go sit with the girls," he said, frowning like I should've already done so.

I no more wanted to sit by them than to gather eggs from Sadie. I wasn't afraid, just didn't want to sit so far from *Maman*, but knew my father wouldn't stand for nonsense.

All the Bromwells watched every step of my dirty feet as I walked the length of the room. Our whole house would have fit in this one room. But it was gone. I swallowed a lump in my throat. They might see my filthy feet, but they would never see me cry.

Alice and her little sister, Frances, sat near the doorway to the kitchen on a braided runner. I knew Alice from school. She sat in the back section for the seventh graders and mostly ignored the younger students in the front section. I was fine with that.

As we knelt onto the rug, I stared right back into Alice's eyes. They were the color of prairie blue bells, and her hair the shade of newly-cut cottonwood. Her full bottom lip carried a pout. Frances was a complete opposite from Alice. Molasses-colored hair, thick eyebrows, and tanned skin. The Bromwell girls were nothing like me and Odette. Our eyes and hair matched. The only difference was size. I was big for my age; Odette needed to grow.

"Blinny is a dumb name," Alice said. "I don't know why Miss Walsh calls you that in school. Ain't proper. I'll call you Blanche."

"Do you want me to call you something besides Alice?"

Alice's blonde eyebrows drew together, then she lifted her chin. "Phew, there are never any girls my age to have fun with."

Odette reached for a doll that Fran wasn't playing with. Fran snatched it away and glared. New tears spilled down Odette's blotched cheeks. I had a good notion to thump both the Bromwell girls, but starting a ruckus was not going to help my mother. Instead, I pulled Odette to an empty rug and held her like *Maman* would have. I slowly rocked on my buttocks, listening to my father answer Mr. Bromwell's questions about the fire. It was hard with two hateful girls glaring at me and Odette sniveling in my arms.

Papa explained how fast the house burst into flames. "By the time I got inside the whole place was an inferno." His voice turned husky. "I need to put what's left of my son in a box before the timbers cool and some wild animal gets at him. Need something tight. I'll have to store it in the barn loft 'til I pick out a spot for a cemetery."

Mr. Bromwell rubbed his chin whiskers. He licked his tongue over his bottom teeth, then grinned in a way to show them. One gold tooth flashed in the lamp light. "Monty, did you finish making that box Uncle Clarence wanted for snakes?"

"Yes, sir, but we've already put a hunnert rattlers in it."

"It'll be big, but we need it for the baby's bones. Dump the snakes in a barrel."

Papa nodded his gratitude.

I dared to speak. "*Maman*'s favorite place is down by the willows. There's a high spot that would work for burying."

Every Bromwell looked at me, and then back at my father to see if he thought it was a good idea.

"I'll decide where," *Papa* said, his tone warning me to keep quiet.

Mr. Bromwell cleared his throat and spat tobacco juice into a coffee can. "Tom and Monty will go with you. Can't send a man alone for what you're about. But first we'll grease your hands."

"When I get back," *Papa* said.

"Better let us tend 'em. Can't do much farming without fingers."

Papa peeled off the gunnysack strips and held his raw, oozing palms out. I shuddered, realizing what my baby brother must've suffered. Heavy with the horrible thought, I hung my head, maybe to never look up again. My eyes were drawn back to *Papa*'s raw hands as Monty smeared gobs of yellowish pig tallow over the burns and to the bedroom door which separated me from my mother.

The men rose and went through the front door. All nine boys scrambled after them.

I wasn't about to be left behind. I hurriedly carried Odette into the room where *Maman* lay. Menthol overpowered the stink of singed clothes piled on the floor.

"Shh," Marvel whispered. "I've rubbed her down good, but I don't know. She just won't say anything. Tuck Odette in beside her mother. Maybe the child's warmth will help."

I eased my little sister onto the bed and pulled the blanket over her. "Thank you, Mrs. Bromwell. I'm going outside."

"Tell Alice and Fran to get their turn at the privy over. I'm going to bunk them on the couches tonight."

I scurried through the long empty room under the watchful eyes of dead deer and dead ancestors. Alice and Fran were in the kitchen, eating cookies from a pickle jar. Neither paid any attention to my presence.

"Marvel wants you to use the outhouse."

Alice sneered. "None of your bees wax what we're supposed to do." She popped a cookie into her sassy mouth, but both girls walked outside, letting the screen slap shut.

Safe in the shadows of the porch, I waited until the glow of the men's lanterns disappeared around the side of the horse barn. I grabbed an old pair of boots from the porch, tucked them under my arm, hurried to the wagon, and burrowed quiet as a mouse under the dry, dusty straw. My nose tickled and my legs itched. I dared to move a little and cleared a small area for my nose and eyes.

An evening breeze moved through the wagon, stirring the straw ever so slightly. Muffled voices carried on the currents. A loud thump. A crash!

I raised enough to see over the side of the wagon.

"Dammit, I told you boys to be careful with that box!" That was Mr. Bromwell's voice.

"Couldn't hold it, Paw!" That was Monty.

Mr. Bromwell jumped to the side. "Watch out! The snakes are all over hell and creation! Watch out! Yow! That was close. Oh hell, we're all gonna get snake bit. Wait 'til morning to catch 'em again."

I dunked back down under the straw. Running footfalls, Mr. Bromwell cursed some more, and then the wooden box barely missed my head when it was shoved into the wagon. I froze, breathing slowly while Monty one-handed himself onto the wagon bed. He sat so close my foot touched his leg. I didn't dare move.

"Tom, you take the reins," *Papa* said.

The wagon rocked as they climbed aboard. The reins flapped. I tried to hold steady. Monty's hand gripped my foot, then his fingers felt my toes and ankles. I held my breath, but he never gave me away, just patted my leg through the straw.

The cottonwood box appeared silvery in the glow of the lantern hanging beside the seat. Handles of leather strips were nailed to the ends and the hinged lid squared even with the sides. No knotholes marred it. It was way too big, longer than I was, but would make a perfectly nice box for *Bébé* Larry.

I never moved, or sneezed, or coughed against the dry, tickling straw as the wagon moved across the prairie. I listened to the low murmur of *Papa* and the two Bromwell boys talking. My eyes stung from lack of sleep and my eyelids drooped. I drowsed to the rhythm of the wagon, feeling as if I were floating away on the Milk River's lazy current. I thought of my house that was no more. It had been a small house, but it was ours. I would help *Papa* build another, maybe one with an extra bedroom for me and Odette instead of a loft and ladder. Maybe a brick house that wouldn't burn. A person needed a house that would last.

The horses finally stopped and blew. I sat up, straw clinging to my hair and ruined dress. The lantern spread a small circle of light.

"Geez," Monty said. "I thought you were a ghost for sure. Where did you come from?"

I heard the lie in his tone and waited for *Papa*'s anger. He twisted on the seat.

"Blinny?"

"I wanna put my brother's bones in the box."

"Child, you're too young for such a thing." He sounded more confused than angry.

"I gotta do it." I shook pieces of straw out of the boots and slipped them on. Way too big, but they'd work, just like the box would work for Larry. I dropped to the ground.

Papa carried the lantern, and I walked beside him toward our burned home. Wisps of smoke still rose from bigger timbers. The rest of the rubble appeared blacker than the night, stinking of smoke and burnt tar paper. Charred wood crackled under my feet; powdery ashes flew up around my legs.

Papa held the light high and moved it slowly from side to side. Nothing looked familiar, then, I recognized a table leg, a blackened plate, and the milk bucket. And *Maman*'s cook pot. I lifted the lid and peeked inside. The old hen was gone, not even a charcoal bite left.

"Over here," *Papa* said.

Monty and Tom hurried to fetch the box they had left outside the rubble. They carried it to us and raised the lid. I watched, but no snake slithered out. Hopefully, whatever essence remained from the snakes would only protect poor *Bébé* Larry.

Carefully as handling *poulet* eggs, *Papa* lifted what was left of the cradle and the corpse of *Bébé* Larry. As he laid the charred remains into the box, something fell. I picked it up, not knowing whether it was part of the cradle or part of my brother, but I would remember the warm, oily feel.

I placed what I believed was a bone inside the box and *Papa* closed the lid. Tom and Monty hefted it up and followed *Papa* toward the barn.

"My hat is down by the garden," I called.

"Go fetch it."

I ran into the night, praying the hat was still by the fence. Prickly dried grass bent under my palms as I touched along the dark ground around the post. Something moved. I felt the brim of my hat. I clutched it to my chest and hurried back.

I climbed back into the wagon, knowing I would recall over and over, maybe for the rest of my days, the pungent odor of burnt flesh, the acrid smell of the burned house, and the silent stench of my grieving father.

Chapter 4

The flatbed truck with Keith's Building Supply written in a crescent on the cab door lumbered to a stop short of my graded construction site. A ruddy-faced man rolled down the window and raised nonexistent eyebrows. "Where ya want it?"

I glanced around, trying to decide the best place to stack the lumber.

"Lady, you've got four sides to the foundation. Pick one."

I didn't like the way he implied I couldn't make up my mind. Also, didn't like the way his face carried the marks of a life spent drinking too much liquor and smoking too many cigarettes. Bet if he had a woman, she left him long ago.

I thumbed toward the tool shed. "Best place is behind it."

"Makes no sense to carry them heavy studs from there to the foundation."

I pointed to the spot. "A nice neat pile right there will be fine."

"Me and the help don't pile nothin' nice and neat. Just unload it."

"Unload it then. I'll do the stacking." He and Alice would make a great pair.

"No need to get uppity. Boss told me you was a woman building yer own house and I'm just tryin' to be helpful." He ground the gears, backed up in a semicircle barely missing the tool shed, cut the engine, hopped off the running board, hitched up his jeans under his beer belly and one-handed himself up onto the truck bed.

His helper was a young guy of maybe eighteen, skinny and pimply and seemed okay. He also climbed onto the truck bed. They released the tie downs and shoved the top boards until they tipped to the ground. The two guys jumped down and pulled them free. Next, they unloaded lengths of pressure-treated wood. "This here is fer the sill plate." One by one, they manhandled the two-by-tens from the bed of the truck.

Before long, sweat ran down the driver's face. His plaid flannel shirt absorbed moisture, looking wet across the back and down his ribs.

I stayed out of his way and welcomed each thud of the lumber. The grain, the knots and the weight of each board was unique, and I would know each one as I measured, sawed and hammered.

He sailed four-by-eight foot sheets of plywood to the ground, then twelve dozen pine two-by-fours. He looked at the haphazard piles, then he glanced at me. "If you're dead set on piling them up, you better tie down the plywood or it'll blow all the way back to Havre."

I hadn't thought of that. "Rope and stakes should do it."

"Yep." He scratched behind his ear. "Beats me how yer planning to put them together all by yerself."

"Beats me, too. But I will, one piece at a time."

He scratched his day old beard and grinned. "If'n you weren't so uppity, I'd drive out every now and again and give you a hand."

I studied him long enough for him to know I wouldn't ask for help.

"Miss Platt, I ain't askin' ya on a date. Just thought you could use some help."

He was just trying to pass along some kindness. Who was I to judge? "I'll call the lumber yard if I change my mind. Who do I ask for?"

"Lem Bierderstad. Born of Norwegian stock and they're proud of it. My folks like me."

I laughed. "Well, I'm Blanche Platt and I'm not sure how my French folks felt about anything."

"Ranch families are hard to explain." Lem saluted in a way learned only in the military, climbed into the cab of the truck and drove off, leaving me alone with my piles of wood and the rich tangy smell of cut pine.

The sun beat through my shirt as I stacked the lumber. The long pieces were heavy and awkward, but I was stronger from digging the footings and working the cement. I had never been stronger. My body no longer produced useless hormones which sap toughness. Instead, it built and stored muscle, preparing me for the later years. I couldn't work hard enough to use up this post-menopausal strength.

Inner contentment eased the labor of stacking lumber, and my mind ran with plans. I should move onto this place. Live in a tent or something. Alice would kick up a fuss, try and make me feel guilty for leaving the ranch. She couldn't understand that I needed to live on land I held the deed to, not live beholden like Odette and I had been after the fire. The shame of it sometimes still haunted me so much I'd have to sit down quickly and wait for weakness to pass.

This time, I sat on a pile of my own treated wood that would be the sill plate, poured a crystal glass of *Maman*'s favorite chardonnay, and wished I'd break down just once and smoke a cigar like Uncle Lanny enjoyed. So far, I had denied myself the indulgence, but someday I would smoke one in honor of him.

The fruity wine tasted sharp and cleared my palette. Too bad a simple glass of fermented grapes could not remove the shame of those long-ago days, too.

~~~~~

Five days after our homestead house burned, a late afternoon heat pressed down on the Bromwell ranch like fire on a hot day. We sweltered, barely able to move, hiding in the shade of the ranch buildings.

Sweat dripping from her temples, Marvel shooed everyone out of her hotter-than-a-mortal-could-stand kitchen. Her eyes and lips squinched in a testy look while she stood guard over the back screen door and told Mr. Bromwell, "I won't ride herd on a tribe of hot, cranky children all evening. You'd better cool 'em off in the river, clothes and all."

Mr. Bromwell tipped his hat back and wiped his damp brow on his long sleeve shirt. "Might jump in myself."

"Oh boy," Eddy yelled and beat all his brothers to the cattle truck. It rocked on its springs as the boys clamored into the back.

Alice and Fran ran like their brothers, but they climbed into the cab. Marvel looked at me and nodded toward the truck. I grabbed Odette's hand and scooted around the side of the house, up the front steps, and through the long room to the bedroom where *Maman* lay unmoving. She wouldn't want us to go swimming with a bunch of boys. What if she woke up and we were gone?

I leaned close to her still form. "*Maman*, if you would just wake up, I could make you happy. We could go visit *Grande-mère's* vineyard and bring home some grapes. And I wouldn't have to get wet in front of the boys."

My mother remained on her side, curled like a baby, knees toward her chest. Had Marvel arranged her into such a position or had *Maman* moved on her own? Was that a good sign? Maybe she was stirring around.

"*Maman*, wake up." I shook her shoulder. It felt limp and moved easily.

Marvel stepped into the stifling room, her sweaty presence using up air. I wanted to chase her away. Send Odette out, too, and sit with *Maman* quiet as could be, but even more, I wanted to be at our homestead, rebuilding a house for her. We needed our Platt privacy.

"Blinny, I know you are prairie shy, but I want you to cool off. If anything changes, I'll ring the dinner bell."

With no choice except to go, I led Odette outside.

"Come on," Eddy yelled from the back of the truck.

Monty jumped down. "The cab is pretty crowded. Best you ride back here. I'll help you up."

I put my right foot into Monty's cupped hands. He lifted me up onto planking and straw. I pulled my dress down over my knees as far as the skirt would go and reached for Odette.

Monty tried to hand her to me, but she twisted and grabbed him around the neck, hanging on as if he were *Papa*. Monty gently pried her arms lose. "Go to your sister." He set her on the bed of the truck.

She curled up beside me, her head bowed and cheeks red. I tried to hide her embarrassment by smoothing her skirt. I couldn't help resent how pinched we looked in the hand-me-down clothes. I hated wearing Alice's old dress, but appreciated not having to wear my burnt one, and I was right sorry for my prideful heart.

But what would the dresses be like wet?

Alice grinned back at me through the rear window. It wasn't a nice one, lips pouty and eyes haughty. She was a sly brat.

Monty hopped aboard and the truck started to roll. "Ignore her," he said and remained standing, balanced by wrapping a hand around one of the wooden slats that made up the sides of the truck. Eddy hung on beside him; Tom hunkered down with Alan and Paul. They were identical twins and the youngest. Harvey, Donald, Richard, and Emmet sat with their backs against the boards, legs sticking out in front of them, rocking with the bump and sway of the rutted road. They all politely kept their eyes turned from me. I silently blessed them for the consideration.

Eddy stole a peek at my legs. He caught a dirty glare from me and didn't look back. He needed a spanking.

The cool dip in the cloudy water of the Milk River lasted as long as it took Mr. Bromwell to roll a cigarette, smoke it, roll another, and puff that one away. After flipping the butt in the river, he hooked his hat on a willow branch, pinched his nose, and jumped off the bank in a great splash. He surfaced blowing water, and then blew a long, sharp whistle around his gold tooth. Instantly, the laughing and yelling hushed as the boys swam for shore.

I hurried from the refreshing shallows by the bank and was the first one to climb out. After pulling at my river-soaked dress, I gathered up Odette, who had refused to even wade. She pulled back, but I lifted her onto the bed of the truck, climbed in beside her, and held her to my side as tightly as my wet skirt glued to my legs. The water and wet clothes cooled me, but *Maman* would have insisted on swimming at our own place.

The truck broke to the top of the coulee.

A flock of Rhode Island Reds squabbled around a watering pan. Four anxious Guernsey milkers had wandered in from the pasture. Three farm dogs ran from the shade of the two-story barn, barking relief that the boys were home.

Our place needed a barn like theirs with a smithy and tool shed hugging the right side. A long roof on the left side covered a tractor, combine, and disk. We could sure use a tall wooden granary, straw shed, bunkhouse and pig run like theirs. The blistering sun, constant wind, and below-zero winters had bleached and peeled them to silvery gray, leaving old paint only in the nooks and crannies. It would take time for the ones we'd build to age to that color. I also wanted big old dogs and a full root cellar dug in a mound with double doors, steps, shelves, and lots of big crocks.

When the truck bounced across a cattle guard, I caught a glimpse of my father on the far side of the corral, turning his saddle horse out to pasture. He waved at us, but headed towards the pump and plunged his hands into a five-gallon pail. Water splashed over the sides.

The truck rattled to a stop next to the house, and Marvel pushed open the screen door. Holding it ajar, she called to *Papa*. "How's the hands?"

"Better," he answered.

"Let 'em sun dry. Fresh air and pig grease work miracles."

My father held his palms upwards toward the evening sun, his body slouched from the weight of troubles. The daily trip to the homestead wore at him, but the return was worse. He fretted constantly about being so far from the livestock.

I jumped to the ground and helped Odette down.

She ran to *Papa* as fast as her spindly legs would go. She looked thinner. I hadn't noticed that before. For the first time, I realized she wanted nothing more to do with me the instant *Papa* returned after working all day at our place.

Didier picked her up as tenderly as he held *Maman* in one of her fits of longing for France.

I took a deep breath. "If you'd let us go to the homestead with you, Odette wouldn't be scared all the time and I could help harvest." I crossed my fingers, willing him to agree. *Papa* and me could do the chores and work the harvest. Maybe I could find something to bring *Maman*. Something to lay beside her cheek, let her smell our land. Make her want to return to it as much as she wanted to return to France.

"Both Monty and Tom are helping tomorrow. You're better off here."

Marvel shaded her eyes with a hand and stared down the road. "Looks like someone's coming."

A spiral of dust rose to the south and moved closer. The rumbling roar of an automobile carried into the barnyard. A long forest-green nose appeared out of the dust, then a huge touring car bumped and slid to a halt. The flared fenders and humped hood were covered by a thick coat of prairie silt.

The driver's door swung open, and a barrel-chested, belly-sagging man hoisted both his legs out onto the running board, then pulled himself upright by using the door as a lever. He stepped to the ground and unfurled to full height, but then his frame settled into a hunch on bowed legs, like his weight bent his knees out.

"Howdy," he boomed.

Those that weren't too shy yelled, "Howdy, Uncle Clarence."

"That isn't much of a welcome for this many children." He held his palm up to his ear which had white protruding hairs.

The kids all yelled, "Howdy, Uncle Clarence!"

This time the loud response made him smile. He sauntered around to the trunk of his car and opened it. He retrieved a suitcase and a tan leather case. "You catch me lots of rattlers?"

Monty stepped forward. "A barrel full."

"Tomorrow we're gonna make a motion picture of vipers." He held the case high so everyone could see the odd shape, oval on one side, flat on the other. "I got the camera to do it, but right now I'm hungrier than a starved rattler for some of your ma's cookin'."

The man's watery blue eyes looked my father over, then he extended a hand. "You the Frenchman they're talking about in Rudyard?"

"Depends on what they're saying."

"Burned out. That your wife's in a bad way. I figure she just needs someone to perk her up. I'll go do that right now." Clarence clumped into the house, Marvel beside him, and *Papa* quickly following.

I chased after them. *Maman* would never want a stranger in her sickroom.

Halfway across the long room, Clarence began tapping the toes of his high-heeled riding boots against the pine floorboards. "Wait a minute, Marvel. I gotta get a rhythm with these old bowed legs."

He pumped his arms and shuffled inside the bedroom, hammering out a merry tune with his boots. The faster his feet flew, the faster his head bobbed, the faster the yellow Bull Durham tag hanging from his shirt pocket bounced, and the faster the red snot rag dangling from his hip pocket banged against his *derriere*.

How dare he enter *Maman*'s bedroom? It wasn't decent. I tried to run between him and *Maman*, but Marvel grabbed my shoulder.

"Little lady in that bed," Clarence sang, his booming voice raspy from too many roll-your-own cigarettes. "Arise and tap your toes."

The nerve of him!

Papa reached and grabbed Clarence's arm. "Now just a damned minute."

The rat-a-tat of Clarence's feet struck even louder. "You want her to wake up, don't you?"

Papa's jaw worked. Red spots appeared by his temples.

Clarence jerked his arm free and jigged around both sides of the bed, head bobbing and feet flying. His shirttail worked loose and wing-flapped as he danced to the very spot next to *Maman*'s head. He bent forward with his nose almost bumping hers.

How could he do that? I should go kick those flying feet. *Papa* should knock him over and step on him. Neither of us did a thing, too dumbstruck to do so.

Maman never moved, blank eyes staring at the ceiling.

For a moment, I thought Clarence was going to kiss her, but the lunatic backed away and jigged for several more minutes before the tapping grew softer and softer. He stopped, crestfallen and exhausted.

I had seen *Papa* mad plenty of times, but never like now. His face was marked with rigid blues veins, livid creases, and deadly eyes. He pushed past Clarence and stood between him and *Maman*. "How could you think dancing would cure grief over a dead son?"

Marvel moved in front of him and placed her palm on his chest. "Didier, you're losing Essie Faye. She isn't eating and now won't even take water. I've tried to get her up and moving but she is just like a ragdoll. Take her to Havre now. "

Papa swallowed.

Did he finally understand?

"You can use our truck. Hospitals stay open all night," Marvel said. "You can't put off death, and your poor missus is headed down that road."

"My girls?"

"They fit right in with mine. And don't worry about your critters either. Let the calves suck the milkers dry. Do 'em good for a few days. The rest will feed off the land."

Papa looked at wet, bedraggled me. "I'm taking your mother to the hospital. I'll be back in a couple of days."

"I'll get us ready," I said.

"You're staying put. Hospitals are no place for children." He gathered *Maman* into his arms, brushed by me, and stepped around Odette who was huddled on the floor by the door.

Papa's strides echoed down the pine floor of the long room.

I snatched a quilt from the bed, grabbed Odette's hand, yanked her up, and chased after him.

Outside, Monty hustled around to the passenger's door of the truck and held it open as wide as it would go.

Papa eased *Maman* inside, tucking the nightgown around her pale, lifeless legs. I handed him the quilt, and he encased all of her still body. He slammed the truck door twice before it caught.

I stood smack in his way, blocking him from going around the truck. "Take us with you," I pleaded. "I'll watch out for Odette. We won't be any trouble. I hate it here. Too many people. Can't I go live in the barn at our place with Odette? I could take care of the cows and chickens." Surely, he knew I wanted the same thing he did. I wanted to be home.

"That's insane," he said. "You can't eat off the land like animals."

I bet I could, but not my frail three-year-old sister. I crumpled inside. Submission is hard to bear. "Promise we can start building a house when you come back."

Papa's eyes grew flinty. "Now quit whining. This has to be. And you be helpful to Mrs. Bromwell. I'm beholding to them for caring for you girls, and I had better not hear of you causing any trouble."

Mr. Bromwell handed over the keys and my father climbed into the truck. He never looked back, or said goodbye to Odette, or to me. Did he blame *Maman* for putting us in this spot by cooking on that burner instead of firing up the cook stove? I could almost hear his thoughts. *Always trying to avoid work. Said she was too tired. And now she just lays like some sleeping damsel in distress while her daughters need a home.*

His thoughts or mine? It would be a long time before I discovered the answer.

The rear slats of the cattle truck grew smaller and disappeared into spiraling dust. Eventually, the cloud of silt faded into nothing.

I stifled a sob, one that wanted to splash out a tub full of tears, but Odette stood beside me, twirling a strand of hair. *Maman* would expect me to watch over her.

The soft pad of Bromwell feet told me they were going toward the house and their supper, but I didn't move -- couldn't move. I watched where the landscape met the sky for any trace of rising dust, any sign that *Papa* was coming back. He couldn't just abandon us in a crowded house where I didn't fit in. My fingernails bit into my palms. The longer I waited the deeper the nails dug.

Odette crowded up against my leg.

Hope for *Papa* coming back dwindled, and I patted Odette's matted curls with a touch as tender as when *Maman* wiped a tear from your cheek.

Behind us, Monty said, "Better come eat before it's all gone."

Odette jumped as if she'd been spooked. She spun toward him. "I don't want to and I don't have to." She plopped on the ground, hugging her legs to her chest.

I couldn't allow her to act in such a way. "Monty, she won't be any trouble. And neither will I. We'll be there in a minute."

As soon as he was out of ear shot, I forced Odette to stand up. "Quit acting like a baby. Aren't you glad *Maman* is finally going to the doctor?"

She struggled to be free of my tight grip. I hung onto her. "*Papa* will come back. He has to. He won't leave us in a house that isn't ours."

She twisted harder. "It's your fault our house burned."

"It was an accident," I said, half believing the accusation. "You're such a brat. I should just let you starve." I held tight to her wrist and stared down the Bromwell's road one last time, searching for any sign of my father.

The blue skyline met the dun-colored prairie without a hint of haze on the horizon. Even the wind flowed as a gentle zephyr disturbing only ripe heads of grass. I was glad the wind lacked the force to kick up a dust devil. False hope would be worse than no hope. *Papa* was not coming back.

"Odette," I said. "We have to go inside. We have no choice." I noticed she had peed down her legs. I quickly pulled some grass and dried them. Her feet looked clean where the urine had splashed. I grabbed a handful of dirt and rubbed the tops and between the toes. "Your dress isn't wet and nobody will notice your undies. It'll be okay."

We walked across the farmyard with heads down, feet dragging, dreading what would be written on the Bromwell faces when we entered. A burned out house, a crazy mother and a father more worried about cattle than his daughters. How could he leave us to suffer their looks of pity?

The moist, stifling kitchen hit with the farm smell of the earthy bodies and cooked turnips. Mr. Bromwell sat at the head of the long plank table with Uncle Clarence on one side, and Tom on the other. The seating order for the benches was the same as the sofas and rugs in the great room, smallest children by Marvel and working up to the oldest by Mr. Bromwell.

They scrunched together to make more room. Pity was on every face.

All sat quietly, clean hands in their laps, and hair wet down and combed. Marvel guarded their cleanliness and manners the same way she guarded her enormous wood stove. She hit the enamel spud pot with her long-handled spoon. Satisfied that we were all paying attention, she said, "Now that everyone is seated, you can quit acting like cannibals long enough for Pa to say grace." She bowed her head, stringy damp hair falling forward around flushed and sweaty cheeks, but her keen eyes roamed over the children.

I squirmed. The sharpness in those hazel eyes had already zeroed on me several times. I ducked my head and stared at the red tulips painted on the oil cloth while Mr. Bromwell said a few words recommending the food to the Lord.

Marvel dished plates to the brim with boiled spuds, chunks of beef, and turnips. She ladled a soupy broth over the top. The portions grew smaller to fit stomach sizes as plates passed to ever younger Bromwells before stopping at Marvel's end.

I needed to bolt back, maybe vomit, but I forced myself to breathe in the heat and smells. How would I ever eat without *Papa* sitting with us and without *Maman* in the bed, maybe to wake up, and with that horrible uncle sitting there eager to eat? It was his fault that *Papa* left with *Maman*.

I stared at my portion, knowing I had to eat and even sop the last of the broth with bread. I could never do it. The longer I stared at my portion; the meat seemed to grow until the beef took on the appearance of the Bromwell bull out in the separation field. Alice kept daring me to go give the bull a pat between the horns, but I ignored her snickers of *chicken* accepting the fact that I was terrified of his size and meanness of eye.

Someday Alice would pay for her ornery ways just like Sadie the hen was supposed to. I planned on sinking my teeth into something that Alice wouldn't want me to. I hadn't figured out what yet, but that spoiled brat would learn not to pick on Platts. *Papa* was beholden to the Bromwells and that didn't allow much room for fighting back, but if a way happened by, I planned on taking it by the horns. My cowardice covered the bull. I held no fear of Alice.

Odette was working her way through the pile of food on her plate. Her tiny fist clenched the spoon and guided it carefully to her mouth. She ate automatically. I looked closer. She might be stuffing herself, but she appeared empty. I touched her leg under the table and she turned her eyes to me. Blank. Then they darkened. She returned to poking in food and staring down the table at Mr. Bromwell and Monty. I sensed her need for our father, maybe more than she needed our mother.

I sighed and shoveled a scoop, chewed, and somehow managed to swallow. It tasted good, and I filled the spoon again. Everyone sopped up the last of the brownish red juices with squares of brown bread.

I cleared the table without being asked and dried the dishes that Alice washed. I cleaned up after the Bromwells without complaint. It was an obligation that would end as soon as *Papa* returned.

The supper cleanup done, I slipped into the long room where everyone had gathered to hear Uncle Clarence's tales. Without a sound, I crossed to Odette and hunkered down on a braided rug. Even though I was mad at him, the pull of a story about that camera lured me in to hear what would probably be a wild tale. Anyone who could move their feet as fast as he could more than likely had a tongue that told tall tales.

Heat from the blistering day still smothered the room. Windows and doors gaped open in hopes a westerly breeze might quicken. A single kerosene lamp cast a warm hue; others were left dark. Even a low-lit flame would add unwanted heat.

Uncle Clarence slouched on the sofa, looking folded, all head and knees. Mr. Bromwell leaned back in his rocker, hands resting on his paunch. Full and satisfied, he rocked in tandem with Marvel. On the wall behind them, the framed tintypes of ancient Bromwells sternly watched over their descendants. Hard work and stern morals stiffened the jut of chins and the lines between eyebrows. The calendar cross spoke of a good harvest.

I made a secret little sign of the cross with my thumb on the cupped palm of my other hand. I wasn't Catholic like the Bromwells, but maybe it would help *Maman.*

Flies and mosquitoes buzzed inside at will. Marvel held her mesh swatter and waved it menacingly every few moments. The motions never once interrupted her rocking, or Uncle Clarence's account of his trip to Russia.

His voice came strong, pride of adventure overpowering the rasp. "In Moscow I searched through several junk stores just to see what wasn't being used by a people who didn't have anything to begin with. I was amazed at the amount of usable items for sale and finally concluded people were selling off their necessities to buy food."

Mr. Bromwell stopped rocking. "Hunger that bad, huh?"

"Skinny people with bloated bellies all over. Bleak place."

Marvel swatted at a fly on her lap, missed, and swatted again. She flicked the dead nuisance onto the floor to be swept away come morning. Her long work day ended the moment her fanny hit the rocker.

After Marvel resettled into a smooth rocking, Clarence went on. "Of course, I wasn't looking to buy necessities, but I kept digging through piles of tools, utensils, and leather goods until I saw a book of Russian poetry. I picked it up to see the name of the author and underneath was a leather case. I opened the flap and the lens of a movie camera stared me right smack in the eyeball." His voice shook with excitement. "And tomorrow, you'll find out why the Russians are crazy about motion pictures."

Mr. Bromwell sat quietly as if he were mulling a vast problem. "It's a shame that some poor fella had to sell his hobby, but by gum, we'll use that fella's camera and take pictures like you said."

"It's called filming. After dark tomorrow, we'll watch us a picture show. It'll be just like taking these children to their first theater."

Mr. Bromwell leaned forward. "Can't be done. The goldamned government ain't strung electricity lines yet. City people's vote is all they care about."

Uncle Clarence slapped his knee and puffed up his chest. "Who's the best inventor you know? I rigged me up an electric cord that runs off the car battery. Long as gas is in the tank, the projector will work fine."

His stories continued far into the night. They helped distract me from worrying about my parents, but the undercurrent of wanting to scream ebbed and flowed. I listened until my eyes drooped. I didn't dare fall asleep in front of so many people and was about to jerk Odette awake when he said, "Blinny, before I came back, I was in your parent's country."

"In Lorraine? In France?"

"Yep. Really pretty country. Did some hiking in the Vosges Mountains and visited some wineries."

"Did you meet anyone by the last name of Martello?"

"That your ma's family?"

"My grandfather is a wine master."

"They work in damned fine country. Would live there myself, but this flatland always calls me back. It just grows in your soul and stays there like some fermenting grape. Suppose those Frenchmen feel the same way about their hills."

Maman sure did, I thought. I didn't tell him that. He talked of the land the way I felt, but he had been rude to my mother and that was not easily set aside.

Marvel stood. "Morning chores come early. Off to bed with all of you."

I led Odette into Alice and Fran's room to our sleeping place in the corner that Marvel had made from several old rugs and a blanket.

Odette curled into a ball and drifted back to sleep.

I sweated under the blanket, but stayed covered to keep the mosquitoes away. Moonlight seeped into the room making murky shadows that resembled the disaster: the pile of dirty dresses appeared like a wrapped baby, a blanket-covered chair became *Maman*, the curtains were the ones burning in the homestead window, the door was *Papa*.

And I waited.

Chapter 5

The concrete had cured for one endless week and three long days. I could hardly wait for Sunday. On that day, my foundation would be hard enough to crack the plywood forms away and let the cement stand alone, ready to support my house. I had stacked red brick along the four sides, hauled enough cinder blocks to build the middle supports and put bags of cement for the mortar by the mixer. I was ready.

While impatiently waiting for the cement to harden, I also had bought a used nineteen foot camping trailer, pulled it all the way from Havre and maneuvered it near enough to the tool shed to run an electric cord.

The decision to move to the construction site was spurred by a need to escape Alice and her nagging, but in truth, I didn't belong on the ranch anymore. My heart was setting aside the familiar sites where I saw my past, *Maman* lingering under the umbrella trees by the river, Monty resting in the west field amid the wild flowers overlooking the coulee. Those images were now stored in a place safe from grief and would surface only when I chose to see them, like I did yesterday when I wandered out onto the land.

A large, hairy clematis surprised me behind a clump of Canadian thistle and I remembered searching for them with my mother. Chokecherry bushes lined a curve in Sage Creek; Monty liked my jelly. The creek itself reminded me of both of them, liquid and nourishing. I never tired of watching the trickle of water meandering through the fields, or the distant outline of the Sweet Grass Hills, or the bottom of a rise that resembled a place on the way to the mercantile, or the piles of dirt scraped away for the foundation of my house. As I pondered on what to do with the mounds of soil mixed with sod, the wind stirred my hair and caressed my cheeks with its flow.

Was that a dust cloud? I squinted up my road and groaned when I could tell it was the Lincoln. I had purposely delayed having a telephone line strung; hoping Alice would get the message that I needed time alone. What was wrong with living like a hermit and letting the land speak to me? It was claiming me in the same way I was possessing it. Maybe, just maybe the contentment of the tiny homestead shack might be rekindled.

The Lincoln slid to the usual skidding halt. Alice rolled down her window. "It's okay by me if you want to be a loner, so I'm not staying. But you need to see this letter I got from Odette's therapist." She flipped the envelope out of the window. "And you need to dig a privy. Here's some lime for it." She opened the door, carefully set a bag down, backed up, did a U-turn, and then disappeared down the road faster that she should drive on gravel.

I left the letter lying on the prairie; a white messenger caught between a tuft of dry clump grass and the dun-colored earth.

The wind didn't even blow it away. It rested there like a beacon warning me not to open and read what I had spent most of my life trying to forget.

The flap to the envelope was tucked inside. I shook the paper open. It was addressed to Alice.

> *Lately Odette has been making progress toward understanding herself. At times, I forget she is a patient, and I think of her more as a friend. There are times she slips into a place where none of us can reach her. It is imperative that her sister fill in the missing information about her*

mother's death so the road to
recovery will be quicker.

The letter continued to the bottom of the page and then asked Alice to speak with me about making a trip to the manor in Great Falls as soon as possible.

I crushed the letter against my chest. How could I rehash our past again with some nosy shrink for a sister who hated my guts? Odette was better off not knowing.

A hawk circled to the north. He plummeted downward, diving for his dinner.

Did Odette really need to consume and digest her past, like the hawk would devour his meal? Knowing her, she'd probably just vomit at any help from me, but I would go.

I sat down on the trailer's hitch, dug a Kleenex out of my hip pocket, and blew my nose. A mosquito lit on my arm and I swatted it away.

~~~~~

Predawn air floated through the open window of the Bromwell girls' stuffy bedroom. A mosquito rode inside on the light breeze. I slapped it away and tried to drift back to sleep. A clatter in the Bromwell kitchen was Marvel shaking the cook stove's dead coals into the ash box. Cows lowed, waiting for grain and milking. A rooster crowed.

Beside me, Odette was still curled in a knot, breathing with the rhythm of a sound sleep. I rose to my knees and looked outside. Shades of pearl gray outlined a few thin clouds. The dim morning matched each day since the fire. The ranch noises hadn't varied, nor the Bromwells.

How could everyone act like nothing had changed? Didn't anybody worry about *Maman* except me? Or care that she was gone? Or care how soon *Papa* came back? Or care whether I was left to watch out for Odette in a house filled with noisy, coarse people? Or that she was acting strange, either quiet or spiteful? She used to be a fun little pest, always curious, always ready to giggle, but now she needed our mother more than I, if that was possible. My chest ached from emptiness and would until *Maman* came back and filled me up again.

I reached for my too-tight dress, slipped the skirt over my head, and tugged the bodice into place. In the living room, I checked the calendar cross. August 28, 1935. Today made nine days since the fire and four since *Papa* and *Maman* rattled away in the Bromwell's farm truck.

Please God, let them come home today.

If He did, I would declare this date a Platt holiday, even buy presents, if I had any money or somewhere to buy them. I crossed fingers, arms, and legs, and wished with all my might.

Kettles clanked together. Marvel cursed.

Foul words? From a woman? I uncrossed myself and scurried, bare feet slapping the floorboards, into the kitchen.

Marvel plunged her hand into a bucket. Water splashed down the front of her white apron.

"What happened?" I asked.

"Come have a look. I won't bite."

I crossed the room to peer into the bucket at her hand. When I bent near, Marvel smelled of sweat and bacon. "What happened?" I asked again.

"Dropped the damned griddle. Bacon grease splashed all over Sam Billy Hell and my wrist. Tarnation and wiggle worms. The cukes are ready to pickle and won't wait for blisters to heal. Gonna be a damned salty stinging mess to do now. Holy jumped-up shit-house Rosie, I don't have time for this."

Marvel pulled her hand free of the water and wrapped it in a dish towel. She plopped herself on the bench by the table, looking as faded as her work dress.

I wanted to give her a hug, but rushed to the massive stove and forked half-charred bacon onto a platter. The kettle of oatmeal smelled scorched. I pushed it to a cooler spot on the cook top and pulled biscuits from the oven.

Marvel unwrapped her hand. Blisters had already formed on her thumb and across both sides of her wrist. "Nothing compared to your father's burnt hands."

Papa's burns were far worse, but that didn't lessen Marvel's pain. "Can't the cucumbers wait for a day or two?"

"Work on a ranch doesn't wait. Your chicken-pecked hand should've taught you that." She hissed at her wrist. "Pssst on pain."

I had not checked my finger since Marvel removed *Maman*'s bandage after the fire and poured kerosene on the gash for disinfecting and toughening. I held my hand up toward the good light of the kitchen window. Only a few fading red marks were left. By now *Papa*'s hands must be healing, too. "Do you think *Maman* is healing yet?"

Marvel looked up at me. "Child, will you fetch the butter from the root cellar."

I paused on the landing of the darkened stoop to let the fresh, sweet air bless my face and arms. I hiked up my dress enough to let the coolness seep up my gangly legs. Did I dare take time to run across the farmyard to the edge of the coulee and feel the air that scampered up from the low lands and the river?

If I was *dang* quick about it.

Still, holding my skirt high, I hurried across the barnyard.

The dim light of daybreak concealed the rugged sandstone cliffs of the coulee in soft shades of brown. The shades of color lied about the landscape. The stark images in the blazing noontime sun told the truth about the prairie – and the truth about me. All day, every day, I pretended to cheerfully wait for my parents to take me home, but as the scorching temperature rose, my ability to appear happy wilted, and my yearning for the quietness of the Platt spread showed. I couldn't help the droop to my shoulders and the frown on my forehead. How could *Papa* leave me behind? Leave me so beholden? Odette was right. Maybe I was the one to blame. No, it was Sadie Chicken. I stepped closer to the edge.

The usually milky river appeared inky in the dense shadows at the bottom and seemed only a simple step away. I could float the river to the town where *Papa* had taken *Maman*.

"Be careful. It's a long way to the bottom." Monty stood a short way behind.

I dropped the hem of my skirt. "How far?"

"Come away from the edge."

I ran for the cellar. My flight might seem obedient to Monty's warning, but I didn't run because of him. I hurried from my own stupidity. Lack of fear at a coulee's edge was dangerous. I had to be more careful. *Maman* would expect me to be at the Bromwells when she came back.

The root cellar's heavy door refused to budge. I took a better grip and tugged it open far enough to set the prop board. The dank wooden steps creaked under my feet; webs brushed my face. I blew at them and wiped my cheeks. A cold draft brought up earth and rot smell. Shivering, I struck a wooden match and lit the candle. Blocks of river ice lay hidden in musty straw in the same way fear for my mother lay freezing in my heart.

I broke into tears. The wetness on my cheeks surprised me, and I scrubbed them away. Why was I such a scaredy cat? I couldn't answer my question any more than I could help worrying.

"Buck up," Marvel would say.

"Hide pain behind a sweet smile," *Maman* would say.

I'd do neither in a root cellar. The privacy allowed me to dwell in self-pity for a moment. Not once since *Papa* left us had I been alone like at our place. *Maman* always encouraged me to roam, explore the prairies, see if I could find the reason why my father hung onto it so hard. I clenched my fists in the quiet confines of the dank underground room, and knowing no one could hear, cried out, "I can't wait too long!"

There, I felt better.

I grabbed a crock of butter from a wooden bench filled with other crocks. I took time to glance into each one. Plenty of sauerkraut and berry jam. Our shelves held only the jars of green beans we had canned two weeks ago. "*Maman*, if you just come back," I whispered, "next summer we'll fill jars like these. Have our own full shelves." Envy and greed were side-by-side in my words, but surely God understood I just didn't want to owe the neighbors a debt too large.

Ducking beneath a spider web, I scurried back up the steps, dropped the door back into place, and hurried toward the house, grateful for that bit of time in the root cellar – a hideaway to expose my deepest feelings. I wished I could stay in the cellar instead of sleeping in Alice's room.

Marvel was cracking eggs into a skillet. Her eyebrows drew together. "Took your sweet time. You been in a jam pot? Fingers a little sticky?"

I wiped at my fingers, then grinned. "You're teasing."

"I wouldn't be if you were Eddy." She clucked her tongue. "Every time I send that boy to fetch butter, he comes back sticky enough to attract bees. Now, set the butter in the center of the table, then skedaddle and tell Odette and Fran to get outa bed. Breakfast is ready." She placed a plate of hot biscuits and gravy from the warming oven into my hands. "Give this to Alice. She woke up with her cycle and has cramps. Odette will have to help you with the dishes.

I marched through the living room. This time my bare feet slapping the pine boards with a flat sound. Shoes with leather heels would echo my resentment much better. Why did three-year-old Odette have to work for lazy Alice? I shoved against the bedroom door.

Odette was fighting her dress over her head, and Fran squatted on the chamber pot. Alice sat in the bed, her back against a feather pillow, blonde hair brushed, and her bottom lip jutted in the perpetual pout. She held her head high and stretched her hands out for the plate. "This is like having an indentured servant. You ever heard of one?"

I placed the hottest part of the plate on Alice's palms.

"Ouch." Alice jiggled the plate as she set it on the blanket. "You did that on purpose."

I touched Odette's shoulder. "You and Fran scoot in for breakfast. Marvel's ready to serve." As soon as they were out of ear shot, I hawk-eyed Alice. "I'm not your servant."

"You gotta work for the food you Platts have been gobbling up." She popped a bite of biscuit into her sassy mouth.

"Maybe you ought to just buck up and go help your mother."

"You're not old enough to know what I'm suffering."

"I know more about blood and birth than you do."

Alice's lips curled in a mirthless smile. "Stay in here much longer and you'll be working on an empty stomach."

I marched from the room, not because I was worried about an empty stomach, but I really needed to swat Alice. I'd never treat company like she did us.

I applied what Marvel called *elbow-grease* to the insides of the iron pot after breakfast. To place myself somewhere besides fighting crusted oatmeal, I let *Maman*'s faraway words whisper in the center of me. I pictured the gnarled, fruit-laden grapevines that looked like stiff little ladies dressed for tea.

Did I hear faint laughter? By the cook stove? But only water bubbled in Marvel's metal canner. Lonesome sadness touched me like a mist after rain. I needed to say, *Goodbye, Maman.* My knees turned rubbery. I wobbled.

"Blinny? What's the matter, girl?"

I blinked at Marvel. "I-I don't know."

Marvel grabbed my arm and propelled me to the bench. "You're white as a ghost. Sit and tell me what happened."

I eased down onto the bench. "I thought I heard *Maman* say good-bye."

"Blinny, it doesn't do any good to fret so much. Puts all kinds of notions in your brain." Marvel headed outside, carrying two bushel baskets with sore hands. As the screen door shut, she added, "I'll need you in the pickle patch. Do you good to be outdoors in the wind. Sweep those cobwebs outa your brain."

It was a relief to leave the quiet kitchen and its lonely feeling. Marvel would chitchat, tell me that picking the cucumbers would chase away my melancholy. I needed that, and I also needed to check on Odette.

Hat brim pulled down against the sun's glare, I crossed the hot ground to the barn. The tops of my tanned feet were browner than I thought they could get; the bottoms were tough enough to walk on the fiery silt, but I hurried with quick short steps.

Odette squatted by the barn door, pestering a new batch of kittens. Such a sad girl with dark hair frizzing every which way and milky skin sunburned and freckled. Her long-sleeve cover-up had been lost to the fire, leaving her exposed to prairie heat that drained moisture from skin like Herefords sucking water tanks dry. Odette needed clothes, a pair of shoes, and a comb of her own. I had a good notion to go through Alice and Fran's box of castoffs. Marvel might let me, but not until the pickles and dill were in the brine.

Odette was jiggling a piece of straw for the kittens to swat. She saw me coming but ducked her head as if I was of no concern. I knelt beside her. "Which kitty do you like best?" I hoped for some kind of response other than dark glares.

She traced the straw in the dirt right under the nose of a kitten. There were four. Two tabbies and two calicos.

I picked up a tabby and held the ball of fur close to my cheek. "This one is awfully cute."

"It'll die now that you've touched it. The mother won't feed it."

"That's the dumbest thing I've ever heard."

"Mothers do that."

How could I explain why *Maman* lay like the dead? I didn't understand myself. I set the kitten down near Odette. With a quick flip of her hand, she brushed it way. The kitty mewed and curled up into a ball. The mother cat dashed from the barn and sniffed the kitten, licking it here and there.

"See, Odette, the cat still loves her baby."

Odette reached out and petted the cat. "I want *Maman*," she said.

"You're not the only one." My words slipped from my heart, hard to give sympathy when I desperately needed some. "Maybe they'll come back today," I mumbled with as much empathy as I could muster. It wasn't Odette's fault that I was all she had. It wasn't her fault that Sadie Chicken burned our house down.

To put some distance between Odette and my feelings, I ambled to the spot near the rutted road where I stood vigil at every chance. I fit my toes in the exact toe prints I left yesterday and the day before. I settled into my marks in the soil with a sigh, hoping Marvel wouldn't yell at me to get my fanny into the garden. Overwork and endless waiting pushed me toward the point of rebellion in the same way wind breaks against a barn. I, too, might howl in protest.

Bromwell's road ran east along a section of wire fence, then up a slight rise before disappearing into the vast prairie. Around the crooked fence posts, sun-bleached rye grass grew high, their long-grained heads tickling knotholes. A family of meadow larks chatted on the top wire, and bees harvested nectar from clover blossoms as I studied the skyline for any sign of an approaching vehicle.

"Ouch," Odette cried behind me.

I scurried back. "What?"

"The kitten scratched me."

"You're pestering it to death. If I was a kitten, I'd scratch you, too."

Tears welled in Odette's eyes. "I'm telling *Papa* on you."

I sighed and returned my attention to the open prairie. It's true, I had been bossy and really couldn't feel sorry for it. Any feelings I had were wrapped up in my own self.

Chapter 6

The very next day after Alice dropped the letter out the car window, her Lincoln again slid to a halt in a great cloud of dust. Prairie silt coated even more of the fenders and doors than yesterday. She climbed out in her usual slow way.

"Of course you don't want me here, but here I are," she said and shook her shoulders in a prideful way. She was trying to be cute, and she was. She even looked friendly. Something none of the family had seen since I moved from the ranch.

"Matter of fact," I said. "I was hoping you'd stop by. I'm ready to rough plumb. You can crawl under the house and run the water pipe to the kitchen for me."

"I'm not crawling under anything. You can skin your knees, but you'll need to seal an elbow joint to come up through the floor. I'll hold the pipe steady from up here." She marched over to the stack of pipe and reached for a piece to cut to size.

A warning *buzz?*

Rattlesnake! Alice jumped back, caught her clog in a rut and sat down hard, skirt flying up, arms flailing. I grabbed a shovel and dashed forward. She was up and running toward the Lincoln. I knocked the coiled snake from the pipes and jabbed the spade down through its head, severing it from its writhing body. Poor little guy had chosen the wrong place to sun himself. I hated the killing. He was young, a foot and a half long and too scared to simply slither away when disturbed.

Alice had stopped halfway to her car. Now she walked back, as indignant as a startled cat. "You'd better check that pile of pipe and your foundation every day until it's closed up. That warm cement's a temptation to every damned rattler here-a-bouts."

A belly laugh welled up. I couldn't help it. I simply hooted. Finally I choked out, "Remember the snake in the outhouse at your folks' place."

Alice's bottom lip quivered. I thought she was going to laugh, too. Instead, she frowned and pinned me with a sharp glare. "Bitch," she said through clenched teeth. She tried not to laugh in the midst of my mirth. She didn't make it. A chuckle broke free, and then she chortled until she snorted.

"I must have been quite a sight running from the privy," she gasped.

I wiped at tears rolling down my face. "A sight I'll never forget, but you had it coming."

"I was mean, but you about drove me nuts. So damned shy. Couldn't say *boo* to you without you causing an uproar. Odette was even worse. That poor girl couldn't even talk until it was prodded from her. I think that's when she lost her marbles."

That sobered me. Alice had crossed into territory belonging only to blood Platts. "Be careful," I said, calmly.

Alice reared back. "You two girls weren't the only ones who suffered during that time. What was it? Nine days? You act like it was a lifetime. Don't you understand that's when our families were permanently sealed? You found a friend in Monty, and I learned to care about Didier. He was so terribly hurt. Who could forgive a wife that purposely killed herself? You never have figured it out. You're more like Didier than your mother."

Again, Alice tromped to her Lincoln and yelled, "I couldn't stand you then, and I can't stand you now." She slammed the car door and spun off in a cloud of dust.

Good, maybe I wouldn't see her for a long time – like never. I might be like my father, but I also felt things like *Maman* did. I knew what it was like to feel lonesome and lost.

The snake's body dangled across the shovel as I walked down the road a good hundred yards. I tossed it in the ditch to make a meal for some bird.

I walked back, admitting to myself that Alice was right about how terribly shy I had been when Didier left Odette and me at the Bromwells, but I had also been smart. Smarter than she figured back then. She had learned the hard way that I wasn't a pushover, and I earned a little respect from her. Not that she ever admitted it. Same as I never let her know that there were times I wished I had her tolerance for family. She bitched and moaned to high heaven, used them as much as they allowed, but she'd fight to the death for all of us.

I rubbed the back of my neck. It felt stiff and painful. And I was at a loss to know how to put Alice's mind at ease about me leaving the ranch. I had come to believe that was the reason for her moodiness. She thought I was punishing her by moving. I wasn't. It was time to go. Somehow Alice needed to release the hold she tried to keep on everything and everyone around her.

I glanced up at the blazing fore-noon sun and lifted my straw hat to cool my forehead. It was every bit as hot as that endless day so long ago when Odette and I were in the Bromwells' kitchen setting plates on the table for Marvel. We were hurrying. Clarence Bromwell wanted to start filming at noon sharp.

~~~~~~

Uncle Clarence stuck his head in the back door. "Marvel, we don't have time for lunch now."

Marvel puffed up. "I don't cook later than noon."

Clarence smiled with the kind of patience reserved for a favorite female relative. "After filming, a plate of sandwiches will be just fine. Besides, it gives you a break, too."

Marvel chewed on that a mite. "Ring the bell. The young 'uns ain't far off. They've been hanging around like a herd of curious sheep." She followed Clarence out onto the stoop, with Odette and me on her heels. The screen door slammed behind us.

He ran the clangor around the inside of a steel triangle hanging from a beam. A loud steady ringing pealed over the barnyard.

Harvey and Donald hurried from the freshly swept barn, Richard and Emmet from the raked corral. The twins raced from the granary where they'd been trapping mice. Tom and Monty tested the two new posts they set in the pig run, and then wandered into the barnyard. Mr. Bromwell, with Fran by his side, rounded the house from where he had strung a length of new chicken wire along the garden's west side.

Sweat stained the rims of the boys' straw hats, and their long-sleeved cotton shirts were rolled to the elbows. Boots protected the boys who were old enough to work. The others ran on bare soles callused to withstand heat or cold.

Uncle Clarence counted heads. "Where's Eddy?"

"If I was a rattler I could bite your butt." Eddy's voice danced.

Uncle Clarence wheeled around and swatted the boy's head, just hard enough to sting. "I'll have no lip outa anyone who's no bigger than a gopher."

Mr. Bromwell frowned. "Come here, Eddy. You're always underfoot."

Eddy's high spirits deflated. He hung his head and drag-footed over to his father. He received another swat. A harder one. He snuck a quick look at me and looked away just as quick.

Poor Eddie hadn't learned yet that pride and falls go together, but I thought it cruel to embarrass him in front of his uncle and us Platt girls. I reached down and patted Odette's tiny shoulder. She clung closer to my skinny leg.

The screen door opened behind us and Alice sighed like she'd rather be anywhere else.

Uncle Clarence stepped from the porch. "Let's film some snakes." He turned and looked at me. "Come on. I know you're prairie shy, but it'll be fun. It's not every day you get a chance to see the filming of a motion picture."

I dang sure didn't want to, but stepped from the porch with Odette beside me. Alice brushed past us.

The four farm dogs set off a horrible racket and raced up the road. A spiral of dust billowed up from behind the knoll. A black model-A topped the rise, then roared into the farmyard. Dust blowing and brakes grinding, it slid to a stop by the house.

"It's Susie Arnold," Uncle Clarence said and then pointed at Marvel. "I don't have time for company."

She spluttered, "I have no idea why she's here. It isn't Sunday or anything."

The doors popped open. Out spilled four gangly blond boys and Cousin Susie. She was scrawny with hunched shoulders, wore a baggy dress, and had fly-away hair the color of sand. Wire-rimmed glasses perched on a hooked red nose that looked like she blew it a lot.

She put one hand on her hip and said loud enough for the cows in the pasture to hear, "I had a notion to come for a visit, and now I see why the good Lord put the thought in my head. Clarence, I haven't seen you in a coon's age."

Clarence snorted and mumbled something. Could've been, *not long enough.*

Mr. Bromwell chuckled and scratched his belly between his buttonholes. "Shoulda said that myself."

Marvel clasped Susie in a hug. "Clarence is making a motion picture, so we gotta be quiet and watch."

The blond boys blended with the brown-haired Bromwells, and Marvel hooked arms with Cousin Susie. She led her forward to stand beside Mr. Bromwell.

The outhouse door opened with a bang and Eddy ran out, pulling up his overalls, a strap forgotten and bouncing against his back. "Uncle Clarence," he yelled, "when we gonna film the snakes?"

Clarence was already striding toward the corral, toting his camera, his step so springy, as if he might break into another toe-tapping dance at any minute. Marvel and Cousin Susie fell in behind Mr. Bromwell as he lumbered toward the corral. Boys converged on the corral at the same time. They crowded close to their uncle, the air pulsing with excited voices, all talking at once.

Curiosity also prodded me. I dragged Odette across the barnyard to the weathered rails.

Everyone, Marvel and Cousin Susie included, climbed the narrow peeled poles. Mr. Bromwell built sturdy and tight corrals. The corral stood eight rungs high with just enough room between the rails to get a good foothold. None of his calves, trying to get to their mother's teats, could squeeze through.

"Blinny," Marvel ordered. "Get Odette up here beside Alice and Fran. Can't have you girls gettin' snake bit."

"Maybe they should be in the house." yelled Susie's eldest son. He was prideful and loud. I hated him on sight.

I boosted Odette ahead of me until we perched on the very top rail. "Hang on tight." I gripped the slippery poles with my hands and feet.

A wooden barrel sat in the center of the corral. A rock held a lid in place. Uncle Clarence raised his hand for silence when we were all settled. "I want to film lots of snakes. How many you think we got?"

Monty answered, "We found a den down the north side coulee. I figure there's a hundred, give or take."

"Got plenty of poles?"

"Yeah, and pitchforks. Also have the .22s and filled our pockets with bullets." Monty nodded toward four rifles resting against the rail, barrels pointed skyward.

"Any shotguns?"

"Pa's and Tom's."

Clarence patted Monty's arm. "I knew you'd have it all figured out. If a Hollywood studio buys the snake film for backdrop scenes, we'll all share in the cash profits."

The Bromwells gasped.

Eddy's chest puffed out with pride as he grinned at one of Cousin Susie's boys.

Clarence cleared his throat. "Everyone, and I mean everyone, keep yourself on this side of the corral once the shooting starts. I don't want snake bites and bullet wounds to deal with."

The tanned, prairie-reared Bromwell boys and the blond Arnolds fairly wiggled with anticipation at the mention of impending carnage. They looked like the greedy crowd waiting for lions to eat Christians that I saw in Mr. Galloway's history book. Monty and Tom entered the corral and stuck the ends of their poles against the barrel. Tom announced, "We're ready when you are."

Clarence aimed his camera. "Let'er roll!"

Monty and Tom shoved the barrel. It tipped. *Thud.* The rock rolled free; the top popped loose. The barrel rolled twice, and then settled. A tangled mass of writhing, hissing, rattling snakes swarmed out onto the packed dirt at the center of the corral. The air droned with a buzz far more terrifying than a swarm of angry hornets. The gray-spotted pit vipers slithered over each other and spread apart. Some remained coiled, ready to strike. Others darted for cover in the shade of the barn. Some neared the fence.

"Watch 'em!" Eddy yelled and poked his pole at an escaping rattler. The other boys worked fast to herd snakes back to the center of the corral. The ground teemed with prairie rattlers, long, short, bulky, pencil-thin.

Uncle Clarence filmed the snakes with their mouths wide, fangs extended, and striking at poles before they were tossed back into the arena.

How could Eve take an apple from one? No wonder God got mad.

Eddy jabbed at a monstrous five-foot grand-daddy and almost toppled from the rail.

"Enough," Mr. Bromwell ordered.

"That's a take," Uncle Clarence said. "Hot damn, you boys done good." He pushed the camera's off button.

Mr. Bromwell yelled, "Shoot'em!"

Tom and Monty opened fire with double-barreled shotguns. The *booms* were followed by the *pops* of the single-shot .22s. Triangular snake heads exploded atop writhing bodies, rattles still shrilling. The rifles were reloaded as younger boys fought snakes back to the center with poles. Another barrage of explosions hit into the mass. Snakes raced in all directions, or remained coiled, tongues flicking to smell the source of danger.

Alice reached across Fran and gave Odette a nudge on the back. Odette teetered. I lurched, but caught her and clutched her tight. I scowled at Alice, who grinned and turned her blond head away. She knew I couldn't do anything in front of her parents.

The boys reloaded and kept shooting. Snake heads their bull's eye. None missed.

I counted dead snakes between volleys of rifle fire. At first, I was glad to see them die, but as the number grew to forty, my stomach heaved. Blood and guts spread on the ground. Gun powder stunk. None of God's creatures deserved to die in such a bloody way. I couldn't imagine what *Maman* would say about the savagery. I covered Odette's eyes.

She twisted from my hand. "Quit it! I want to see." She licked her lips, eyes roaming to where the shots rang out. One shot blew holes in the heads of two snakes. "Did you see that?" she asked, pointing. Her violet eyes shone and her cheeks were flushed.

I looked where she pointed. Monty stood there, gun to his shoulder but he wasn't pulling the trigger. His face appeared stony. Why was he mad? He walked toward the gate. He glanced up at me as he passed by. He wasn't mad. His eyes clearly showed a sadness like I'd never seen before. I wanted to jump down and walk with him. Ask what was wrong, but I didn't. He leaned against the gate and watched his brothers as they continued to slaughter the snakes.

One thin rattler slithered by the edge of the barn. "Hurry, hurry," I cheered under my breath. It disappeared into the barn's shadow and reappeared desperately wriggling toward the outdoor privy. It disappeared into a crack under the weathered door. My relief lasted only a moment, and then an idea occurred. First person to use the privy would have a rude surprise.

The echo from the final rifle shot faded away. Silent and devoid of any expression, the Bromwells studied the mess of dead reptiles for movement.

"Should be safe," Mr. Bromwell finally said and dropped to the ground. "Use the hayforks to load 'em in the wagon, boys. Save the big ones for skinning. We can all use new belts." He grabbed the tail of one and held it high. It stretched to the ground. The sun caught its sage-colored scales and grayish underbelly. "This guy has gotta be long enough to go around old Saul at the Hingham Café."

I waited a moment more, then helped Odette to the ground and walked straight toward Alice, brushed by her, and hot-footed for the privy.

Alice laughed. "Made you sick enough to pee your undies?"

I pretended to speed up, listening for Alice's footfalls. Sure enough Alice ran around me.

"You're first after me." She disappeared inside. The privy door slammed shut.

I counted, "One . . two . . . " The bloodcurdling scream happened on seven. The privy door flew open and Alice beelined out, underpants flapping at her ankles. "Snake," she screamed hysterically.

Mr. Bromwell ran toward her. "Are you bit?"

"I saw it just in time. It's coiled in the back corner."

"Then pull up yer pants and quit yer yelling!"

Alice pointed at Uncle Clarence. "It's all your fault!" She bolted for the house.

The Arnold boys were laughing their heads off and holding their sides.

I didn't laugh. Instead, I savored a sweet feeling. Alice might be five years older, but she sure wasn't five years smarter.

As usual, I checked down the road before going in the house to help make sandwiches. Was that a thin spiral of dust? *Papa?* The cloud of dust grew wider. My heart leaped and almost choked me. *"Papa!"* I clasped Odette's hand. Together, we charged up the road. The shape became a truck, then disappeared on the far side of the rise. The dogs erupted and charged forward. Finally, the International bounced into full view, blew by us, and slid to a stop in the barnyard. The door opened and *Papa* climbed out, the dearest sight I ever saw.

Still, hand-in-hand, Odette and I dashed back toward the truck.

Odette pulled free of my grip. *"Papa! Papa!"*

He grabbed her up.

"Where's *Maman*?" I cried.

He gazed down at me like every sad thing was piled onto what he had to say. His words came with stark simplicity, "She's gone to heaven."

I couldn't think of what he meant. I needed him to hold me, but Odette filled his arms. She burrowed her face into his shoulder as if she hadn't heard. I wanted to scream. Make Odette understand, like I suddenly did. The word heaven locked onto *Maman*. I couldn't separate them.

"Blinny," *Papa* said. "Odette will understand later."

How did he know what I was thinking? Could he read my dark thoughts? The ones that shamed me? No, he didn't know what I really wanted to yell, but didn't dare. *You didn't take her to the hospital in time! Why didn't you take her right away? You let her die.*

"You let her die," I cried.

His face hardened, chin jutted. "You will not say that to me. She died because she wanted to."

I spluttered. "She did not. She wanted her baby."

Marvel rushed to me and gathered me into her arms. I sobbed against her bosom. She patted my back. "That's enough," she whispered in my ear. "You have to buck up."

I pulled away, embarrassed by my tears.

Mr. Bromwell stepped forward from where he and Marvel had gathered with their children and the Arnolds. "Right sorry about your wife," he said. "Come inside and tell us what happened."

Marvel fussed at *Papa*'s side. "When was the last time you ate? I'll round you up something."

Food? How could she think of eating? My mother is dead!

"Can't stay," *Papa* said. "I need to harness the team and take my girls to Rudyard."

Despite my tears, I felt relief. This time I was going with him.

Marvel's eyebrows lifted. "Rudyard?"

Odette hugged *Papa* harder. The planes of his face appeared thinner, and the black shadows under his eyes ran down to his cheekbones. My hope deadened at the expression in his eyes.

Papa said in a voice so low that I strained to hear the words, "I wired my uncles, and they sent train fare for Blinny and Odette. They'll live with my uncles in Kalispell."

Marvel chewed on her bottom lip. "You're sending those girls off?"

I gasped and held my breath, my stomach retching. I didn't spew vomit, just held it in.

"They're better off with family. I'll bring them back when it's time."

At that moment, my heart hardened against *Papa*, and I realized for the first time what my father lacked. He lacked good sense. Why send us hundreds of miles away to relatives I had never met when we needed him most? The exasperation written on Marvel's face said she knew it, too. She should tell him some of her sound logic.

But all she said was, "I'll see what I have to send with the girls."

I couldn't believe it.

"No need," *Papa* said. "I'm outfitting them in Rudyard."

Marvel studied my father. She shook her head. "I ain't used to telling folks what is right and wrong, but it ain't right for your girls to be away from all they're used to. Can't they stay with us?"

She spoke a glimmer of good sense. As much as I hated being at the Bromwells', I quailed at the thought of going so far away. "Please, let us stay. I'll help Marvel with chores and you can come see us. Odette wants to stay."

She glared at me and burrowed into his shoulder as if I stood between them even though she was the one in his arms.

Papa spoke in a flat tone, "Platts take care of Platts, and will until I can bring you back."

Marvel's lips pressed together, ending her questions. But questions filled every part of me. I could even feel them in my toes, and the first one boiled to the surface. "You want me to take Odette all the way across the Rocky Mountains all by myself?"

"The conductor on the train will watch out for you."

"How will I know when to get off?"

"Blinny, I'll explain on the way. Right now I'm going to harness the team. Fetch your things."

"We don't have anything. It's all burnt up."

Papa's cheeks reddened. "Come along and help me with the team." He tromped away, packing Odette on his hip, expecting me to obey without protest.

I followed silently – for now. Anger would soon overcome my fear and my father *was* going to listen. We would refuse to leave him by himself. He needed us, even if he didn't think so.

Our wagon, the one with sides tight enough to haul grain, had been pushed up against the north side of the barn near the lean-to. The pulling collars and harnesses were stored in the wagon bed under an old tarp Mr. Bromwell had lent to *Papa*. We'd be leaving with two hand-me-down dresses, one bonnet for Odette, the hat *Maman* gave me and a castoff tarp.

I felt castoff; as though I was no longer needed.

Papa stood Odette down. "Stay with your sister. I can't hold you and harness the team at the same time." He walked to a small holding field behind the barn, whistled and rattled a grain bucket. Joey and Johnny stepped lively across the pasture.

I willed them to plug along, stretch out time, delay what *Papa* was set on doing.

Odette pulled away from me and ran forward. She stumbled into the back of *Papa's* leg. "Get back or you'll get stepped on," he said. "Blinny, watch out for her."

I dragged her out of the way as he led the horses to the wagon.

Odette finally quit struggling and leaned into me. "I want *Maman*," she mewled like a kitten for its mother.

Papa slipped a pulling collar over Joey's shoulders and coupled it. The draft horse accepted the heavy leather as if it weighed nothing. He was well muscled, sixteen hands tall, and willing to work.

Please Joey, just this once run away! But he never twitched, accepting the bit into his mouth as he had the collar over his neck. *Papa* buckled the bridle around his head, led him along the right side of the wagon tongue, and connected the front of the harness to the neck yoke.

The harnessing was going too fast, quicker than ever before. Why couldn't *Papa* be as slow as he had been when I waited forever on the sooty ground beside *Maman*?

What ground was she laying in now?

"Stop!" I cried. "Where is my mother's resting place?"

Papa, acting as if he hadn't heard, nudged Joey's hip toward the tongue and attached the two pulling chains to the single tree. Then Johnny was in his harness and beside Joey.

"Blinny, get into the wagon."

"Did you bury her in Havre?"

He touched my shoulder and pointed to the wagon seat.

I locked my jaw and climbed up the spokes of the wheel and onto the seat. He handed Odette up to me. We sat on the sturdy wooden seat, but I didn't feel solid. My stomach churned and my mind buzzed. *Papa* plain made me mad. How could he send his family away? He'll be all alone. What sense did that make?

I made one more plea. "Please. We want to stay with you."

"Enough." He hoisted himself up onto the seat beside Odette, who slid as close to him as she could.

Marvel's kitchen door should fly open as the wagon wheeled through the barnyard, but she just watched through the window. Alice sat on the stoop, regal as a fairytale princess. She didn't smile or wave. I expected her to gloat, but she ignored me, her eyes on *Papa*. Monty, Mr. Bromwell, Harvey, Tom, and the twins nodded as we rolled by.

"I'm obliged to you," *Papa* said.

Mr. Bromwell spat in the dust. "Crazy damned Frenchman." He and his sons broke off into different directions to return to their chores.

Marvel hurried through the kitchen door. "Wait! I can't let you go hungry." She handed a cloth bundle to Monty, who loped to the wagon and handed it up to me.

I couldn't say thanks. *Papa* slapped the reins on Johnny's rump. Their step quickened. I turned and looked back – twice: first time to see if anyone was waving, second time to say thanks under my breath.

I rode quietly. My only movement was one thumbnail picking at the other. This ride was worse than the one after the fire. At least then, I knew why. We had left the homestead to seek help. There was no reason for this trip. I could keep house and run the tractor just like *Maman*.

I closed my eyes and tried to see *Maman*, but saw only her unmoving face after the fire. That image was seared into me by fire and death. Somehow, I had to find *Maman*'s real face again. I needed to be at the homestead, remembering her in all the places where we laughed and told each other stories.

Chapter 7

Alice was bound and determined to help me. She showed up more and more, couldn't get it through her thick skull that I wanted to be alone with my building. Then she showed up with a request that sounded like a cover for something else.

"I know you're avoiding me," she said. "But I need you at the ranch."

I lifted my ratty straw hat and scratched at the sweat running freely down my temple. It didn't ease the throb I suddenly felt. "I'm busy."

"Oh, poof. You're always busy. It's time to take a break."

"I'm getting ready to set fence posts."

"I am not digging holes."

"I thought you're the one who wanted to help."

"Did I say anything at all about helping? You have to come home and talk to Junior. He's bound and determined to plant pumpkins. Just like his dad. He'll lose money on 'em for sure. And we can't afford to waste money, as you well know."

"Junior is forty-five years old. Let the man make his mistakes."

"So you admit it's a mistake?"

"What does Steven think about it?"

Alice scowled. "He's as bad as his brother. Platt men are damned disgusting."

Thunder rumbled in the west. Huge clouds, dark and roiling, sailed above the Sweet Grass Hills. As we looked skyward, a flash of electricity bolted downward, followed by a sharp crack.

Alice jumped. "Where the heck did that come from?"

"We'd better go inside until it passes over. Looks like those clouds are angry enough to dump hail, and they're coming fast."

"I'm heading home. I should've known you'd refuse to talk to Junior."

Wind rushed over us, kicking up dust from the graded soil. Choking, I grabbed for my hat and held it against my nose and mouth. "Come on," I yelled and raced to the camper. The wind yanked at the door as I fought to open it.

Head down and skirt billowing, Alice charged inside. A clap of thunder chased in behind her.

I pulled the door shut and set the lock. The trailer vibrated as if the wind was hitting from all directions and rain backwashed against the windows. Then a blast of hail struck the metal roof. I covered my ears. The smell of water and newness seeped inside through vents and cracked caulking. Rain dripped inside near the table.

I slid a bowl under the leak and lit the kerosene burner. "Coffee sound good?"

"I'll have a cup, but I don't feel like chitchat in this racket."

I hadn't planned on chitting or chatting. Also didn't plan on letting her goad me. "The storm will be gone in a few minutes. Darn, we needed a nice gentle downpour, not a gully washer."

Alice eyed me. "Why won't you help me with Junior?"

"Why didn't you even say goodbye when Didier took us to the train station after *Maman* died?"

"Whoa. That's outa left field."

"Do you have any idea what that train ride was like?"

"No, and I don't want to know."

"Of course you don't."

"It's no wonder you're a recluse. With an attitude like yours, nobody wants to be around you."

"Then why are you dead set on me staying at the ranch?"

"Damned if I know." Her voice sounded loud as the hail suddenly lessened to rain. The stream running from the ceiling turned to watery plops in the bucket.

I handed her a hot cup of leftover coffee.

Alice slurped once, stood, shoved open the door against the wind and tossed her coffee outside. She looked at me for a long moment. "You ought to tell Odette about the train ride, and the shrink still wants to know what happened when your mother died."

"How can I explain what she did? Or my father's guilt? I don't even know the whole of it. Maybe you need to tell me."

Alice avoided my eyes.

"I would tell my sister anything she asked about, but she hasn't. I go through this with every new therapist. I've told and retold it, and it doesn't do Odette one bit of good. What could I say that would make a difference?"

Alice ran her hand along the edge of the doorjamb. "How can you stand staying in this dinky tin box? It's awful and *you know* that. Punishing yourself won't pay the piper."

She didn't bother to shut the door.

I stuck my head outside and called after her, "Let Junior have his pumpkins. He'll make them pay."

Why had I asked Alice about saying goodbye?

After Alice left in a huff, I closed out the rain and wiped up the puddle by the door, took my coffee to the one soft chair and picked up my manuals on house building. I read the first paragraph about laying brick and mortar up the sides of the foundation. Movement caught the corner of my eye. A grasshopper hopped from the counter to the table. I snatched it and held him up. "Too wet for you outside, too. Well, I don't mind sharing if you stay out of the grub." It looked like he winked at me. "I think I'll just call you Mr. Simpson after a station agent. He looked just like you."

~~~~~

I met Mr. Simpson at the Rudyard train station when *Papa* bought the one-way tickets to Whitefish, Montana. He looked like a grasshopper, all legs, barrel chest, and a flat face. He wore a green visor above his bloodshot eyes. He gave me a nod when he handed the tickets to my father. It was almost like he understood I couldn't help staring.

He wrote down the message *Papa* told him and then his finger rapped the telegraph key faster than I thought possible. The metal base fairly jumped from the *tat-a-tats*. How will my great uncles ever make sense of the message? *Papa* expected me to trust in the uncles. Said they'd be waiting at the Whitefish depot. My eight-year-old doubt ran stronger than my trust, and I crossed my fingers that they understood what *ticks* and *clicks* of a key meant.

Papa paid for the words and nudged Odette and me out the door and onto the loading platform. He leaned his back against the clapboard depot, appeared to be resting, and not near as upset as he should've been.

I set Marvel's sack down on the wooden planks beside my newly shod feet. The shoes were sturdy brown oxfords. For the first time since the fire, I wiggled my toes inside leather. Plenty of room.

Odette wore a new pair of high tops and a new ready-made dress that actually fit. *Papa* had looked through all the dresses on the rack at the mercantile, but they were either too big or too small. I really wanted to discard Alice's tight sweaty hand-me-down and hoped the uncles had better luck finding me a dress. How could I have such a thought? The uncles shouldn't have to buy me anything.

Surely, *Papa* would change his mind. Maybe I could plant a seed of doubt, make him worry. "How will I recognize them?"

Papa jerked, startled from where ever his mind had been.

"How will I know the uncles?" I asked again.

"We stayed at their farm when we first came over. Don't you remember?"

"No. I don't even know their names."

"Lanny and Tyson." *Papa* peered down at me. "How many little girls will be getting off the train? They'll know you."

"What if they're not there?"

"You stay at the depot until they come."

"How long do we have to stay?"

"Until I get a house built."

"How long will that take?"

"I have to finish the harvest, build, and...."

"And what?"

"Odette needs a mother and I need sons."

His words stopped me cold. I stared at his glum profile. What was he thinking? "How are you going to find a wife out here in the middle of the prairie?"

"One what?"

"A mother!"

He just turned his head and looked out across the railroad tracks to fields of un-grazed blue stem and Indian grasses.

I stretched my back and lifted my face to gaze up into the watery blue heavens. I was too numb to ask the Almighty for help, but the currents of a westerly breeze cooled my flushed cheeks. A chicken hawk circled high to the left. Run home little mouse or gopher or prairie dog. The hawk's wings collapsed. It plummeted toward earth, swooped, and then flapped back into the air. I squinted. Nothing dangled from his claws. I sighed. Whatever the hawk was after had escaped. At least it had a home. Mine was a pile of ashes and a grave somewhere in Havre – a town I didn't know.

"Why can't you come with us and stay with the uncles?"

"I won't leave my land."

I needed to say it was my land too, but didn't. My hope dimmed. My heart knew leaving was close. "How many miles is it?" I asked, just to make *Papa* say something.

"About two hundred miles to the Whitefish depot," he answered as if this was any ordinary trip, like going to the Sweet Grass Hills for a Sunday picnic. "The uncles will pick you up there."

Mr. Simpson stepped out onto the platform and tipped his visor against the glare. "The Empire Builder's right on time. Won't be long." He relaxed against the front of the depot next to *Papa*, smoking a stogie like Uncle Clarence had on Marvel's stoop. It had been the only thing about him that smelled good.

Papa and Mr. Simpson discussed crops and how hot it was. They should've been worrying about Odette and me. Couldn't they see we were afraid? Throwing a fit would be useless. My father's bad decision was made, and once he made up his mind, *Maman* was the only one who could change it.

How could she die? I wanted to scream that too.

A funnel of black smoke approached from the east and a long-winded whistle mourned across the grasslands, followed by several short blasts. A bright headlight glowed enough to match the midday sun, making the Great Northern locomotive look like an approaching one-eyed serpent. The earth vibrated as Engine 2584, bell clanging, pistons pumping, huge wheels turning, powered past in a cloud of steam.

Odette pressed hard against me, and I grabbed my hat against the strong draft until the train stopped.

The conductor looked important dressed in a blue uniform. He jumped from the lead passenger car and placed a wooden step on the platform below the door.

He nodded to the station agent. "How many?"

"The two girls. They're traveling to whitefish."

He looked down at me. "Are you young ladies ready to climb aboard?"

My father's jaw was hard and determined.

He can't really do this. He just can't.

Papa spoke low and firm, "Blanche, get on the train."

My feet wouldn't budge. Odd how badly I wanted to stay with someone who was doing such a bitter thing.

"Blanche." His voice spurred me, and I picked up the top of Marvel's cloth sack, clutching it so tightly my nails bit my palm. Turning too fast, I bumped Odette and she toppled forward. I caught her in mid-air and guided her up onto the wooden step.

Odette tore from my grip. "*Papa!*"

He stepped forward and gathered her into his arms. "Hush child, I'll come for you soon." He hurried up the steps and carried her onboard.

I followed, blindly, obediently – a child without choice.

The conductor led *Papa* to the rear of the car. "Put the girls next to my seat. I'll keep an eye on 'em."

Papa set Odette down on the seat by the window and waited until I squeezed by him and sat down. Odette's sobs racked against my own hidden ones. I clutched her to my side, hugging as hard as she did.

Papa gripped my other arm. "You carry the Platt name, and it is your job to take care of your sister." He turned away and strode stiffly down the aisle. He disappeared without looking back. Odette cried harder. She fought to chase after him, but I held her tight.

I stared at the empty doorway, willing him to come back. How could he send us away? Made no sense, and why did he say I carried the Platt name? We all did. The sounds of the engine grew loud. The whistle tooted twice. The bell clanged as the train jerked, slipped, and moved forward. I peered out the window and looked up and down the length of the platform. Then I searched the street behind the station. No sign of Didier.

That was the first time I thought of him by name. He would never be *Papa* again.

And I never should've asked for revenge on a poule.

The depot disappeared in the distance. My last glimpse of Rudyard was the top of the grain elevator sinking into the prairie's horizon.

Odette buried her face under my arm. Damp tangles stuck to her sweaty head. She trembled and smelled as if she'd run a long ways. "*Papa* hates us," she said, "but I hate him more."

Her tear-filled words echoed in my mind as I rocked her back and forth like *Maman* would have done. "We're going to the uncles and we can't change it. Haven't I always taken care of you?"

But who is going to take care of me? I had never gone anywhere, just lived on the homestead, attended a one-room school on Bromwell's land, and went to Rudyard only when Didier sold wheat.

My own tears started silently. Keeping my head down, I wiped at them with the back of my hand until they dried. When I finally calmed enough to open my eyes, I saw a maroon rug covering every inch of the floor. Rows of fancy seats matched the rug in color. I smoothed my palm over the fabric. It dented and rose. What was the material called? Why was the name James J. Hill painted on the outside of the train? Why was a picture of a white goat on the engine? And why was a telegrapher called an agent?

Where was the privy?

The end door opened and a man dressed all in black except for a white collar entered the coach. A white beard circled his round chin and a mustache joined the beard on both sides of his mouth. His nose twitched. Reminded me of a rabbit. He wore a cap with the word *Porter* stitched on it. His skin matched his jacket. How could the sun make anyone that dark? The black man walked down the aisle, holding the seat backs one after the other, talking to folks. Now and then his nose twitched and he smiled wide. When he worked his way to us, he stopped and peered down at Odette.

"Are you the one I heard caterwauling?" he asked in a voice that sounded too deep for a rabbit.

Odette shrank against the seat, face tear-blotchy and scared; her nose needed to be wiped.

How dare he say something mean to a poor child just sent away? He no longer looked like a nice rabbit, but a skunk. I pulled a rag from the patch pocket of Alice's hand-me-down and handed it to Odette. My eyes never once left Porter's face. "That was a lie you just told. My sister was not crying that loud."

His nose twitched. "By jiggers, we got us a spitty kitten onboard."

I heard the tease in his voice, but shot him a scowl anyway.

"Little Miss, if you need to use the facilities, the one for women is up that way, first door on your left. Lunch is still being served in the diner car."

My feet nudged Marvel's bag. "We brought our own food, but we'll need a privy."

"That's the facilities I was telling you about. Called the Ladies' Lounge. There's a water fountain by the door."

His brown eyes twinkled at me and his nose twitched again.

I dared to ask, "How did you get that color?"

He chuckled. "The man upstairs made me that-a-way. Just like he made you sassy." He held out the back of his hand. "Go ahead, give it a good rub. It feels the same as yours."

I so wanted to touch him, feel that skin, but I shook my head and asked, "Why is your name on your hat?"

"That's my job's name. I take care of folks riding the train. You traveling by yourself?"

"My sister and I are going to our Platt uncles cause Platts take care of Platts."

Porter scratched his hairy neck. "You need anything, come find me." He moved away and disappeared through the door at the end of the car.

I now knew that facilities was a fancy name for a privy, where to find water, and that trains even had a dining car. The dark-colored man had left me a gift of knowledge. I owed him my thanks.

My hat squashed behind my head when I leaned against the white napkin covering the top part of the seat.   Odette slumped against my side and soon breathed deeply, a rattle in her throat, like the one on the wagon trip to the Bromwell's after the fire. Only this trip was worse. She wasn't in the back of the wagon covered with straw and curled against *Maman*. She had only my side.

Lulled by the *tick* of the wheels on the rail joints, I stared out the window at the passing prairie, picking out mounds that resembled the ones at the homestead.   According to Mr. Galloway at the mercantile, the windy land rolled with purpose, each swell giving a place for blue stem, wild rye, and switch-grass seeds to catch and root. He had taught me how the seeds matured, then the wind or birds took them to the next mound. He explained how the constant re-seeding produced a fine rich soil for Didier's crops.

On each weekly mail trip, *Maman* took Odette and me on a slightly different route so we could picnic on new knolls and gather plants for Mr. Galloway to identify. Didier called him a worn-out teacher from the Blackfeet Indian Reservation, but *Maman* admired him because he had taken great pains to learn the flora and fauna of the Montana prairie. I figured he liked to share his knowledge so he could make *Maman* laugh, even on days when a letter had not arrived from *Grandmaman*.

Mr. Galloway owned the two buildings in Goldstone; the mercantile where we picked up the mail and a dance hall where ranchers brought their families for a good time on Saturday night. He always saved a dance for *Maman*, and one for me. *Papa* didn't think much of Mr. Galloway, but I liked him and was sad when he sold out and moved on. I hoped he was happy wherever he was.

Odette woke up and whimpered, "I need the privy. Hurry."

Strangers filled *all* the seats *all* the way to the door. I ground my teeth, and grabbed Odette's hand. We walked the length of the car, lurching from side to side as the coach rocked. The eyes of the strangers stung worse than all the Bromwells watching my dirty feet. My cheeks burned and were probably the color of chokecherry juice. So many people should never know about someone needing to use the privy.

With both hands, I shoved open the heavy door Mr. Porter told us about. The train lurched. We stumbled inside the Ladies Lounge – such a fancy name for a place to pee.

Three white wash basins with odd metal handles lined one wall of the small room. On another was a counter with three chairs and three mirrors. Each mirror had a light above it. Okay, everything is in threes, but where were the holes? Behind that narrow door? The handle didn't budge. I twisted harder and rattled the knob.

"Just a bloomin' minute!"

I jumped back from the door. The angry voice was a woman's and sounded like Marvel scolding Eddy.

Odette crossed her legs. "I gotta go."

"My little sister has to go real bad. Aren't there three holes in there?"

No answer.

Odette fidgeted.

I rattled the doorknob again.

The sound of rushing water came from behind the door. It opened and out stepped a lady with arched eyebrows clenched together. "It's very impolite to rattle the doorknob when it's locked." She stood blocking the door with her wide bottom.

Running for cover was impossible, so I pushed Odette around the woman, through the narrow opening, and shut the door behind her. I stood in front of it, facing the lady, who backed up a step. "I'm right sorry," I said. "I thought everything was in threes."

The wattles under the lady's chin quivered. "That is the silliest thing I ever heard. Where's your mother? I want to talk with her about your behavior."

"The tent preacher said bad people earn fire and brimstone. *Maman* was good, so I guess you'll have to look in heaven."

The woman's eyes went directly up, looked at the ceiling, then she zeroed back on me. "Appears nobody has taught you manners. Maybe I should." She reached out to pinch my arm.

I pulled back. "I don't take to strangers touching me." The woman was meaner than an old hen. I was raised to respect my elders, but *Maman* wouldn't like this one pinching me.

The woman tried to stare me down, but I won and her eyes dropped first. She turned to one of the bowls and twisted the handle. Water gushed forth. As she washed, I noticed her navy blue and white daisy dress had not been pulled down proper and her white slip showed crooked. After drying her hands on a towel that pulled from a roll, she sat down in one of the chairs and kept a watch on me in the mirror while she combed her hateful brown hair.

Odette finally opened the privy door.

The woman scolded, "Go back in there and flush."

Odette cringed at the harsh words.

The passageway door opened and in stepped a lady, grander than anyone I'd ever seen. She wore shiny gray trousers made of slippery fabric. Her shirt clung to her bosom and a fur-edged stole drooped on her shoulders. Her blond hair was rolled along the sides, held in place by black netting. She carried a black square case.

She looked from me to the mean lady. "Is something wrong?"

Her voice held the concern I needed. She was on our side. Even Odette could tell and grabbed onto a long leg covered with the shiny trousers.

The daisy-clad woman half stood and pointed at Odette. "That girl didn't flush!"

A tinkle of laughter rose from the grand lady. "She's probably never seen a flush toilet. Did you show them or just yell at them?"

"How dare you question me about correcting impolite girls?"

"How dare you pick on these children?"

The daisy woman humphed and squeezed through the door, broad rump jiggling the flowers, one side of the dress still hiked up. The slip clung to the backs of her doughy legs.

I grinned at the elegant lady. "Thank you, Madam."

"You're welcome." Her eyes shone with a mischievous glint. "Vengeance is mine saith the Lord, but I say a small victory is sweet."

Imagining the daisy woman walking down the aisle, skirt hiked, and the strangers watching, I nodded in triumph. "She earned her just rewards."

"My name is Lydia Worley. What do I call you?"

"Blanche Platt." I extended my hand to her. "Mrs. Worley, I didn't mean to make trouble."

"You didn't. And please call me Lydia." She reached into the cubicle and pushed a silver button on the wall behind the hole.

The swishing sound happened again. I reached in and pushed the button too. The water swirled and disappeared down a hole. I saw the railroad tracks whizzing by below. "How does it work?"

Lydia chuckled. "It's magic." She sat down in front of the mirrors and opened the square case. It was filled with jars and bottles. "I noticed when you girls boarded the train that you're traveling alone."

"Didier's job is to take care of our stock and build a new house. Mine is to take Odette to the uncles."

Lydia picked out a flat jar, twisted the lid off and painted scarlet on her perfect lips. "A couple of weeks ago, the Havre Daily News carried a story about a farmer named Platt being burned out, and that he lost his son in the fire. Is that your father?"

My breath caught. "You know Havre?"

"More than I ever wish to."

"Where's the cemetery?"

Lydia's eyebrows rose. "Well, that's a surprising question for someone your age, but the top of Tank Hill is where the cemeteries are. That's out on Highland Park Road."

"My mother is buried there, and I'll need to find it someday. Say goodbye to her like I said goodbye to my baby brother in the snake box."

"I'm so sorry. I didn't know your mother died, too." Lydia's fine lips turned down. Pity glimmered in eyes that had been bright with humor only a moment ago.

I didn't like pity. She didn't have to feel sorry for us. "We'd better go."

Odette and I both took a long drink of water from the fountain, then hurried back down the aisle, past a soldier dressed in a brown uniform who winked at me, past an elderly man sitting with his legs stretched into the aisle. His wife nudged him, and he pulled them out of the way. We scurried past the daisy woman without looking at her.

"I'm hungry," Odette whimpered after we were in the safety of our seats.

Marvel's sack fit between us. I pulled out the loaf of bread and block of cheese that *Papa* had bought at the mercantile. I tore off a chunk of bread and broke a piece from the cheese.

Odette nibbled away and gave me a weak smile for the first time since leaving the Bromwells. Poor little mite always tagged after me when I wanted to run with the wind in my face, or she pestered when I wanted to read one of *Maman*'s books. I tricked her lots of times just to get away. Now I hugged her close. She had lost so much: her home, her baby brother, her mother, and now Didier.

My whole forehead ached, and I rubbed above my eyebrows before breaking off some cheese for myself. I ate slowly, savoring each bite. The food filled the hollow spot in my tummy and quelled the green-apple pain.

Miles sped away. The monotony of watching the prairie through the window grew hypnotic. The whistle blew, two long, a short and a long for each of the little towns. Chester, Lothair, Galata. Their names, painted on grain elevators or depots, appeared then faded from sight, as did the spires of white churches.

"Oh, *Maman*," I whispered. "I remember the Lutheran one in Rudyard."

I'd seen it when *Maman* took us girls for a walk while *Papa* unloaded wheat at the granary. We had strolled past a church with a white cross on the belfry. She cupped her work-reddened fingers near her mouth and whispered, "They think they're the only ones going to heaven, but they'll have to pass by us tent-goers to get in."

We giggled, proud that we'd be waiting by the pearly gates.

"Come on," *Maman* had said. "I want to show you something special." We walked to a house with a big bush hanging over a white picket fence. *Maman* touched a branch. "Girls, Mrs. Sanvick said we could have a start of these lilacs. They bloom in the late spring with dark purple blossoms, almost the color of our eyes. Each tiny star-shape blossom in the cluster will be our way of seeing the many prisms of the prairie."

I studied the clumps of brown flower carcasses and couldn't imagine that they had ever been purple, or that we could see the prairie in them. I whispered back, "The prairie doesn't have prisms."

"No. But it has edges that run parallel to each other. Someday you'll come to recognize the lines that divide yet hold prairie people together."

Maman's funny notion puzzled me most of that winter until I realized I had witnessed a sharp prism of isolation and its parallel side of loneliness when Larry was born. Both caused by time. The baby wouldn't wait long enough for me to run to the north field for *Papa*, so I stood at the end of the bed and caught the baby between my mother's legs. She told me how to tie the cord in two places. I did it, then took *Maman*'s butcher knife that *Papa* kept sharp for slaughter and cut the slippery, bloody cord. I quickly handed the still baby to *Maman*. She stuck her finger in his mouth and cleaned it out. His lungs filled with air and he screamed. As he cried, chest sucking in and out, she cleaned him with a rag dipped into warm water. He didn't like it one bit.

I understood his dislike at being pushed from *Maman*'s warm safe womb. In the same way I was seeing another prairie prism flashing by at the speed of a train – a parallel of not knowing anything except prairie and not wanting to learn different.

The train rolled near a lush stand of cottonwoods, elms, and willows. The trees broke the sameness of the prairie with their dusty green leaves; some near the top were already turning gold. The branches tossed in a stiff breeze. Leaves broke free and scampered along the ground until caught against tall grass or fence posts. I almost felt the currents of the wind against my arms and shoulders as I had felt the twists and turns in the prairie air all my life.

Movement among the trees caught my attention.

I strained to see into the shadows. Men and boys milled around in the afternoon shade. Even in the heat, sweat-stained hats perched on their heads and long woolen coats draped their hunched shoulders.

Hoboes? Pity filled the soft spots in me as I answered my own question. Yes, they had to be the homeless people Mr. Galloway had told me about even though *Maman* shook her head at him. "Now, Mrs. Platt, your girls need to know what is happening beyond your homestead and this mercantile." *Maman* hadn't liked it, but he continued, "Even with drought and hard times, be glad you live on a farm. City folks have no place to grow food and no money to buy it. I've heard about soup lines that stretched for blocks."

I had wanted to ask about soup lines and blocks, but *Maman* tapped the tip of her finger on her lips. She never wanted to talk about unpleasant things. I wasn't quite sure why. How bad could soup lines and blocks be?

Through the thick window of the train, a young hobo's bleak gaze met mine, his eyes soulful as a calf separated from its mother. He didn't appear much older than Monty. As the train passed, he vanished as though he'd never been, but his haunted look remained in my mind. I shivered at this first understanding of homelessness and hunger. Maybe going to the uncles' house wasn't the worst thing that could happen.

Someday we would return to our homestead.

I didn't remember the uncles and couldn't imagine what they were like. Did they really want two young girls underfoot, even for a little while? I shuddered and willed my father to keep his word to come for us soon.

Chapter 8

On July 1, 1982, I felt grimy to the core. Sponge bathing in a wash tub of sun-warmed water kept me clean enough, but my skin itched for a neck deep soak in a tub filled with steaming water and bubbles.

I also needed to borrow a couple of ladders to use as scaffolding, my pickup needed gas, and I missed Winnie, my eight-year-old mare. She understood me, maybe the only living, breathing thing that did. I had finally strung enough barbed wire last Sunday to enclose a small field where she could graze without wandering off. I also needed to fetch enough bales of hay to get her by until the rest of the fencing was completed.

Time to go to the ranch.

The sun rode the sky straight up noon by the time I forced myself away from laying out the studs for a wall frame. I tossed my work gloves on the two-by-fours, gathered up my basket of laundry, and jumped into the stifling pickup cab.

Windows rolled down and left elbow hanging out, I breezed along. McFeeters' mailbox looked as if someone had sideswiped it. I still hadn't dug a posthole for the standard galvanized box I'd bought at the hardware store in Rudyard. I couldn't decide what would survive wayward farm machinery, snow plows, or mischievous teenagers. Besides, it didn't hurt to keep picking up my few pieces of mail at the ranch. Maybe I'd leave it that way, as an excuse to visit from time to time. Or force me back – which would it become?

McFeeters' house lay hidden inside a four-sided wind break of elms, Scotch pine, and caragana bushes. They were quick growing and hardy. I'd plant some next spring on my north and west sides. I wanted to keep the east open to see the fullness of the sunrises from my bedroom window.

I drove past McFeeters' driveway feeling a tug of guilt. I should stop by. The old farmer was laid up with gout and wouldn't be able to bring in his harvest. The neighbors would help. I would, too. The time away from my building was an itchy scab on my soul, but all those years ago he helped Didier raise his new barn.

A few threatening cumulus clouds scudded eastward. Might rain if they didn't break up. The prairie needed a lot more moisture than the quick downpour we had the other day.

I passed by Bromwells' road and the unused school at the corner of their holdings. Fran Bromwell had been the teacher since 1960, the year after a tractor ran over her husband's back, leaving him crippled and only fit for light chores. When the one-room school closed, Fran moved her family to Rudyard and taught middle school. Teaching suited her. Unlike Alice, she'd inherited Marvel's good sense and used it in the classroom. No child raised on the modern prairie was going to forget what their great-grandparents accomplished. She made sure they understood the miracle of flush toilets and hot showers.

The clouds had gathered into a threatening overcast by the time the pickup finally rattled across the cattle guard, and I entered my father's spread, 37,000 acres of prime short grass prairie. The working ranch supported Alice, my two half-brothers, and their families. The Platt name was secured by six strapping grandsons. Didier would have been proud.

The Platt Road ran for two miles into his land. Behind barbed wire fence, fields of barley and oats lined the road. Cattle was the mainstay, grazing north and east of the ranch buildings.

I wheeled past cylinder-shaped metal granaries, the prominent red barn, the holding corral and cow chutes, the white-washed hen house, long narrow bunk houses, tool sheds, and a horse barn with roping corrals. Four barking farm dogs raced ahead of the pickup's front tires. A hired hand waved from the roping corral.

Didier's ranch house rose to the west on a swell overlooking the pride of his life – his acres upon acres. Two wings had been added to either side giving the home a look of stability and making it appear more enduring than when I first saw the tall narrow house my father built after the homestead shack burned. The ranch also had two houses for my half-brothers: one a few miles towards Bromwells' spread, the other in the east section, closer to the ghost town of Goldstone. My father's land encompassed it all. How many more acres he would've acquired if cancer had not taken him was anyone's guess. His greed for land never died until it was laid to rest with him.

Fran's Chevy was parked by the bent willow fence. So were two 1980 Ford pickups. One red and one white. They belonged to Anna and Claire, the twin daughters of Ralph Connor who owned a spread north of Chester. I had grown fond of the girls after my two half-brothers snuck off to Havre, married them at the county seat, and brought them home without telling Alice what they were up to. Alice's reaction still brought a smile to my lips. She can throw a fit when she wants to.

Alice's Lincoln was missing. Her sister and daughter-in-laws were here without her? Odd. But company or not, I'd wash my clothes and soak my skin.

I parked in Alice's spot, grabbed my laundry basket from the pickup bed and took four steps toward the fence and stopped.

I wasn't ready to go inside. I set the basket on the hood and leaned against a fender. Currents tugged at my straw hat. I pushed it tighter on my crown. I don't remember how many straw work-hats I've owned, but none ever fit as well as the one *Maman* bought for me from Mr. Galloway at the mercantile. I still had it, choosing to wear it only when life pressed down on me.

The clouds broke on the wind and the sun blasted down on my shoulders. A Western meadowlark sang as if morning had come again. He was answered in the same manner. Somewhere, a calf bawled. A small herd of range horses in a holding pasture kicked up their heels and galloped along the fence line. Their tails flowed and nostrils flared. Were they happy or sad the rain had passed them by?

Grasshoppers scattered in front of my boots as I wandered through clump grass toward *Maman*'s place – the site where our little homestead house had stood. Humbly, I approached the piece of prairie where my family had lived.

After Didier passed away and I stayed on to help Alice, I had slowly cleared away the charred wood that would still burn. I kept the fire going for a couple of days and then turned under the ash and blackened soil. Slowly I broke apart the river rock that had formed the fireplace and chimney. I hauled them down the coulee road to the Milk River and one by one dropped them in a deep cloudy pool.

The next spring I had driven to Rudyard and visited Mrs. Sanvick. She had gladly given me starts from her purple lilacs. I planted the shoots in the ground where the ashes would keep them fertilized until they rooted strong enough to survive the extreme weather.

And they did. Through the years they had matured into bushes, shading a green nook in the midst of the beige prairie. I sat down for a moment on the bench in their shade and thought of our family before the fire. *Papa* and *Maman*, Odette and me. And *Bébé* Larry. What had become of us?

The rustle of stirring lilac leaves reminded me that I already knew the answer and that dwelling on it did no good. I wandered back to the house for a good thorough scrubbing.

Noisy laughter carried from an open kitchen window as I pulled open the screen door to warm fragrances of honey and chokecherries.

Tall blonde Anna screeched. "Oh, it's you, Blinny." She patted her chest. "I thought a ghost had invaded us, but you're all brown and wrinkled."

Medium-sized and redheaded Claire sniffed. "And apparently ripe."

Short tanned Fran shook her brunette pageboy. "I think she looks great. All strong and hardy, but maybe a tad gamey."

I stepped inside and sat my laundry beside a bushel of pea pods. Then laughing at the women's cries, I gave each one a sweaty hug. "I'm here to wash clothes and soak in the biggest bathtub."

"That's Alice's," Fran said. "I'd think twice before using it."

"She won't know the difference. Where is she?"

Fran slowly poured a crock of honey through another sieve. "We ran out of jar lids. Seems our boys used her supply as targets. Had all five dozen nailed to fence posts in the west field. Which reminds me, why in the hell aren't you building out there? Alice has been on the warpath since you left. Don't know what's wrong, but something is biting her butt."

"I don't care what's gnawing at her, I'm off to soak." I grabbed my laundry.

Fran took the basket from my hands. "You go ahead. I'll throw these in for you."

I liked Fran.

The room Alice had shared with my father was in the right wing. I entered through white French doors. A rustic bed made of peeled poles rested in front of a knotty pine wall. A settee sat by a bay window. Photos of Alice, Hyatt, Junior, and Steven hung beside a ceiling-high pine wardrobe. Near another set of French doors, a black and white pencil etching of Didier standing at the edge of the coulee crowded the wall. He stood proud, yet looked haunted.

I ducked my eyes and went into the sunroom and the massive porcelain tub. After filling it with hot water and a good portion of Alice's gardenia bubble bath, I slid into the steaming water and laid neck deep under the suds. I rested my head against the rim and closed my eyes. Muscles sore from lifting lumber relaxed.

A light tap on the door? Alice got back and couldn't even leave me alone in a tub of water? I slit my eyes open.

Fran's head poked through the doorway. "I hate to disturb you, but we need to talk." She tiptoed into the room as if her footsteps were the intrusion. She perched on the vanity stool and stared at her cupped hands laying in her lap.

I blinked my eyelids a couple of times. "Okay, I'm done peering at you as if I wished you'd go away."

Fran broke into a grin, then rushed through the words. "I'm worried about Alice."

"Why? She's the same as ever."

Fran's cupped hands tightened. "No Alice's moods are more volatile. One minute nice, the next she bites off the head of whoever happens to be closest. Junior and Steven are avoiding her like they might catch mad cow disease. One thing for sure, nobody wants to be the target of her next tongue lashing."

I blew a soap bubble off my nose. "Sounds pretty normal."

"This is different. She constantly rants about how Odette blames you for her problems. Did you really burn down the homestead house?"

My nose itched. I rubbed it with a wet hand. A bubbled shot into my nostril. I sneezed, blowing bubbles every which way.

"Bless you," Fran said.

I glared at her. "Odette is a schizophrenic. Blaming other people for their problems is what they do. According to my sister, everything, real or made up, is my fault."

"Alice has been to see her a couple of times."

My frown returned. This was new.

Fran added softly, "I think she misses Didier more now than when he first passed on. She talks about him all the time, making excuses for his inability to love anything but his land."

"Alice is hiding something."

Fran's eyes rounded. "What?" she whispered.

"Damned if I know, but I'm done playing her games. She can carry whatever is biting her to the grave for all I care."

"Blinny, you're as bad as she is. I'm going to pray for both of you."

Fran tiptoed out, quiet as if she'd never entered.

Just before she closed the door, I said, "Tell Anna to have a couple of her boys fill my gas tank and load up two ladders and as many bales of hay as they can get in the back of the pickup. I need them to hook the horse trailer to my pickup. I'm taking Winnie home."

"This is your home." The door latch clicked shut.

I groaned and slid beneath the fragrant bubbles.

I still smelled of bath water and Gardenias when I reached down and patted Winnie's neck. Been too long since I rode her into a lather. She needed the workout as much as I did. As we loped back toward my trailer I noticed a flash of sun off glass. I reined Winnie in, tipped my hat back, and straightened my legs in the stirrups. Alice's Lincoln was parked near the tool shed. Now what the devil did she want? I hadn't been home more than an hour.

Winnie broke into a trot at my nudge.

Alice leaned against the front fender of the Lincoln and watched me dismount, unsaddle Winnie, scoop oats from a gunny sack and dump them into a feed bucket.

While waiting for Alice to say what was on her mind, I rubbed down Winnie's back and shoulders with a towel and brushed her with a curry comb.

Of course her first words would be critical. "It's the first of July and the walls aren't framed and the roof isn't on, but you have enough time to use my bubble bath?"

"I'm right on schedule. The trusses will be here in two weeks. By then the walls will be up and waiting."

"No they won't."

My eyebrows rose. "The walls won't be up?"

Alice blew through her lips as if she was addressing a complete idiot. "No, the trusses."

I waited for further explanation.

"If you'd get a damned phone hooked up, I wouldn't have to drive twenty miles to give you messages after I've already been to town and back."

"Who called?"

"Lem from the lumber yard. His boss won't guarantee delivery for at least three weeks. Said there was some kind of delay with the truss company."

A slow burn rose in my chest. "Did he give you a date?"

"Didn't know." Alice studied the flooring studs. She walked over and tried to wiggle one.

"They're solid," I said.

"Still can't understand why you asked this Lem character to help set and anchor them. You should've asked the boys."

"My brothers told me not to ask. Used chores as an excuse. Of course I didn't really want them to."

"Those boys are my sons, but they're Platts through and through. Stubborn and single-minded. In fact the only Platt that made any kind of sense was your Uncle Lanny."

That was the first time Alice admitted liking my uncle. Took me so much by surprise that I admitted, "I still miss him."

Alice shifted her weight to the other foot. "Odette called this morning asking what I remember about him and Tyson. She should be asking you."

"Alice, don't stick your long nose where it doesn't belong. Odette's relationship with our uncles is my business."

Alice threw her hands in the air. "That's just what I said." She shook her head and left without another word.

I called after her, "Your tub is great. Thanks for sharing." My words fell on her stiff back as she climbed into the Lincoln.

Her car disappeared down the driveway but our sharp words stayed. Maybe Fran was right. Alice was getting terrible. Nothing but criticism spewed from her. During the years we worked my father's land we managed to be civil. Now nothing but anger lay between us, and it was getting worse. She claimed her demands to rehash the past was for Odette, but I was beginning to doubt that. She needed something from me, and evidently I wasn't providing it. If only she understood how hard I tried not to remember the long terrifying train trip and the reason Didier sent us away. I had been so afraid of not finding my great uncles on that dark and scary loading dock. My father had told me there were five of the Platt boys: his grandfather, his two uncles still in France and the two in Kalispell. He, Maman and I came on the ship with them to America. He said I should remember, but I hadn't.

I looked at my hammer and leather apron, but couldn't reach for them. My mind wouldn't come away from the memories of my uncles. Sometimes I missed them so much tears smarted. I never was really sure whether my tears were for them or for what sent me to them.

~~~~~

The Empire Builder swayed from side to side, wheels singing a consistent rhythm against the rails. Drowsy, I half-opened my eyes to check Odette who huddled beside me on the train seat.

A voice boomed, "You're finally awake?"

I bolted upright, throwing my arm across Odette.

"Sorry." The man who had spoken looked like last year's seed potato. Wrinkles sagged around his eyes, mouth, and under his chin. Even the creases in his navy blue jacket drooped, but his crabby look disappeared into the sparkle of his blue eyes.

The conductor held out his hand for a shake. "I didn't mean to shoot you out of a cannon. Just wanted to introduce myself. Thorpe told me about you and your little sister. Said your father is sending you to your uncles in Kalispell. They'll pick you up at the Whitefish Depot. I'll make sure you get there safe and sound. You may call me Mr. Fleming. Or would you prefer Oscar?"

I slipped my hand into his wrinkled one. "Mr. Fleming will do."

"I've work to do, but I'll be back shortly."

The curve and swell of the prairie stretched ahead, behind, and straight south for as far as I could see through the window. I stared hard at the passing grassland, fixing views of the September-brown land into my mind like photos in an album, knowing it'd change quick enough as soon as the train entered the mountains.

The passengers visited. A laugh. A cough. The wind howled against the glass. Odette didn't settle down, just kept picking at my skirt; it seemed as if a wind had gotten a hold of her deep inside.

Meadowlarks darted across the land and were lost to sight in the ever changing landscape seen through the window. I wanted to reach out and grab onto the prairie, not see it passing without sound. I needed to hear killdeer call to one another, to hear the wind rustle through the dry grasses, and to hear the flies drone around the scattered Herefords – all the sounds of my life.

The train's whistle echoed long, long, short, and long. The *tick-tick* of the wheels increased to a faster *clickety-clack-clickety-clack.* We sped around a sweeping curve. My breath caught. The Rocky Mountains had grown from a distant blue haze into jagged thrusts of pink-hued rock towering over flanks of dark evergreen forests.

I heard a different tone in the rails and straightened up far enough to see downward. "Odette, we're on a bridge. Look how the river winds like a piece of dropped ribbon."

"I don't want to and you can't make me." She closed her eyes tight and turned her face away.

The river below disappeared, the way everything familiar in my life was vanishing. I knew coulees and rivers and flatland. I didn't know mountains.

I didn't know anything about uncles either.

Mr. Fleming approached and held onto the back of my seat. "We're coming into East Glacier. Wanna see a real live Indian chief?"

"My father said not to get off the train until Whitefish."

Mr. Fleming shifted his wrinkles into what could pass for a smile. "You can tell your uncles you shook the hand of a medicine man who knows all about the earth and such."

I was tempted, but Didier had said to stay on the train, and he might be right about this. "We'd better not."

The soldier who had winked at me earlier stood and watched eagerly through the window, holding onto the back of a seat for balance. A grandpa helped his wife to stand. She straightened her skirt and fluffed her snowy hair into place. Looking eager and happy, they walked forward in the car.

Lydia stood up, stretched, and looked back at me. I couldn't make out the meaning in her expression, but it seemed to be sad. She nodded to me and disappeared through the door, leaving me sad, too. I was scared and angry, but not sad in the way her look of pity made me feel sorry for myself.

The wide woman with the daisy-covered *derriere* struggled onto her feet and smoothed down the back of her skirt. She glared at me, then blustered out, complaining that none of the so-called gentlemen had offered to carry her bag. I checked through the window and was more than glad to see the daisy woman lug a heavy suitcase across the boards and disappear into the depot.

At the opposite end of the loading dock, a few passengers gathered around a man dressed in white leather, a feathered war bonnet trailed down his back. Shiny red and black beads were sewn into diamond shapes on the leggings. His skin was a lighter shade of brown than Mr. Porter, not red at all. His face was thin with a hawk nose. Beside him stood an Indian woman dressed in a fringed dress and a girl about my size. Beaded headbands topped off their fat brown braids. Moccasins were laced part way up their legs. The girl laughed at something the Indian woman said.

They must be her grandparents. They seemed nice, like the old couple on the train. I had never known my *grandmère* and sure needed her now. If only she wasn't across the ocean. Suddenly, I wanted to ask the chief who has great wisdom and knows all, why had our home burned. Why had *Maman* gotten so sick? And why was Didier so bone-headed?

I couldn't sit still one more minute. I was used to doing chores and wandering the land. Sitting in a seat for endless hours was terrible, and I was so filled with questions. Didier would never know if we got off just once. I grabbed Odette's hand and rushed down the aisle.

My new shoes squeaked with every hurried step as we crossed the platform. The Chief's eagle eyes met mine, and he winked like the soldier had. Must be a way of saying *hello*. I winked back.

"Can you tell–" A gust of wind plucked my hat from my head. It scampered down the platform. I dropped Odette's hand and darted after it. Another gust caught the brim and blew it around the corner of the depot.

I raced after it.

There!

I ran down the steps and across a graveled parking lot, reaching to grab the brim. The wind whipped, and my hat wheeled away from my fingers. It rolled, sailed, twisted, and flew into some scrub brush. I dashed for it. It stuck on a bramble. I tugged. A rip of straw. It tore free.

Oh no. My hat had torn.

I blinked back tears and checked the hole. Thankfully, only a little snag. I stuck it back on my head, pulling it down tight and turned around to tell Odette it was okay. She wasn't there. Where on earth? I dashed for the steps of the loading platform. Odette wasn't where I'd left her. The Indians were gone. I looked to the right, to the left, and across the tracks. No

Odette. A cold sweat broke out on my tense muscles. My legs felt weak. Why hadn't she followed me? She better not be hiding. Be just like her. She loved hide and seek. Please God she can't be playing that stupid game now. She was such an imp. *Maman* called her a minx, and she was, but this wasn't funny. We had to get back on the train.

I ran into the midst of the milling people, but couldn't see her. I charged inside the depot, looking in every direction. I spotted a swinging door marked *Ladies* and dashed for it, shoving it so hard I bumped the daisy woman coming out.

"For crying out loud, you again," she said and blocked my way. "I can't understand how your father could put you girls on a train without supervision. You're a hell-un. You'll be in prison before you're twenty."

I pushed past her and looked inside each privy. Not there. I raced back outside. A car sped around the end of the depot. I dashed to the end, but couldn't make out any children in the car.

Where to look? Where to look?

I couldn't believe Odette had vanished like a rabbit into brush. She was more trouble than a dozen scattered chicks, and I got mad. Anger is a blinding force. I needed to stomp and scream. Instead my tears made it impossible to see. I needed help. I scrubbed my eyes with my fists and scurried to find Mr. Fleming.

His familiar droopy figure stood beside the passenger car. I ran my hardest toward him.

"Hurry up!" he called.

"I've lost my little sister!"

"One of the ladies found her in the parking lot, trying to get in a car. Good thing too. We could've lost her. She said you were playing hide and seek."

"Where is she?"

"On board with the lady."

My racing heart slowed. Remorse filled the places that had been drained by fear. *Dang* hat. *Dang* wind. It was their fault. I clambered aboard and hurried down the aisle, searching for the little brat who couldn't be trusted to stick with me. My conscience pricked, told me I was the one who ran off, worried more about a hat than my sister.

Odette sat perched on Lydia's lap. The two of them were laughing, having fun.

Lydia saw me out of the corner of her eye. Her smile turned down, and she pinned me with a solemn look. "Never leave your sister alone like that again. Scared me half to death finding her like that. I just happened to notice her."

"I know, ma'am. But my hat--"

"What's more important, Odette or your hat?"

"Odette is, but the hat--"

"There's no excuse."

"It's the only thing I have from *Maman*."

Lydia drew in a quick breath, like she really understood, but then she shook her head. Her eyes darkened, the lines around her mouth stiffened. "Your sister is a precious gift." She tightened her arms around Odette and leaned her cheek against the springy curls like I'd seen *Maman* do.

I didn't like it. "Come on, Odette."

Odette leaned tight against Lydia. "I'm staying here."

"Well, you can't." I grabbed her arms to lift her down, but Lydia tightened her hold.

"Blinny, there's one thing I know, it's hard to face the realities of loss. Your home and mother are gone. If you can't be responsible for your sister, someone else should."

"No, ma'am. Platts take care of Platts."

Lydia stared at me until I swallowed, but I didn't look away. She sighed, and without any more arguing, released Odette, who slid off the silken gray trousers. "Go with your sister, honey. I think she's learned her lesson."

If it was Lydia's intention to heap guilt on my head, it worked. It lay right beside Sadie Chicken burning up our house, and right beside my vengeance. I couldn't get Odette and guilty me back to our seats quick enough.

I sat staring out the window, feeling bad for leaving Odette alone on the loading dock, but I was also upset with Lydia for scolding me. What if a hat was all she had left of her mother?

Odette curled into the corner up against the armrest and wall. She looked at me. Her violet eyes round and questioning. "Did I really scare you bad?"

"I was afraid we'd miss the train. The uncles wouldn't know where we were."

Odette met my look straight on. "I'm sorry, Blinny. I just wanted to make us laugh like we laughed when *Maman* hid from us and we found her." She grinned like a little imp.

A smile tugged at my lips. I tried to stop it, then gave up. "You really did get me good, but you have to stay right by me. Promise?"

The Empire Builder worked upward through bald-faced mountains on the north side of the tracks and forest-filled on the south.

Mr. Fleming leaned over from his seat and pointed out the window. "That's Great Northern Peak." When we rolled by a tall, skinny, stone pillar with a needle-like top, he said, "That marks the Continental Divide. You're right smack on top of Marias Pass." We rode the rails down into what he called the drainage of the Middle Fork of the Flathead River.

The river that followed the gap between the mountains fascinated me. Unlike the muddy Milk River meandering at the bottom of a coulee near our homestead, this water ran ever-downward – fast-flowing and pure, clear as drinking water from a deep well.

Shadows eased onto the mountains. Forests turned into blotches of ebony below towering peaks, outlined against a sky the color of deep purple lilacs. The train jerked around curves, yet the clicking of wheels was slower than on the prairie. The moon disappeared behind sable clouds. In the darkness I faced a loneliness I had never met before. I had no one to say what was right or wrong, do this or do that. Could I make those choices by myself? "I'm only eight-years-old," I whispered.

In the dimly lit passenger car, people rested and some snored. Mr. Porter wandered back into the passenger coach. With his gray hair tufted up on both sides of his hat and his whiskered chin, he still resembled a friendly rabbit. He walked the length of the aisle, lurching with a little hop to his step as the Empire Builder sped straight and fast. "Yours is the next stop. About a half an hour, or so."

There it was. Everything about me felt sick. I swallowed and held my chin high.

The time was close. I tried to take Marvel's advice. *"Buck-up,"* she had said. *"Sometimes that's all a girl has."*

I stroked Odette's hair, gently pushing it away from her sleeping face. "It's time to wake up. We're almost there."

Odette's eyes popped open, alert and guarded. "I don't want to go to the uncles."

"Don't be frightened. Didier wouldn't send us to a bad place." I hoped not, but my own fear was thick in my throat. I never thought he would send us away or talk about a new mother. If he found one, would he have new children and forget us? What if she was a widow with children? Little boys? Didier wouldn't need girls. Lack of faith in my father seeped into the very core of me.

A few seats ahead, a man looking somewhat like Mr. Bromwell cleared his throat and spat into his handkerchief; another rose and headed to the men's privy.

Lydia entered the car from the far end, carrying a folded bundle. "I'm bearing a gift to make up for scolding you. Let's go to the lady's lounge and open it.

I didn't dare. "Our stop is pretty soon."

"I won't let you miss it." Her brown eyes seemed as bereft of hope as *Maman*'s had been when I found her crying in the midst of labor. Lydia seemed to be suffering the same kind of hurt. I wanted to ask what made her sad, but I needed to stay put.

Lydia spoke to Odette, "Would you like to come with me?"

Before I could stop her, Odette slid from the seat, green-plaid dress hiking up around her thighs. She grabbed Lydia's outstretched hand.

Quickly I yanked her skirt down. "Odette, we can't go. Get back up here."

Odette ducked her eyes and reached for Lydia.

"Blinny," Lydia said softly. "It'll be all right."

Against my better judgment, I rose.

Lydia nudged my shoulder. "Go ahead. Odette and I will follow." She herded me along and I didn't like it. I halted. Odette bumped into me. I glanced back at her. The spitting man loudly harrumphed to clear his throat. Lydia jumped. I did too. Odette broke into giggles and we hurried into the ladies' facilities.

Pale and nervous, she closed the door and stood in front of it. She clutched the package to her chest. She looked like a child that wanted to tell something but was afraid.

"What is wrong?" I asked.

"I'm just anxious to give you this." Lydia shook out a blue checkered dress with a white rounded collar, narrow lace, and pearly buttons. "I noticed a girl just a little bigger than you in the dining car. I talked to her mother about how your family was burned out and she agreed to sell me the dress. I want you to have it."

I gasped, "But I might tear it."

Lydia shook her head. "The cloth is sturdy and the color would be very nice on you."

I wanted the dress more than anything, but I didn't touch it. "Why would you buy me a dress?"

"When families lose everything they have, other people pitch in to help. I saw a way to do that." She sounded so innocent and eager.

"My father said Uncle Tyson will buy what we need."

"I have no doubt, but please let me give you this. What you're wearing must be uncomfortable."

I agreed with that, and I really hated Alice's hand-me-down. "But I can't repay the debt."

"Please take it."

The softness of the fabric surprised me when she handed me the dress. I held it up in front of me and looked into one of the mirrors. Plenty big enough.

Lydia smiled. "Go in the little room and try it on. Then let us see."

"It's pretty," Odette said.

It was. It really was. I drew the dress to my cheek and smelled the freshness of new cloth. Yet I hesitated, torn between desire and guilt. Pride won. I stepped into the cubicle, thinking how much better I'd look to the uncles in this dress.

With hardly enough room to turn around, I tugged Alice's old dress over my head and wiggled into the beautiful one. I held my breath for fear of ripping the sleeves, but they hung loosely. I fastened each little button and even dared to touch the lace.

I opened the door.

Lydia sat on one of the chairs in front of the mirrors, Odette nestling on her lap. They stared at me, then Lydia's eyes shone with wetness. She blinked several times. "The dress is perfect on you."

"I never expected to own one so fine."

"I'm glad you like it." Lydia sighed and moistened her lips. "If I had a little girl, I could buy her lots of dresses."

Odette looked up at her. "I want one, too."

Lydia smiled down at her. "We'd have such fun picking out a whole bunch."

My chest tightened. The green apple feeling hit full force, running up my throat. I didn't know what Lydia was up to, but I knew I didn't like the way Odette was taking to her. It was almost like she was sitting on *Maman*'s lap.

"C'mon, Odette. We'd better go back to our seats in case Mr. Fleming comes to tell us to get ready."

Lydia ran her fingers through Odette's tangled curls. "I have so many empty rooms. Odette would fill them with joy. There's a huge yard and I'll build her a playhouse. She'll have lots of dolls. These are hard times, but I promise to provide. She'll be happy with me."

I suddenly realized my hat wasn't the only thing left of what *Maman* had given to me. "I've changed my mind about the dress. I can't be owing you anything."

"I'll just have to toss it in the basket if you don't keep it. What a waste that would be." Her tone pleaded.

I didn't want to let my sister out of my sight by changing in the privy. I yanked the dress off and struggled back into Alice Bromwell's. It pinched and smelled sweaty, but it was a gift clear of owing. "We have to go."

Lydia squeezed her arms around Odette. "You've already proven you can't watch her properly. I'd be good to her. I promise I'll go see your father and tell him where she is. In fact, you come and stay, too. He'd probably be happy having you girls closer to the homestead. Lots of families are taking in children, what with the depression and all. My friend, Dorothy, just took in three boys from a mother who couldn't even feed herself. Hard times are tough on families that didn't have much to begin with. I'd love to have you, and when your father is ready for you to go home I'll take you."

Lydia sounded so reasonable, so sure of what she was saying. I was tempted, but said, "*Maman* would say you're wanting what doesn't belong to you. You'd better let go of Odette or I'll scream for Mr. Porter and Mr. Fleming. They'll call the train bull, and if he's anything like Bromwell's bull, you won't like it."

Odette squirmed in Lydia's clasp, she pushed at the pressed arms. Lydia relaxed her grip and Odette slid free.

"Ma'am, us Platts stick together. Get your money back for that dress."

"You still owe me. You just learned how much your sister means to you. That lesson's worth more than money." Lydia lowered her face between her knees and moaned.

For a moment I wanted to pat her back and tell her not to hurt so much in her heart; instead, I grabbed Odette's hand and shoved the door open.

Lydia spoke behind me, "I just wanted a more perfect world. One where little girls are looked after."

We fled to our seats and safely disappeared behind their high backs. I tugged on the sleeves of Alice's dress and relieved the pressure for a moment. Lydia's dress had been so wonderful. I wouldn't soon forget how it felt.

Minutes later the train slowed and entered the outskirts of Whitefish, Montana. Small rectangles of light shone from houses not far from the tracks. I tried to imagine the families inside. The train jerked twice before settling to a full stop. My breath caught and released slowly, calming my snaky feeling.

I helped my little sister from the seat and grabbed Marvel's bag. Hand-in-hand we walked the long aisle and stepped out onto the platform. I wobbled, feeling as though I was still train-walking instead of on solid ground. I couldn't even trust the *dang* ground. I was more scared than mad, but it felt good to swear inside.

People milled around, none I recognized.

Conductor Fleming touched my shoulder. "Wait with me until we find your uncles."

The depot loomed into the fresh night sky, a huge dark building. A big-wheeled hand cart loaded with luggage rattled by, pulled by a hunched fellow. Two men approached from the far end of the depot. They disappeared for a second into the building's shadows, then re-appeared, outlined by the lights from the windows. One man was enormous and lumbering, the other puny and precise. Both wore suits, with Fedoras perched on their heads.

The smaller one spoke to Mr. Fleming. "I'm Tyson Platt. This is Lanny. We've come for our grand-nieces."

It seemed forever before I could get past the lump in my throat enough to speak. "I'm Blinny Platt and this here is Odette."

Uncle Tyson sized me up in a kind way. A smile of welcome touched his aged eyes. He held his sloping shoulders square, his hat sat at a jaunty angle, and his coat had been brushed. He was cleanly shaven and wore glasses. Nothing about him spoke of meanness. He looked nice.

He spoke to Conductor Fleming. "Thank you for watching out for our nieces."

Mr. Fleming nodded. "They're good girls."

Uncle Lanny bent over, reached out and shook my hand, his paw completely engulfing it and my wrist, but the squeeze was careful not to hurt. His face was a combination of broad planes, wide forehead, spread out nose with a blubbery flat tip, cheeks uneven, one caved inward, the other round. A scar angled from his left eye across his shrunken cheek and disappeared into a shaggy beard. He smiled. "I know I've been hit with an ugly stick, but I'm nicer than he is." He nodded toward Tyson.

I blurted, "You're a mighty big Platt."

"And you're a mighty small one. We'll see if we can get along. Are you bossy?"

"Odette isn't."

"You'll fit right in. Where's your luggage?"

"Marvel's sack is all we have and I can carry it fine."

"Good, cause I ain't gonna." Uncle Lanny lumbered after Tyson, who was already walking toward the side of the depot.

Conductor Fleming gave me a nod. "Go on with you. They're nice enough blokes."

"Thank you for your help." I pulled Odette along, hurrying to catch up.

I had to look back. Mr. Fleming had disappeared inside and the train rolled forward. A window framed Lydia's face. She waved and mouthed, *I'm sorry*.

I waved in return. I'd never forget Lydia. She hadn't meant harm, just offered what she thought was a better life for Odette. Right then I promised myself that someday, I'd go to Havre to find *Maman*'s resting place and thank Lydia for the lesson. Tell them both how much I owed them. Odette was a pain, but she was a Platt and my responsibility – one that *Maman* left me.

I scurried across the platform, dragging Odette. Under a street lamp in the parking lot, Uncle Lanny waited beside a black car as big as Clarence Bromwell's green one. Tyson was already behind the wheel.

I opened the back car door to a pungent blast of dog smell. I pushed Odette inside and squeezed in after her. Two enormous black dogs straddled us, paws heavy and sharp on my thighs. Dodging wet tongues and slobber, I managed to slam the door shut as Uncle Tyson fired up the engine. The dogs shifted, squishing me.

Uncle Lanny reached across the seat and boxed the biggest dog on the snout. "Get over, you big lug, and give 'em some room."

I shoved the dog aside enough to breathe. "What's he called?"

"Pooch. The other's Mutt. They hold the title to the car. It can't go anywhere unless they're in the back seat. Dog law or something." Uncle Lanny settled in the front seat as we hurtled through the night. Before long, his deep breathing ended any chance I had of asking more questions.

Uncle Tyson drove in silence. His clean-shaven jaw, pointed nose, and chiseled cheekbones were barely outlined in the dark car. The sky was pitch black. No stars or moon. A few rain drops hit the windshield and ran down. Then more. Tyson turned on the wipers and their rhythm matched Lanny's snores. I loved the sound of the rain hitting the car and the wet sound of the tires on the road. It had been so long since I felt raindrops. I wanted to hold my hand out the window, but didn't dare; instead, I tried to see the land, wondering if it was all tall mountains.

We sped through the rainy night, dogs panting, and the tires humming – so different than the wagon trip from the Bromwells to the depot in Rudyard.

Chapter 9

"Stop your infernal pounding and come eat." Alice set a wicker basket down in the shade of the camper and spread a blanket as if she'd been invited to do so.

I kept driving nails into two-by-four inch studs. The wall frames were almost done and I had hoped to go to bed tonight with them completed. The lumber yard finally committed to a delivery date for the trusses. The walls had to be up in a couple more days. Lem was coming tomorrow to help raise them. I didn't have time for Alice or want to stop and eat.

She lifted a pie from the basket and set it in the center of the blanket just like *Maman* used to.

A pie? What kind? I threw the hammer down and walked over to her.

"For as long as I've known you, never once have you packed a picnic basket and asked me to join you."

"I want to explain something about your father."

"Why should you try to explain my father?"

Alice's cornflower eyes grew hard. "Maybe, just maybe, you shouldn't ask me that. Why can't you simply listen, and store it in that hard head, and then pass it along to Odette to help her."

"I think the only reason you want to talk about Didier is that you miss him. Although, I'll never understand why. All I ever saw between the two of you were fights and moody silences."

"Sit down and eat."

After I knelt on the blanket and then wiggled around to sit Indian style, she handed me a tuna sandwich. It tasted like fishy mayonnaise laced with onion and dill pickle. It went down good.

"Blanche, you have no idea what went on in my marriage. Didier talked to me in a way he never could with you. Maybe I should keep it that way. Just between him and me."

She had my attention, but I wasn't about to give her the satisfaction of letting her know. "Fran thinks you're worried about something. Says you've never been so moody."

Alice cleaned bread from her teeth with her tongue. She was trying not to get mad. She slurped water from a jar, smacked her lips and said, "Didn't know I was such a hot topic."

"Do you have cancer?" I asked softly.

She blinked a couple of times. "You think I have cancer?"

"That or some other awful thing."

She jabbed her thumb towards her chest. "I'm not sick, never been sick, and don't intend on getting sick."

I swallowed a bite of sandwich. "Then why are you acting like a hen sitting on eggs. You're pecking at everyone."

"Cause it's high time you heard how difficult it was for Didier to put you on that train and for you to quit blaming him for every bad thing in your life. Odette does it too."

"He earned the blame."

"Maybe so, but after Essie Faye died, he sent you to the one place he knew you'd be safe."

I never thought of that. Was it true?

Alice pulled a folder from the basket. "You know, you girls weren't the first family he lost. He was so devastated by losing Essie that he wrote this. I think it took him many nights to put his feelings in words."

The manila folder was bent and dirty along the top. The back showed creases in several places. "Looks like it used to hold a lot more. How much have you kept to yourself?"

"Kept for you."

"Why now? What's changed?"

"You weren't ready to see these before, probably still aren't, but it's high time. Needs to be done before you both croak of old age." She handed me the folder like she expected me to open it and read while she sat and watched.

"I'll read it later."

"It's going home with me."

I held it toward her as though I didn't care. We battled in silence, her will against mine. She won, and I opened the folder. Inside was a sheet of lined paper torn from a writing tablet and the stub of a pencil, sharpened by a jackknife. The look in Alice's eyes told me it was Didier's. I rubbed the painted, teeth-dented wood between my fingers, picturing my overworked and over-worried father with a tablet resting on his legs, pencil in his hand, searching for words to write. He wasn't schooled, knew only farm work, yet he wrote poems. Out of respect for his urge to record what he felt, I read:

> *The man that was me wrote the unbidden,*
>
> *The rhythm wouldn't, couldn't stay hidden.*
>
> *Words flowed from exhaustion buried in he,*
>
> *Earned by him doing what never should be.*
>
> *His daughters sent away on rails of iron,*
>
> *As he watched, hidden behind the grain tower,*

Choking back bile in a throat way tight,

'til the last of the train was lost to sight.

Unending grief, and he cursed at his trials

as his wagon rolled the childless miles,

moved by a team simply given their head

by a man with a spirit totally dead.

Finally his fields, the ones of his own,

appeared in the dusk looking darker of tone.

Hues of caramel touched his over ripe grain.

He needed to harvest 'ere the next rain.

But now he had time, he would hurry no more.

He'd gather the crop to calm his heart sore.

A house he'd rebuild, and find a new wife,

to sire sons and put an end to the strife.

He guided the team past his house all burned,

And away from the charred chimney he turned.

But magnet of sorrow it drew him once more,

And forced him to write of a lad and a war.

Mortar shells blew holes in houses of stone.

He ran and he ran, terrified and alone.

He fell near rubble, the church o' his youth?

He saw the lone cross, a symbol of truth.

Oh God let this be your heavenly sign,

spare my family, they're all that is mine.

Finally he reached the house he called home.

Part of the roof blown down on the loam.

Inside his mother and sister lay entwine

hugging in death as if they were fine.

The pool of blood that ran below them

was darker, far darker than ink from his pen.

*Parts of his father scattered
the ground.*

*The lad that was still
wanders around*

*inside the heart of the man,
that was me.*

Some of his words were written hard and bold, others scrawled and childlike. He had suffered as he wrote. I crushed the poem to my chest. Tears stung but I refused to let them flow in front of Alice. I'd save them for a time when I could grieve alone on the prairie that my father so loved.

Alice shook her head. "Your father wasn't educated in words, but the truth of him is there if you look for it."

I covered my sorrow with sharp words. Alice was getting too close to where I harbored past memories. "Didier's feelings are here, but what good were they? They were buried all day every day, coming out only at night by himself? What good is that? The man preferred the horses and his barn to his daughters. He felt safer with the hay, prairie dust, manure, and urine than us. How in the hell can I forgive that kind of father?"

"Why do you insist on being such a shrew?"

"Call me names all you want. I know what I know, and I know for sure he milked the cows, fed the chickens and slopped the hogs before he felt the sadness he wrote down. My so-called father turned his back on two little girls and walked away, leaving us totally at the mercies of strangers."

Alice's eyes narrowed. "You always find fault. I still don't know how my brother could love you."

"Leave Monty out this. We're talking about Didier. The one you chose to marry. I didn't get a choice. I just got stuck with a hard man who called himself a father, but didn't act like one. Did he leave any writings about why *Maman* married him? Or are you keeping that secret, too?"

Alice paused as if she knew why, but said, "Monty came and talked to him that first night after you left on the train. I can tell you Didier was bent with grief." Eyes closed, she was quiet long enough for me to think she was through ripping at my feelings, but no, she started again.

"Didier remembered every tiny painful detail of the wagon trip back to his homestead after putting you on the train. How tired the horses were, how empty he was. It haunted him for years."

I groaned. "Stop now."

Alice clasped her hands in her lap. Her shoulders hunched. "I'd like to shake you."

Let her try, I thought.

But she only said, "Don't you see? Didier needed to write down the grief he could not talk about. Didn't have time to learn how. His job was to build the homestead into a paying ranch for Essie Faye's daughters." The words lay between us a moment. "He wasn't worried about Odette going to the uncles because he knew you'd care for her."

Alice put the folder back into the safety of the basket. She reached over and lifted a piece of pie onto a paper plate. Apple slices oozing from the crust, she handed it to me as though nothing had been said or any emotion was connected to her picnic.

I accepted the slice, barely aware of doing so. My father had lost his whole family to German artillery. I had lost a mother and a brother. Was his loss more than mine?

~~~~~

Odette and I became town kids. We lived in a two-story house, attended a three-story school, and walked to Main Street for ice cream cones. On the Morning of October 23, 1940, I lay in bed listening to wind-blown tendrils of our weeping willow brush against a second-story window in my uncles' Victorian house. I smiled at the whish and slash, imagining Uncle Tyson's grimace as he must be hearing it, too. For each of the last five springs, I had held the ladder steady for him and listened for when declared, "I've pruned enough." But in the October winds, the once-again overgrown foliage reached the windowpanes. I expected Uncle Tyson to have a choice comment at the breakfast table.

I hugged the goose down quilts up under my chin, closed my eyes and listened to weak spots in the clapboard siding creak from the first cold of coming winter. Something scurried in the attic.

According to the engraved pocket watch Uncle Tyson gave me last Christmas I had lain wake again 'til after midnight. Odette was a worry. She was quiet, distant, and moody, same as *Maman* had been after *Bébé* Larry's birth. Not that Odette ever possessed *Maman*'s fun sense of humor. My sister was now eight-years-old and had become plain mean. Just yesterday, I caught her in the back yard, cutting night crawlers in half.

Her reasoning was worse than the cutting. Said she wanted to hold a few up for show-and-tell, explaining, "I couldn't figure out which end was the head. I didn't want to dangle them upside down, so I cut them in half, figuring the head side would wiggle. Both ends wiggle. I gotta keep cutting 'til I find the pea dinky brain." She made sense. I simply left her alone with her murderous chore.

What would *Maman* do? Leave Odette cutting? With worm juice all over? If only I could talk to someone. Marvel Bromwell came to mind. I hadn't seen her since I was eight-years-old, but I remembered her passing along sensible advice.

Uncle Lanny would only say I was making the usual teenage mountain. Uncle Tyson would frown and worry along with me, but he didn't understand the ways of anything except the ledger books in his office. I considered several of the church ladies, but they weren't Platts. Odette was family business. That left my cousin Elaine, Tyson's only child, and the only Platt woman I knew.

Since the first day we arrived, she insisted we call her Aunt Elaine instead of cousin, because she didn't want to explain to the whole of the town that we were third cousins. We'd be much closer than that. Aunt would do just fine. I should be able to confide in her, yet I hesitated, couldn't settle my mind to it. She was God-fearing and stern, and quite unbelievably, Odette seemed to like her. I didn't.

I refused to worry for the next few minutes and burrowed deeper into the quilts, listening to the groans of a bigger-than-necessary house. One good-sized square room with doors opening to bedrooms was all I deemed useful. Why have rooms on top of one another with fourteen steps to climb? It made for a long trip to the privy in the middle of the night. My first request of Uncle Tyson had been chamber pots for Odette and myself, but he had insisted that his heart pumped at a strong, steady pace because of climbing the stairs in the middle of the night. He claimed it kept the blood from laying in one side of the veins too long.

Uncle Lanny had snorted at that idea. The same evening, he brought home two porcelain pots, each creamy-colored with painted daisies and a lid.

"Pretty enough for a queen's heinie," he had said, sending me into shock and worry over what *Maman* would say about such talk as heinie and one-sided veins, but she'd probably laugh at Uncle Lanny and surely say that flip-flopping in bed should help as much as climbing stairs. My tossing last night had not been from worry about veins and blood. It was directly related to my sister's sorry attitude.

Odette's bedroom was across the hall which had seemed strange at first. The night we arrived at the uncles' house Tyson had led us upstairs. "You girls share this room for tonight. The house won't seem so strange. Tomorrow is time enough for you to decide who gets which bedroom. We'll keep you across the hall from each other. You'll still be close, but you need your own space to grow, just like a row of carrots need thinning to let them grow plump."

I had never considered having my own space, didn't know if I liked the idea or not, especially if it made me plump, but I needn't have worried. At first Odette would slip into my room in the middle of the night and climb into my bed, curling against me, crying lots of tears. After a few months, that had stopped, and I was glad. Having my own room, my very own place was the best thing ever.

I finally forced myself from the warmth of the four-poster bed. The metal springs rattled just like Alice Bromwell's bed used to. I was surprised to recall such a minor detail. Could be I held too much pride at not sharing my bed or my room like Alice did with Fran. Of course, Alice was the brat in that set of sisters, and as far as I could see, Odette was well on the way to surpass Alice's spiteful ways.

I checked the weather through the double-hung window. Windy and overcast. Low, water-laden clouds would hide sunrise over Columbia Mountain. On clear mornings, I used to ask the rising arc if I'd ever see the other side of the Rockies, the prairies and my father again. The years passed, and my yearnings for the homestead lessened. The uncles' two-story house became home.

Wind howled in the eaves and rattled the window. An icy draft brushed across my feet. The half-open door creaked and the lunky, lazy Retrievers padded inside. Their noses had roughened over the years, bellies hung lower, and more whiskers were gray, but they still searched me out every morning as soon as my bed rattled.

"Old buddies, what can I do about Odette's sorry behavior?" All the answer I got was sad eyes and wags of tail. I slipped into the hall and turned Odette's doorknob. Locked again. I rattled it and pounded on the door. "Time to get up."

She didn't answer on the first call, nor the second. I kept calling until she sleepily answered, "Go away."

I should just let her fail school. "I don't care if you ever get up," I hollered.

Uncle Lanny's door cracked open. I couldn't see his craggy old face, but his gruff voice said, "Blinny, do you have to yell?"

"I'm trying to wake Miss Brat."

His door closed, and I hustled back into my room to dress. Today was Wednesday, the day of the week to wear my favorite dress with tiny violets the color of my eyes. I removed it from the walnut wardrobe and held it tight for a moment. Besides having a sharp tongue, vanity had laid claim to some of my thoughts.

The crisp percale slipped on easily over a cotton slip and smoothed down over me. The top no longer lay flat, but swelled a little in the proper places. I checked my face in the mirror. Aunt Elaine told me thirteenth birthdays and pimples went together. She was right and I hated them. Thankfully there were no new ones today. After a good brushing, my ebony hair smoothed into waves over my shoulders. The color of my hair and eyes were the only features I shared with *Maman* and Odette. They were petite and wispy; I was gangly and firm. Maybe I took after an ancient grandmother, maybe a third or fourth great. I wondered what they were like.

I removed the chamber pot from under the skirted stand and carried the queen's bowl to the door. The dilapidated straw hat *Maman* had given me hung on a peg beside a black velvet cloche for church and a wide-brimmed sunbonnet. I plopped on the old straw, padded out into the hall, banged twice on Odette's door, scurried past the uncles' rooms, and careful not to spill, glided down the dark stairs into the kitchen, dogs leading the way. They stopped and watched me stuff my feet into my oxfords by the back door.

Outside, frozen grass crunched underfoot. I paused for a moment to savor the granite-colored shapes huddled in the predawn: maple trees, lilac bushes, unused dog house, chicken coop, stable used as a garage, and the privy. I breathed in the tang of pine. This green valley's perfume was heady stuff compared to the prairies. No wonder *Maman* loved the vineyard in France. It must've smelled lush in the morning dew. I was surprised at my comparison of the two. Odette's bratty attitude had caused me to dwell in memories long buried. I needed my mother to deal with her.

The overcast above the mountains pearled into soft gray. A few rays might pierce through the clouds. The neighbor's rooster crowed.

I was dawdling again. I scooted to the privy, emptied the pot, and did my business.

Odette's window was still dark as I hurried back inside and shut the door in the dogs' faces. I didn't have time to trip over them while fixing oatmeal and toast, and I didn't have time to fight with Miss Ornery herself. I was building up a good bit of steam over my sister.

I quickly filled the coffee pot and placed it on a back burner of the new Hotpoint electric range. "The Hi-speed Calrod is the fastest, most durable electric cooking coil in the world," Uncle Tyson had bragged when it was delivered. I loved the stove, knowing that a good portion of his monthly pension went to make my cooking easier.

Uncle Lanny's footsteps thumped on the stairs before he poked his head inside the kitchen doorway. His wet gray hair was combed back, face freshly shaved, and eyes shone with *good morning*.

"It's only a week 'till Halloween," he said. "Decide on the costumes yet?" He crossed to the cupboard where his cup normally sat on the second shelf. "Where in the blue blazes is my mug?"

"In the cabinet by the sink. Handier place for glasses and cups."

"I thought you were done turning the house upside down and inside out," Lanny grumbled.

To divert his train of thought, I asked, "What would you suggest as a costume? I can't think of what to make. Ghosts, witches and bums are all boring. I want something exotic enough to win a prize."

"Tell you what," Lanny said, delight shining in his dark eyes. "We'll sneak over to old man Petersen's farm and cut off the horse's tail so you can go as Lady Godiva. That'll give those church biddies something to judge." He laughed and plopped in his chair at the foot of the pine table. "They'd be judging 'til Kingdom come. And don't worry about the horse. We'll give him the swatter by the back door. He could stick it in his teeth like so." Lanny stuck the end of a fork in his mouth and made swatting motions, like a horse swishing his tail from side to side.

Uncle Tyson cleared his throat. He was framed in the doorway. "Is this a stable or a kitchen?"

Lanny grinned around the handle of the fork. "Stable. What are you doing sneaking up on people?"

Tyson ignored the question and carried the ledger he worked on over coffee to the table. He looked down at Lanny still clenching the fork's handle in his teeth. "When are you going to grow up?"

"At the rapture."

"Hellfire and damnation claimed your hide long ago unless there's a big change in your attitude."

Lanny blew on his coffee and took a loud slurp. "I git along jist fine with the devil and his helpers. Takes work to earn their respect."

The twists and turns of their fussing was part of every breakfast and as satisfying as the oatmeal I scooped into two bowls. I placed the steaming mush in front of them.

"I've got it!" I said. "We'll dress Uncle Lanny in an angel costume and win the prize for the most improved."

Tyson's eyebrows shot up, and he pointed a bony finger at Lanny. "You earned that." He chuckled as he dripped honey on his cereal. "Where's Odette?"

"Still upstairs." I crossed to the hallway. "Odette! Your mush is getting cold."

My sister finally pattered down the stairs, flew into the kitchen, and slipped into her chair. Her black curls tangled around her thin face and half-hid her thick-lashed eyes. She avoided our looks and started eating.

"Odette," Uncle Tyson said. "When you sit at this table you will greet us before gobbling food."

She looked my way, her eyes gleamed, like a conniving kitten. "Good morning, Uncle Tyson. Did the tree limbs scratching on the windows keep you awake, too?"

He peered over his glasses. "Why yes they did. You're a good girl."

I simmered. She was not a good girl. She needed a good swat. "Odette, if you--"

Lanny shoved away from the table. "If I don't show up soon, the lumber yard may shut down permanent." He opened the door, dodged the dogs as they bounded inside and closed the door behind himself, having once again avoided the inevitable quarrel between Odette and myself. I needed his frank advice, not desertion. Uncle Tyson also avoided me by sticking his nose into the ledger book. Neither uncle was any help, choosing to ignore Odette's moods, and hoping she'd outgrow them.

Odette scraped up the last bite in her bowl and shoveled it into her mouth. "Uncle Tyson, may I please be excused?"

"Of course, child. Run along."

She bumped my arm on purpose when she brushed by.

I really needed to talk to Aunt Elaine about Odette's lack of concern. She just didn't care what anyone said to her.

Uncle Tyson glanced up from the book. "Between that tree and your sister, I'm all befuddled this morning. I'm just gonna cut down that crying, sobbing, weeping willow."

"Next spring I'll prune and you can hold the ladder."

Uncle Tyson sipped his coffee, then shivered. "It's colder this morning. Better wear the knit hats and mittens that Elaine made you. If she sees you walking into her class without them, she'll be hurt."

I scarfed down lumpy oatmeal. With the solid mass in my stomach, I cleared the table, ran upstairs and put on Aunt Elaine's knitting. She did do nice things for Odette and me. I should appreciate her more, but I never saw how I could pretend enough to overcome Elaine's put-on ways.

I banged on Odette's door. "Hurry up, I need to talk to Aunt Elaine."

Odette threw open her door, rushed past me and charged downstairs ahead of me, slamming the front door in my face. I'd find some way to straighten her up. I called *goodbye* to Uncle Tyson and stepped out into a sharp northeast wind that blew straight out of Canada and down the canyon of the North Fork. Odette waited for me at the gate, looking every bit the innocent.

"I thought you were in a hurry," she said sweetly.

This time I passed her like she wasn't there. The wind pressed my wool coat against the back of my legs, scooting me into a faster pace.

Odette lagged behind.

Along our route to Edgerton School, the houses were an assortment of clapboards. They all had sheds, wood piles, outhouses, vegetable gardens, lilac bushes, and wooden rockers on the front porches. Telephone poles marked every corner as if a writer had added an exclamation mark to separate the blocks. I liked to think of things as parts of grammar, wanting everything clear and precise. Concrete nouns and verbs, exact punctuation, prepositional phrases, adjectives, and adverbs, all neatly diagramed, precise and clear. Unlike Odette's behavior.

How could I help her be a little girl instead of a mean old hen?

Maybe Odette longed for the homestead, like *Maman* yearned for France? I doubted it, but she had a space inside that wasn't filled. I had no idea what would fill it, but I had to come up with something before she got lost to me in the same way *Maman* did. She had slipped away to where she couldn't return from.

I glanced back at Odette, drag-tailing behind and waited for her to catch up. "Don't you even care if I get to school early? I told you I need to talk with Aunt Elaine before first bell."

Odette shrugged, the familiar vacant expression entering her eyes again. I wanted to shake the absent look away, but her shutdowns stayed until she chose to answer.

"Okay, you can walk the rest of the way by yourself."

I ran up the steps of the three-story brick school with worry in my mind as weighty as the oatmeal in my stomach. I rattled the door, hoping someone would let me inside.

Mr. Johnson, the janitor, pushed the door open only far enough to say, "You have ten more minutes before the bell."

"I know, but I really need to talk with my aunt Elaine before everyone comes inside."

He shoved the door open a little more and I had to squeeze by him. He watched me climb the two flights of creaky hardwood stairs. Glad to be out of his creepy eyesight, I hurried down the waxed hall.

The door to Aunt Elaine Cada's eighth grade classroom was ajar. Voices carried from within. Aunt Elaine was visiting with her friend, Mrs. Dunbar, a first grade teacher.

I stopped dead still and listened to my aunt say, "I'm worried about my father. He's too old to take care of those girls, let alone support them. I still can't believe he bought that new stove. The old one was working just fine. Didier can just come and take his children back to the prairie."

I shook my head, unsure if I had heard right.

Mrs. Dunbar said, "Blinny and Odette have been here for a long time. It's their home now."

"You don't understand. They're in *my* childhood home. I was raised there, and my father holds the deed. It's his house and no one else's. Not one board belongs to that good-for-nothing Lanny or those girls. Someday the house will be mine. Mine to sell. The money is going to be my nest egg and pay for my retirement trip to the Holy Land. I've earned it. That big house about broke my back after Mom died."

"Blinny's a hard worker. She's helped you by keeping up the place."

Aunt Elaine continued her rant as though Mrs. Dunbar hadn't said anything. "And besides that, I taught school, took care of my children and a deathly sick husband. I was actually relieved when he died. Can you believe that? Glad the man you love is dead? And soon I'll have to take care of my father."

"Your father's healthy as a horse."

"He won't be if those girls keep pestering him. The other day, he was sleeping in his chair and didn't hear my knocking or the dogs barking. I could see him through the window, still as death. Right then and there I knew the girls should go home."

"Elaine, it's good for you to let off steam, but you're getting close to a hissy fit again."

"I am not."

"You told me to warn you."

"If I told you to poke yourself in the eye, you'd do that too?"

"See?"

I heard Aunt Elaine take a deep breath. Her voice came again, "The good Lord knows I tried when Blanche and Odette first came. Frightened little things. I tried hard to mother Odette, but Blinny stood over her, ever-watching, ever-protecting, ever-sassing. Nobody had a chance to claim the child's affection. Do I feel guilt at giving up? Probably. Selfish, too. But I'm going to make sure my father doesn't change his will and give the place to them. Be just like him. Blanche and Odette have become like his second family. He's probably thinking I have plenty without his inheritance."

"You don't really think that."

"All I know is, it's time for me to enjoy the fruits of my labors. And walking the streets that Jesus walked is going to be my reward."

Mrs. Dunbar stepped to the door.

I wanted to run, but before I could move the door flew open all the way, and I was frozen in place, blocking the doorway.

Mrs. Dunbar stood there like a dug carrot, drooping and out-of-place. I think she just wanted to sink into the ground.

I met my aunt's eyes. Her cheeks flushed, but she said, "Good morning, Blanche. You're early. Who let you inside?"

I never uttered a sound and went straight to my desk, fourth one in a line by the outside wall. It's strange what the mind ponders when it's in shock, like how I had to address my aunt in the classroom as *Mrs. Cada*, never *Aunt Elaine*. I watched her staring at me. She wondered how much I had heard, and I wondered how much she thought I heard. Right now, I saw only the rotten-to-the-core part in her. The Platt part was unrecognizable. Green apples churned around in the oatmeal. I felt the same as I had when my father said he was sending us away: helpless, confused, deceived, and mad clean down to my toes.

Who owned the uncles' house or where I'd go if something happened to them had never entered my mind. Besides who would think of them dying? I shivered at the thought. Right now, I desperately needed to see Uncle Lanny.

The tardy bell rang. The students scuffled inside, talking, thumping books on desks. I felt numb, far away, removed, isolated. Was this what Odette felt? I pulled back from the feeling, knowing I could do nothing now. And anyway, the uncles were not about to die before I got home.

Mrs. Cada stepped to the chalkboard, a frown creasing her brow. She looked nothing like Tyson, with thick glasses on her long nose and painted rouge on her high cheekbones. She even plucked the hair from her pointed chin. I could tell because she missed a couple. As far as I was concerned right then, her plain heart-shaped face held nothing remarkable or memorable except the self-righteousness she used to rule her classroom, Tyson, her children, grandchildren, and Odette. But not me. Never me. No matter how hard she worked at it. Or so I thought.

Those overheard words shook the very foundation of the house I lived in. The one I called home – but it wasn't. Could I swallow my sinful pride and beg her to let us stay? I didn't think I could pay that price.

The morning's current events class opened with more disturbing war news. Mrs. Cada pointed out the countries on the European map in the order they had fallen during the summer of 1940. Denmark, Norway, Belgium, Luxemburg, and then the Netherlands joined Poland and Finland as German conquests. All small, different colored spots on the map that Mrs. Cada pulled down like a shade over the blackboard. Then she pointed to *Maman's* country, saying, "Not only has France been defeated, but also the people of London are being bombed every night. How much longer before they, too, give up?"

The pall of the war hung over the classroom as frightening events too big to understand.

The lessons dragged from boring history to never-ending math problems. Fidgety at first, I finally settled down by searching out each cobweb missed by the janitor and counting fly specks on the windowpanes. The windows were placed high enough so students could not spend their time sightseeing.

What did a little sightseeing hurt?

The lunch bell finally rang at 11:40. I hurried to the principal's office, told him I was sick and needed to go home. Then I hurried toward the lumber yard and Uncle Lanny.

Chapter 10

Good as his word, Lem had arrived with two of his hunting buddies and the walls were finally in place and ready for the trusses. They had refused pay, hopped in their pickups, honked their horns and drove away. In the quiet after their leaving, I had an urge to sit and just look at the skeleton of my house. My very own house.

~~~~

Spurred by Aunt Elaine's claim on Uncle Tyson's house, I walked fast to see Uncle Lanny at the lumber yard. I unbuttoned my pea coat, almost hearing her telling me I'd catch my death. Why her betrayal now? She had provided good counsel since we came, helped us ease into town living and shopped with us for clothing and school supplies. She was also concerned about our souls and took us regularly to the First Presbyterian Church on Main Street. But I'd seen her temperamental side plenty of times.

No matter how I figured it, I couldn't understand why she hated Odette and me so much. We were Platts. Her nieces. She could have her house for all I cared. We just needed to stay until we were done with school. A teacher should understand that.

I shortened the mile-long route to where he worked at the lumber yard by cutting across empty lots and small fields on a web of well-worn paths. I avoided brushy areas near the rail spur where hoboes might lurk. Aunt Elaine said the tramps were a blight and should be run off by the sheriff, but deep down I figured hoboes weren't all that bad, just people without money and homes. But who knew? It didn't make sense to doubt my aunt's advice.

I skirted the creek-fed mill pond and walked between stacks of fragrant milled pine. My uncle was with a customer near the end of the row. I hung back, watching Lanny lug his hulk around in his unimposing way.

He glanced my direction, took a second look, left his customer standing there, and walked toward me faster than I ever remember seeing him move. He no longer appeared soft or unimposing.

"What's the matter?" he called before he was halfway to me.

"Need to talk," I called back and strode toward him, fighting back the emotional relief at seeing him.

"What?" he asked again when I got close enough not to have to shout.

Before I could answer, Uncle Lanny's mouth dropped open, then he spluttered, "Good Lord, my whole family has showed up for a visit. What's going on?"

I spun to see what he was staring at, praying it wasn't Aunt Elaine. Uncle Tyson clipped toward us between the perpendicular stacks. I stared down the row, trying to see if Uncle Tyson looked as sick as Elaine said he was. His step was brisk, his hands swung with his fast pace. He held his shoulders back and head high. He was a tad thinner than last winter, but that was all.

I blurted before he drew close enough to hear, "What happens to me and Odette if you and Uncle Tyson both die?"

Lanny eyed me with one brow cocked, making his scarred face appear quizzical instead of the confident look he always wore. The whine of a saw shrilled. He asked loudly, "What would make you worry about that?"

The sharp metal screech in wood sent chills down my back worse than chalk grating against slate, but the sound prevented Tyson from hearing my answer. "I overheard Aunt Elaine saying the house belongs to her when Uncle Tyson dies, and she's selling it to go walk where Jesus walked."

"That damned Elaine. I—" Lanny interrupted himself as Tyson closed the gap between us.

Tyson's brow wrinkled into a questioning frown at me. "What in the world are you doing here? You're supposed to be in school."

Lanny took off his leather gloves one finger at a time. He spat on the ground. "She's worried about us dying."

Uncle Tyson opened and closed his mouth, then said, "Blinny, if the good Lord grants it, we have lots of years left." He retrieved a yellow piece of paper from his inside jacket pocket and unfolded it. "This is a telegram from your father."

My reaction was pure and simple disbelief. The only words from Didier since he put us on the train had been a letter each Christmas detailing the homestead, livestock, and crops.

Tyson cleared his throat and read, "*Will marry Friday. Arrive Kalispell Sunday.*"

I gasped as if I'd been butted by one of Bromwells' calves. The black and white one that I was sure the mean bull sired. The saw shrilled again. "Is that all he says?" I yelled over the saw's whine.

Uncle Tyson held himself erect, but I noticed he was not as square-shouldered as usual. His lips thinned to a grim line. "Each word on a telegram costs money, and your father is frugal."

Lanny's scar turned red along both sides. A vein pumped in his temple. He spoke through clenched teeth, "That's a nice word for cheap."

The saw shrieked.

"Why would he come now?" I shouted. The saw quit when I shouted *now*, and both uncles jumped.

Tyson met my eyes. I thought for a moment he was going to draw me into his arms, but he didn't. He never hugged. Neither did Lanny. Neither did I, not since Odette forgot about *Maman* and didn't want hugs anymore.

"If we knew why," Tyson answered, "we'd tell you."

"Is he going to take us back with him?" I croaked, barely able to push the words around the lump in my throat.

"Blinny," Uncle Lanny said. "You have a right to be upset. Just don't panic. It's about time Didier came to see you girls."

Don't panic? My emotions ran amok. This was my home now, and I wouldn't let Didier uproot Odette again. Didier would have a fight on his hands if he tried to take us. I had been a scared little girl when he put us on the train, but I wasn't scared or little anymore. I was thirteen and strong – standing five-foot, seven-inches in my socks the last time Lanny measured me – and I would do battle if I had to.

Lanny grinned. He knew my temper, and knew it was woe to anyone who didn't treat Odette right. My father had not.

I didn't return Lanny's grin, and that was a first. I looked Tyson straight in the eyes. "You want Didier to take us?"

"Hell no." That was the first swear word I ever heard from him. "I should've adopted you and Odette when you first arrived."

A glimmer of hope. "Can you do it now?"

"Don't badger me with a bunch of questions I can't answer. Your father is bringing a bride and that's that." Tyson flicked his fingers against the bad-news telegram and stuck it back into his jacket pocket.

I turned to Lanny. "Is it possible to choke on unasked questions?"

"They'll be answered soon enough."

Uncle Tyson retired to his room as soon as we arrived home from the lumber yard. He was fed up with repeating, "I don't know why your father's coming. I don't know what the new mother is like. I don't know what's expected of you."

I flounced from room to room until I could no longer stand the quiet in the big old house that Aunt Elaine claimed. I had to get out and talk to someone. But who? Mrs. Tiffany was the only one I could think of. She was my Presbyterian confirmation teacher, looking out for me at church, and watching my ways. I liked her and stopped by her house regularly for a cup of English tea. I had dismissed her as someone to ask about Odette because my sister was Platt business, but news of my father's arrival would spread as quickly as one church lady could tell another. I might as well start it.

I drew on my red woolen coat and stuffed a sugar cookie in my pocket without wrapping it. Sticky granules would lay at the bottom for a long time, but I didn't care.

Mutt and Pooch rose to follow me off the back stoop. "You stay put," I ordered, sounding mean even to myself. Their heads drooped and tails quit wagging. "Sorry, guys." After a couple of scratches behind the ears they flopped in front of the door again.

Mrs. Tiffany lived north of us in a modern ranch-style house at the foot of Buffalo Hill. I hurried up her front walk, admiring its compact single story.

Her black cocker spaniel was tied to the front porch railing with a rope just long enough to give the dog a chance to beg anyone passing by. Pepper was a habitual mooch – fat, sassy, and mischievous. She waddled up to me as fast as she could and I passed along the sugar cookie.

The front door opened and Mrs. Tiffany stepped out. "Spotted you from the window. Come have tea." She and her dog looked so much alike: round tummy, impish eyes, and a feisty grin. She enjoyed life and had a hard time maintaining the dignity required of a Sunday school teacher. Today she wore a silken housecoat and had a layer of crimson on her cheeks and lips. Her gray hair was pulled up and held with a ribbon. To church, she wore a black cape over a shirtwaist dress and no makeup. I liked this version better.

Inside, she pointed at the couch in the living room. "Sit and tell me what is wrong."

My worries had been roiling like well water splashing into a trough. They brimmed over the top, and I started leaking tears. Dumb. Dumb thing to do. It was just my father coming for a visit.

Mrs. Tiffany chewed at the edge of her bottom lip. Her eyes twinkled. "Blanche, has some dashing young man pestered you into something you shouldn't be thinking about?"

I sniveled and shook my head. "I wished it was something so simple. I'd just knock his block off."

"Aha, so you are fighting them off." Her *tsk-tsk* sounded close to laughter. "Believe me, it's a whole lotta fun when they catch you."

My cheeks burned. "No boys dare chase after me." I wiped away my tears and stood.

"Oh, I'm sorry, Blinny. I tease too much, but laughing is better than fretting like you're doing. Now sit back down."

I eased back onto the couch. I really wanted to talk, but my Platt business hid behind a life of keeping family separate from others. I just couldn't spill the words.

Mrs. Tiffany eyed me through her glasses. "If you ever need a place to stay, come here. I need a companion and I sure could use you to get things off the top shelves. Same as I could help your mind get some peace. Talking is better than stewing."

"My father is getting married and is coming to see us with his new wife." There, it was out.

Mrs. Tiffany looked more puzzled. "Why is seeing your father so upsetting?"

"I don't know."

She clucked her tongue and her tone grew confessional. "I had a father who was as mean as they get. Smacked me and my sisters right and left. I've been in the process of forgiving him for the last thirty years. Still trying to, like the good book says, but some things keep cropping back up. Do you need to forgive something?"

"No, he does."

"Well, frankly dear, I don't understand. Take a deep breath and see if you can put your anxiety into words."

It was a simple request. One I couldn't do. "I'd better get back. Odette will be home from school soon."

"She's old enough to be alone for a while. Do her good." Mrs. Tiffany sniffed and rubbed the end of her nose as if something had tickled it. "Hope I'm not coming down with something," she said reaching for her hanky. She blew her nose and then looked at me. "Guess I might as well tell you. I have noticed Odette's strange behavior. She's sulking in Sunday school. Won't do her lessons."

"I've told her to, but she won't listen. She spends most of her time up in the attic. What would make her do that?"

"Some people turn into real loners. Why don't you go up there and talk to her where she's comfortable?"

"She'd just think I'm spying. I'd better be going."

Mrs. Tiffany reached out to me, but held back from touching my arms. "I know you're not the hugging kind but I'm going to say bless you. Take those words with you." At the door she added, "I've told you plenty of times I need a house girl and I'd just as soon it was you. Come stay with me."

"I can't." I left with her blessing ringing in my ears.

I carried soup bowls, silverware, the salt shaker and pepper mill to the heavy the oak dining table. The sturdy furnishings in the Uncles' home suited me. I needed solid things with purpose, the rest were just unnecessary adjectives. Like Didier's marriage coming without any warning.

The front door flung out. Odette banged it shut and scowled at me. "I looked all over the school yard for you."

"I came home early."

"I had to search for you when I have three whole pages of arithmetic to do. That dumb teacher. Somebody ought to whack her with a paddle."

"Didier is coming and bringing a new wife." I figured that news would slow down her unimportant tirade over a few pages of numbers.

Without so much as a blink, Odette climbed up on the chair in front of the solid desk. She squirmed on the hard desk chair, pencil in hand, acting as if she hadn't heard the announcement about our father's arrival.

I ignored her slouched back and swinging feet, and crossed to the double-hung window beside the front door and pulled back the lace panel to see if Uncle Lanny was coming yet.

The dogs were curled close to the gravel road, heads up, ears alert to the direction the car would come. Pooch and Mutt waited for Lanny. I waited for reassurance about Didier's arrival.

A dusty odor tickled my nose as I dropped the curtain back into place. I sneezed.

"Bless you," Uncle Tyson called as he light-footed it downstairs. He passed by me, walked into the parlor, sat down in his chair, and opened the *Daily Interlake*. The paper's rustle conveyed he was not answering anymore of my questions.

Odette brushed her hair out of her eyes and glared at me. "If you'd quit your racket, I could get my numbers done."

"Aren't you worried about Didier coming?"

"Why should I care?" She pressed the point of her pencil against the tablet until the lead snapped.

"Because he'll have a say about us."

Outside, Pooch and Mutt erupted into noisy welcomes, and I ran to open the door. The dogs charged through almost knocking me down, and Aunt Elaine breezed inside. Her normally neat hair was mussed from the stiff north wind and wisps of gray had escaped from the bun at the back of her head. Her face carried a look of something's-wrong-and-I'm-gonna-fix-it. She appeared as windblown on the inside as the outside.

I didn't like her look, but shut the door before we all blew away. Besides, I couldn't very well tell her to leave her own future house.

Elaine hurried to the archway of the living room and peered down at her father. Uncle Tyson lowered his paper halfway to his lap. "It's a cold evening for you to be out visiting."

Elaine pushed her unbuttoned coat away from her sides and placed both hands on her hips. "Blinny left school at lunchtime today and you need to find out why."

The dining table was between me and my traitor aunt. I dared to say, "Didier's coming to stay."

Elaine would have blown a big bubble had she been chewing gum. She wiped spittle from her mouth with the back of her hand.

Uncle Lanny appeared in the doorway to the kitchen, still holding his lunch pail. "Elaine," he said, "I believe it's Didier's honeymoon. Never thought our old house would be used as a lover's nest."

Aunt Elaine pointed at Odette. "Lanny, a child is present," she said in her teacher's voice.

Legs swinging and with a grin of satisfaction, Odette enjoyed the high drama that always occurred between Lanny and Elaine.

Lanny set his lunch box on the cupboard and faced Elaine with a tease in his eyes. "No matter their age, everyone should know that a lover's lair is supposed to be filled with laughter and tender mercies. From the looks of you, Elaine, you need a damn good tryst somewhere."

Tyson dropped his newspaper on the floor. "Heaven help us, Didier's not even here yet, and the squabbling starts. Elaine, we've no idea why he's coming except to see his girls."

"I don't want him to get any notion about staying."

Rotten me couldn't help giving my aunt more to rankle about. "Maybe his new wife doesn't want to live on the homestead."

Elaine inhaled deeply through her nose and exhaled slowly. Her deep breathing didn't help her righteous dismay at a possible further intrusion by Didier. She moistened her lips and spoke directly to Uncle Lanny. "I believe it's time for honesty. It isn't right that my father has to care for another man's children. He needs peace and quiet for his old age. Odette is nothing but aggravation. Blanche is an upstart and needs a good swat. And you, Lanny, are a sucker for both girls. They need a father's control. Now that he's married, he'll be able to take them home."

I didn't want her talking about us leaving. She might cement the idea in my uncles' heads. "Aunt Elaine," I said loudly enough to get her attention. "Odette is about finished with her homework, and we are about to eat. Should I put a bowl on for you?"

"No, I do not want to eat, or change the subject. And you need a good tanning in the woodshed for running from school without telling me first. But I don't expect anyone will do it. You need your father's firm hand on your smart ways."

Odette clapped her hands and smirked at me. "She sure does. She thinks she knows everything, all the time."

I gave my sister my getcha-later look.

Elaine's eyes looked toward the ceiling for help, then shot back at Uncle Lanny. "You've ruined those two girls, just like you've ruined other things."

He pinpointed Elaine, eyes glittered hard. "Watch yourself before you say something stupid like you manage to do more often than not. You have a spiteful, mean tongue. It's time someone told you."

"You're bound for hell, Lanny Platt," Elaine said through her teeth. She spun, put on a high-moral face and sweetly kissed her father on top of his head.

He waved her away. "All I want is some peace and quiet before dinner, and tell me how that's possible with the lot of you. Go home, daughter."

Elaine stalked out the same door she had blustered inside, the storm of her irritation leaving us with drained emotions.

The uncles ate without conversation, and so did Odette. She ate silently watching us as she had watched the hullabaloo with Aunt Elaine. We were more fun to watch than a Saturday matinee.

For myself, I didn't dare to speak. I had provoked Aunt Elaine and Uncle Tyson knew it. Very few times had I earned his disapproval, and his silence heaped guilt on my head.

Uncle Lanny pushed back his chair after cleaning his plate and looked at me. "I think it's time for you to come with me to the woodshed."

Tyson's mouth dropped open. "She's too old for corporal punishment."

Lanny ignored him and took my hand. The lightness of his touch conveyed no spanking was forthcoming.

Outside, a harvest moon hung in the east above Columbia Mountain and the back yard shimmered in cold pale light. A neighbor's cat yowled in a hungry, lonesome manner. I understood the plaintive cry. I felt the same lonely hunger for a father's love, but Didier cared only about his fields and livestock – and now a new bride. Did he love her like he had *Maman*? Had he loved *Maman*?

Uncle Lanny led me to the weathered shed on the back part of the lot. The door groaned on rusty hinges. He struck a wooden match and held the tiny torch inside the inky interior. He crossed to a kerosene lamp sitting on an upturned log and lit the wick. The light glow filtered around pitchy stove-length logs. Blond wood chips littered the dirt floor. A maul and splitting iron were propped beside the chopping block. Several axes leaned against the wall by the door.

Lanny rolled a log from the pile, set it upright, and sat down on it. Knees sharply bent, he leaned forward and rested his arms on his legs, dangling hands between them.

I perched on the chopping block aware that I might not like what my uncle was about to say. The rough cut surface prickled through the cotton of my dress.

"I know you're upset about your father's arrival," Uncle Lanny said without preamble. He was as serious as I had ever seen him. "No father should dump his daughters on someone else's doorstep and cause the hurt Didier did. Taking it out on Elaine won't help. She did a mean thing, but she didn't know you were listening."

I was far beyond wanting to talk about Elaine. Her hurtful words this morning didn't count. Didier's coming was the right-here-and-now crisis, not the somewhere-in-the-future demise of my uncles.

"Maybe," Lanny added, "you're afraid of change. Not that I blame you. Your life changed the day of the fire in a way that left you desperate to know what would happen next."

"It was Sadie's fault."

"Sadie who?"

"Sadie Chicken."

Lanny snorted. "Corporal punishment is always an option."

"I'm sorry, but I wanted *Maman* to boil the old laying hen because I got pecked bad every morning. Our shanty house caught on fire because of stewing that mean old hen."

"So you're at fault?"

I blurted out from deep inside guilty me, "*Papa* got rid of us right afterwards."

"Cursed thing your father did. But blaming yourself is more cursed. I'm telling you to put those thoughts away. Don't dwell on something that was out of your control. You weren't at fault."

I wanted to believe him, but I had requested the death of an enemy and lost *Maman* because of it.

Uncle Lanny breathed deeply, his wide chest expanding, then relaxing. "However, you have no reason to fear. If Didier decides to take you and Odette back to the ranch, the prairie isn't unknown to you, like this valley was. Coming here worked out okay, didn't it?"

"You'll miss me."

"Never said I wouldn't. But surely you can think of a few good things about going back home."

I wanted to touch his kind face, reassure him that I'd be okay even if I didn't want to return to Didier's care. Instead I uttered the only thing I could think to say, "Well, one good thing. Aunt Elaine could quit worrying about her inheritance. Why is the deed only in Uncle Tyson's name? She said it was. Does that mean you don't own the house, too?"

Lanny cleared his throat and spat in the wood chips. "You're meddling where you don't belong. Now git along inside and clean up the supper mess."

I walked toward the back door of the house. The sound of the maul striking the splitting iron rang in rhythm with my steps. I kicked a pebble in the path. I didn't know which worry to let nag – Elaine's betrayal or Didier's marriage or Lanny's not owning a house or leaving Kalispell. Nothing was obvious. All had unfinished endings, like a sentence without a period.

I looked over my shoulder at the woodshed and muttered, "I'm not afraid of going back to the homestead. I'm afraid that the new mother won't be the one Odette needs." The words weren't completely true. I was worried about the mother, but was also concerned about Didier's house. I had learned that the roof above your head could burn and crash down, leaving you without a home to call your own. I had also learned, that no matter how much the uncles loved me, their house was not mine. Their hearts were mine, but not the wooden structure I called home – nor any of the furnishings. My only possessions were my personal things the uncles had bought for me. I was beholden to Uncle Tyson and Uncle Lanny, but I didn't truly belong here. I was just a needy relative.

Would the new wife think of Didier's house as hers? That Odette and I were only needy relatives?

I needed a deed to my own house.

Chapter 11

White hair whipping around her face, Alice put hands on hips and looked up at me. "Are you going to come down off that roof? I didn't drive over here to just stand and gaze up at the top of your house in hopes that you might speak to me." She sounded grouchy as usual.

I looked over the edge. "You were the one smarting off about getting the roof done before the snow flies," I said in a syrupy voice, and then disappeared from her sight.

Silence. Noise of her climbing up the ladder carried on a wind that kept the temperature bearable on the hot roof. Alice's head appeared. "Geez peez. It's only September third and you're almost done. Come down. Let's go visit Fran. I haven't seen her in a couple of weeks. We can talk on the way."

"Don't have time, but come up and sit. Tell me what's on your mind. For a tight-lipped flatlander you're yakking all the time anymore."

She climbed up onto the roof and sat legs spread out, back hunched. "Someone has to get you thinking about something other than this house."

"Me thinking about this house keeps *me* going."

"Your problems are of your own making. You're getting worse than Odette. Which reminds me. She called. For some insane reason she wants to see you on Halloween. Makes no kinda sense."

Odette actually called? I slid another length of asphalt shingles into place. "Maybe she's reliving the past. End of October is when you and Didier came for us. Don't you remember your horrible honeymoon?"

Satisfaction sparked in Alice's eyes. She was proud of whatever she was thinking. "Tyson's death wasn't the worst of it. We had to sell pumpkins on my wedding day. Didier was so damned proud of his crop. It was like he sailed to China and discovered them. Take the pun'kins and me to town. Sell one, marry the other. I shoulda let him marry the pumpkin. But I went along. Anything to keep my parents shut up and to get away from my bossy brothers."

I didn't encourage Alice, but she kept babbling.

"Yes in-dee-dee," she said. "He was proud to marry me and have a baby in the bargain. Said he appreciated my parents' trust. But I wouldn't have married him unless I wanted to. He never did figure out I really wanted to make a life with him."

"He knew you loved him."

Alice shook her head, lips pursed with denial. "I did not. He knew it and didn't care. It was high time for him to have a wife again, and I was handy. He was worried about turning forty and wasting his virile years. My pregnancy proved my fertility. He gave my baby his name. I had to bear his sons like Ma did for our spread – like Essie Faye should've. He never did comprehend her choosing to die."

"She wasn't any crazier than he was."

"Oh I don't know. He seemed pretty smart to me. He searched the churches and dance halls and decided there wasn't a single woman who was pretty enough to look at all winter. Just like a man. Put looks before anything. Guess that's why he was so eager to get me into his bed." She licked her lips and tossed her hair. "I'm damned good to look at."

Alice was trying to goad me. I knew she knew I knew it. I wasn't going to fall into her trap this time. I would not argue with her, but that didn't stop her rattling on every time I stopped pounding the hammer. I drove more nails, drowning her out.

"What's wrong?" she yelled over the racket. "Don't want to hear that? By God, a Bromwell couldn't be having a bastard, she could just marry one."

I shook my head and kept nailing.

Alice laughed. This time she sounded merry, enjoying a good joke even if it was on herself. "Not that I'm calling Didier a bastard, but he was mighty close. You know he made my folks wait for an answer. Took their parental worry and yanked it good."

I slid another piece of roofing into place, lining up the overlaps.

This time, Alice waited until the nail was driven. She appeared lost in thought, mulling over a memory. "I came with the folks for his answer. They wanted me to stay home, but I threw a fit. It was my life and I'd have a say in it." Alice spoke with a tremor, an emotion I'd never heard before. She looked beautiful, glowed with vitality, looked twenty years younger. Her eyes danced like a vixen's. The memory obviously brought her pleasure, but I'd rather listen to the hawk calling his mate as they soared northward.

"I really didn't know Didier," Alice said. "Had no idea about the depth of him." She glanced at me, her eyebrows drew together. "You never did understand him. Only saw the hard-nosed man who worked every daylight moment. But I'm telling you he was also a lonely man who filled tablets with the rhythm of the prairies and his longings for a son."

Her private moments with my father should stay that way, yet I laid the hammer down, squirmed into a comfortable hunch, arms around my knees, and looked south across the prairies. For years, Alice had buried too many secrets behind tight lips. Maybe she was loosened up enough to let some slip out. Why I cared was as baffling as her now wanting to talk. I wanted to forget the past, but couldn't help wanting to know. It was like putting my hands over my eyes, yet peeking through my fingers.

Her voice sounded confident, her memories accurate. "When my folks drove me up to your father's holding, I noticed the height of the house he had built. I asked him about it. He said, he chose a spot on the highest swell and built high. The wind moaning around the eaves didn't matter. Two levels and a standup attic satisfied his need to see his place from afar. He had made sure to build a house that would mark his land with a long shadow. He had lived in the barn for two years, building in the twilight after the chores were done, board by board, nail by nail, and then writing his poems late at night."

"Alice, my father wasn't a hero, but I've come to understand his need to build a house. What I don't understand is why you're telling me all this. Why not forget the painful past?"

Alice straightened. Her shoulders reared back, chin tipped up. "My past isn't painful. When our marriage vows were done, we were sealed. I knew it when he kept snatching glimpses of my cleavage. I didn't expect to feel so drawn to him. My belly was already thickened with the baby, but he didn't mind, said that signs of fertility made him happy, and that I looked great in my pale blue dress. We desperately needed to find a room for the rest of the day, but oh no, he just had to drive a hundred and eighty miles to spend our first two nights at the fancy Many Glacier Hotel." She laughed and clapped her hands. "We almost drove in the ditch when I unbuttoned a few more buttons so he could have a better look."

That was enough. "You always controlled Didier with sex. It was disgusting."

"I did, didn't I? Made it fun."

"Your sex life doesn't interest me. Unbelievable that you'd sit there and talk to me about it. Can't you let me live in peace?"

"You're a sexless woman. I'm trying to stir your juices before you shrivel up and stay an old maid forever. You need a man to bring color to your cheeks. You look like hell."

"I gave *you* my years. Helped raise your boys." I grabbed ahold of the shingle hammer. "You'd better get off the roof."

"What? You gonna hit me with a hammer? If I died right now on your roof I'd be happy. At least you'd finally react to something. Now go help your sister. Then find a man and jump in bed."

She clamored away from me and down the ladder. The ladder tipped. Away from the roof! It thudded to the ground. The witch! I scrabbled to the edge. "Dammit, Alice. Put the ladder back!"

Her car door slammed. I slung the hammer. The engine fired. The hammer clanged on the Lincoln's trunk and bounced to the ground. A cloud of dust rose. The wind blew it my way. *Dang* her hide. She left me stranded on the roof top and I didn't even have the hammer to finish the shingling with.

I sat on the roof's edge and dangled my feet over, contemplating the drop to the ground. Nothing to do except to sigh loud and long. I slid away from the edge, content to sit and watch shadows of evening creep along the prairie, see the depth of color unseen under a full sun. The sun-dried sagebrush appeared lizard-green instead of dull brown. Dun-colored prairie grass became shades of gray, running to black near the ground. The land became saturated with quiet hues of purple and pink as the sun lowered. My few meager buildings also became grand, dusk hiding the imperfections of rough-cut planks and unpainted boards. The shadows lent a look of naturalness to the buildings, same as they gentled the harshness of the windswept terrain.

Contentment on this land and in this house was finally mine. I had waited for years to live in a place where I belonged and would wait no more. I patted the roof, then lowered myself over the edge and dropped to the ground, very glad to have chosen to build a single story, and very glad to overcome the anxiety of youth. I had done my share of stewing about Odette and worrying about my father's coming for us. I had known he would take us from the uncles' house without being told.

~~~~~

An unrelenting anxiousness clouded the next four days – an unfair amount of time. Inmates waiting capital punishment had it easier. At least they knew their fate. I only knew my father was coming with a new wife. I worried in a way I had never felt before. My usual stewing was caused by some dumb thing Odette pulled, like some nasty trick or not doing what was good for her. Didier's arrival threatened my living with the uncles. How could one person have such control? Especially one who had forfeited his family for a homestead.

I sighed in a mewling sort of way as I dusted the hall table near the parlor where Uncle Tyson sat in his lumpy wingback, listening to his old cathedral radio. The 12:00 o'clock news announcer aired his rich pronouncement against Italy for joining forces with the Third Reich and invading Greece. With hardly a breath to recover, he blew right into the weather report. Hard winds and snow in the high elevations. Rain and cold in the valley. A gloomy forecast, just like Didier's pending arrival.

"Blinny," Tyson said over a commercial for Gillette Blue Blades, "Your moaning and groaning sounds worse than two soldiers shivering in a rain-filled fox hole. I'd like to listen to this in peace. Take Odette for ice cream, or you may see a full-blown Platt fit."

I was surprised at even a hint of a tantrum from my even-keeled uncle and poked my head through the doorway. "I'd rather stay and see the fit."

"No you wouldn't." Tyson dug a finger into his vest pocket and tossed me two quarters. "Out with you."

I caught the coins and hightailed down the hall, thankful for an understanding uncle and his excuse to give me something to do. I stuffed the dust rag in the box under the kitchen sink, grabbed my pea coat from a hook, and plopped on my ratty hat, glad I still had *Maman*'s gift to cover my worrying head.

Mutt and Pooch warmed themselves in a sunny spot on the back stoop. I stepped over them and their skin didn't even twitch. Only their tails thumped against the rotting boards.

"Where's Odette?" I asked them.

Their tails whumped a couple of times and settled back into the same spots on the warm wood.

Gravel crunched in the driveway. Odette rounded the south-side corner of the house, clumping on Tommy Walkers made out of two tin cans and twine.

"Uncle Tyson gave us quarters for ice cream."

Odette wobbled. "Shut up, you're gonna make me fall." She finished the last six steps to the porch and kicked free of the cans. Twine marks indented her palms, and she rubbed them against her overalls. "I don't want to go," she said and lined up the cans to step up on them again.

"You have to go. You're driving Uncle Tyson nuts clanking around. He's close to a fit."

Odette pressed her lips together and gave me an evil eye. "I won't go and you can't make me."

"Why does even buying you a treat have to be a battle?"

The screen door squeaked, and Uncle Tyson held it open. "Odette, run along. Your sister has enough on her plate without fighting with you."

Odette kicked the cans up beside the porch and walked toward the street, arms stiff to her sides, knees bending only enough to move. Her fat, lively braids bounced against her stiff back. She was doing her zombie death walk and wouldn't speak to me until it suited her.

I should have told her we didn't have to go when I caught up, but selfishly said, "I've been upset since getting the telegram. Can't you understand that?"

She walked beside me for a few moments as though I wasn't there. I honestly tried to think of something more to say, but couldn't and was relieved when she fell back a couple of steps.

An autumn breeze swirled and caught the skirt of my brown corduroy jumper. I smoothed it back into place. The pressure of my hand brushed the nap of the fabric into a darker shade, same as Didier's telegram had changed the color of my mood to black. His words had so easily altered my secure place. I had grown used to living in town, going to school, and caring for the uncles and Odette. To live with the father who sent me away and with a stepmother I didn't know sounded unbearable. I would probably never smile again for the rest of my whole life. Not that I deserved to.

Odette still trailed a few steps behind. Her frizzy braids dangled over her ears and down her shoulders, one in front, the other in back. She had relaxed to her normal amble. Freckles sprinkled the fair skin across the pert nose. Thick curled eyelashes added depth to her violet eyes. She might become even prettier than *Maman* was, but too much beauty could also turn my willful sister into a temptress bound for the Presbyterian abyss.

What made me think such a thing? Odette was just a kid. What did I know about temptresses and harlots? I didn't even understand the recent strange sensations in my own loins. I wished I knew how *Maman* would've handled Odette, and what she'd tell me about my surging teenage emotions.

Why couldn't I be granted one short talk with *Maman*?

Odette lagged farther behind as we strolled south toward Main Street. That was fine, better than walking beside a sister who wouldn't talk to me anyway. We angled down a path alongside Griffin Baseball Field, crossed the single rail spur, and entered a crowd of Saturday afternoon shoppers relaxing in Depot Park. Some rested on benches, some bought meaty hot dogs from a steam vendor, and some clustered to watch the practice drills by Company F of the National Guard.

Boots clumped. Hands slapped against rifle stocks. A deep voice barked orders for a close order drill. One hundred and twenty proud Guardsmen, four abreast, approached the park.

My heart tightened with pride at the cadence; the rhythmic beat confirmed these men were willing to fight for us.

The formation filed past where Odette and I stood watching. One young guardsman, shoulders proudly back and in perfect step with the others, grinned shyly at me. He wore black dungarees, a plaid flannel shirt and an ill-fitting jacket. His boots showed signs of a barnyard. He seemed a little like Monty Bromwell with brown hair and browner eyes. The soldier was gone in a few sharp steps. He had reminded me of Monty, the boy who called to be careful of the coulee, and who had handed me Marvel's flour sack filled with food. I wondered if my long ago friend might go to war and hoped he wouldn't have to fight in *Maman*'s France.

War talk was everywhere, even at school. My cocky classmate, Sam Johnson, constantly talked about the battles in Europe. "What if the dirty pickle-sucking Krauts attacked us right here in the good old U-S-of-A? Hell, now that they've captured Frenchy, they'll bomb England into a heap of stones, or into the ocean. That tiny little island might just gol-damned disappear."

Last week, I had checked the blackboard map to see just how small England was, and doubted it could fall anywhere.

The guardsman and his squad rounded the block and marched into the park. Their drill was over.

"Come on," I said, tugging at Odette's arm. "Let's get our ice cream."

She planted her feet and stared behind me. A hand clasped my shoulder. I spun to see who. A stooped, scrawny woman stood practically in my face.

"Are you the Platt nieces?" she demanded.

I stepped back to avoid the aged breath. "Yes. I'm Blanche and this is Odette."

The woman's pale forehead and downy cheeks were scored so deeply that I wanted to smooth them out with the palms of my hands to see the eyes and mouth clearly. The bits of visible eye showed calculating sharpness.

The woman cleared a rattle in her throat. "Lanny Platt is a gambling, murdering bastard." She pushed past me.

I caught my balance by grabbing Odette's shoulder. "What did she say?" I asked.

Odette shrugged. "Who cares? I want my ice cream cone."

I ignored Odette and stared after the woman hurrying on spindly legs down the block, weaving quickly through parade spectators crowding the sidewalk. She would tell me why she slandered my uncle, or I'd know the reason why not. I caught up to her in front of Sam's Barber Shop. "What did you mean?" I stopped myself from grabbing such a frail old person to halt her rapid pace. No telling what would happen. She might have a heart attack.

The woman hoofed along faster, boot heels striking against the cement, arms swinging, and shoulder purse bouncing. She looked like a banty rooster as she brushed past several ladies standing in the center of the sidewalk.

I bumped a buxom matron who frowned at me. Another in a fur coat shook her head and glared. I ignored them and matched strides with the old woman.

"Who are you?" I asked as we rounded the corner of Second and Main. I dodged Mr. Higgins who was coming toward me and caught back up beside the woman. In the flow of shoppers, we passed the Army Goods Store, Alton Pearce Drug, and JC Penney.

At the street corner, the woman finally looked at me. "I have nothing more to say to you."

"Madam, I respect my elders, but it is totally unfair to slander my uncle and not explain why."

"You're a rude big-footed girl. Bad as your great-uncle. Leave me alone or I'll call the police. Anyone can see you're harassing me."

I spluttered, "You harassed me."

The woman was already crossing the street. She disappeared into Holland's Grocery. I fumed with the notion to follow, but how could I? Uncle Lanny would just have to explain.

Odette should be straggling along somewhere behind me. She wasn't. "Dam," I muttered and hurried down the block, glancing into stores in case she was hiding from me like she'd been known to do. Blast her ornery hide, she wouldn't even stick with me against a mean old witch. This time Odette really was going to get a snake twist on her scrawny brat wrist.

Automobiles with big front fenders and sloping backs were angle-parked along both sides of the street. I checked between the cars and the boxy bed of a Ford pickup. At the end of the next block, I crossed Center Street and into Depot Park. Thank God. There was Odette seated on an isolated bench under a maple tree on the far side of the gazebo.

A man appeared from behind the depot and approached her. He was bent from the weight of a pack. He wore a long ratty coat and floppy dirty hat. He sat down close beside Odette.

I went cold.

Odette laughed. Was she talking to him? What was she doing? I dashed across the lawn, fuming, she should have enough sense not to talk to a strange dirty man. She didn't know filth from apple butter.

"Odette," I yelled. "Come here!" The man jumped up and scuttled back toward the tracks, taking any evil intent with him. Finally, I skidded to a stop in front of Odette. She grinned up at me in a gotcha kind of way. Her forearm squished under my grip.

"You knew I was watching? You talked to that man just to scare me?"

"I asked him to sit with me."

"Do you have any idea how dumb that was?"

She yanked out of my grip. "It's your fault. You're the one who ran off chasing a witch."

I sat down sure that my knees were going to cave in any second.

Odette slid to the end of the bench and stared off into space.

Wind stirred and a flurry of golden leaves rained down on us. The swaying limbs released their burden as if shaking off their clothing. Bare branches reached upward, like fingers praying for the snows of winter. I silently pleaded for a blizzard to fill the Continental Divide and keep Didier on the other side. Even though Odette was the worst kind of adverb, I just didn't dare give the responsibility of her to anyone, especially an unknown stepmother. What would the new wife be like?

"Why didn't you come with me?" I asked softly, hoping to pry loose Odette's reasoning.

"I didn't feel like watching you fight with an old witch."

"I wasn't fighting. I just wanted to know why she called Uncle Lanny a murdering, gambling bastard."

"He is."

"What?"

"He gambled away his own house."

"How do you know that? Look at me!"

Odette stared me in the eye and held steady. Violet eyes searching violet eyes. She finally answered, "Stella told me."

"Who's Stella?"

"Angie's aunt. That old lady is her great-grandma."

"You knew her?"

Odette shook her head. "I've just seen her with Angie, but she hates Uncle Lanny 'cause of what he did."

"What did he do?"

"Gamble and murder."

"Oh, for crying in the bean bucket. Our uncle didn't kill anybody. Sadie did." I gasped. Why did I say that? A chicken didn't set the fire. It was an accident. Uncle Lanny had told me that time and again. Didier's coming, the old woman's accusation, and Odette's meanness was too much. Tears smarted. I peered through them and saw a satisfied smirk on my sister's face.

"This makes you happy?"

Odette lips turned down, like Alice Bromwell's pout. "You're worse than that witchy grandma."

"I ought to snake twist your wrist."

"If you don't buy me licorice ice cream, I'm going to tell Aunt Elaine that you stole my treat money."

I looked down at the one person who looked like *Maman*, but Odette was sly, secretive, had a smart mouth and a mean streak. I had absolutely no idea what to do with her. I fished a quarter out of my pocket and handed it to her. "Here's the money but we're going home right now. You're going to tell Uncle Lanny what you know about that old lady, and what she's saying about him."

I lagged behind fast-walking Odette, catching up every time I thought of one more scolding thing to say, only to drop back to the sluggish pace my black mood demanded. This was the first time I'd ever walked behind Odette. I should be racing to tell Uncle Lanny what the witch said, but my feet dragged. Maybe I didn't want to hear what he might say. You idiot, I thought. Angie's great-grandmother had me upset. Might as well confront Lanny head on and rid myself of her uncalled-for insult. My stride lengthened.

Odette checked over her shoulder and saw I was closing in again. She broke into a trot until we entered our block, and then ran up our driveway. She stopped by the back porch, pointed her skinny index finger at me, and yelled, "I'm not doing anything you say. Ever again!"

Uncle Lanny stepped from the woodshed. "What's all the caterwauling?"

I snatched Odette's arm and marched her across the backyard to him. "Tell him right now." I shook her arm.

Odette glared up at him, her eyebrows so tightly drawn that her eyes became slits. "You're a gambler and a murderer," she said like a judge condemning a felon.

I could tell that was probably the most surprising statement Lanny had ever heard. He scratched the back of his neck. "I don't recall any particular murder in my past that you two need to know about."

Odette lifted her chin, brow smoothed, and lips smirked. "Angie's great-grandmother says so and I believe her."

Lanny shrugged. "Don't bother me a bit what you believe."

"Uncle Lanny," I spoke up. "You've a right to your secrets, but Angie's great-grandmother slandered us Platts. Made me mad enough to want to punch that frail old lady, except she might've had a heart attack. I could be standing here right now as a murderer, waiting for the police to haul me away."

He took his good time about leaning the axe against the shed. He no more wanted to explain than he wanted to go to Sunday morning services. He attended church only for Odette's and my sake. Now for the same reason he'd explain.

"People hold grudges," he said. "Nothing will ever change that old lady's opinion of me."

Suddenly I realized Lanny looked cold even with the heat of a fine October sun beating down and his wool work jacket buttoned to the neck. His arms were tight to his sides and he shivered. He rubbed at a temple as if a bad headache pounded near the surface.

"Are you sick?" I asked.

"Caught the cold you had last week."

I straightened like I'd been jabbed unfairly. "I didn't have a cold."

"Don't feel so good to be blamed for something does it?" Uncle Lanny moistened his lips. "I don't talk easy about what I can't change."

He made me want to shake the clear truth from him. Plain and simple truth was all I needed. "You don't have to change anything, but it isn't fair I have to fight battles without knowing why."

Lanny shook his head as if to deny what we were discussing. "It's time you girls learned that not everything goes the way you want. You need to learn not to worry so dang much about who owns what house and who says what about who."

Odette shook out of my grip, ran across the yard, and up the back porch steps. "I'm not worried," she yelled at us. She opened the screen door and let it bang behind her. The inner door slammed.

"She's been weird all day," I said. "Even before that old witch said what she did. Why did...?"

Lanny put his arm around my shoulders and led me to the house. "Blinny, I want you to stop with your incessant questions." His voice was sharp.

Afraid to push any further, I left him resting in the sun and stepped into the kitchen to put potatoes and a meatloaf in the oven for dinner. I had been hard on Odette and the feeling of it weighed on my mind. She was probably in the attic again. It was where she hid out. I climbed the stairs to see if she'd settled down enough to set the table.

My footfalls tapped against the hardwood steps. She'd know I was coming. I cracked open the narrow door. Voices sounded on the far side of an old wardrobe. Who was she talking to? A chill worked through me. I crept toward the voices.

"Odette?" I said softly.

She sat cross-legged on the board flooring, a quilt wrapped around her and hair stringing into her eyes. Her clothes were piled beside her.

Her eyes challenged mine. "I don't want you here."

"Who were you talking to?"

Her pale skin flushed, colorless lips thinned. "None of your business."

I rubbed my arms. "I'm sorry for being mean to you today."

She blinked. "*Maman* said you would be, but I didn't believe her."

"Odette, you know that *Maman* died and our father is on the other side of the mountains."

"I visit her in heaven, but we can only talk when *Papa* can't listen."

I pressed my fingertips against my lips.

She scowled. "Don't look at me like that!" She dropped the cover and stood. Her nakedness was so thin, so pale. She grabbed up her overalls and pulled them on. "You don't know anything about me or even care. You just came up here to get me to set the table."

I reached out to touch her. She dodged out of the way and ran for the door. The noise of her running down the stairs echoed in the dark attic. I shivered and hurried to the door. I looked back to make sure no one else lurked about.

Chapter 12

Even through leather gloves, the bricks felt rough and gritty, the way I was becoming. The skin on my arms and neck looked like gnarly bark, my waist and hips narrowed so much the pants rode low and baggy. My hair needed to be brushed, not squished by my ratty straw hat. I didn't smell very good either. I had changed. The only consistent thing about me was the hat. *Maman*'s gift. I wore it more often now, leaving my work hats hanging on nails in the shed. I needed *Maman* with me for the tedious brick laying.

I filled another bucket with mortar and scooped a trowel full and flapped it on the top of a row of bricks that were two feet up on the north side. The south and east sides were only bricked halfway to the eaves. I needed to come up with a better scaffolding than a board between two ladders. Time to build one eluded me as one finished row of bricks led to another unfinished one.

Placing brick on top of brick seemed never-ending. The monotony would end, but when? Alice hadn't even stopped by to pester and pick. Not that I missed her. Usually she showed up at the most aggravating times. Laying the bricks proved different. I'd welcome a break. The irony was that she hadn't come when I almost wished she would. A good argument always released my pent up steam. Why I'd even welcome Lem if he stopped by. Didn't expect him though. Last time he was here, he said he wouldn't come back until he received an invite. He added that anyone with an ounce of flatlander in their veins always had time for a visitor. I should treat his conversations with more than a nod between hammer blows. Rude had been added to my repertoire of faults. Temper, jealousy, pride and now rudeness. Age held no boundary for personal shortcomings. They just kept piling up.

All work and no break from the repetition of placing brick upon brick added to the flaws. I was cranky, but I did love the red brick. Its weight, coarseness, and color appeared eternal, like part of the earth it was made from.

I can't say why the brick brought me to thinking about Uncle Tyson's veranda and waiting behind the ivy-covered lattice watching a spider, but it did. More likely it was the boredom just like on that day I waited for Didier to come to Uncle Tyson's home.

~~~~~

No amount of pouting or worrying would make it happen any faster. Or put a halt to it. Didier would arrive when he arrived. To help pass the afternoon, I hustled upstairs to retrieve my library book from the bedside table. I held *The Good Earth* against my chest. The well-worn classic smelled of ink and many hands. I embraced comfort from the sense that so many people had read the words I now enjoyed.

Would that sense of connection be lost on the isolated prairies? Returning to the homestead was beyond comprehension, so was leaving my very own room. I flopped on the bed to memorize each detail: tiny cracks in the plaster, the slight slant of the blue curtains on the window, and the nick in the dresser I kept rubbing with lemon oil.

Concentrating on the familiar imperfections calmed my growing apprehension, and I determined to stay in control. Pretense was the only way to do so. I'd be a highborn lady and contain myself with precise movements. I would calmly read and calmly wait for Didier on the veranda.

I glided down the hardwood stairs to the main floor with all the elegance Princess Elizabeth possessed.

Uncle Tyson sat reading in his favorite overstuffed chair. He had shoved it closer to the parlor window with the good light and a good view of the road. He lowered the ever-present newspaper. "Your Highness, will you please settle yourself someplace?"

I stepped over Mutt and Pooch to kiss his temple. His skin tasted of Burma Shave. "Your Uncle Lordship, I'll be on the veranda reading."

"That's a good girl. Your poor old uncle needs a snooze."

His voice sounded reedy and I noticed a grayish pallor. "Are you all right?"

"Old kings need naps, but with royal ladies wagging their tongues, it's quite impossible."

I felt dismissed and wanted to retort, but he did look like he needed to doze.

The dogs padded through the doorway to the veranda ahead of me and flopped on the sunny boards at the top of the steps, guarding the front door like they guarded their bowls. A flop of a tail now and then was the only sign of attentiveness.

I squinted against another bright fall day and crossed to the shade of a rambling Virginia creeper. The vine with frost-browned leaves clung to a wraparound lattice and made a shady private nook at the south end of the veranda. I gracefully lowered my royal self onto Lanny's cane-bottom rocker and sat hidden in the shadows, not for rest, but for concealment. My first sight of Didier would be mine alone, and not shared by him looking back at me.

Once more gloom over his arrival descended on me, and I still hated myself for pestering Uncle Lanny about his past. Compassion for my uncle and worry over my father stuck like twin barbs in the bottom of my sock -- step, jab, step, jab. Pretended lady-like elegance could not overcome my worry or guilt.

My index finger marked the place in the book; the words remained unread. I left Wang Lung to brood about the babies he'd have and reached over to part a hole in the stiff leaves. Didier should come up the block from the south. Did good things arrive from a southern route? Dumb thought. It didn't matter if he arrived from the north, south, east, or west. He was my father, and I was duty bound to him.

A barn spider dropped to dangle near the lattice. He wiggled, dropped a few more inches, only to stop and wiggle again. He descended in the wiggle-drop pattern until he reached the floor.

After watching his efforts I didn't have the heart to squish him; instead I tapped my toes to spur his escape over the edge of the boards. I kept tapping until he was safely away, and then peered through the leaves again, as if drawn on a thread like the spider. Check and wait. Check and wait.

Motor sound. Quickly I checked through the hole. Gravel crunched. I drew back, took a jagged breath and peeked again. Tenseness ached between my shoulder blades. Why was I so fearful?

Mutt and Pooch jumped up and charged off the porch, barking. A black Pontiac coupe rolled to a stop in front of the house. Didier got out. His sable hair still had the deep wave at the front, but was cut shorter. A hint of ebony whiskers shadowed his clean-shaven face. Black jacket, black pants, black shoes, his Sunday best. The last time I saw him he looked like a homesteader, worn-out overalls, rundown boots, hair to his shoulders. I was leery of both images, knowing I was at the mercy of a father who loved only his land.

He stooped to pat the dogs, who were downright glad to see him.

Their treats tonight might be docked, I thought as I waited for excitement to erupt at seeing my father for the first time in five years. I remained cynical, distrustful. Not the way a daughter should feel.

Even from this distance I noticed a spring in his step that hadn't been there before. Pride, too, evident from the set of his shoulders and the tilt of his head. He looked happy. I couldn't remember ever seeing him carefree. Was that thanks to the new bride?

Didier opened the passenger door, and a honey blond woman stepped out. She was short, pleasingly plump, and a familiar pout rode her bottom lip. Alice Bromwell? Didier had married Alice? Alice was Odette's new mother? All the distrust in me reared up and erupted in utter dismay. How could he be so stupid? He didn't care one whit about Odette, or he wouldn't give her a selfish, spoiled, pouty mother. Odette needed a true protective parent in the worst sort of way.

As Didier and Alice walked hand-in-hand toward the veranda, I noticed a slight bulge in Alice's dress. She's pregnant! Didier had got her pregnant! And before they were married. That's why Alice married him. Had to be.

I remained in the shadows, unmoving, same as the spider hid somewhere under the house. I flinched when the front door opened and Odette stepped out onto the veranda to stand before the newlyweds like a scared curious kitten. One wrong move by Didier and she'd scratch him and run for the attic.

Didier halted at the bottom of the three steps. "Odette? You look just like your mother."

"I don't remember her." Then Odette did a remarkable thing. She raised a hand to her cheek and held it there. "Do I really?" Her question was timid, so unlike her usual combative self. Her voice sounded like it had before the fire, like when she was just a sweet innocent child.

"Exactly like your mother. Same color hair and your eyes are so much like hers. She'd be proud of you." Didier climbed the stairs, pulled her to him, and kissed her cheek. "You smell like Ivory soap."

Odette shied away and stiffened her neck and shoulders. Arched like a spitty kitten, she spat, "I don't remember you either."

Didier stepped back as if slapped and bumped into Alice, who teetered on the top step. He grabbed her forearm and steadied her. "Don't stand on the steps. Get up here beside me so I know where you're at."

Alice stepped closer, but shot him a look that clearly said don't push too far.

He turned from the glare and frowned at Odette. "Where's your sister?"

I shrank more into Lanny's chair, knowing full well I had to greet him. Delaying only stretched out the anxiety, but I was curious about my father, needed to sit and watch, except my eyes focused on Alice. I was waiting for some sign of how she would be with Odette. Alice was only five years older than me. Eighteen and very pregnant, yet she seemed at ease, like she belonged beside my father. Would she be able to handle Odette? Only one way to find out. I bit my bottom lip and rocked forward to stand. The chair creaked.

Through the dappled shadows, Didier's eyes met mine.

"Blinny?   Why were you hiding there without saying something?" censure already in his voice.

"I was getting used to how you look," I said. "You're different." I stepped out of the shadows, but not close enough to receive a kiss, wondering if he even considered greeting me as he had Odette. I didn't want him to. The place in my heart where love for a parent should be was filled with the memory of him hurrying down the aisle of the train and disappearing through the exit, leaving me alone and in charge of Odette. Somehow Didier needed to replace that image. I didn't think he could.

He stepped closer and brushed a kiss on my cheek. Old Spice aftershave clung to him; the scents of dry loam and baked rocks were buried under the spicy aroma.

"Blinny, you remember Alice?   We were married yesterday."

Alice grinned the smile I remembered, the one that was meant to be friendly. "Hi, Blanche. You sure have grown into a tall girl. You're already twice as tall as your mother was."

Until this moment, I had never minded my height. Five-foot seven-inches wasn't all that tall. Some girls in school were taller. However, the tease in Alice's eyes made me feel inferior. "I know I'm blessed to have long bones to carry my weight. Makes me strong, too."

Didier laughed. "That's good. We can use some of that strength on the ranch. Where are my uncles?"

"Probably hiding out. Letting us have time with you." I was sure Lanny was doing that, but Tyson should've stepped out when the dogs barked. I nudged Odette away from the door and reached to turn the knob.

Noise of another car coming fast up the gravel road drew our attention. Aunt Elaine's Ford sedan skidded, nosed up against the rear bumper of Didier's coupe and rocked to a stop. She hopped out. "Didier, so good to see you." She breezed up the front walk, neat rayon dress clinging to her legs, stylish padded shoulders, classy alligator shoes. She was combed and brushed, ready to greet her cousin and his bride. She quickly climbed the steps.

Didier held out his hand and shook hers warmly. "It's good to see you, too. This is my bride, Alice."

Elaine engulfed Alice's hand in hers. "Welcome to the Platt family. I'm glad we have a new member."

Alice raised her chest and tried to suck in her tummy. She half-smiled, her eyes gleamed wickedly. "Guess that makes you shirttail relations to my tribe of brothers. We're whatcha call prairie Bromwells."

I choked. She had brought Elaine down from put-on-airs better than I ever could. Five years ago, Alice was a greedy spoiled brat. Still was as far as I could tell. She might fool Didier with an act of sweetness and goodness. Not me. But at that moment, I kinda liked her. Maybe her remark about my height was a cover-up for Didier putting her on display. Then again, she might just be as hateful as before.

Elaine looked at me. Her cheeks reddened. "Why are you staring off into space instead of asking us inside?"

"I was just opening the door when you drove up." I turned the knob and shoved.

Mutt and Pooch pushed past me, went inside, and padded straight to Uncle Tyson, still in his overstuffed chair, head lolled to his left shoulder. Mutt's ruff rose and he yowled. The eerie sound coiled through me like a cold rattler and settled in my heart.

Elaine shoved me out of the way, bumped Odette into the wall, and ran to Tyson, placing a hand on his forehead. Instantly the color drained from her face. She leaned down and placed her cheek under his nose. "Oh... my...God," she cried. "He's sleeping in Jesus!" She threw her arms straight in the air and jiggled as if a force had hold of her; her hands waved above her head and her silk-clad breasts bounced. "Sweet Lord. Take him home!" She chanted home over and over, her tone reaching a higher note with each chant until I put my hands on my ears. I thought she might fly away, too. Elaine stopped dead still, listening, arms still in the air.

"He's on his way," she cried and collapsed to her knees beside Tyson's chair, clinging to his legs, sobbing loud enough to wake the dead. Or at least startle the heck out of them, I figured through a fog of disbelief.

I pressed forward to stand beside Elaine. The air around her was stifling, as if her sobs depleted the oxygen. Sweat broke out under my hair. Could Uncle Tyson really be gone? I had kissed him only moments ago. I peered closely into his vacant pupils. No eyes should be so empty. I reached to touch his dear cheek. The instant my fingertips touched his skin, I knew he had gone to join *Maman*. She would no longer be alone with *Bébé* Larry. Uncle Tyson would take care of them just like he'd taken care of Odette and me. *Maman* and Larry were the quiet sort. Tyson would like that. A pain pricked in my side like a stitch from running too hard. I wobbled, knees weak.

Odette squeezed around me and stared at Uncle Tyson if she was enjoying a new experience. She tried to push his eyelids closed, but they only went halfway. He appeared to be sneaking looks.

I was too horrified by Odette's grotesque pleasure to shove her away. Helpless, I turned to Didier, hoping he'd take charge of her. He stood behind me, Alice pinned to his side. He looked stunned. She appeared calm, as if death was an everyday occurrence; the look was earned by living amongst the natural elements on a ranch. We all understood death.

"At least Uncle Tyson died reading his paper," he said and stepped away, drawing Alice to the couch in front of the fireplace.

Didier was somewhat sad. Alice, I couldn't tell. No way of knowing, but felt she held sympathy for us in her strange and guarded way.

Thankfully, Odette turned her back on Tyson and walked to the overstuffed chair by the fireplace. The chair seemed to swallow all of her except her huge eyes that worked the room with an insatiable curiosity.

Elaine's crying softened to whimpers, then escalated again to weeping, then to keening.

I wanted to put a gag on her and wake up my dead uncle. Because I could do neither and because there was nothing else to do, I dropped on the rug beside Elaine close enough for her to feel my presence, hoping to give her some kind of comfort. I hated her for wanting Odette and me gone, but the death of a parent overrode bad feelings with ones of sorrow.

Lanny burst into the room from the kitchen. His hulking form slowed as he looked at Tyson. Then me. "He's gone?" The disbelief written on his face was more hurtful than Tyson without life.

Elaine caught her breath and shrieked again in a drawn-out, eerie way.

Lanny jerked as if hit by the sound. His worn face paled, then turned red, the scar a livid line running from eye to beard. "Elaine, stop it! You sound like a gol-damned cat caught in a chimney."

She rocked back on her haunches. "My father is dead."

"Elaine, shut up that racket or he'll be damned glad about it. He was a man of peace, not a--" Lanny's voice broke.

Elaine sucked in a sob. "You're cruel. I'm sick to death of you."

Lanny inhaled deeply through his nose. "You're right, Elaine. I was cruel and I'm sorry about it." He gritted his teeth, striving for control.

He shouldn't try so hard. I wanted to run to Lanny and throw my arms around him, ease the hunched look of him, but I couldn't move, rooted by the unexpected pain that filled the Platt house: Lanny fought his anger, Odette watched with morbid pleasure, Didier curled his arm along the back of the sofa, Alice tucked in his curved arm, Elaine glared through tears. And me – I was unable to say or do anything.

Elaine suddenly rose like a demon out of the Presbyterian abyss, hair streaming from her bun; her eyes were red, lips a line of hatred, hands claw-like. "Uncle Lanny, I've never understood why Father let you live with him. Or Didier's brats either. I want you all out of my house as soon as we bury my father."

Uncle Lanny stood with his arms stiff to his sides; his hands were balled into fists. I thought he might strike Elaine. Then he shook his shoulders and stretched his fingers until his hands hung relaxed. "We'll leave now." His words were soft, too. But the undertone was iron.

Didier jumped up and in three quick strides stood face to face with Elaine. He looked like a parson pleading a case of mercy. "Elaine, good Christians don't--."

Elaine snorted, cutting him off. "What do you know about Christian? You sent away your own flesh and blood when their mother died and saddled two old men with them. It wore my father out. Killed him sure as I'm standing here." Elaine drew back her hand to slap Didier.

Lanny caught her forearm as she swung forward. "No need for the show, Elaine. Only people here are us Platts. Find someplace to sit while I go for a doctor."

Crazed and without any good sense left, she yelled, "Get out and take smarty pants Blinny with you."

Blood rushed to my ears. "Aunt Elaine, when Uncle Tyson was alive, this was our home, but not anymore. Sell it and have fun in the stupid Holy Land." Tears sprung and I swiped at them.

Elaine hugged herself, holding on as if she was afraid to let go. "At least somebody understands," she moaned and crumpled to the floor by Tyson's knees.

Aunt Elaine thought I understood? How could she be so blind? Plain mad replaced my disgust and other overwrought emotions. I fairly simmered.

Lanny, Didier, Alice, and I looked at each other. The meaning in that long look was stronger than any of Elaine's hateful words. The quiet of our eyes meeting was a moment of relief in a room smelling sick from the stench of death and raw emotions.

Alice rose from the couch, smoothed down her dress, and crossed to Odette. She took the fey hand and led her to us. "Let's go home," she said.

There it was. We were going home.

"Can Lanny come with us?" I asked my father.

"It's up to him."

Lanny cleared his throat. "I'll work for room and board. Don't want any pay. We'll pack up and follow you in the dogs' car, but first I'm going next door to telephone Dr. Higgs and the funeral parlor." Lanny disappeared through the kitchen doorway, mumbling about Tyson being too old fashioned to have a newfangled telephone installed.

I heard him fill the tea kettle. It clattered onto the stove. The back door banged shut.

Didier took charge and led Elaine to the sofa. She threw herself face down, sprawling with her dress hiked, tops of her silk stockings showing, garters indenting the pale flab of her thighs. Didier did the decent thing and threw a ripple-weave afghan over her shaking body. The yarn coverlet settled around her in a blaze of yellow, orange, and green stripes.

"Go pack up, Blanche," Didier said. "You too, Odette."

I fled, my sister followed. From the head of the stairs, I called to Elaine. "You should've been nicer to Uncle Lanny. He's Tyson's best friend."

Chapter 13

I slapped mortar, set a brick, squared it up, and tapped it firmly into place for a whole long week. Row upon row. The boredom of brick laying seemed endless as I stood on a wobbly make-shift scaffolding of a plank cross-beamed between the rungs of the two stepladders that I had taken from the ranch. I'd meant to build a sturdier one – didn't get around to it, making do, but carefully. A fall was the last thing I needed. I hurt all over. The brutal work of laying brick ached in my shoulders and neck. The small of my back would never be the same. I was almost to the point of calling Lem.

I dipped to refill the trowel and reached up to plop it on top of the row of bricks. The board waggled, the ladder rocked, I grabbed for balance. A freshly laid brick broke loose. I caught my balance and the ladder settled. The scoop of mortar and the brick lay on the ground below me. *"Dang,"* I muttered and gingerly scooped up another load, spread it and set a brick.

A cloud of dust billowed from the road. Company coming. I sighed. My arms, back, and legs needed a break. I was tired and getting careless.

Alice coiled from the Lincoln dressed in rubber boots and gloves, jeans and a straw hat. "Stole my ladders, huh?" she called as she approached.

"You need new ones. They're so wobbly I just about fell."

"Need a hod carrier?"

I grinned. "It's about time you showed up. I need more mortar. It'll also help to have you to squabble with." I handed down the bucket.

Alice grabbed it. "I don't squabble. I tell the honest to God truth. You're the one who gets huffy." She hurried off to the cement mixer.

Oh the relief of her sharp tongue. I almost liked her. I caught myself before I said so. Wouldn't do to let Alice know.

She handed the bucket back up to me and just had to start telling the *honest to God truth* about my sister. "I guess you think Odette was happy when I told her you're building this house."

Good thoughts about Alice vanished. How dare she tell her before I was ready? "Why did you tell? I wasn't going to until it's finished."

"That's stupid. Just like bricking up this wall by yourself is stupid."

"Go home."

"The quicker you get your ass in gear and finish the wall, the quicker I can leave. Hurts me though that you pretend you're glad to see me, only to order me to go home. I expected you'd want to know how your sister is and if she's getting any better, but no, you just holler at me. Well, I'm gonna tell you anyway. She's better. Clearer in her mind than I can remember. I never knew Essie Faye, just seen her laying like a lump of coal killing herself in my bed, but I think Odette is like her in more ways than looks. She feels too deeply. Was hurt by things you or I would brush aside." Alice paused for breath. "Maybe you shouldn't go see her. One look at you might send her right back to hiding inside her head."

I waited for Alice to finish. Why, I don't know. She shot me with a couple more arrows, then abruptly stopped as if expecting me to erupt. I didn't blow, just scooped a trowel full of mortar and slapped it on a brick.

Behind me, I heard her walk away. I slapped my trowel down and jumped from the ladders. "Alice! I'm sick and tired of you driving off in a huff. What can be so wrong that you can't talk to me about it? We've been to hell and back. Buried our parents, fought the prairie, brought in crops, raised your boys."

She spun in her tracks and marched back towards me. She shook her finger. "You ought to know."

"I know two things. One, you want everyone to do exactly what you say and nothing else. Two, I'm not going to. I need to be here working, keeping busy. Your boys work the ranch far better than I can now, and I don't like sitting around. Can't stand it. You should understand that. I didn't leave to get away from you. I left to find myself."

"Well fine. I hope you're happy with just you and yourself." She hopped in the Lincoln before I said another word.

Who in his right mind could understand her or the harsh words that flowed between us? I clamored back up on the scaffolding. It rocked and settled. I mortared and set bricks as fast as I could with my sore-to-the-bone hands. My righteous anger at Alice spurred me same as my righteous anger at my Aunt Elaine spurred me to pack Odette's and my things as fast as I could. Alice and Elaine should spend time together. Ruin each other.

~~~~~~

Uncle Tyson's hall closet must have something to pack our clothes into. A stack of pillowcases. They'd work. My fingers rubbed against a row of blue hens Elaine had cross-stitched on the hem of the cases after we first arrived. Her so-called Christian duty to a couple of motherless girls. She had put on a good act.

Every knitted and crocheted and hand-stitched thing made by her should be pitched. The practical part of me cautioned against satisfying my righteous anger; we would need the warmth of handmade mittens and such on the windswept prairies.

I shoved open Odette's door. She was nowhere in sight. How could she sneak off without me hearing her? I had been right here in the hallway. Shaking away a shiver, I tossed a few of the cases on her bed and checked under it just to make sure she wasn't hiding. Only thing under it was her un-emptied chamber pot. She wouldn't even do that simple chore to make her room smell better.

Why worry about it when Uncle Tyson lay dead, and I was packing to leave? The best thing to do was to tend to my things then start on Odette's. She figured it that way and hid to make sure I did.

I returned to my room and stuffed anklets, undies, camisoles, garter belts, and long cotton stockings into two of the pillowcases. I poked in my two new brassieres. The kitchen door thudded. Lanny was back already! I snatched up the two pillowcases, lugged them downstairs, and dropped them on the landing.

Lanny appeared at the kitchen doorway carrying a tray with the tea kettle and cups into the parlor.

"Put your stuff in the kitchen," he said. "We'll keep our leaving among Platts for the time being."

"I have lots more to pack."

"We'll worry about that later. I need to talk to Elaine."

The grandfather's clock in the dining room bonged seven times as we crossed to the parlor. Didier sat in Uncle Lanny's horsehair chair, Alice perched on the padded arm. Odette huddled on the floor, leaning her head against the armrest at Elaine's feet, carefully monitoring me, Lanny, Didier, and Alice with eyes like the bottom of a well.

Elaine still lay face down under the afghan, not talking, acting more stubborn than my sister ever had. She ignored Lanny's offering of tea, pretending as though she didn't care that he had called Dr. Higgs.

Lanny tried to calm her down, but why? He should whop her wide bottom. Then, I realized he was treating Aunt Elaine with true charity. He might be mad as a hornet, but he knew how to hold it in check. He was a better person than me. I would have stung her.

We waited in silence for Dr. Higgs. The clock on the mantel chimed the half hour. Lanny lit the logs in the fireplace and the crackle and flare seemed out of place. Alice's cup clinked against the saucer.

My gaze returned time and again to my father. The look of him seemed so different, yet a turn of the head, or a gesture was familiar. I tried not to stare or appear too curious. He should think I didn't care about him or that he married. How could I adjust with Alice as his wife? *Maman* should be sitting beside him. Alice Bromwell didn't belong with us. I just couldn't picture her a Platt. Not ever.

Pooch and Mutt erupted into a ruckus that made everyone jump except dead Uncle Tyson. A knock pounded, the front door opened, and Dr. Higgs bustled into the parlor carrying his Gladstone doctor's bag and a good amount of fresh air.

The man was bundled in a black overcoat and hat that was pulled down around his ears; the black garb conveyed the seriousness of his mission. He crossed straight to Uncle Tyson, set his bag on the floor, undid the latch, pulled out a stethoscope, and pressed it against Tyson's still chest.

Odette scooted across the floor to peer inside the open bag and inspected the contents with great interest.

Dr. Higgs straightened. "Dead, all right."

Uncle Lanny's jaw was set like steel, but he managed to sound like he held respect for the doctor. "Elaine needs you more than Tyson. She's gone off the deep end."

"I'll check her after I call Wagner and Campbell's."

"Mortuary's been contacted."

"Good. We'll get ready for them. Won't take long to sign the death certificate."

The details concerning the disposal of my uncle's body sounded so ordinary, like an everyday occurrence. But not to me. Touching Uncle Tyson's corpse had been like putting my brother's burnt bone in the snake box. The feel of dead skin covering dead flesh would stay with me, same as the hot charred bone had.

After the men from the mortuary wheeled Uncle Tyson through the door, and after a whispered visit with Dr. Higgs, and after two shots of brandy, followed by a cup of hot tea, Aunt Elaine came to her senses in a mess of tears and apologies – but not until after Dr. Higgs left did she beg us to stay for the funeral services.

"No," Lanny said.

Elaine stood up fast and wobbled. She righted herself and threw the afghan around her shoulders. "Uncle Lanny, I said I was sorry."

"No," Lanny repeated.

Still wrapped in the blazing stripes she fell to her knees at his feet, wailing, "What will everyone say if you're not a pall bearer? His very own brother not lowering him into the ground?"

"You kicked us out. If Tyson could see the way you're behaving, he wouldn't go either. I'll not be a hypocrite for your pride."

"He's your own brother."

"And he knows how much I respect him. Now, I'll not put up with one more idiotic thing coming from your mouth." His tone left no doubt.

Elaine pressed her lips into a thin, tight line and put her forehead on the floor, like a servant bowing to a master. "Please, Uncle Lanny, I can't bear the gossip."

Lanny hesitated.

I thought for a moment that this time he really was going to slap Elaine. He reached down instead and pulled her to her feet and led her back to the couch. "Blinny and Odette need time to pack," he said. "We'll stay the night, but come morning, we're leaving. You dealt this hand with greed and jealousy. You'll have to live with the shame."

Odette scrambled up beside Elaine. "I'm not going. I'm staying," she cried, looking prickly and mean.

Finally, the outbreak I'd been expecting. I checked to see what Didier thought of Odette's refusal to go. His expression told me nothing. He just sat there with Alice perched beside him. I noticed he slowly stroked her back, running his hand all the way to the curve of her buttock. She leaned closer to him.

I shot them both a look. Neither of them saw it.

"Odette," I said. "You have to come."

"No, I won't!" She grabbed onto Elaine, clutching fistfuls of dress under the afghan. "Don't send me with them. Blinny beats me. And Lanny hates me."

My aunt looked a mess. More hair hung loose than was tucked into her bun, her face was blotchy and her nose drippy. She brushed Odette's wild black hair back and stared right into the girl's eyes almost nose to nose. "You will go with your father. Understand?"

Odette shoved Elaine's hands away and bolted for the stairs. The noise of her running up the second flight echoed down to us, then the attic door slammed shut. She would set the lock.

Elaine stared at the stairwell as if she actually expected Odette to come back down. She slowly turned her glare on Didier, who had moved his hand to rest on Alice's bare knee.

"Now do you see," Elaine spat, "how much that child needs the control of a father? How could you leave her with two old men for five years?"

Didier flushed, rose in a huff and stomped up the two flights of stairs. The thuds of him pounding on the attic door carried throughout the house like a bass drum at a funeral parade. "Open this damned door right now!"

I caught Alice's brief expression as she looked up the stairs, impatient and spiteful. She'd had enough of the whole business and her new husband should know that. I could read her like a book.

Her eyes fixed on mine for a moment. A hint of a smile touched her bottom lip. The true Alice had been well-concealed for everyone's benefit. Relief welled in me. I knew how to deal with this Alice. Then I saw something indiscernible as she lowered her gaze and smoothed her skirt down over her knees. Could be, she knew me better than I thought.

Lanny swore a string of words I had never heard. He yelled up the stairs. "Leave Odette be. She'll not come down till she's ready."

Didier clattered back downstairs and grabbed Alice by the hand. "We're spending the night at the Kalispell Hotel," he said, more to her than the rest of us.

"That's not necessary," Elaine said. "You can stay in Tyson's room. His bed is empty." She broke down into another round of blubbering.

Didier shook his head. "If I'm not welcome in this house tomorrow, I'm damned sure not staying tonight." He guided Alice to the front door. She gave me a look that said she was sorry for my uncle dying and stepped outside.

After the door shut behind my father and his bride, I hung onto the exchange between us. Alice hadn't changed, and she had let me know in the middle of a family torn apart.

Disbelief at losing Uncle Tyson and flabbergasted at Elaine was one thing, but Uncle Lanny scared me. He'd been angry plenty of times, but never so deadly serious. He was wound up, and I was afraid of what could happen if he snapped. A storm tearing limbs from trees might be safer.

And Odette could rot in the attic with the spider webs.

And Uncle Tyson was being laid to rest without his Platt family. He shouldn't be buried like that. Elaine's attack on us hadn't bothered me like it did Lanny. I understood. She had cared for a dying mother, a dying husband, and supported her children, all at the mercy of circumstances. She must have felt the same helplessness I had on the day of the snake shoot. No, before that. I had felt it under the sting of all the Bromwells' eyes at the table the day Didier took *Maman* away. I had been a child left to the mercy of strangers and could do nothing about it.

Elaine's reward for her sad, narrow life depended on selling her family home. Trading a house for a trip to the Holy Land was the dumbest thing I could imagine, but walking those streets was Elaine's choice.

She had traded us for a trip.

Chapter 14

Lem acted as if I was the last person he wanted to help, but showed me the foam channels I needed to install before the fiberglass insulation could be stapled in the attic. What kind of a mind could dream up such a simple way for air to flow from the soffit vents to the ridge vents? Genius, and I was glad somebody figured it out and glad Lem knew how to explain the concept to me. Lem also sold me a couple of sturdy stepladders, a heavy plank that would fit between their rungs and helped me tie down the rolls of insulation, channels, and ladders into the bed of my pickup.

I really needed to apologize to him for being so caught up in building that I couldn't carry on a proper conversation. "Lem, how would you like to share a chicken cooked on a spit next Sunday?"

He raised his light-colored eyebrows. "Depends on your motive. I'm in the habit of saving myself for ladies who appreciate a gentleman."

He looked so unlike a gentle man. I burst out laughing. "I just want to make up for treating you so rudely."

"I won't argue with that. What kinda sauce goes on your chicken?"

"I make one out of tomatoes and jalapenos."

"You're so scrawny, I never thought of you as a cook. Just a feisty female."

"That's a pretty good compliment. I don't mind feisty a bit. See you about three in the afternoon?"

"Better cook two chickens. I eat a whole one." He ambled back into the lumber yard. He was whistling as he went. Sounded almost like Uncle Lanny.

Before leaving the busy town, I ate a decent burger at the Dairy Queen across from the rail yard and enjoyed a walk to the library. A stack of Ralph Moody, Louise May Alcott, and Ralph Waldo Emerson classics would while away the evenings, and I bought several sacks of groceries that included two plump chickens and oatmeal. Tough to start a day without a bowl.

I drove home slowly, relaxed, feeling grateful for a day not spent in hard labor. My house was finally enclosed: roof on, bricks set, windows in place, and doors hung. The drive home slipped away in contentment, and I was surprised when I pulled onto my roadway. Where had the time gone? Lost in perfection, I couldn't remember when I had so enjoyed a day.

I parked beside the tool shed. Something was different? I felt it before I heard it. A ruckus inside my trailer? Barking? Snarling? A dog? How the heck did he get there? I had checked the latch when I left. It had been tight. I reached for the screen door. The growls grew vicious. A piece of paper floated free.

Alice's handwriting?

> *It's about time you cared*
> *for something besides your own*
> *ornery hide and that mangy horse.*
> *If you can tame this fine fellow*
> *enough to get inside, you'll get*
> *along fine.*

She had left a sack of dog food beside the steps. If she was anywhere near I'd choke her 'til her pouty bottom lip touched her stubborn chin. I stole over to the window and peeked inside. Savage jaw and canine teeth hit the glass. I jumped back. He fell out of sight. I leaned in for another look. Teeth bared, he barked against the glass.

My shotgun leaned in the corner behind the chair. Even if I stuck my arm inside I couldn't reach it, and I wasn't about to lose flesh trying.

The dog quieted, but the ruff on his neck stayed ridged and his eyes glared hatred at me through the windowpane. He was white with black Border collie markings on his head and rump. Gray splashed his shoulders. Part coyote? Maybe. Sure looked like a crossbreed. A wild one. More than likely a coyote bitch got mixed up with a sheepherder's wandering dog and had a litter.

"Where did you come from?" I asked through the glass.

Snarls, low and mean.

I had absolutely no idea what to do except kill Alice.

"Well there's nothing to do but wait till you pass out." Hoping that would happen quickly from lack of water. Poor guy shouldn't suffer on account of Alice's stupid ideas.

My stomach rumbled. The hamburger hadn't lasted long. I gathered short pieces of sawed-off wood and piled them loosely over some dried grass. I got a kerosene lantern from the tool shed and a box of matches.

A lively fire soon burned, and I laid two of the bricks on burning coals. On top of them I placed one of the steaks I bought. The fat sizzled and smelled rich. I savored the smoky beef-laced wind.

You're smarter than a chicken.

I laughed – deep and delighted. "Yes I am. And smarter than Alice and a wild dog put together." A plan formed, and I clapped my hands in childish glee and my ire seeped away into a self-satisfied bubble of knowing I'd sleep tonight in my bed inside the trailer. I'd just open the door and he'd run for the steak. My glee died in its tracks. The fire would scare him and he wouldn't leave the safety of the camper. I'd have only a split second to get out of the way of his bared teeth. My puffed up attitude sunk. There was more to this than simply opening the door.

I picked the hot steak off the brick, tossed it a few feet in front of the door and scooped handfuls of dirt on the flames.

The work bench in the tool shed might be high enough. When I set it up against the camper, the metal clunked.

Vicious growls, claws raking the inside of the metal door.

I snarled back

Vile and hateful growls.

I propped the screen open with a shovel handle, shoved the door open, and jumped for the bench.

The wild dog leapt from the trailer

I grabbed the roof.

He hit the ground running.

I scrambled one leg up on the edge of the roof.

He snatched the steak.

I hoisted to safety. Metal creaked and dented, but held.

He snatched the steak, rounded the tool shed, and disappeared into the prairie.

I shook my arm in victory. "Take that, Alice!"

My jubilant adrenalin surge calmed. I felt hollow. Surely I didn't expect the dog to stop and thank me for supper like Mutt and Pooch used to.

~~~~~~

The very last day Odette and I lived in Uncle Tyson's house Pooch and Mutt's nails clicked against the hallway's hardwood floor outside my bedroom. They pushed through the door. "Today, we're going for a long ride in your car," I whispered woefully. Parting with my very own room saddened my prideful heart. The brass bed rattled as I sat up and scratched between their ears.

I rose and crossed to the window. Low clouds hugged the Rocky Mountains. The sun would soon rise unseen behind the complicated shades of gray. It was fitting that these dense clouds hid the fiery orb lifting over the high peaks. I was as gray inside as the shroud in the sky.

The dogs flopped on the floor and watched me strip my room bare, packing even the curtains, bedding, and scatter rugs. I recalled how Uncle Tyson had taken me to the mercantile and waited patiently while I fingered chintz, organdy, and muslin curtains. I'd chosen the blue muslin, blankets of a darker blue, and a multicolored Oriental rug. I refused to let Uncle Tyson's patient gift to be sold to strangers at the yard sale Aunt Elaine was sure to have.

The queen's pot was already cleaned and packed safely between the blankets.

Wondering if Odette was still locked in the attic, I opened her bedroom door. She snuggled deep in her covers; her tousled hair barely showed. Poor girl, I thought. She's the same age I was when Didier put us on the train.

I sat on the edge of the bed and uncovered the face that looked like *Maman*. She tried hard to appear sound asleep, but the very corners of her lips twitched as she fought back laughter. Humor was the last thing I expected. I tickled her cheek right beside the corner of her lips.

Odette giggled a sound of true merriment. Her violet eyes opened. "I hate you," she said, trying to sound fierce, but her voice quavered as she held back giggles.

I longed for more of these times when Odette seemed at peace, not angry at unseen forces, not fighting a battle I couldn't share. "And I hate you, but up you get. We have to pack."

"I'm not going," she said firmly.

"I know." I rolled her out of bed. "Didier will be here soon."

I packed her bedding while Odette put on her plaid shirt and overalls. Then she sprawled flat on the bare mattress and watched me, same as the dogs had; her eyes followed every movement, an unspoken question in them. I could not explain to her any more than I could to the dogs that we were going and had no voice in it.

I checked in the closet, under the bed, and deep in the dresser drawers for anything overlooked. Nothing. Odette hopped from the bed, grabbed two bags and ran downstairs. I sighed in relief. Maybe she wouldn't cause a scene.

We had Lanny's few possessions alongside our huge pile stacked on the veranda by the time Didier arrived. He left Alice in the coupe, strode up the walk and stopped short of the steps. "That's a mountain of belongings," he said without a greeting of good morning or anything. "Don't know if we can take it all."

"We'll make 'em fit," Lanny said and grabbed an armful of pillowcases.

He and Didier silently loaded our boxes and bags into the two cars. We had arrived with nothing and were leaving with so much packed and stuffed away. Memories of Uncle Tyson were also tucked away into every nook and cranny in my heart. I was not leaving him behind.

Didier started on Lanny's small pile. "Is this all?"

Lanny spat on the ground. "I only wanted my personals and a few of Tyson's books. Elaine can damned well sell everything else. Maybe buy herself a Jewish prayer rug while she's over there." My uncle's anger had not abated like I thought it had when I first saw him sipping his morning coffee. Instead, his ire simmered and erupted in spits on the ground and sarcastic words.

Odette held her peace until every last thing was crammed inside the vehicles. "I won't ride with those two stinkin' dogs. They'll slobber all over me."

"You need to ride with your sister," Didier said.

Odette's chin jutted out, body stiffened, eyes flashed. "I'll not ride in the same car with Blinny. She bosses me all the time. You just wait and see how awful she is. Besides maybe I'd like to get to know my father." She batted her lashes at him as if she were a sweet innocent.

Alice leaned out of the open window. "Oh for pity sake, let the girl ride with us. I can use the company."

Didier didn't look happy, but he opened the coupe door and held the seat forward for Odette to climb inside. She slid over to sit right behind Alice.

That was fine by me. At least Odette had had a choice about something.

The gray heavens opened and lavished rain on the lush Flathead Valley when we drove away. It was so different than when I left the thirsty, empty prairies.

Narrow Highway 2 climbed, plunged, and snaked toward Marias Pass, but Uncle Lanny didn't seem to appreciate the danger of the wet, unfamiliar road. He kept his foot hard on the gas pedal, window down, left elbow hanging out, an unlit cigar clenched in his teeth and a coffee can filled with peanuts braced against his leg.

Bundled in my wool coat and Aunt Elaine's knitting, I clutched the arm strap and held on to the floorboard with my toes curled in my oxfords as we sped around every curve whether sweeping or sharp. I screeched as the tires grabbed the watery blacktop when we hurled around the *Devil's Elbow*.

Lanny eased up a little until we reached the next straight stretch, then gunned the engine again. He reached into the coffee can and tossed a couple of peanuts to Mutt and Pooch.

I glanced back to see if Didier was keeping up. The Pontiac was nowhere to be seen. "We lost Didier."

"He knows where we're going."

Damp, frigid air gushed in Lanny's window, circulating the rank odor of the two panting black Labs throughout the car. Mutt had passed gas again. Pooch hung his nose across the seat just behind my left ear.

"Phew, you guys stink." I let go of the armrest long enough to reach back and thump Pooch. "Lay down. The peanuts are gone."

Pooch licked at my hand, liquid-brown eyes pleading.

"Quit picking on the dogs," Lanny said around the butt of his cigar.

I itched to pick an argument over anything and wiped Pooch's slobber off my hand on Lanny's shirt sleeve.

Lanny ignored me and drove even faster.

The minute we crested the Continental Divide the rain ceased. We shot downward on dry blacktop for thirty miles through East Glacier and twelve more into Browning. The rain-starved foothills flattened on the other side of Cut Bank. Thatches of gamma grass had matured in the shady bottoms between mounds and scarps. The prairie fought back by letting wind-scattered seeds catch, take root, and survive like a seasoned veteran giving and taking punches yet staying on his feet.

Sun burnt wheat stubble now whiskered both sides of the road. Didier had mentioned this year's harvest had been the fullest in the last few, providing plenty of money to buy next year's seed and to get by on. He had sounded proud, so different from the father I remembered, bent against work and worry.

I checked behind us, and Didier had caught up. The front of the Pontiac coupe remained visible as we traveled mile after mile on the straight ribbon of asphalt that divided the vast grassland.

The Rudyard grain elevator finally appeared in the distance. The tall wooden port rose like a beacon, announcing where we would turn north. The endless straightaway miles were almost over.

We turned left off the highway and rattled across the railroad tracks we'd been paralleling all the way from Uncle Tyson's and into the small farming town.

Didier, now tight on our tail, honked his horn and pointed at the mercantile.

We all piled out to use the facilities. Earth beneath my feet had never felt so good. An invisible force flowed over me, swirling my hair and tugging my skirt. I braced into the wind I remembered. It smelled of grass and soil. A flock of sparrows banked against the currents above the mercantile roof. I wanted to run out into fields and spread my wings, let the sweet prairie breezes blow me along same as the birds soared.

Instead, I took my turn in the facilities.

North of Rudyard we rode Didier's bumper onto the gravel of Montana Highway 255, then fishtailed on the washboard road until Lanny raised his heavy foot off the gas pedal. Once the car settled, he goosed her again.

My toes curled in my shoes and I hung on. Thirty miles to the Platt homestead.

Finally, the brake lights on Didier's coupe flashed. The car turned left, vibrated over a cattle guard, and sped up the Platt road. At breakneck speed Lanny swerved the sedan toward two skinny ruts marking the entrance to the Platt holdings. The sedan flew off the gravel, jolted across the poles of another cattle guard, went airborne for a split second, and bounced back on the two-track road. We disappeared into a cloud of prairie silt. A blanket of dust rose behind the coupe. My uncle slowed only so we wouldn't choke. I was sure Lanny didn't care about visibility. He hit every possible bump, rattling the dogs, the car, and my eye teeth.

I waited until Didier was well ahead before I rolled down the window to breathe in the smells of dry grass and sage. The tangy dusty aromas reminded me of my mother. I tried not to dwell on missing her, but this first close-up view of the Platt ranch brought back the inner ache.

On a knoll where *Maman*, Odette, and I had eaten lunch, the image of *Maman* lingered in the toast browns of the prairie grasses and in the colors beneath the browns. Pull a handful of seemingly dead grass and right at the root line search for a hint of deep green – the promise of life to come. She would always be part of the landscape, appearing in different places where the three of us had played. First as a mother thin and graceful, then cumbersome with child, and then wistful and wan; then she was gone, leaving behind loneliness: an emptiness she hadn't prepared us for.

Maman had taught us many lessons, but never about living without her. Her instructions dealt with daily living: how to brush your teeth with baking soda and salt to keep gums strong. How to heal a cut with kerosene and to stand proud while the sting of it shot through nerve endings, how to find laughter while sweeping offal out of the chicken coop, how to look for pleasure in the hearts of wild flowers, inside the husk of a wheat kernel, within the palm when walking hand in hand.

Whatever happened to my joyful mother who had taught us with an arch to her eyebrows and a playful grin on her lips? I couldn't tear my eyes from the landscape. I needed to go visit her grave. I'd ask Didier to take us the first chance I got.

"Not much to look at," Lanny said.

"I see my mother."

"I figured you were pulling up memories."

The first shapes of distant buildings appeared, and I leaned forward. Last time I had seen the rough-lumber outbuildings was when I hid in the wagon to put *Bébé* Larry in the box. The barn, chicken coop, pig pen, granary, and outhouse had been sad shadows against a starry night that reeked of burnt tar.

Didier's two-track road angled beside a field of rotting pumpkin vines and ran past acres of wheat stubble. The car rattled across another cattle guard, swung around a new barn that dwarfed the old one behind it, past the bunkhouse where a tall, lanky ranch hand stood watching, and into the yard near the charred rubble of *Maman*'s homestead house.

"I expected him to clean up the mess," I mumbled, wondering if mess was the right noun to describe the blackened wood representing death.

Uncle Lanny braked. Tires slid in the silt. He wheeled hard to the right and skidded to a stop next to a bent black-willow fence which separated the new ranch house from the barnyard.

I let go of the dash and stared up through the windshield at the house Didier had built.

The house was foursquare with a pyramid roof. I counted three levels including one with a front dormer window. The eaves were deep and the front porch was wide. He had painted it all white, even the trim. The only break from starkness was a porch foundation made of gray field stones.

Lanny stared, too. "Didier built hisself quite a house," he said with a note of approval.

I opened the car door and stood gaping. "I never imagined us Platts having a house so big." I was none too sure I approved. Where would I fit in? Alice now occupied my father's house. I knew her bad side – the lazy, pouty, selfish, and mean part I had confronted at the Bromwell home. How much of this land and house would be hers? What would become of me and Odette if she produced male heirs for Didier?

Alice was already opening the white front door, with Odette right behind her. Looked as if Odette had found a friend. Good, they deserve each other. Then I felt bad. What a terrible way for me to think. Odette was my sister and Platts stuck together.

Odette turned just before she stepped inside the house. She stuck her tongue out at me, did a flip of her head and disappeared inside. Something in her demeanor was wrong. She wasn't just a mean little kid. Her perception of life ran to the evil side. She saw bad in everything. Maybe living here on the prairies would change that, but I doubted it. Alice certainly couldn't help Odette, not with her attitude.

Maman, what am I to do?

I let the dogs out of the backseat, and Lanny flung open the trunk. He carried an armload of stuffed pillowcases to the porch and came back for more. "You gonna stand there gaping or give me a hand?"

I didn't want to help unload. I needed to explore, go for a walk in the fields, listen for meadowlarks and visit the pigs, the cows, check out the hens. I wanted to feel the ranch the way I had before the fire. See if I could regain the freedom I'd once had and feel our land without the hurt from being sent away.

I grabbed an apple crate from the trunk. "You look out of breath, Uncle Lanny. Why don't you sit for a minute?" I really didn't like the way he appeared. He'd driven like a crazy man, but I had arrived safely. I wasn't sure he was so safe. "What's the matter?"

"Leave me be, girl. I'm all right. It's hard on an old man to be uprooted. You ought to know that." He sat down on the steps.

Didier ambled down the rise and across the farmyard toward the man on the stoop of the bunkhouse as I lugged the last box to the porch.

The ranch hand stepped down into good light and took off his hat. He looked familiar. Monty? Alice's brother? The one who cared enough to warn me away from the dangers of the coulee? The one who looked at me with soft sorrow when he handed me Marvel's sack? It was him. I hurried down the rise. Would he remember me? Be my friend again.

"Monty," I said and extended my hand for a shake.

His warm hand curled around mine. "Blinny."

My blood pumped warm and fast. We would be friends.

Didier cleared his throat. "I won't need you till next Monday so you might as well ride on home. Be sure and bring that milker when you come back."

"Pa will expect my wages next week." Monty nodded to me and walked towards the over-sized new barn.

After Monty disappeared through the double doors, Didier reached over and chucked my chin. "It's good to have you back."

His light touch to my chin was the closest thing he would ever do to admit he hated sending us away. A small surge of respect for my father reentered my heart. Maybe I didn't understand what he suffered after the fire. I smiled at him. We were Platts and would stick together.

It felt nice to be standing beside my father, sharing a moment of quiet while gazing on what he'd built in the five years I was gone.

"What part of that tall house do I get?" I asked.

"You'll get used to the wind in the eaves. Odette can't run off to the top floor if you're already there. Be easier for you to keep an eye on her."

My respect lessened. We were banned to the rafters. What other limits was he about to impose?

Didier nodded toward the west. "I have in mind to build you a house on that rise by the west field. You remember the spot?"

Build me a house? My chest surged with surprise. I glanced west. From here I couldn't see the knoll, but the look of it was clear in my mind. For hours I had sat there under a spring sun watching him plant wheat, wishing I was old enough to sow the fertile seeds.

"I remember," I answered, studying him, wondering why he would plan a house for me.

He was watching me as closely as I was him. We were like two strange animals sniffing about. "I have a spot picked out for Odette too," he said without dropping his eyes. "Plenty of men would be willing to marry for a house on my spread. And I'm planning to buy a couple more sections."

Even with a wife and baby on the way, he wanted me and Odette to stay on his land. Why? The answer popped into my head. "You expect us to marry so you can have more ranch hands?"

"Daughters marry, need a place. It's what you want, isn't it? A house of your own?"

How had he guessed?

"You're the same as me, Blinny. I've sensed it from the time your mother and I first built on the homestead. You're part of this land as much as I am."

So he thought he knew me better than I knew myself? He was wrong about that. "What did you get by marrying Alice?"

"A wife and child."

I looked him in the eye. "And her brothers to help. We both know they'd never let their sister's crops go un-harvested."

My father answered in a tone that told me I was crossing into dangerous territory, "It's saving the land, isn't it?"

I didn't have an answer to that. Apprehension wiggled around, but why? I gazed back toward the west field, feeling the pull of the wind, the pull of the prairies. Storms, snows, and wind had eroded deeper creases in the coulees, but the grasslands rolled in unchanging drama. Even the depth of the tire tracks in the two-rut road was the same. Under the weight of the farm machinery, the soil had hardened into an unyielding crust.

Year in and year out, my father's battles with the elements had hardened him the same way. My distrust was also unyielding. Could I learn to live with him? Be a part of this ranch? Uncle Lanny was not the only one who had been uprooted. I loved Uncle Tyson's house and the school and my friends as much as I loved the prairies. Where did I fit? I felt divided.

Chapter 15

The rolls of insulation were hung. Finally. My hand ached between the thumb and forefinger from using the stapler. I sat on the trailer steps, put my thumb in my mouth and felt sorry for the poor digit. My house looked good. The red bricks sound, roof solid, and doors straight. Miracle.

My whole place had taken on the look of a home.

I lifted my face to the breeze and wished my Uncle Lanny could see it. He had been my steadfast friend.

~~~~~

In 1943, an April breeze wandered down the north side of the coulee through tufts of dried grass, rippled across the spring flooding of the Milk River, and dallied with new buds on canopy trees and willows. I lifted my face to the draft of fresh scents rising from the bottom, letting the promise of rebirth steady my impatience.

Didier had promised to build me a house three years ago and that still hadn't happened. I took matters into my own hands last fall on my sixteenth birthday and picked the perfect spot in the west field to build. I paced it off, pounded stakes, and ran twine to mark the foundation for a cozy squat house, but January blizzards had rotted and broken the twine. Fibers of tan jute dangled from the knots. I picked one free and twisted the shaggy cord around and through my work-roughened fingers as if the bite of roughness could bring about the miracle of building.

Didier wasn't in a hurry to buy lumber. His excuses ran from lack of money to the opinions of local busybodies. Girls had to stay on the ranches until, by some miracle, a hardworking boy came along and popped the question. Walk down the aisle and a bride could then have a house built somewhere on her father's holdings.

I certainly hadn't walked down any aisles, and I didn't have much use for old fashioned notions. I simply wanted my promised house without a vow of matrimony.

The lone boy I might consider couldn't force words past his shyness. Monty and I had stolen long meaningful eye talk, but had never held hands. Nor had we talked about anything except the ranches and chores and crops. I dwelled on his sparse words, repeating them, picking out each noun and verb, hoping for a hint of how he felt, but only his eyes spoke with meaning.

The few times our fingers brushed in passing a pitchfork, or halter, or rope, or a plate of food the heat of his skin lingered on mine, feeding my curiosity about what it would feel like to be held in his arms. Maybe he would kiss me. I had kissed my mirror a few times practicing, but the cold touch of the glass could not answer my yearnings.

Just yesterday I sat with Monty in a harsh prairie wind rubbing straw on a newborn calf we had pulled from a cow, and I purposely placed my palm on the wet calf right next to Monty's hand. I felt the new life of the calf and the warmth of Monty at the same time. The power of both rested me like a dream that wouldn't let go. I kept slipping into a sensation soft with comfort. The longer I held the side of my hand against Monty, the more dreamy I felt. I had to get beyond my own shyness and get us talking soon. Spring planting would be done in a couple of days, and Monty would return to the Bromwell spread until harvest time.

The calf had bawled and struggled up onto wobbly feet. I also struggled to my feet, holding my hand against my mouth, waiting for Monty to say something; surely he felt what I had. He merely wiped the calf puller with a hunk of gunny sack and tossed the rag in the back of Didier's truck. "I'll see you

Monday," he said and mounted his range horse to go to the Bromwell ranch for the weekend.

I watched him ride away without uttering a word.

But I was tired of waiting on a boy that couldn't talk and tired of living with Didier and Alice, watching them spoil their son and turn Odette into a housebound loner. Not that Odette cared. She preferred to stay indoors with Alice, who never criticized or made her do anything that consisted of real work. They played together at taking care of Alice's son, Hyatt.

I couldn't help compare the day Alice went into labor to the day *Maman* gave birth to *Bébé* Larry. Didier had whisked Alice off to the Havre Hospital at the first sign of a cramp, leaving me in charge of the ranch.

The day *Maman* went into labor, I was also left in charge, helping the best way a child could. Odette had been so frightened, and I didn't have time to comfort her as she clung to my skirt, crying, me scolding her to be quiet, but she didn't. She scrambled under the bed and sobbed below the mattress as our screaming mother pushed our baby brother out.

Maman had held the baby toward Didier when he returned from the fields that day. You have a son." Her smile was weak, but prideful.

Didier rushed to her and leaned in close. "Thank you, my sweet girl." He kissed both her cheeks, then took his son from her and gingerly folded the baby into his strong arms. My father walked out of the house as if we no longer mattered, crooning words about the crops and animals they would raise. He acted like his son cost *Maman* nothing.

I wanted to chase after him and yell about the pain I had witnessed, but *Maman* shook her head at me when I stepped toward the door. I choked back the words of anger for her sake. She was protecting him from what the birth had cost her in strength, and I wouldn't add worry to what little she had left.

Spoiled Alice had Didier beside her with nurses and a doctor to help. But I imagined the pain was the same and wondered how Alice handled it. Was she brave? I figured she was as tough on the inside as she was on the exterior. Alice had grit. She just happened to also be a self-centered witch.

When Didier returned from Havre without Alice, he appeared tired around the eyes and anxious.

"What's wrong?" I asked.

"How many calves so far?"

He was worried about his cattle, but not so worried that he left Alice to labor alone like he had *Maman*. I couldn't help but snap. "Twenty-six. Monty needed to pull only three."

Didier ignored my tone. "Alice has a son. I'll go back for them in a few days." He looked none too happy about another trip, as he walked to the corral to saddle up and check on the herd.

Five days later, Odette squealed at the sight of the dust-laden Pontiac coup bouncing up the Platt road. She ran down the porch steps to the bent willow fence. I couldn't recall ever seeing her so excited; she fairly danced along the fence line.

The Pontiac slowed to a stop and Odette scurried to the car.

The door opened and Alice's shapely legs touched the ground. She remained seated and pulled the blanket away from the baby so Odette could see.

Alice and Odette appeared enchanted.

I couldn't help but go see, too. I stood beside the car in the sun and wind as Hyatt Platt curled his fingers around my finger and around my heart. He was so much like *Bébé* Larry, with downy hair and deepest blue eyes.

I stole time a month later from chores and carried him to see the pigs, chickens, and horses. I continued the daily visits as he grew to be a heavy armful, then helped him toddle to the pens. Alice never intruded with our walks. She left me alone, and I her.

Despite Alice's and Odette's feminine efforts, Hyatt turned out to be a roly-poly ruffian by his third birthday. Every time he managed to escape outside, he would race across the ranch at breakneck speed toward anything that moved or looked the least bit exciting.

Didier was crazy about the tough blond boy and railed at Odette if he caught him loose and on the run. My father chose to ignore the fact that Odette never quite grasped what was going on around her. She inhabited another world and preferred it, becoming more and more like *Maman*. Once in a while, I'd overhear her talking and answering herself. The talking happened less the longer we were at the ranch, but she would do other odd things, like hold her hands over her ears and cry out for no reason. When I tried to ask her what was wrong, she'd just shake her head and run off, disappearing into the prairie for hours on end. And sometimes I swore she liked our father. Her eyes shone when he entered a room, but she never said anything to him. Other times she told me he was a devil and she hated him. She sought his approval though. Lots of times she'd be the first to hop from the table if he asked for something and bring it to him. She glared at him if he acknowledged her effort.

What Odette needed was to live away from Alice's catering and needed a strong hand to make her pay attention. Didier had the strong hand, but instead of worrying about his daughter, he made a fool of himself every time Alice swished her tail or brushed her bosom against him. Alice flirted with him unabashedly, and didn't care who watched.

I found it hard to believe that Alice was in love with my father, and I questioned her open intimacy, which seemed more like playacting for my benefit. So far, her waistline stayed trim, no outward sign of forthcoming Platt sons.

I mentioned Alice's lack of children to Uncle Lanny when we were riding horseback along the fence of the separation field, checking to see if any defiant cow had broken through to get to her yearling.   The calves bawled on one side and mothers bellowed on the other.   The noise of the cattle got me to thinking of Alice and I asked, "Uncle Lanny, isn't it strange that Alice hasn't had any more babies?"

He shrugged. "Let it alone."

A cold wind whipped my hair below the brim of my felt Stetson and nipped my skin inside the turned up collar of my sheepskin jacket. "But she's fertile. We know that."

Uncle Lanny took a stogie from his shirt pocket and stuck it unlit into the corner of his lips.   He chewed on it, and then spoke around the butt. "You're not really worried about that, are you?"

"I—"

"Blinny, you're talking all around what you really want. Quit worrying so much about a place to build a house.   Your father needs your help and he knows it.   He'll eventually get to it."

But Uncle Lanny also grew tired of Alice.   I was in the house garden, on my hands and knees, planting a row of early peas when he ambled through the gate.   He pushed soil over my row of seeds with the toe of his boot and tapped the earth down, working down the row until he stood almost on top of me.

I sat back on my heels. "What's on your mind, Uncle Lanny?"

"I don't fit here."

He had my full attention.   My eighty-year-old great uncle was trying to say goodbye.

Lanny straightened like a younger man. "I've decided to look up my sisters in Vermont before they die, or I do.   They're both widows and might need a brother around. You know we Platts take care of Platts."

"I need you around."

"No you don't. Not anymore. You're in your element here. As much of a farmer as your father."

He was trying to spare my feelings amid his hurt at leaving me. I could hold on and make him feel guilty, but he'd been on my side for so long that it was now my turn to be on his. He needed his freedom.

I swallowed. "I know living on the ranch has been hard for you."

"Not as hard as some things. Before I go you need to hear a story. Let's go sit on the fence rail."

Him asking me to sit was like telling me this was important and I had better listen. He was going to open a door that he'd never wanted to before. I could still close it. Instead, my curiosity forced me to climb the rungs and balance against the fence post.

Lanny leaned against the railing near my knees, letting the rays warm his neck muscles. "Remember the old woman accusing me of being a gambler and a murder?"

I nodded solemnly.

"It's time for you to know. See if you can use it to help you have a past less painful than mine."

I had waited a long time to hear his story and now that the time had come, I wasn't at all sure I wanted to hear it.

Uncle Lanny cleared his throat. "Back in 1910, I gambled my savings in a small chemical company that was dabbling in synthetic fibers used to make cloth. I did good. Four years later, I withdrew my money to buy a corner lot on Nob Hill near the Conrad Mansion.

"I planned to build a house large enough for a family. I was ready for a wife and children. A man has to work to that point. Got to be willing to give up being single. Let a woman boss him around. You'll be good at that, Blinny." Lanny was delaying, talking all around what he wanted to say.

"Is it so hard to talk about?" I asked.

"Some hurts last a lifetime." He sighed. "I helped the builders in the evenings and on weekends. I mortared my own fireplace using a combination of shale slabs and river rock. I'd come to think of the round and flat surfaces of the polished stone as chapters in my life. People would naturally think the highlights would be contained atop the rounded stones, but the flat ones held the key.

"Good things happen when everything is on an even plane, like setting the soles of my worn-out boots on the dock at Ellis Island. I can still hear the flat planks of the pier respond to my heel-toe steps. *Welcome, welcome,* they sang. Most of the folks back in the homeland couldn't understand why I left, but I slapped my boots along, knowing that here in this new land, I'd find a place for myself and Tyson."

My curiosity about Platt history sparked. "My father said you helped him come from France, too."

"Him and two of my sisters. Your great-aunts still live in Vermont. Now, where was I?" His eyes grew faraway, as if seeing 1914 and his house again. "I had met Lilly Mae Bickle. She was a spitfire, full of righteous indignation, turning down suitor after suitor, saying she'd marry when she found a man who understood that women need to vote, sit on school boards, have jobs besides cooking and cleaning, live in decent homes and have protection from drunken husbands.

"She was the kind of a woman that filled a man's heart, and I was determined to have her and have plump children with her dark hair and blue eyes. Oh, how I wanted her children. I bought her a diamond ring, but held back until the last wall of my house was painted and the final coat of mahogany varnish applied. I wanted to dazzle her with the stability of the building and myself. The day I brought her to my house, I knew her answer would be yes. She couldn't refuse, but she did.

"I loved her more for the denial. I'd always chased the impossible, desired more than what was available, even crossed an ocean to find a home. Miss Contrary Lilly Mae Bickle would be mine.

"Two months later, the vows before a preacher were done, the ring was on her finger, and she moved into my new house. My life was set. Good paying job at the lumber yard, a home, and a wife who would give me a family of my own. A son or daughter to share our life.

"Four years later, Lilly Mae still hadn't conceived a child and learned she never would. She grew restless, claimed keeping track of me wasn't enough. Those infernal suffragettes got their mitts on my Lilly Mae about the time winter was hard on the heels of October."

Lanny's frustration echoed in his tone and the slump of his shoulders. I didn't know if I wanted to hear more, but he'd started this, and I had to stay beside him.

"What happened?" I asked.

"Oh, she fought hard for women rights, working in the thick of the November elections. They planned a rally one night. I had wanted her to stay home, told her it was too dangerous.

"Women already had my respect, and I damned sure wasn't going to stand in a crowd telling the world about it. I held the door open for her, shutting it hard after she passed through. I'm sure she jumped like the dickens. I watched through the window as she walked away. She tripped on the gutter. I remembered I reached out as if to catch her, but she righted herself and disappeared around the corner."

By now, I really wanted my uncle to stop, hear no more about his private affairs. Something bad had happened to Lilly Mae.

He looked at me. "Heard enough?" He knew very well I had.

"You don't need to tell."

"You need to hear about wanting something too much." He cleared his throat. "That night, at midnight, something was wrong. I knew it. She was headstrong and willful, but never let me worry.

"I found out that after those women paraded through town, they wanted to be where men were men. Show they belonged. They traveled from bar to bar. Those fools left Lilly Mae in Mel's Saloon playing five card stud. I knew she liked to play cards. Even knew that her bridge club wagered, but never this. Anger black and thick hit me."

Had my uncle killed his wife like the wrinkled old lady said? "What did you do?"

"Ran to Mel's Saloon and charged inside. The dealer told me she wasn't there, had left two hours ago, owing a large sum of money to a couple of high rollers. They fed her whiskey and took her vouchers. The anger in me turned to horror.

"The search for Lilly Mae lasted four days. Then a fisherman working the banks of the Flathead River snagged her dress and pulled her ashore. Some figured she killed herself because she couldn't have a baby, others thought some man had violated her. I knew what happened. She killed herself, but the gambling and money wasn't why. It was the helplessness of an empty womb and me not understanding. Why I didn't go with her to the rally, I'll never know. I sold my house to honor the gambling debt and let Lilly Mae's mother believe I gambled away the house."

Lanny searched my eyes. "Now you know the simple truth about your gambling, murdering uncle." A wheeze rattled inside his chest. He looked old and sick. He took his handkerchief from his hip pocket and honked his nose. "Blinny, the lesson here is, my overpowering desire that my house be filled with children, cost me the one person I loved."

I understood he was leaving me with a gift. I just needed to ponder it some. "You did the right thing by paying off the debt."

He nodded, satisfied that I would be okay. "I want you to drive me to the depot tomorrow. You can have the dogs' car if you give them plenty of rides and let them take care of you."

My mind was filled with his story, wouldn't let go of it. Would I be strong enough to sell my very own house to pay someone else's debt, or even my own?

The next morning, after Lanny loaded the dogs in the backseat of the car, he looked at me and pointed at the passenger side. "Hop in. I'm gonna give you a dang good Lanny Platt ride. When the snows are drifting and you have to go somewhere you'll be dang glad I'm not here driving."

I hopped inside, took a solid grip on the armrest and dash. "Go," I yelled.

Lanny stuck a cigar between his teeth, lit it, blew smoke at the windshield, and revved the engine. He fiddled with the radio knob, checked the gas needle, and jiggled the gear shift.

Was he nuts? "What are you doing?"

"A pilot always checks his instruments. We're gonna fly!" The tires slid in the dirt, grabbed hold, and we zoomed out of the farmyard.

I hung on for twenty miles, laughing every time we sailed over a rise or fishtailed in the gravel. By the time we arrived at the depot we were high on speed and daring.

Reality set in as I stood on the loading dock while the train roared by in a hiss of brakes and clang of bells. I hugged him tight even though he never hugged.

"Write to me." I let him go.

He stepped up into the train, then turned back and leaned out. "The best way to go, is just do it." He vanished inside.

I held my hand over my quivering lips until the train disappeared. I would recall his words at several more hurtful partings.

Mutt and Pooch guarded me day and night after Uncle Lanny left, just as the uncles did when I had appeared on their doorstep. The severe cold of last January had kindly taken the last of the aged dogs' reserve and they moved on to where dogs go. I liked to think of them romping across heavenly fields on their big padded paws and slobbering on saints.

Lanny wrote twice from an address in Sugar Hill. The letters stopped. As far as I knew, he might be buried in a plot for an unknown. Lanny would like that, and that's all I had left of him. A car that no longer started and two wooden crosses where the old dogs were buried.

I put my face into the chilly April breeze that had brought on my thoughts of Uncle Lanny. I so needed the house that I had marked off and not just the weathered stakes with twine hanging on them. With a defiant sigh, I tossed the rotted piece of twine I had been working through my fingers into the wind and walked back toward the ranch building and the waiting chores.

Chapter 16

I stretched up to reach the peak of the roof with a loaded paint brush. The new sturdy ladder wobbled. I clutched a rung and leaned into it. That was close. To steady myself I looked out across the prairies toward the Sweet Grass Hills.

The wild dog sat at the edge of sight, just close enough to make him out against the dun-colored grasses.

My battered straw hat shaded my eyes as I stared, unmoving.

He stared back, and then disappeared. He had been around though. The cleaned-out pie plate I filled with scraps each night and set behind the tool shed testified to his appetite. His paw prints tattled on him. Eventually he might pay me a visit and make friends, or he might not. Didn't matter. I hated tossing leftovers. He was welcome to them as a reward for visiting. No one else dropped by. Finally I had been left to work in peace.

It was kind of lonely though. Maybe I should take an afternoon off and invite Fran on a picnic in the Sweet Grass Hills. I'd been admiring them every day and should go tromp around in them for a while. Fran would probably be glad for a get-a-away–hard thing to have her husband home all the time.

My stomach suddenly felt hollow. Sadness pressed down. I'd give anything to have Monty underfoot for just one more hug.

A dust spiral was coming up the road? Alice! I hadn't seen her since she left the dog inside my trailer, and I planned to yell at her.

Calmly, I dipped the brush into the gallon of white paint. The trim at the highest point of the peak was finished by the time she pulled to a stop, sending up dust.

"If you don't quit skidding to a stop, I'll be dead from black lung," I yelled when she opened her car door.

"I don't hear the dog so you've been sleeping in that nasty trailer. No wonder you're crabby," she yelled back.

"The dog was no problem. He came right out, talked awhile and left. We had a nice visit."

Alice stuck out her tongue before she waggled a paint brush at me. "Figured you'd be painting trim."

"Only one bucket of paint."

She held up an empty coffee can. "I'll do the bottoms of the window sills." She stepped from the car, looking kinda cute standing down there in bib overalls and tennis shoes.

"Why don't you go into Rudyard and show the bar bums in Casey's your cute new bibs? Might get yourself a date for dinner."

Alice high-stepped over to the bottom of the ladder and shook it.

I hung on. "Git away from there!"

"Gawd, you're bitchy." But she stepped back. "In fact, you've been a real pain in the ass ever since Monty went missing."

That's when I did it.

I tipped the paint can and a glob of paint splattered down on Alice. It caught her on the left shoulder.

She glared up at me. "You think I'm scared of a little paint?" She wiped her brush in the paint on her shirt and walked, pretty as you please, to the nearest window. She smeared the white latex on the sill.

"Getting rid of you is harder than getting rid of that dog," I mumbled, climbing down to pour paint into her can.

We painted the afternoon away without speaking again. It felt peaceful.

Just before she left, she opened her yap. "I'm sorry I mentioned Monty. I know you've never gotten over him. Hell, you've waited forty years. He isn't coming back. Missing in action means that in all the carnage his body was lost. You've got to put that to rest."

She was trying to help, but her words cut to my very core. "I know he died, and I made my peace a long time ago."

"Not from what I see. Same thing with Odette. You need to see her."

"Go home."

My stomach rumbled after she drove away. I hungered deep. Never felt so empty. I went inside the trailer and barely fried a rib steak, leaving it red and juicy. I wolfed it down sitting out on the steps watching the sun lower over the hills and thinking back to the first house I had planned.

~~~~~

I faced the wind in the west field, and I hungered in my soul. I was sixteen years old and lonely. I yearned for someone to talk with, to laugh with, be with. Memories of *Maman* and Uncle Lanny weren't much comfort when I was filled with unsaid words. Didier stayed absent in his drive to build the ranch, and Odette dwelt in her own world where she hated me most.

A calf bawled from somewhere deep in the coulee. I listened, waiting. Another bawl. It sounded like Chester. I'd have to fetch him before Didier came across the motherless scamp. My father said the runty calf wasn't worth the time it took to chase him down. Calves were money, but so was time.

I couldn't blame Chester for wandering. It wasn't his fault his flighty mother refused him teat. Day after day, I'd held the feeding bucket until he sucked his fill from a hard rubber nipple.

Another bawl – an angry sound. I ran toward the cries, worried that he had caught himself on something. Then I picked up the sound of a horse on the river road.

The horse and rider broke into view. The calf struggled at the end of a rope behind them.

Monty.

I quickly brushed pieces of dried grass from the front of my work dress and pushed my hair away from my face. The wind blew strands right back into my eyes and plastered my faded skirt tight against my legs.

Monty tightened his reins and the horse halted. "I found this little guy in the river. Stuck in mud up to his belly."

I held back my windblown hair. "He's always in trouble. Thank you for helping him."

Monty tipped the brim of his hat back from low on his forehead and smiled. A rarely seen dimple dented his right cheek near the corner of his mouth. I melted same as I did each time he smiled enough to show true amusement.

Monty scanned the area. "What are you doing out here on foot?"

"Daydreaming. Come see."

He slid off his buckskin mare, leaving Chester tied to the saddle horn, and walked beside me to where my house was planned.

Monty's strides were longer than mine as he paced around the perimeter of stakes and broken twine. "You need more width," he said.

"I want a house that hugs. I want the walls near. I want them to hold me." The words startled me. My deepest feelings should have stayed inside.

Monty's brown eyes softened, the look around his mouth tender, almost sad. Slowly he reached for me, hesitated, then drew me into his arms. "I'll hold you."

I let him, as surprised by his boldness as he was.

He didn't move or speak, just encircled me in his firm arms. I couldn't remember ever being held. Odette had hung onto me when she was small, but that was it. Didier had never hugged, nor had the uncles. I tried to recall my mother's arms around me, but couldn't remember any feel of encirclement. The closest time was Monty's hand around my ankle in the wagon bed when I hid under the straw beside the snake box. His touch then had been warm and reassuring.

It was more so now.

I slid my hands around Monty's lean waist and held onto his back, feeling the muscles and ribs. My cheek lay against the coarse twill shirt and solid chest. He smelled of sunshine, dust, horse.

He cleared his throat. "I came to tell you I've enlisted in the Army. I leave for Fort Lewis tomorrow."

I stayed inside his embrace, letting him hold me upright at the news. I'd fall if he let go. War news on the radio and talk at the Mercantile were sad, sorry affairs. But this news was about Monty. He might die. I squeezed him until my arms grew numb, then I let them fall.

Monty looked down at me, questioning and a little uncertain. Was he also feeling something new and confounded by it? He whispered into my ear, "It could be that I've always loved you, Blinny."

"And it could be that I knew that."

"Could you love me back?"

"I can't remember when I haven't."

We didn't kiss. I thought we might. His face so near. Instead, we sank to the ground with me still in his arms and laid side-by-side in my someday house, shoulders touching, fingers interlaced.

Rain clouds drifted away to the south, taking their moisture with them to dump on Murphey's spread or maybe Dalen's.

"We needed that rain," Monty said, his thumb rubbing against my fingers.

My fingertips tingled from the pressure of his fingers stroking mine. "Jordan's," I said to cover my urge to get closer, let him absorb me, "over by Goldstone got a good dousing yesterday."

Our words were going all around what needed to be said. Monty was leaving. How could that be? To war?

"I'll come back," he said.

He was too shy to kiss, so I kissed him.

The following morning, weak light filtered through the open barn door, leaving the recesses behind the manger dark as night. I didn't need to see much. From habit I sensed when I reached the feed bin. My fingers found the coffee can and I scooped it deep into the grain. Nutty dust tickled my nose. A milk cow shifted her weight; another bumped a sturdy neck against the stanchion. A tail flapped against a haunch; bovine urine hissed and splat down on the straw-covered planks. Hardly aware of doing so, I dumped the mixture of oats and barley into the first manger, dipped again, and carried the can to the next stall.

In the thousands of moments since yesterday, I had constantly relived the wonder of Monty's arms tight around me, and I repeatedly heard his words. *"I love you,"* he had said without hesitation or shyness. The only other time I had heard those words was when *Maman* whispered them at bedtime as she tucked the blankets around me. Monty's declaration also covered me like a cozy quilt and comforted the loneliness I had known so long.

I poured the grain into the wooden manger. The silken swish, gush, and spill begat an urgency I'd never felt before – Monty could not go to war without holding me one more time. I milked with impatience spurred by fear. He might be gone before I got to the Bromwells.

The last cow was finally drained. I turned them out to pasture and carried two heavy buckets of milk across the dewy barnyard toward the house. I glanced at the sun. Plenty of time. The Bromwells shouldn't leave for a couple of hours.

Would all the brothers go see him off? Or just Marvel and Hank? Why not just me? What if they left early? Before I could ask permission to give him a ride? Milk sloshed as I charged up the kitchen steps.

Alice, still in her chenille wraparound, flipped a pancake on the cast iron griddle; Hyatt perched in his chair on top of several Montgomery Ward catalogs, banging a fork against the tabletop; Didier lathered his hands with Ivory soap at the kitchen sink; Odette's chair was empty, but hallelujah, from the looks of her plate she'd already eaten and was getting ready for school.

I plunked the buckets beside the separator. "After I drop off Odette, I'm driving Monty to Rudyard. Okay?"

Didier dried his hands, folded the towel in half, and draped it over the bar by the sink. He looked at me as if trying to piece together thoughts that didn't mesh. "Why would Monty be going anywhere? He knows he's to start sowing pumpkin."

Monty hadn't told him? I didn't know how I felt about that. I blurted, "He's leaving to fight the war."

Didier's stubble chin dropped open. Understanding of what I said registered. His jaw snapped closed, dark eyes flashed, lips thinned with impatience. "That damned kid is leaving me high and dry. He ought to know his duty is right here. Soldiers need food. We grow it." Didier looked at me like I should know that. Suspicion entered his expression. "When did you talk to him?"

My cheeks grew warm. I felt guilty for no reason.

Didier glanced at Alice. The air between them chilled. "Monty," he said, "was supposed to start seeding yesterday, but I never saw hide nor hair of him. What's going on behind my back?"

Alice's face hardened, shoulders stiffened, lips clamped; what words she might have said froze behind the block of ice she'd become.

"Answer me," Didier said coldly, taking a step toward her.

The sudden animosity between them surprised me. I couldn't tell if the tension was about me or something else.

"Nothing's going on," I answered for her. "Monty found Chester and brought him home. That's when he told me. I only want to send him off like a good neighbor should. If the dogs' car was fixed, I wouldn't have to ask."

"And I ain't gonna fix it for a sass mouth. Sit down and eat. You'll start planting the pumpkins, and Alice'll take Odette to school."

Alice set a pancake smothered with maple syrup in front of Hyatt. "Let her go," she said.

My usual hesitation at any help from Alice disappeared. I didn't question her taking my side. I just hoped Didier listened to her.

Didier shook his head. "I said no."

A gleam entered Alice's sharp blue eyes. She tossed her shimmering mass of blond hair back. Her chin relaxed, and she moistened her pouty bottom lip with the tip of her pink tongue; the whole time her gaze challenged Didier. She knew how to get her way and was willing to do so.

"We never eat breakfast alone," she said to him in a throaty voice. She tightened the belt of her robe, making the fabric pull across her ample chest. "Do you have time to eat with me?"

Didier's gaze never left Alice's face, as he dug in his pocket. "I don't like things kept from me." He tossed me the coupe keys.

I snatched them in midair and ran upstairs, wondering what caused the undercurrent of tension between my father and Alice. Seemed like it was more than me wanting to see Monty or using the coupe. I drove their car all the time, so why such a mountain over it this morning? Surely, Didier wouldn't care if Monty and I chose each other, but I didn't have time to mull it over. I pushed open Odette's door.

Odette was stretched out on her bed, fully dressed and pretending to be asleep.

"Get up. I'm taking you to school early."

Odette squirmed and made a show of settling into a comfortable curl. She opened one violet eye. "I saw you in that house without walls. You were doing the naughty."

"That's such a lie. Get up or I'll snake twist both your wrists and scrawny ankles."

"You're not my boss. I have a father and a nice stepmother. They're my bosses and I only do what they say."

I grabbed her ankle. "Your bosses said to take you to school."

She kicked free, stuck her tongue out at me, slid from the bed, ran downstairs, and slammed the door behind her, same as she did every morning. Force, run, slam. The slam accentuated her helplessness at no control; she only wanted to be left alone.

Maman, Maman, your Odette has become impossible. Maybe crazy, I thought for the first time. Her anger and reclusive ways were growing worse. I understood that much, but so far had been unable to convince Didier she needed help. He ignored it, same as he ignored *Maman*'s need for help.

When I slid beneath the steering wheel, Odette smiled slightly. "I don't blame you for wanting to see Monty. You might never see him again."

No malice touched her tone. I had not heard a kind word from her in a long time. Mostly, she yelled spiteful words or ignored my existence.

"I'm glad you understand."

She rode quiet until just before we arrived at the school. "Do you think I look like *Maman*?"

Her question surprised me. "Why do you ask?"

"Was her hair the same color as ours? We don't have a photo of her or anything."

"All of the keepsakes were lost when the house burned down."

"Not all. You got to keep your hat. I don't have anything that *Maman* gave me."

A lightness touched my mind, a relief from worry. She did care about *Maman.* "Odette, you have so much of our mother. Your eyes and hair are the same color as hers, but there is more. You have the same makeup."

"I remember that *Maman* wanted to have fun and laugh. I don't like that."

"You used to. You and *Maman* were always playing jokes on me. I miss it." I braked to a stop in the school yard. "In fact you and *Maman* were best friends."

"You're lying. I've never been a friend to anyone and I never will be."

"*Maman* would hate your attitude."

Odette mulled that over. Her expression appeared faraway, same as *Maman*'s when she thought of the vineyard.

"Right now, you look just like her when she was missing her home. It's almost like I'm seeing her. She was so pretty."

Odette pushed down on the door handle. "I only see her as a dried up bag of bones. I don't miss her." She hopped out and carefully shut the door without a sound.

The coupe sped down the county road toward the two ten-foot peeled logs that held aloft a plank with Bromwell's Rocking B brand burned into the wood. Below the framed entrance was a shallow pit topped with lodgepole. No wandering herd would dare step on the slippery poles that gapped at least three inches apart. A five strand fence of barbed wire was strung on either side of the opening as far as the eyes could see.

The coupe rattled across the lodgepole and hit the two track road, bouncing me high in the seat, but I kept driving as fast as Uncle Lanny would have. A cloud of dust billowed up behind. Bromwell's ranch buildings sat a mile back into his spread, and I knew they had spotted the rising dust already.

Four mangy mongrels charged the tires, barking like Satan himself had arrived with all kinds of evil intent. Mine was simple. I wanted to see the boy I loved.

The Bromwell sons waved from the barn door, the corral, and the pig run, then disappeared back to their chores when I parked near the stoop.

Marvel stepped out onto the porch. Her usual placid features were pinched around the mouth and eyes, her forehead lined as if she had a headache. I knew it was heartache instead. She was sending her favorite son to a place no mother wants her child to go.

I slid from the car. "Mornin', Marvel. I'd like to drive Monty to the depot if it's okay." I expected a glare or challenge of some sort, but she only nodded.

"He'll be ready to go after he brings the yearling herd up from the river. I'd hoped he'd just sit in the kitchen and talk to me. I don't know how I'll get along without him."

"I was afraid you had already left for town."

"I'm talkin' to ya, so we ain't." Marvel chuckled at her own cleverness. "Come in and catch me up on Hyatt. I don't hear near enough. Didier keeps Alice too close to home. I wanted a hardworking man for my daughter, but he's working hisself into an early grave. I've told Alice she'd better be pushing another son for him, but she says God will give them one when he's ready. What does she know about what God will do?"

Marvel grabbed my forearm and pulled me inside the kitchen. I dug in my heels, wanting to run find Monty, but then I allowed her to pull me along, wouldn't do to upset her more than she was. The room smelled of pork sausage, yeast, and strong coffee.

Marvel set a cup in front of me on the tulip oilcloth. I still liked the colorful red blossoms even though they were blotchy with age. Marvel's kitchen reflected her – old and faded from life's wear and tear, but still of good quality and useful.

"Yesterday," I said, "your sweet Hyatt slipped out the front door and hid under the porch. Liked to scare Alice to death. I found her down by the old barn, tears flowing faster than she could wipe them away. She figured Hyatt had followed Odette to the old barn."

"So why would that be upsetting? Kids like to play in barns."

"My father nailed boards across the doors and windows. Says it's unsafe, but Odette slips off after we are in the fields and spends hours in there."

Marvel clucked her tongue. "He ought to just tear it down. Damned rattlers have a habit of getting in old unused buildings."

I shivered. A faint memory of *Maman* in the old hayloft appeared for a moment.

Marvel touched my forearm. "What's the matter, child?"

I rubbed my forehead. "Anyway, Alice and I couldn't find Hyatt or Odette. It took another hour before Hyatt started bawling loud enough for us to find them under the porch. Apparently, Odette had found him, crawled into the hole, and wouldn't let him out."

Marvel sighed. "Kids do mean stuff, but Hyatt's only three. That could give him nightmares for a long time. Did Odette say why?"

"Took me all evening to pry loose the answer, but she finally said she was playing Hell. Said she wanted to know what it's like for *Maman*. Can you believe that? She thinks *Maman* isn't in Heaven."

Marvel's work-worn hand guarded her mouth, as if she didn't dare say what had popped into her mind. Her eyes filled with sorrow. She blinked a couple of times and dropped her hand to curl around her cup. "Your mother died when Odette was only three, like Hyatt is now. I think your sister was scarred by it in some way we can't understand. Poor girl may never be right."

Boots sounded on the stoop, and Monty poked his head inside. He saw me first thing and the brown in his eyes shone with welcome; his smile was wide enough for the dimple to dent. The look of him filled the room. He was lean and tough, sun darkened and handsome, sure of himself, yet shy.

I melted.

"Want a ride to the depot?" I asked, more to cover the rush of emotions than needing an answer.

Monty glanced at his mother.

"She can come with us," I said, meaning it. "I'll bring her home."

Marvel looked from me to Monty and back again. A grin spread across her face. "Looks like I figured right. Glad you two finally know it, too. Go on with you. I got beets to plant."

I ducked my eyes from her searching ones. So did Monty. Both of us bashful in the newness of our feelings.

Marvel grabbed up her packets of beet seed from the window ledge near the sink. She waved us outside like she was brushing crumbs from the table. She walked Monty to the car, gave him a hug, pushed him gently inside and shut the door.

I could tell she was crying as she walked toward the garden. I slid under the wheel.

Monty said, "Drive."

It was better just to leave. My heart ached for Marvel's grit. She always did right.

We seemed tongue-tied until we passed under the Bromwell signboard, and rain clouds moved in from above the Sweet Grass Hills.

"Rain's coming," Monty said. "Did your father plant the pumpkins yet?"

"Started today. He was upset to lose you."

"I need to strike out, find my own way. The Army will take me places."

I had to ask. "Why did you leave it to me to tell Didier you're going?"

Monty turned his eyes from me and stared out the passenger window so long I expected him not to answer. Finally he said, "He's a hard man. Cares only for his land. I figured it was better to leave without an argument. Guess I didn't think how it'd be for you. I should've."

My heart tightened. In a day and a half Monty had told me of his love and admitted wrongdoing. What more did a girl in love need? "You'll come home?"

"I will."

We rode silently for the rest of the trip to Rudyard, content to spend our last moments the way we worked together - a stolen glance, an accidental touch, a nod over a job completed. This was the way we were with each other, sharing a quiet romance as powerful as the soil that held the prairie grasses against the winds. Our love had been secured before we spoke of it and would hold against the forces of separation.

We waited on the depot's loading dock, watching for the train to come whistling down the tracks from the east. The moment I saw it, I turned to Monty. "You have to hold me."

I stayed inside his tight arms until the rumble and gush of the engine passed and the train stopped.

Monty kissed my lips, the touch of him so tender. We both knew the other would wait. Our eyes said as much.

I stayed on the depot platform until all that was left of the train was the plume of smoke rising. After it, too, had faded, I walked down the tracks, tucked my best skirt behind my knees, knelt, and lay my ear against the hot rail until the hum grew faint and died.

Monty was on his way.

Maybe to fight the Nazis.

God keep him safe.

I really needed him to come back already, and I had to have that house in the west field.

Chapter 17

There was a day, May Day, 1943 to be exact, that I did go searching for my mother's grave. My grief over Monty leaving spurred me to seek *Maman*'s final resting place. I hoped it had a few willow trees nearby.

~~~~~~

It was nineteen days, six hours, and forty-five minutes since I held my ear to the rail and heard the last of Monty's leaving. I snapped shut my Elgin watch and rubbed my thumb across the engraving of a tiny cottage tucked between two oak trees. Uncle Tyson chose the house scene because he sensed my need. I missed my thoughtful uncle. I tucked the watch safely in my skirt pocket.

I once again stood inside my house without walls, bracing against a raw wind and twisting the same piece of twine tight enough against my fingers to distract me from Monty's memory. A gust caught my ratty straw hat, and flipped it from my crown. I stepped on the brim before it flew away and plopped it safely back on my windblown curls. I probably looked like Medusa with snakes for hair. I snugged the hat tighter, trying to control the tangles with an old hat that was too small and riddled with holes. A sadness of the tender kind had grieved my heart at the first sign of a tear. I cherished the hat more as other spots wore through. *Maman*'s love never once had a hole in it. The hat reminded me of that.

All these thoughts of hats and holes and hair brought me right back to fretting about Monty. How did he look with a GI haircut? In an Army cap? I tried to picture him in uniform, marching, and taking orders. He sure didn't need to be taught how to fire a rifle. I was relieved Monty would be an infantry soldier with a rifle he knew how to use. I sure didn't want him to be a daredevil pilot in an airplane.   Just yesterday at the Goldstone Mercantile, I listened to the reporter on the radio bark out the 12:00 news.   *"Yes Sir, folks, our fly boys shot down Admiral Isoroku Yamamoto's plane in a US aerial ambush. Japan's navy is now minus its commander-in-chief. That's one brave bunch of boys."*

The clerk and I had faced the radio and saluted those courageous boys in their fighter airplanes.

I tucked my love for Monty into a safe place inside my heart, tossed the twine by a stake, and moseyed along the half-mile stretch back toward the ranch house to fix supper.   Fried potatoes and juicy steak sounded good.

The farm truck rattled in from the south field as I neared the barnyard.   A calf bawled from behind the wooden slats enclosing the truck's bed.   Didier yelled through the open side window. "I'm shooting that damned calf of yours." He braked to a stop and added, "The *batárd* won't even come for grain. I've chased him for the last time. Get in the back and shut him up."

Didier never used a French word that I could remember. Not even when the homestead shack burned, or when the grasshoppers ruined the wheat four years ago, or when a late blizzard last spring froze calves with their afterbirth still attached. My silent father always survived by working harder.

Why the outspoken anger over a wayward calf? Each and every calf, chicken, and pig was important to the ranch. Money in the bank, but Didier disliked this particular orphan.

Didier had the collar on his jacket turned up and his Stetson pulled down around his ears.   Even in the cab of the truck, he appeared cold. He needed his supper, a shave, and the answer to whatever was bothering him.

I closed my mouth tight and climbed aboard.   Chester nudged my shoulder until I held him around the neck and laid my cheek against his warm slick hide. He smelled of dust and cow.

Easier to embrace a calf than people. Shouldn't be, I thought, and missed Monty and his hugging all the more. I kept my cheek against Chester until Didier parked near the barn and helped me lower the calf to the ground.

"He's not worth the effort," he said.

My jaw tightened. "He's a stubborn loner because losing a mother does that to animals and certain children."

"Don't start about Odette. She's gonna stay in school."

I wasn't about to let him get away with ignoring the problems Odette faced, and I wasn't going to let him avoid mine. "I want to start building my house, then move Odette in with me so I can school her. She doesn't belong in a classroom with a bunch of kids. It makes her even more withdrawn."

Didier put a chaw of tobacco in his mouth, worked the bit of cake around, and then looked me in the eye. "Blinny, I've told you, I'd start on that house when I have the time and money."

I pressed the point, "Might be enough sound wood in the old barn to start on the foundation."

"Can't tear it down."

"It isn't used for anything."

"Girl, that rotten old barn is good for one thing. Reminds me every day how damned hard this prairie is on buildings. The sun bakes 'em, the wind beats 'em, and the snow freezes 'em. Those boards stay where they are so I won't take this land for granted."

That was more explanation than I usually got, and I understood his attachment to the old barn. I really did. But I also understood he was putting off his promise. This one time he was going to do what I wanted. Someday Monty would come home and that house needed to be ready.

"I want to get married," I said plainly.

"It's about time. I've planned all along you'd wed and live in the west field."

"I want my house on the swell overlooking the coulee. How many acres are you deeding me?"

"Who'd you pick?"

"Monty Bromwell."

Didier flushed, his lips tightened. "I won't have it. He just up and left with the spring planting undone. He's worthless. Can't be trusted."

I had figured there might be an argument about my age, but never who. "Monty is the boy I want."

"Want doesn't count." Didier slapped his work gloves against his leg. "Dammit, I should've known when he came asking for you."

"When did he come asking what?" I probably looked as confused as I felt.

"The night after I got home from sending you girls to your uncles. He came riding in announcing hisself and saying his Ma sent him over to see if I made it back okay. None of their business."

"Marvel was just worried about us."

"The boy sat there staring down at me, like I was some kind of a criminal. He finally asked about you girls getting on the train."

My chest tightened. It hurt too much. My heart ached to the very core. Monty had loved me even then. I should've known. "Saying we can't marry makes no sense."

Didier snorted. "No wonder he didn't object about working here. The sneaky bastard had his sights on my land all along."

My temper flared. "Is that when you started planning to marry me and Odette off so you'd have ranch hands to work this precious land of yours? I can't believe you'd do that. We were only eight and three back then."

Didier blanched under his day-old whiskers. Guilt showed all over him. "You're damned right. Why shouldn't a son-in-law help? Doesn't hurt to make plans. You know very well it takes twelve years before a son matures enough to do a man's work."

"That's a sick way to think," I blurted.

His lips thinned. "I'll hear no more about Monty or that house." He walked away, muttering.

I overheard the word "selfishness" and knew he meant me. How could he think I wouldn't marry Monty just because he forbade it? My life's partner would be my pick, whether Didier liked it or not. I turned my smarting eyes away from the wind and fed on the words about Monty coming to check like they were a thick steak cooked rare, oozing red, but delicious.

Then my dratted brain just had to ask, *would Monty want me to leave Platt land?*

The wind tugged at my hat, and I reached to hold it in place, but instead, I lifted it free and let cold air sweep through my hair. I doubted Monty wanted to live anywhere except the prairies, and he understood the west field belonged to me. He'd struck out on his own, but surely he'd come back. A chill settled in my bones. What if he didn't? I choked on the question as it sprung into possibility for the first time. I had closed off all thought to the reality of war. My father now opened the worry, and it was red and raw. I desperately needed to flee to the train depot, go find Monty and bring him home where we could find shelter in the west field. I needed that house for Monty.

At the same time Didier walked into the deep shadow cast by his tall house, yelling and squawking erupted from the far end of the chicken coop. Hyatt burst from behind it, squeezing a yellow chick in his grasp, a hen chasing him, Odette chasing after both.

Didier held out his arms to the boy. Hyatt dropped the chick and sailed into safety. The hen slammed into Didier's boot with a thud, feathers flying. She screeched as if she'd hit a coyote's jaws. She scrambled up and hightailed it back toward the coop, the squalling chick trailing after her.

Odette dodged to get out of the way, tripped, and belly-whopped face down in the dirt. She also scrambled up, madly brushed the soil from the front of her dress, and then pointed a finger at Didier. "You need to spank Hyatt 'til he's bloody. He's terrible and you make me babysit a brat all the time. Even if you're my father, I hate you."

Didier laughed. "Wasn't his fault you fell on your face."

Odette puffed. "You never take my side. You always choose him over me." She flounced away, running toward the front porch.

Didier shifted Hyatt in his arms. The boy sat higher, looking like he owned the farm and everything in it, including chicks with angry mothers. He was like the calf. Once their minds were set on something, nothing stopped them from going after what they wanted.

I, too, had my heart set and possessed a will strong enough to find a way. Surely, Monty would care about my feelings in the house built for us on my promised land. He would. He'd love me even after I spent a day in the hot dusty fields, even when I stood too long in a rain-soaked wind, even when I cried about a crop ruined by hail, or when I railed at God in the midst of grasshoppers swarming over my corn patch. Monty would stick with me, but would I stick if he wanted me to leave?

I told myself yes, even as doubt lurked in the recesses of my mind. No. I refused to think that. Monty was my partner. We equaled each other in chores and working the land. We held equal love for the prairies, the elements, and the need to produce crops. Calling him a soul mate was not good enough. He had been the one who held me when no one else did.

I tried to piece together the real reason Didier objected to Monty, and why he delayed building my house. Did he think I was trying to take part of his land? Keep Monty from helping? Or me not helping?

I hurried after Didier and caught him by the crook of his arm. "Are you still punishing me for *Maman* boiling Sadie on the propane burner? Is that why you won't build my house?"

He jerked his arm from my hand. "I'll hear no more about it."

"I blame myself, too."

"Blanche. No more. I just want to eat my supper and do the milking." Didier hoisted Hyatt higher in his arms and stepped across the bent willow fence.

I inhaled until my chest hurt, then slowly, ever so slowly, released the pent up air. Odette was right. He never listened to either of us.

Maybe I should listen to myself and finally just go visit *Maman*'s grave and ask for absolution. At least square myself with her. The more I thought about going the more I needed to go, but Didier would not be told about me visiting my mother's grave. He didn't care anyway. I'd figure out some way to get the car and go—the sooner, the better. Were my eyes watering from the chill? I'd like to blame the elements, but my heart hurt, too.

Monty, come home.

The sound of a car coming fast drew my attention to the road. Marvel Bromwell's black and tan Hudson rattled across the cattle guard, swung wide of the manure pile, and slid to a halt short of the black willow fence. She opened the car door and pulled herself out. Her sturdy weight settled on swollen ankles. She wore a standard house dress and common-sense oxfords, with an elegant beaver stole snuggled around her shoulder - a sure sign she was on her way to a meeting of ranch wives.

Marvel stretched the kinks out of her back, leaned over and looked inside the car. "Fran, be polite and get out."

Fran slid farther down into the seat.

Marvel glared at her. "If you want everyone to think you're a shy mouse, go ahead and sit there like your tail is caught in a trap."

Fran tucked her chin and ignored us.

Marvel spied Odette perched on the top step. "Why don't you come and talk to Fran? Show her what it's like to communicate?"

Odette didn't move. She was even more of a cornered quarry than Fran.

Alice pushed open the screen door. "Evening, Ma. No need to pick on Odette and Fran."

"Don't Ma me. They're both twelve-years-old and still want to hide like baby chicks under a hen. But you're just as bad. You haven't shown your face at your family home for two months, and I'm mad as grasshoppers at you."

Alice stepped through the doorway. She held the door against the tug of the heavy spring and eased it closed. She leaned her back on it as if guarding her den. Her pouty lips curled into a half-smile. "How's Pa and the boys?"

"Asking ain't the same as seeing," Marvel stated.

Alice straightened weight square on her feet. "I invited you and the boys for Hyatt's birthday and not one of you showed up."

"Couldn't. You planned his party on the day we had to have your father in Great Falls at the heart doctor's office. We didn't get the invite until the next day. You shoulda asked sooner or come by and talked it over."

Alice's cheeks grew red.

"Oh pooh," Marvel said. "Don't get on your high horse. I ain't here to cause an uproar." She glued Didier with a hard look as if the mix-up was his fault. "You keep these gals too close to home."

"Alice can go where she pleases."

Marvel digested that with a frown puckering her brow. "I've come to get Odette for the 4H doings this evening."

Odette paled. "I don't want to go."

Didier spit his chaw near the corner of the fence. "Don't have to." He stood Hyatt down and gave him a nudge. "Go say hello to your grandmother."

Hyatt obeyed, head down, feet dragging. His toes and ankles were filthy from playing barefoot in the barnyard, but he didn't seem aware of them like I had been mine when I walked the length of the Bromwell living room that first night after the fire. I shivered from the sudden recollection. Even after eight years, the harm done returned unexpectedly in bits and pieces. My toes felt grimy in my boots.

Hyatt reached Marvel and her features softened. She patted his head. He allowed two pats before he hiked up his britches, scampered up the steps, and grabbed Alice around the leg.

Marvel clucked her tongue. "He's as shy as Odette and Fran. The whole Demonstration Club jumped all over me last week. Said we keep our children so isolated that we might as well lock 'em up in cages. Made me feel like a damned zoo keeper."

Didier snorted.   "That's none of their long-nosed business."

"Even Grandma Severud said we can't keep the girls tied to the ranches. They gotta socialize or they'll never amount to a hill a beans. I had thought Odette shouldn't even be in school, but maybe the girls do need some fun in order to bloom."

"I agree," I spoke up. "In fact, I'm taking Odette and Alice shopping in Havre tomorrow? We're going to have a picnic and everything. Fran can come, too."

Didier looked at me. "First I've heard of that."

"I've been thinking about it for a while. We need some new fabric for summer dresses." My reason for going sounded plausible even to me. I silently patted myself on the back. I would search for *Maman*. Yes, I would.

Marvel bent into the car again. "Fran, get out of there now. Blinny wants to ask you something."

Fran slid from the car, but stood by the open door as if she might jump right back inside.

Marvel looked at me. "Hard to turn a caterpillar into a butterfly if it fights cracking the cocoon."

Fran did appear as gloomy inside as she appeared on the outside. Her chocolate eyes set under a perpetual scowl behind dark bangs that needed pulled back or cut. As far as I was concerned, she was a hidden clause and needed a pair of commas to separate her from all those brothers.

"Fran," I said, "Would you like to stay here tonight and go to Havre with us tomorrow."

The solemn girl raised her eyes. I wasn't sure what I read in them. Her narrow face didn't change expression, but she nodded.

"Okay, that ties it," Marvel said. "I wasn't for all that 4H stuff anyhow. Growing vegetables and livestock is all we do and getting a blue ribbon doesn't make the steaks tender or the green beans fresh." She glanced at the sun. "I'll be late if I don't shake a tail. I'm going to demonstrate my new blend of prairie tea." She opened her purse and took out a couple of silver dollars. "Fran, you'll need to buy yourself something."

Fran reached for the coins as though reaching for a forbidden cookie, a sweet bounty she hadn't expected. She seemed less dark for an instant.

Marvel snapped shut her coin purse and climbed back into the Hudson. I hurried to her window before she drove off. As soon as she rolled it down, I blurted, "Have you heard from Monty?"

"Shucks almighty girl, I should've told you right off. We finally got a letter today. He said he was allowed one letter to his folks to let them know he arrived at Fort Riley. He said to tell you he'd write as soon as basic training was over. I'll give you his address when you bring Fran home."

I almost burned the supper biscuits as I stewed about the army not letting boys write to their girlfriends. Why just the mothers? My selfish heart pouted. I missed Monty.

Dinner and the evening milking were done before I went in search of Alice to convince her to go with me. We tolerated one another only because we had to share the same house and family. I had expected sparks aplenty when Odette and I first arrived, but none flared, leaving me to chalk up Alice's prior bad behavior at the Bromwell ranch to the clannish male-dominated environment.

Sometimes I even admired how Alice found ways to calm Odette. Like yesterday morning when Odette pitched a fit about having to help Didier with the milking instead of me doing it. He needed a sprocket for the tractor, and I had to go to Rudyard for it. Odette didn't want to get up, didn't want to pour grain in the feed trough because her nose plugged up, didn't want to smell cow poop. All Didier wanted was to make her sick for a week. Alice calmly went upstairs brought down her red silk scarf and tied it around Odette's nose, patted her on the head and said, "You are now the best damned bandit around these parts. Go rob those cows of their milk." Odette did it. And miracle of miracles, she did it without more fuss.

Amazing, I thought as I went into the living room to find Alice. She wasn't in her usual place on the sofa flipping pages of a magazine or a catalog. I checked the kitchen and Hyatt's room before I heard giggling from the third floor.

Alice's voice carried as I reached the doorway of Odette's room, "I'm not going to Havre on some lark with Blinny. She gets the dumbest ideas."

"Me, either," said Odette.

"I wanna go," Fran said. "I've never gone anywhere without Ma and Pa."

I stepped inside the room. Odette and Fran sprawled on the bed, belly down, feet bent up in the air, and were looking over the edge. Alice sat on the floor with her back against the mattress, Hyatt cuddled beside her, and a book was opened on her lap—a nice picture of family harmony, like my memories with *Maman*.

True sorrow reared its ugly head in the form of green jealousy. Alice with her pouty, bossy ways was closer to Odette than me. While Odette returned Alice's indifference with tolerance; my care earned hatred. However, I knew Odette's obedience to Alice was simply another way of punishing me.

"Alice, Marvel was right. We are prisoners if we have to devise excuses for going somewhere." I had never thought of the ranch like that before, but it was true. We only went to the store in Goldstone, or Rudyard for farm supplies. Once a year we went all the way to Havre to sell pumpkins and shop for shoes.

"Why won't you come?" I asked.

Alice didn't even blink at my barely civil tone. "Hyatt would drive me nuts."

"Aw, come on. Let's have a little fun."

Alice's eyebrows arched. "What's your idea of a good time?"

"I want to go for a walk in the Havre cemetery and see the tombstones."

Her jaw dropped. "That's the last thing I'd call fun." She shivered. "Sometimes you give me the creeps."

"What's creepy about finding out where people are buried?"

"Just is."

"I want to pay respects at my mother's grave."

Alice leveled her cornflower blue eyes into mine. "Well, why didn't you say so? I'm not some kind of disrespectful person to the dead. I'll go." Alice's eyes shone and her lips appeared pleased. She'd given in mighty quick. She was up to something.

Odette looked at Alice as if Judas Iscariot himself sat there. "I won't go," she said to me. "And you can't make me. Boss, boss that's all you do." She rolled off the bed, walked in a huff to the door, and held it open. "Get out of my room."

Alice rose and picked up Hyatt. "Come on, Fran. If Odette wants to be a brat, we don't want to be around her." They trooped out.

Odette stood by the door, glaring at me. "Now Alice hates me and it's your fault."

"Maybe so, but a good way to make up is helping her with Hyatt on the trip."

Odette pointed at the doorway. "Just leave. All of you leave me alone. I'd rather sit in the dark than see any of you."

I left, but paused and placed my ear against the closed door.

Suddenly it opened. I caught my balance.

Odette stood like a miniature Nazi, shoulders back, eyes blazing, and spine stiff. "There is no one here but me. Why are you spying?" Her tone sounded puzzled.

"Sometimes I hear you talking."

"That's a bald-faced lie. Who have I got to talk to?" She shut the door. Sealing herself from me.

I leaned against the wall. Her anger left me weak.

But tomorrow I would find my mother's resting place and say a proper goodbye.

Chapter 18

Alice yakked at me nonstop for the whole half an hour it took me to carefully measure and cut four different angles in a piece of drywall. I pushed it up into place at the back of the closet, held it with one hand and my knees, and drew back with the hammer.

Clank came from right behind me.

The piece of drywall tipped. I missed the nail head with the hammer and knocked a hole the size of a grapefruit in the sheet rock.

"Sorry," Alice muttered behind me. "Damned square fell off the sawhorse."

I tried hard not to lose my temper, but she kept slamming tools around and yammering about the past. I slid the drywall down to the floor. "Alice, why are you still upset over old stuff? It's been years since I took Odette to Lydia."

Alice eyed me back, her look calculating as if she were trying to figure me out. She raised her chin. "It wasn't right. Didier grieved over you girls until I was worried for his sanity."

"Tell me, just when did he worry about our sanity?"

"How can you say that? He worked himself to death for his family and their heritage."

"Why are you grieving for him now?"

"Same reason you still grieve for Monty."

She had me there. Monty was my love, never to be replaced. "Why do we always end up arguing?"

Alice almost said something, but she caught herself and locked her jaw like closing a door on a safe. She wasn't going to talk about what she didn't want to. Not now, maybe never.

"I hope," she said, "that this house makes you as happy as you think it's going to. Odette didn't find happiness in the one you took her to. She went over the edge and never returned. The same might happen to you."

"You think this house is where I'll finally go nuts?"

"You're well on the way."

"Leave it alone," I said evenly. "I've been caring for Odette since before *Bébé* Larry was born. You should know I'll do what is right for her and myself."

Alice threw her hands in the air. "Oh, you've been a *true* martyr."

She stomped out through the two-by-four walls and dragged back a new piece of sheet rock from where it was stacked in the room that would become a living room. She leaned it against the two-by-fours, pushed past me, and grabbed the damaged one. She set it in front of the new piece and quickly drew around the cut line.

"I'll hold while you saw," she said.

In a matter of minutes, we held the newly-cut piece in place and I pounded it along the top. "Halloween is next week, "Alice said as I started down the left side. "Are you gonna drive to Great Falls like Odette asked?"

"I don't know yet." I drove a nail.

"The inside of this house can wait for one day."

It could, but I wasn't giving Alice any kind of assurance about whether or not I'd go. I planned to, even told her once I'd go, but she'd pestered me so much she deserved to stew. "It's beyond me why you're so dead set on me seeing Odette." Alice wouldn't tell me, but maybe if I kept asking she'd slip up and say something without thinking.

Alice drew in a sturdy breath. "Because she knows something you need to know, and I can't tell you what it is."

I was surprised she'd given me any reason at all and waited for her to explain.

Alice wet her lips. "I'll never understand why you thought Odette would be better off at Lydia's."

Air seeped back into my lungs. "I didn't expect you'd tell me some deep dark family secret, or tell me why you can't find a hobby except pester me to death. But I'll tell you, taking Odette to Lydia was the only thing that made sense, and she wanted to go. I probably should've let her go when Lydia first wanted to give us a home. Didier should've had to make a decision like that, not me."

"Just exactly when are you going to quit blaming him for everything bad that happened to your family? He was just a man who fought to hold his land. Grow up and go see Odette. Maybe you'll learn something."

"What can Odette possible know that I don't? She's probably thought up some way to feed me poison. I'm her worst enemy. She made it abundantly clear even on the train that a total stranger was better than me, and she was only three-years-old at the time. Ever since then, she's says that I ruined her life by not giving me to the lady on the train. And maybe I did."

"Hello in the house," Fran's voice called from outside.

Alice and I exchanged surprised glances. "What are you doing here?" I called as I hurried down the hallway.

Fran stood just outside the open front door. "No front veranda?"

"I'm building a back deck to watch the sunrises and–"

"And shade in the evening," Fran finished for me. "You've always liked your sunrises." She entered my house for the first time.

A steady hammering came from down the hall.

"What's Alice up to?" Fran whispered and crossed the living room toward the racket. "Besides sticking her nose where it doesn't belong."

It was good to have an ally against Alice's moods. "She's in Odette's room. Even if my sister never spends a night in it, I'm going to hang a brass plate over the door with her name just to keep your sister quiet."

Alice knelt nailing the bottom of the drywall as we entered. She dropped the hammer and stood. "Fran, why aren't you in school teaching those brats?"

"Good afternoon to you, too." Fran scanned the half-finished room. "This is going to be nice and cozy."

"It's way too small," Alice said. "Why are you–"

"I called a sub and took the day off."

"To come see Blinny's house?"

"Of course not. I took the day off because I'm tired and drove out to the ranch for some rest and relaxation. Thought I'd soak in that big tub of yours like Blinny did before we–"

"Shoulda called first. You're as bad as Blinny with the phone."

A slight frown shadowed Fran's face. She pursed her lips and swallowed. Her eyes sought mine. She appeared disappointed by whatever she saw in my face, but said, "You should have a phone. Junior needs Alice to go into Rudyard and pick up a part for the combine." Fran looked back at Alice. "He says he wants it now."

An angry flush crept up Alice's neck. "He's got a wife that can do his errands."

"The girls are in Havre, shopping for Halloween costumes for the grange party."

Alice's flush receded. "Hard to believe an old lady like me is so indispensable. Every time I turn around those boys need some damned thing."

"Spoken like a true martyr," I said.

Alice stuck her tongue out at me and stuffed her gloves into her hip pocket. "By the way, my tub is not communal."

Fran and I broke into giggles after Alice waved her fingers in a *ta-ta* way and stepped through the door.

"I don't give a fine rat's ass if you two laugh at me," she called. "And you both better be at Junior's party next Sunday." The front door closed.

"She's getting worse," I said.

Fran's smile faded, brown eyes turned worried, bottom lip trembled. "Alice insists we go to all those birthday parties she throws and doesn't even remember that Mom died five years ago today. I wanted her to go to the cemetery with me." Fran swallowed and put her shoulders back, bucking up like Marvel always did.

"What are we waiting for? You have flowers for the grave?"

Her eyes shone. "No, I brought a picnic basket with chokecherry jelly sandwiches just like you did when we went to Havre looking for your mother's grave."

I hugged Fran and led her out to the car. She opened the passenger door for me. "You better not huddle in a corner of the car seat like a mouse," she said.

"You remember?"

"Blinny, how could I forget? I was twelve and you were my first escape from Mom's eagle eye."

"Marvel just wanted you to be happy."

Fran slid behind the wheel. "I am."

The prairie drifted by as Fran drove down my road to the highway. The passage of swells and dry fields grew hypnotic, and I drifted back to the time the two of us went searching for Mère's resting place.

~~~

I was sixteen and going to search for my mother's grave. After a restless night, the morning sky pearled, the cock crowed, and the cows bawled just like any other morning. Shouldn't have. Everything ought to be turned upside down and in as much turmoil as I was. Today I would finally search for *Maman*'s resting place, see the plot that Didier had chosen. I had always pictured a gentle knoll shaded by a leafy elm. I couldn't fathom the gravestone, though I tried. Didier never talked about the cemetery nor took us to see her grave. I never found the words to ask why, and now I needed to keep my visit to the cemetery private. Why did I feel that way? It was normal for a daughter to search out where her mother laid buried, but I knew he would find one excuse after another to keep me working.

Again I asked myself, "Why?"

I sighed and concentrated on what kind of flowers to take for the grave. Patches of buttercups were the only wild flowers blooming this early in the spring and their short stems would never stay tied together. Dandelions? I was no longer a child bringing weeds to her mother. I needed something more meaningful. Something we had shared. Like chokecherry jelly. We loved to pick the berries from bushes along the river bottom, boil the fruit with sugar, and pour the hot fragrant juice into glasses, and top with melted paraffin. *Maman* always smacked her lips and declared, "Nothing tasted better than chokecherry jelly atop biscuits on a stormy winter morning, except grape jelly made from the pick of the vineyard."

When my mother lay like a corpse in Alice's bed at the Bromwells, I whispered in her ear, "I haven't tasted that grape jelly yet. Get well and someday we'll visit the vineyard. Bring some grapes home enough to fill a shelf in the cellar with jelly. Chokecherry, too." My bribe fell on ears that could no longer hear, but for the past two years, I'd kept the chokecherry part of the bargain. Now, I'd spread some on bread and sit by *Maman*'s mound. We would visit while I ate.

I milked and gathered eggs before I descended into the dank root cellar, swiping spider webs from the stairwell with a corn broom. Everything needed a good scrubbing before the first vegetables were ready for processing in July. Odette could certainly change the mildewed straw and scrub the shelves.

A pleasant picture of Odette slaving away at something constructive tickled my mind as I searched though the jars of preserves. Apple butter, wild plum, but no chokecherry. Wasn't there any left? I searched through them again, pulling jars from the back row. In my haste two pints clunked together. One rolled onto its side and fell off the shelf. I caught it inches from hitting the ground. I took a deep breath and moved a jar of apple butter over to set the pint down. Tucked behind was a jar of deep red chokecherry jelly. The last one. The glass felt cool to my touch, and I held it to my cheek.

Odette called down the stairs of the root cellar, "Alice says if you want us to go, you'd better come on."

I was surprised that Alice had sent Odette to tell me anything at all and hurried up the steps. Odette stood holding onto the door, acting like she wanted to slam it in my face.

"I should've locked you in," she said, "then I wouldn't have to go." She ran for the house before I could say a word.

I felt weak in the knees and my legs shook by the time I got to the porch. Why was I so upset? Odette said miserable things all the time. I sat down on the steps and rolled the glass of jelly back and forth between my palms, trying to understand the restlessness I'd felt since looking at the dawn. It was as though the first golden rays relayed a message I couldn't grasp.

What was I trying to remember?

I recalled Odette asking Lydia for jelly and bread on the train. It was when I stepped out after putting on the pretty dress. The dress! Lydia! The lady who had wanted to swap the beautiful dress for Odette. I had almost forgotten. Maybe Odette wouldn't be so awful now if I had let her go then. I also recalled how she protected us from the Daisy Woman. I should thank her for that and see how her life had worked out. I'd try and find her before going to the cemetery. My shakes calmed with that decision.

Odette scarfed down her cereal at the kitchen table. Alice was bribing Hyatt, one bite of oatmeal, one peach slice from a #2 can. Sticky juice flowed down his pudgy arms. Fran silently stirred her oats, looking as if any morsel would cause her to barf.

And Marvel thinks Odette is worse than Fran? Both would put Job of old to the test. I shook my head and set the jelly in a picnic basket. I dished up a bowl of gooey porridge, poured cream on top, and sat down beside Fran. "It's going to be a long day, Fran," I said. "You'd better eat."

"She's planning on buying penny candy," Alice said as she handed Hyatt another peach slice. His empty hand flopped away from his mouth. Juice sprayed. Alice jumped back. "Dang it, I don't want goo all over me." She wiped at a spot on her creamy linen dress. It had capped sleeves, gored shirt, and square neckline showing just enough cleavage. A bone comb held her blond hair up in a silken coil. She was dressed to the nines and a looker. No doubt about it. Strange? She hadn't primped that much for church last Easter.

She looked me up and down. "You're not going to town dressed like Annie Oakley, are you?"

"I don't think the coffin dwellers are going to say a thing about my dungarees and Uncle Lanny's old sweater. And besides, I'm planning to sit on the ground and share lunch with Mère."

Odette's face blanched. "I already know our mother quit talking and died. You harp about it all the time."

"I don't do that," I declared, annoyed at the sudden guilt running up my neck to my cheeks. Odette never cared what I said, but this careless remark had struck her deep.

Odette grabbed the sides of her chair and hunkered down like a stubborn donkey. "You're meaner than snakes and I'm not going anywhere with you. You'd feed Adam the apple and laugh about it."

"Oh great," Alice said. "I want to go have some fun, not listen to you two squabble. Odette, quit acting like an ass and get in the car. Take Hyatt with you."

Alice scrubbed sticky juice from his pink skin and handed him to Odette, then looked at Fran. "Go, I'll bring you a cookie to eat in the car."

Alice's eagerness to leave surprised me. I didn't ask why, just put the question beside all the other ones clanging inside my noggin since I woke up. They were worse than the dong of a cowbell around the neck of a grazing milker. Start, stop, start, stop. I needed the cow to take a nap.

Fresh spring colors trimmed Rudyard: new lime-green growth flittered on elms, the undersides of cottonwood leaves shimmered silver, emerald grass sprouted around the foundations of homes. I stole a few minutes to drive slowly by Sanvick's house to see if the violet lilacs were in bloom. Leaves showed on the bushes. Florets were forming, but the colorful clusters had not opened. *Maman*'s prairie prisms were hidden within tight little buds, same as my dormant memories of a baby born and burned, of a mother quiet and gone, of a train ride and return were held tight within me.

Alice let out a low groan. "Are we going to stare at bushes, or go? Tell you what. Me and the girls are just gonna go visit Cousin Susie Arnold in Gildford. You can pick us up when you're done traipsing on graves."

Caught completely off guard, I blurted, "Why would you want to visit Susie?"

Alice shrugged. "I haven't seen her in a long time. Thought it was time. Does it matter?"

"You stinker. You never intended on going to Havre. Why didn't you just say you wanted to see Cousin Susie?"

"I didn't tell Didier why you wanted to go to Havre. I understood your need for privacy."

Alice had avoided my question like I usually dodged answering what I didn't want to. "Fair enough. I'll keep quiet about your visit." It was odd for Alice and me to form a pact, especially one to keep Didier from knowing where we were going. Alice usually fussed over him, trying to keep the family steady and peaceful. And I wanted to keep peace with her. His anger I shrugged off, hers made me see myself.

I accelerated onto Highway Two and picked up speed.

I glanced sideways at Alice a few times on the thirteen-mile drive to Gildford. She acted calm and ignored me until I turned from the highway and stopped at the railroad tracks and waited for a freight train to roll by.

She fidgeted until the caboose cleared the crossing, and then said, "Cousin Susie lives at the north edge of town."

Three blocks later, she pointed to a two-story clapboard that was freshly whitewashed and well kept. "That's it. Cousin Susie and her kids used to visit us on Sunday afternoons. Don't you remember her showing up when Uncle Clarence filmed the snakes?"

I hadn't asked for an explanation. Her volunteering one puzzled me more than her secrets. "I haven't forgotten."

Alice groaned, slid from the car, smoothed her hands over the front of her dress, and shook the skirt. The creamy fabric lay perfectly on her shape. She looked at Hyatt who scrambled out of the car.

Odette's scowl ruined the prettiness of her violet eyes and best dress, but she got out. Before she shut the door, she announced, "I wanted to buy a treat in Havre, but I won't go with you."

"You should come with me and pay respect to *Maman*."

"I don't need to." She tried to slam the door, but Alice held onto it.

"Fran, get out," she ordered.

Fran shrunk against the seat. "I'm not going in there. I don't like 'em." Her voice broke and tears gathered.

Alice looked ready to belt Fran. "I don't have time for your foolishness."

Fran glared back. She wrapped her arms around herself and huddled in the corner of the back seat as if she wanted to disappear into the upholstery.

"Fran can come with me," I said.

Alice fluffed the ends of her hair. "Suits me. And don't be late picking us up. Didier will have a fit if we're not home in time to milk." She herded Odette and Hyatt up the veranda steps. The door opened and they vanished inside.

I stared after them for a long moment. "Fran, why don't you ride up here with me and tell me about them?"

"I'll come up, but I can't tell you anything about 'em." Fran's skinny legs hoisted over the seat back, and she slid into the front seat, pulling her skirt down proper. The frown still set deep on her brow, her lips pressed together like a clam.

I sighed. The thirty-mile trip to Havre was going to be a long, one-sided conversation.

Scudding thunder heads darkened the prairie as we wound past Black Butte. I held the steering wheel tight, fighting against a wind pushing from the northwest. All I needed was to end up in the ditch with gloomy silent Fran.

I had made up my mind to try and locate Lydia too by the time the road dropped down through Black Butte. Odette's comment at breakfast wouldn't let go of my mind. Maybe it was time to see her and then go to the cemetery.

The strength in the wind lessened near the bottom of the hill and my hands relaxed on the steering wheel. At last, the Havre rail yard lay before us. An orange and black Great Northern train engine was pushing boxcars into a siding, but I didn't watch the switching like I normally did. This time the canopy trees covering the town held my attention. Somewhere under them I hoped to find Lydia. It was worth a try anyway.

The highway led us down onto a main street busy with pedestrians and automobiles. I turned south and went a block to the mercantile.

A blast of grit-filled wind thrust against the car door when I tried to open it. I shoved harder. The wind picked my straw hat from my head. I caught it in midair and tossed it in the back seat. Cripe, first Alice pulled her trick and now a storm on the day I wanted . . . what did I want?

Absolution.

A mother long buried could not absolve me from demanding too much for a birthday present. I was on a fool's errand, but had to try and come to terms with my guilt over the fire.

"Come on, Fran. You can buy some candy then we'll walk around the corner. I want to talk to Mr. Larson at the shoe shop." Thunder grumbled, warning of lightening in the coming storm. Several huge raindrops splat near my feet. "Hurry up and we'll beat the rain."

A peppermint stick protruded from her cheerless mouth when we pushed into the shoe repair shop. The bell above the door jangled.

Mr. Larson glanced up from his workbench where he was inserting a shoetree into a pair of lady's shoes. He was scrawny and hump-backed, dressed in black dungarees and a plaid, oily shirt, pockets stuffed with papers, pens and a bag of Bullduram. He seemed as comfortable as a pair of old boots, and working on boots that smelled like barnyards and sweaty feet would take a kind heart. He wouldn't mind helping me.

"You're the Platt girls, aren't cha?" he asked in an easy-going voice.

I stepped farther into a shop dimmed by brown walls and racks of shoes. Fran hung back.

"Yes, Sir. I'm Blinny. I am looking for Lydia Worley and wondered if you know her."

"I know most of the feet in this town. She lives over on Fifth. Big house with a playhouse sitting under a giant elm. Can't miss it."

"She has children, then."

"Nary a one. Strange ain't it?"

"Thanks," I said, wondering who the playhouse was for.

Outside, the angry clouds roiled directly overhead. The hit-and-miss raindrops became a deluge. We ran for the car. Even with Lanny's heavy sweater the tops of my shoulders and the back of my neck were soaked by the time I jumped into the coupe.

Fran clamored in the passenger side and pondered me through wet lashes and leaking bangs. She doubted if I knew what I was doing. Did I? Would Lydia remember me? Or even want to see me? "Fran, don't worry. We are just going to find a lady who helped me out once a long time ago."

"I don't worry." She stuck another peppermint into her mouth.

The drumming of the rain on the coupe lessened. The tires splashed rooster tails as I drove slowly, taking up precious time, waiting for the rain to stop, waiting for us to dry out a little. The dripping houses and trees reminded me of Kalispell. I wanted to get out and walk along the blocks to look at the different homes, see if I saw one like I dreamed of building. A foursquare – too big. Next corner was a Prairie Revival – too spread out. Middle of the next block stood a Tudor – too formal. A Victorian – too old-fashioned. Small houses, big houses, none fit what I wanted. A lot of the homes were painted white. I wanted a yellow or red brick. The beige or reddish tones would blend with the grasslands, same as I wanted to meld with the house: live unobtrusively, care for the land, and enjoy the wind, the sun, the night sky.

My desire to find Lydia first and then the cemetery crowded out my impulse to walk among the dwellings, and I turned onto Fifth.

"Look, Fran. There's the playhouse." I pointed to a miniature cottage that looked right out of the pages of the picture book Uncle Tyson had kept on his shelf of classics. The roofing shingles were pink, white, and brown like cherry, vanilla, and chocolate frosting. The walls resembled the texture of crisp gingerbread, and the window was shiny like spun sugar.

Seeing the playhouse put away all unease. Any lady who owned a playhouse like that would take time to talk for a minute or two.

I held back a moment and just gazed at Lydia's yellow and white-trimmed house. It rose two stories with a steep gabled roof. A wide covered veranda joined together a bay windows and a turret. Spindle posts were painted in a merry ringed pattern of yellow, brown and white. The bright colors made a person feel like happiness was just beyond the door. I couldn't imagine why anyone would want a house so big. Maybe that was why she had been so lonesome on the train. Her big fancy house lacked the closeness families share. Underfoot and in the way might aggravate, but in a place as small as the homestead house you never felt alone.

I reached out, took Fran's hand, and walked up the curving brick pathway. Hand-in-hand, we approached Lydia's dignified house. We crossed the sweeping veranda practically on tiptoe; any loud noise and we would scurry away.

A brass knocker hung below the door's leaded-glass window. I rapped it three times, waited a few moments, and then struck it again. I peered through the glass. No sign of anyone.

Was I disappointed or relieved?

Fran pulled at my hand and pointed in the direction of the turret. "Look over there," she whispered.

Branches on a trimmed hedge wiggled. A gate swung inward. Lydia appeared like a ghost from the past: silk blouse, dressy trousers, blond hair caught in a web of black netting – so much like I remembered.

Then deep inside a hard knot gripped. I had told myself for a long time that I needed to thank her, but instead anger churned.

She hadn't changed at all. Some mark of penance should show. A "T" for traitor branded on her forehead would do. How could she betray my childish trust and ask me to give away my sister? And then as an afterthought try to include me, the big gangly sister. Frustration kindled at my unbidden thoughts of revenge. I couldn't help it. I had come to thank her, but I didn't feel one bit thankful. She had asked an eight-year-old to give away her tiny sister and then tried to cover it over by saying hard times were at fault.

Was this why I had wanted to see her? To accuse and not to thank? In my heart, it was.

Lydia climbed a set of steps on the far edge of the veranda. Her eyes held the look of recognition I had hoped for. She remembered.

"Blinny, you still have the straw hat."

I had to respect my elders. My hands trembled as I removed my hat and held it out like a precious crown sat on my palms. "How could I possibly let it get away from me at the train depot?"

"That was scary for you." Lydia's tone was bittersweet.

A mark of penance?

She reached out for Fran's chin and tipped her face upward.

Fran stiffened, but didn't pull away from Lydia's touch.

"I don't believe you're Odette. She had the most astonishing violet eyes. Yours are just as striking, but bright acorn."

Fran blinked a couple of times, flushed, and almost smiled. "I'm Fran, Alice's sister."

Lydia freed Fran and glanced at me. She was still calm and gracious, but for a second I saw the haunted, lonesome lady I remembered; the slight slump in her shoulders and the pain in her eyes gave it away. She was covering her memories too.

"Alice is my stepmother. The reason I'm here is to thank you for teaching me that my sister was a gift from *Maman*." Where did those words come from?

"And have you watched out for little Odette?"

"I've tried." I struggled not to be upset, trying to understand. Lydia existed in a life void of children, never knew the tranquility like my mother enjoyed after *Bébé* Larry was born. Lydia lived in an empty house.

Lydia touched her lips. "My goodness, I can't believe you're a young lady now. I remember you as Mr. Porter's spitty kitten. You suppose he still looks like a rabbit?"

She remembered even that. She really had helped fill my desperate lonely need on the train. My feelings slipped a shade closer to forgiveness.

She opened the door. "Please come in. We'll have tea."

Fran locked her knees. "I don't want tea. I want to go."

I didn't want tea either. I just wanted to leave and deal with my feelings. How could I be so mad at her and yet like her? "We don't have time for tea. I have to get back before evening chores."

"Are you sure?" Lydia's lips turned down. Her shoulders sagged. "I'd enjoy a chat like we shared on the train."

How could I refuse? "Just a quick one." I gave Fran a nudge toward the foyer. She lost her balance, and I snatched the back of her dress before she tripped on the doorsill. Fran pulled from my grasp. She looked scared as snakes.

"I don't blame you, Fran," Lydia said. "This big old house frightens me sometimes. I have an idea. Let's have tea in the playhouse. I haven't been inside it since the neighbor girls grew up."

I had to ask, "You never had any girls of your own?"

"Never did." Lydia's eyes glistened and she cleared her throat. "Why don't you go ahead while I brew the tea? I'll be along in a couple of minutes."

There was no way out. I followed along behind Fran who almost ran toward the child-sized door with a little window shaped like a heart.

I just didn't know what to make of Lydia. She was a sad sight in her childlessness. No wonder she'd tried to steal Odette. Maybe I should have let her. Maybe Odette would be happy now. I shook my head and blinked my eyes. How could I even think that?

Fran and I crowded inside. I had to tip my head slightly to stand upright. Light from a west window cast a cozy glow on soft yellow walls. A spider's spun net covered half the window. I checked. Only a few flies hung laced in the gossamer web.

Dolls that Lydia must've bought for the neighbor girls filled a pair of corner shelves. I reached for a porcelain bride with ribbons and paper flowers in long yellow curls. Dust flew. Cobwebs clung to the back of the veil and hair.

"The floor's dusty," Fran said. "But I like this little house."

Fran and I sat on the floor with our backs against the wall, knees bent, legs crossed. We waited, childlike, uneasy and pressed for time. My plan had been to thank Lydia and leave for the cemetery, not sit bunched together in a house so tiny we couldn't stretch our legs without touching the opposite wall.

Lydia finally bent through the doorway, carrying a tray filled by a silver pot, cups, shortbread, and pickles. She promptly handed it to me, then knelt, and wiggled around until she too sat cross-legged. We were so close our knees almost touched.

I reached across Fran's knees and set the tray in the only open space on the floor. The silver tea service glowed like a camp fire.

Her fingers arched and delicate, Lydia poured and passed us each a cup.

I blew on the hot liquid, wondering how pickles and cookies would taste together. Sweet and sour. Same as this visit. I searched for something to say. "I noticed you bought dolls."

"I did, didn't I? Surprising that you would remember that."

Wasn't surprising to me. Of course, I remembered the words of a lady who offered a fancy dress for my little sister. It hung between us like a bad memory that needed to be purged.

I sipped my tea, hoping the hot liquid would dilute my sudden churning anger. I felt terror again, heard my frantic footsteps against the loading platform as I dashed to find Odette, only to discover her on Lydia's lap inside the train car.

Again, I searched for words. "Did you build the playhouse yourself?" I asked for lack of anything else to say.

"I did. Planning it and pounding nails brought me a sense of accomplishment. I even learned how to use an electric saw." She straightened her shoulders. Pride swelled in her eyes.

Her passion touched the part of me that wanted a house of my own. "I've started planning my house. There's a spot in our west field that I staked out. Someday, I'll build on it."

"The fun part is the planning. The rest is work."

Lydia held her cup in the palms of her hands as though they needed warming, her eyes searching me. "Blinny, what's wrong?"

I set the rattling teacup and saucer on the floor. Tea splashed into the saucer like anger spilling from the bowl of my resentment. "Asking to take Odette was a lot meaner than what the daisy lady did."

"I know." She set her cup down too and locked her fingers together in her lap. She glanced at Fran. "Blinny and I went through such an emotional trauma on the train. I hope you don't mind if we talk about it."

Fran shrugged, *who cares.*

Then Lydia honed in on my eyes. "The day before I got on the train, I learned I could never have children. Never have a little girl of my own. I think I went a little bit crazy." She wet her lips. "No, I was a lot crazy. No excuse for what I did."

"Why did you?"

"I was dying inside, then all of a sudden, I find a little girl that had been rejected by her father. It seemed so unfair. Odette's wane scared face pulled at my very core as the miles sped away down the tracks. I could be her mother. I thought of nothing else. I grew to love your sister sitting on that train. It was like I had gone into labor, and I did a dumb thing."

Lydia reached toward me. Her hands dropped. Her eyes never left mine as she said, "I still can't believe I bought you a dress and tried to bargain for Odette with it." This time when she reached out, she touched my knee. "Will you please forgive me?"

Again, a thought pricked my mind. Odette might be a happy child now if I had let her go, but how could I have? She's a Platt. But I sat wishing I had. My guilt was worse than Lydia's. I cared more for my own needs than Odette's. I cleared my throat. "I thought I'd already forgiven you when we waved goodbye at the train depot, but I hadn't. I do now."

Lydia's eyes blurred. "Thank you."

Mine also watered with tears of the healing kind and with tears of compassion. She was so terribly sad and alone. I blinked mine away. "We really have to go."

I drank the last of my tea. "It must be noon already, and we still need to find the cemetery. Can you point me in the right direction?"

"Which one?"

That never occurred to me. "There's more than one?"

"There's Highland, Calvary, and Sunset. They're side by side up on Tank Hill. Just drive up Fifth past the college."

Lydia walked us to the car and gave me a hug. The third person to do that. Just before she shut the car door for me, she said, "Blinny, don't want something too much. You have a forgiving heart and I want you to stay that way."

I wondered about her words as I drove away.

Beloved wives, angel babies, dearest husbands. Crosses, lambs, praying hands. Anderson, Stephens, Weisler, Hunt, Gibbson, Connor. On and on. Hundreds of stones. Up and down, back and forth, I walked the rows of gravestones. Fran tagged behind.

The wind cut through Lanny's protective wool as if it were netting. Fran huddled against my side whenever I stopped. I lost track of time. Hours slid by in the search of names. I checked every single one in all three cemeteries and none proclaimed that buried here was Essie Faye Platt, Beloved Wife and Mother.

The last stone in the last row had lichen running like tears down the shady side. Harold Longnecker at rest. He wasn't dearest or beloved, had just lived and died. I perched on his stone and looked at Fran, her cheeks burned raw and her hair had been whipped into tangles, but she had stuck with me for each and every marker.

A dirty black pickup bounced through the gate at the far end of the graveyard and followed a lane to the asphalt-shingled building at the back of the cemetery. I had checked it when we arrived and found not a living soul. Now, a man got out and went inside.

I grabbed Fran's hand. "Come on."

We hurried down the row of withered, wiry grass until we reached the hard-packed roadway that dissected the graves, same as streets divide a town.

I walked toward the building as fast as Fran would let me drag her. I finally dropped her hand and left her to tag a few steps behind. One side of the double doors was propped open with a gnarly chunk of cottonwood limb. I stepped right through into the murky interior. The man's head jerked up from a huge ledger book lying on a counter below a weak dangling light bulb.

My cheeks warmed. My hand reached to straighten my hat. I gawked at him, knowing I looked like a rat's nest. Never had I seen anyone so extraordinary. A Grecian nose, with strong, angular cheekbones, deeply grooved forehead, dense lashes fringed friendly sapphire eyes.

"May I help you?" he asked.

My knees, already weak from tramping on lumpy grass, turned watery under his gaze. Pleasure touched his eyes. "It's okay," he said with a hint of conspiracy. "I won't bite."

Then I grasped why he seemed satisfied. He knew he was too handsome, and knew I was flustered because of it.

"Are you the caretaker?" Dumb thing to ask.

"I am. But tell me why a pretty girl like yourself is so upset?"

He'd called me pretty. My face flushed. Red cheeks.
What an awful betrayal God had given girls. I wanted to be cool
and collected, but that princess part of me was nowhere to be
found.

"I am looking for Essie Faye Platt's plot. Didier Platt
bought the plat." I couldn't believe I had blurted something so
stupid.

He laughed, those eyes twinkling.

I laughed, too. "You must think I'm a country bumpkin.
I sure feel like one."

Still chuckling, he flipped pages in the ledger and ran his
finger down the pages of names beginning with a P. He scanned
again. "I can't find a record of a Didier or Essie Faye Platt. Are
you sure she was buried in Havre?"

His question had never occurred to me. "I always thought
so," I mumbled.

"I'm sorry, but they aren't listed, and as far as I know,
this record is complete. If she was buried here, her name would
be in the book. Is it possible she's buried under another name?"

I shook my head and turned away without even saying
thanks. I had to get out of the little building and gulp air. I never
dreamt *Maman* could be anywhere else. I caught myself from
hurrying away and stepped back inside. "May I look at every
page?"

"I have to prepare for a funeral tomorrow, but help
yourself." He grabbed a pair of work gloves. "I just thought of
something. Death certificates include the place of burial. You
could go to the courthouse and look up your mother's." He took
his handsome self out of the shack without another word.

I was mortified at how I acted every time I confronted a problem I had no control over, like the fire, *Maman* dying, Aunt Elaine's betrayal. And now. Why did my thoughts run away about things completely removed from the real issue?

Fran crowded up beside me to look through the pages. I had to give her credit. She had stuck right with me, like her mother did.

The light from a dangling overhead bulb was feeble, but I could read the handwritten names clearly. There were two sections, one by plot number and one alphabetically. Starting with Shilo Abel, I ran my finger down page after page, reading each name until I got the last. Harry H. Zumoto.

That was it.

I closed the book of dead people and looked at my sidekick. "Thank you, Fran, for being my friend today."

Fran's face beamed brighter than the dangling light. "Maybe your ma is buried in Rudyard."

Chapter 19

The leftover soup bones clunked into the pie pan I had left behind the tool shed. Tallow and savory beef clung to the bones. The dog would sleep with a full belly tonight. Three days of eating stew was enough for me. Could be I made too much knowing the dog needed a coat of fat under his hide for the coming winter.

The wind and shade behind the shed were chilly – end of October chilly. I shivered and stepped around the corner to where the lowering sun could warm my bones.

I don't know who was more surprised the dog or me. His hackles raised. Mine did too. In a calm low tone, I said, "Well, hello. I wondered when we'd come face to face." His ears perked. "You wanna make friends?" I figured he didn't.

He looked me over, decided I was Satan himself, and hightailed it into the prairie, leaving me to feel lonely. I whistled and called, but saw or heard nothing, yet I knew he watched, a silent animal afraid to come to me.

Yesterday, Alice's smart remark had been, "Odette is afraid of you, always has been. Just like that dog you're feeding."

I had mulled on Alice's assertion all day. It could be true. Odette used to hang back at the uncles, eyes following my every move at the most unnerving times. I'd turn from the kitchen range and she'd be just inside the doorway, quiet as a mouse, watching. Or I'd be on the veranda and sense her on the other side of the Virginia creeper, peeking through the leaves. Or I'd catch her spying on me and my friends during lunch hour at school. I grew to think it was just another way for her to torment me.

I ignored Odette after we came back to the ranch, lost myself in the work and cared less if she watched from afar. Could be she didn't trust me anymore than that dog did, or any more than I trusted our father. Didier had broken my trust, but what severed Odette's trust in me? I'd spent a lifetime protecting her, but all she had given me was angry words or odd behavior before she'd run off to her bedroom or out to the old barn.

~~~~~

I drove from the graveyard toward Gildford, seeing, not only the wavering blacktop, but every twitch of the ditch grass and each grasshopper's eyes as its body splat against the windshield. Oncoming cars whizzed by. Farmers waved as they rumbled passed in their farm trucks. I didn't wave back. I couldn't have put two words together if I had to. The questions flowed like they always did, ones without answer.

Where was *Maman*? Why wasn't she buried in Havre? Was she in the Rudyard cemetery like Fran suggested?

Fran rode beside me, chattering like a little sparrow with a fresh egg. She hadn't hushed her mouth since we left the cemetery. I was now the one who huddled like a cornered mouse.

Why hadn't I talked to Didier about visiting *Maman*'s grave? Instead, I had searched three whole cemeteries only to learn she wasn't where I believed she was. I shifted back and forth between anger at myself for not asking and anger at Didier for being so closemouthed. At last the Gildford grain elevator towered in the horizon.

"You turn here," Fran said pointing at the rail crossing. "But look out."

An engine chugged down the tracks, followed by a string of boxcars. I fidgeted. Why didn't the boxcars end? I just wanted to pick up Alice and Odette and go home, curl up in my bed and never move. Melodramatic I know. Couldn't help it.

"Cousin Susie is hateful for what she did," Fran said plain and simple.

I came out of my woebegone self. Fran seemed to have shrunk and hunkered into the corner of the seat, same as she had been for the entire thirty miles into Havre. Gone was the brave little girl who tramped graveyards reading each and every tombstone.

"What did Cousin Susie do?" I really wanted to know the reason Fran had returned to her sullen self.

"She and her son were mean to Alice."

I paused at that. "I remember her sons as loudmouths, laughing at me like I wasn't a person."

Fran curled her lips downward and shook her head. She was disgusted. "Cousin Susie used to bring her brats to visit. But then Alice cried a lot, and when she cries my mom and my brothers will do anything to make her happy. The way my brothers acted, I figured one of them would end up in jail for shooting Cousin Susie and her whole Arnold family. Every last one deserves it."

The caboose, with a mountain goat painted in a circle on its side, rolled by. The tracks cleared.

Fran touched my arm. "Aren't you gonna go get Alice? She'll be mad if we don't hurry up. Remember the house is just around the first corner."

I did as Fran directed and sat with the car idling. "Go tell your sister we're here."

Fran cringed deeper into the seat. "I won't do it."

I cut the engine and opened the car door. Another freight train rumbled down the tracks by the depot. Coal smoke blew downwind into Arnolds' yard. The bell clanged uninterrupted, the whistle blared, boxcar wheels clacked against rail joints. I wouldn't want a house anywhere near a railroad.

New grass stood high enough to mow near Arnolds' foundation. A duck-shaped welcome sign was nailed above a brass knocker. Beside it a plaque read, *Clean shoes make for clean floors. Wipe and enter.* A door mat had *WELCOME* painted on the burlap.

The clean and neat trappings appeared friendly enough. Nothing like Fran's version of the Arnolds. I rapped the brass knocker.

A matron about the same age as Marvel answered the door. I didn't recognize her at all. Her mouth was down-turned, jowls hung, eyebrows like little umbrellas, shoulders drooped. She was an upside down U if I ever saw one.

"I'm sorry to disturb you," I said. "I'm Blinny Platt and I've come to pick up Alice."

"She and her brat aren't here."

I blinked. "Where are they?"

Cousin Susie's glum features hardened with impatience. "Don't know and don't care," she muttered.

I held my ground even though I wanted to hightail it back to the Pontiac. "I dropped them off here this morning and I'm supposed to pick them up here."

"You had no business leaving them on my doorstep. I told them to leave."

"Why?"

"None of your business."

"Where did they go?"

Cousin Susie placed her hands on her hips. "Like I said. Don't know and don't care."

"Mother," said a male voice behind her. A man appeared in the doorway. Tall, blond, plump. He fairly glowed with his blond hair and pale skin, so unlike his dark, harsh mother. He looked exactly like Hyatt would look in his middle twenties.

I was face to face with Hyatt's father. I knew for certain sure.

"Hi pretty girl. I'm Gerald." A wide grin spread his lips. "Alice stayed only a few minutes. I believe she walked to the mercantile. I watched her from the window as she dragged that kid away."

His blue eyes gleamed with a leer like I had never seen before. "Is that cute Odette your sister?"

That pricked my defenses like a thorn in a tender spot. I backed up, hackles rising.

Gerald chuckled. "If she's as ripe as you are when she gets red cheeks, I'd like to tease her plenty."

I gaped like a flabbergasted dope. He was too pushy, too curious about a young girl, and I was so taken back I couldn't spit out a single word.

"I'll bet she is," he added, smugly.

I found my tongue and my temper at the same time. "You'll stay away from her if you know what's good for you. You never, not ever, mess with a Platt." I hurried from the porch, trying to control anger of the survival kind. I didn't know how to use the rage that poured through me, but I would shield Odette from him or any man. Alice, too. And Fran.

"Bring her back for a visit anytime," he called. Under his loud laughter, I could hear his mother scolding him. I shivered and got into the Pontiac.

Could Alice really have conceived a son by someone so horrible?

Alice, Hyatt and Odette sat on a bench in front of the mercantile, looking cranky. Alice grabbed up Hyatt and hurried to the car as soon as I stopped.

Odette rose, patted her skirt into place, and ambled toward the coupe. She was smiling for the first time in a very long time.

Alice yanked open the passenger door. "Fran, get in the back," she snapped. Fran instantly pulled the back of the seat forward, and scrambled across it into the rear seat. Alice leaned in and sat Hyatt beside her, and straightened back up. Her noggin bonked on the car roof. "Ouch," she cried and bumped into Odette.

"Ouch yourself," Odette yelled. "You just stepped on my shoe."

"I hate two-door cars." Alice rubbed at her head, turned to Odette and pointed to the backseat. "Hurry up!"

Odette bent over her shoe, acting like her shoe had come untied.

Alice thumped the back of Odette's head. "We ought to just leave you."

Relaxed and smiling, Odette finished tying her lace, straightened, and stepped through the opening like a princess getting into her coach. She sat in the spot beside Hyatt. Her eyes shone as if a court jester and his clowns had just put on a show.

Alice shoved the back of the seat. It thudded into place and she hopped inside. Without looking at me, she said, "Don't ask."

I glanced in the rearview mirror at Odette.

She mimicked, "Don't ask." Enjoyment bubbled away inside of her. Something bad had happened, and she wasn't one bit sorry it had.

Alice groaned. "Blinny, quit eye-balling Odette. It's none of your business what happened. Take us home."

"I saw Cousin Susie's son and I know."

Alice's cornflower blue eyes met mine. "You know diddly squat."

Odette spoke up. "Cousin Susie said Hyatt was no kin to them and that he didn't look anything at all like her Gerald. I thought he was knockout cute. No wonder Alice likes him better than our father."

"Hush up." Alice reached back and took a swipe at Odette's knee.

Odette jerked away. "I can't see why. Just because Gerald told you he didn't have any idea what teepee Indian studded you, doesn't mean I can't like him. He'd be more fun than either of you."

Alice reached over the seat and pinched Odette's leg.

Odette screamed and slapped Alice's hand. "I hate you all." She hid her face against the side panel.

"Are you two done?" I didn't get an answer so I shifted into reverse, backed onto the street, and drove silently to Highway 2.

A few miles later Hyatt's rattling snore rose from the rear. I glanced in the mirror. All three kids were napping like kittens after nursing – returning to the ranch satisfied them as much as a belly filled with warm milk. I, too, wanted to get back to the safety of the ranch and curl up in my bed.

I glanced sideways at Alice. "I already knew Didier wasn't the father. He told me the first day I came back."

"You know nothing."

"Cousin Susie's son is. I could tell the moment I saw him."

Alice moaned and put her hand to her forehead like it was apt to split. "Yes, he is Hyatt's father. Yes, I loved him at one time. Yes, he hurt me. Are you satisfied now?"

How many times I had wanted Alice to be paid back for her spitefulness? Now, I felt sorrow for her pain. "I am not glad you were hurt."

"Thank the Lord for that," she snapped.

"Still in love with him?"

"His parents sent him away as soon as they learned about my pregnancy. When I heard Gerald finally came home, I wanted him to see his son. Family is important and I wanted Hyatt to know his natural father. I never realized how awful Gerald Arnold is until today. He never truly loved me, just wanted to poke me for his pleasure."

"Alice, that's crude."

"What he did back then was cruder."

I had to agree with that.

Alice laughed bitterly. "You knowing my sordid past doesn't make us friends." She clammed up and stared out the window as if trapped in a different world, one of hurt that went deep inside.

I didn't tell her that I already had three friends. Lanny, Monty, and Lydia. That was enough for anyone.

The disappointment at not finding my mother's resting place made the long silent drive home from the Havre graveyards longer. The miles finally ended when I drove the Pontiac onto Platt land. Alice perked up a little. The kids in the back were still asleep. I was just relieved when I saw the long shadow of Didier's tall house running down the swell to the barn, chicken coop, pig pen, and granary. It was as though the house absorbed the whole farmyard onto itself. The shadows of the outbuildings also stretched outward and mingled with the rich prairie soil. The Platt spread drew on itself like we drew on it. We were home at last.

The veranda was empty. Didier should be watching for us, but the whole ranch seemed deserted in the quiet sort of way evening brings. Chickens rested on their nightly roosts; pigs wallowed in their pens waiting for fresh milk; calves slumbered in the open field.

Odette shoved out of the backseat as soon as I slid from the car, pushed past, and hightailed it toward the old barn.

"Come back here," I yelled. "You know the eggs have to be gathered before dark."

She ran faster and disappeared through a loose slat. Well, she would tend to the eggs whether she wanted to or not.

Fran helped Hyatt into Alice's outstretched hands and got out. She yawned, worn out from walking all over the cemeteries and the ride home, but she said, "I can get the eggs."

"Miss Odette will do it if I have anything to say about it." I stomped toward the house to fetch the basket. Felt *dang* good to be angry instead of weak with the inertia I'd dwelt in all the way home. I planned to keep the juices of anger flowing until Didier told me where my mother was buried.

I slammed into the kitchen. No milk buckets sat on the stand by the back door. He was milking, wouldn't leave the cows with full bags even when he heard us come home. Cows first, anything else came after, including my need to know about *Maman*. No matter how distraught I was I had to wait until the cows were turned out to evening pasture.

Although, I needed that time, I didn't want to admit it. How could I possibly convey the anguish of searching for *Maman* and not finding her? Anger would surely spill and we'd argue.

I'd use the time to send Odette to the coop and maybe settle in my mind what to say to my father. I grabbed the egg basket and headed down the rise to the barns.

Didier had nailed half a dozen boards across the side door of the barn. I yanked on one. It groaned, acted as if it would give way, but held firm. I tried each one and none broke loose. For crying out loud, he'd pounded enough nails into them to seal up a tomb. I tried to squeeze in through the opening where Odette slipped inside – too tight.

Nothing for it but to go get an axe. I stomped to the tool shed. The longer that brat avoided gathering eggs the angrier I grew. I grabbed a hatchet and tromped back to the boarded up door.

I finally whacked the last board free and entered into odors that matched how I felt after all the upset of this day – worn out and abandoned.

"Odette," I yelled.

I stepped farther inside the dank, dismal barn. I had not been inside the decrepit structure since we'd come back from the uncles. I had avoided it, kept myself away from memories of *Maman* laughing in the hay with us.

Why?

That should be a good memory like the ones in the picnic places, the mercantile, and even the ruins of the homestead. But in my mind the barn sat apart. A vague shadow crossed my thoughts. To brush it away, I again called, "Odette."

Shafts of evening light filtered into the murky building by the open side door and cracks between the planks of the walls and in the roof. Picking my way carefully, I passed broken-down stalls to the ladder leading to the hayloft. I stared up at the square opening. I really didn't want to climb up there. A few pieces of dried hay clung in the joints where the rungs were nailed to rotting studs.

I closed my eyes and again saw *Maman* handing Odette and *Bébé* Larry up to me, and then she drew her skirt through her legs in the modest sort of way and climbed up. We burrowed into the sweet Timothy hay. *Maman* laid in the soft nest, telling us of the ship crossing the Atlantic to a new and wonderful paradise that turned out to be prairies and wind and lonesomeness. *Maman*'s melancholy in the ocean of hay was a palpable thing. Odette and I feasted upon her stories, yet tasted only the frosting; as children we never looked for the inner filling, never considered that my mother starved with longing.

Was that a man's laugh? My eyes flew open. I strained to hear. A flurry of feet – mice or rats. I was acting like a scaredy cat and didn't much like it. The dark opening to the hayloft beckoned. To find Odette, I had to climb up. I set the egg basket down.

The old boards creaked, but held my weight. A spider web tickled my cheek. I wiped at my face with a hand grimy from the ladder and hurried up the last two rungs into the loft thick with dust. I squinted into the dimness. "Odette, I know you're up here. Better come out or you'll be sorry."

She materialized from the dark back corner, like a mist above a pot of heating water. I couldn't see her features, only the outline of her body. One hand behind her back, she skulked toward me until light from an overhead crack lit her face. She wanted me to see her look of pure hate.

"Get out of here," she screamed. "This is my house!"

I was used to her hatred, but her tone sounded different from the usual screechy spite. Goose bumps tightened on my arms. Fear of my own sister entered my heart. Never before had I felt she could hurt me without remorse. Now I did.

But I wasn't easily damaged. "Why are you so upset?"

She planted her feet squarely and glowered. "Leave."

"What's in the corner that you don't want me to see?"

Odette pulled an old pitchfork without a handle from behind her back and jabbed the tines in my direction. "I'll kill you same as you killed our brother and mother."

"What are you hiding?"

"None of your bees wax." She jabbed the air.

I snatched the bottom tine and yanked the fork from her fingers.

She fell back a step. A sly grin creased her lips. "Maybe it's time you knew." She dug in her pocket, pulled out a wooden match, struck its sulfur head on a floorboard and held the flame high. "You'll like what you're about to see."

I followed her across the planks. In the flickering light I saw a cubbyhole made by stacks of old wood. "Is that a box behind the wood?"

"It's my bed. I sleep on it all the time and you don't even know it." She dropped the burning match and stepped on it. "I'm not blistering my fingers just so you can look." She struck another match and lit a candle that was propped in a peach can.

I eased forward to stare into the corner.

"You don't even recognize it, do you?" Odette puffed up, haughty in her sarcasm. She swore damnation at me.

I should snake twist her arm, not let her talk to me like that, but I didn't and picked up the can with the candle and held it high. I made out an old mussed-up quilt on top of a dirty gray box about five-feet long. Short leather straps were pounded to the ends for handles.

A perfectly nice box for *Bébé* Larry.

"It can't be the snake box?" I whispered.

Odette's violet eyes burned into me like coals in a fire. "You're just too stupid. Can't even believe your own eyes."

"That's plain dumb. Didier buried *Bébé* Larry right after the fire."

"Where is the baby buried? Did you ask our precious father?" She pushed her palms toward me as if to ward off anything I would say. "Don't even try to make an excuse. You didn't even care enough about our baby to ask where his grave is."

"Odette. I don't know why. I just didn't. But I will."

Her lips turned up in an evil smile. "I sleep on him and *Maman* all the time."

"What?"

"*Maman*'s in the box."

"She can't be. It's too small." Brainless thing to say.

"Look for yourself," Odette taunted and scurried to the ladder. "Our mother won't bite, but watch out for *Bébé* Larry."

I heard Odette scramble down the ladder without taking my eyes from the snake box, heard her feet thud to the floor, heard the old planks squeak under her steps, and heard the side door slap shut. The wind whistled through the cracks. I shook with chill, but had to pull the collar of my sweater away from my sweaty neck.

I knelt before the box, terribly fascinated by Odette's shrine in the murky corner. I tugged the musty ragged quilt off the box. Dust flew. I sneezed – the sound loud and disrespectful.

How could Odette sleep in such a place without choking?

The hinged lid was still squared even with the sides. I rubbed at one corner of grime-covered cottonwood until the spot showed the silvery color I remembered. I bowed my head and drifted back to the wagon ride. Tickling straw had covered me, the hard box laid against one side of me, and Monty, my Monty, patted my ankle, conveying his sorrow at the loss of a brother.

"Monty, I need you now." I shivered from the need of him and felt betrayed he had left me behind.

Again my mind had strayed to something beside a problem that demanded full concentration. I couldn't fathom why Didier hadn't buried my baby brother. Or why I hadn't asked about him. I massaged the palm of my right hand and felt again the warm oily feel of the bone. The pungent odor of burnt flesh and acid smell of the burned house welled in my memory.

I knew *Maman* wasn't inside the box like Odette said. My sister had lied to punish me, same as always. Did I dare raise the lid? I so wanted to know if it actually was a bone I had dropped inside the box. Call it morbid, but I truly needed to see *Bébé* Larry's remains. I wanted to ask his forgiveness. My vengeance against mean Sadie should have been left to the Lord.

Had Didier found a better box to use as a casket or not? I just did not want to think that he had neglected to bury *Bébé* Larry. It was too horrible to contemplate. I lifted the lid. My eyes widened as far as they could go; bug-eyed and unblinking I tried to understand what I saw. I threw the lid back. It slammed against the plank wall. I crashed to my knees and hung onto the side of the box. I stared without understanding.

Maman's sable hair lay wispy around her dear face. The once beautiful skin was now a leather sheath stretched over bones. She was curled into a ball, knees to chest. The fabric of her nightgown outlined her shoulder, rib, and spine bones.

I reached inside and touched my mother. "Oh *Maman*," I cried. "What happened?" I sucked in air. Didier! What have you done?

I collected myself enough to close the lid.

Bébé Larry! Was Odette right? Had Didier left him in the box? He couldn't have. Unthinkable. I gasped. Could I look again? This time I carefully rested the lid against the wall.

Pieces of his charred cradle stuck out from beneath *Maman*. I couldn't make out any of *Bébé* Larry. *Maman*'s body concealed his bones and ashes in death same as her body had held him while he formed inside her. A charred rod-like object lay along the edge of the bottom beside *Maman*'s knees. Was it bone or wood? I couldn't tell. I reached inside, gently sliding my hand by *Maman*, trying not to disturb her. I fingered the rod into my palm. Oily, cool to the touch. I guided it up the side and held it toward a shaft of light. A chair leg. All these years I thought I'd given *Bébé* Larry back his bone, and I hadn't.

I didn't know how to feel about that.

I turned from the box and vomited, retching until I was empty. A cold sweat beaded under my hair, and I needed to curl up on the floor, but somehow I put the piece of wood back in the snake box and shut the lid.

I leaned my cheek against the box. "Don't worry, *Maman*, I've found you. You've waited eight years, but I'll bury you in your favorite place by the river."

My foot slipped on the ladder rung. I grabbed and hung on, clinging to the slivery old wood as if it were solid enough to hold me. I slowly regained sufficient sense to realize it was only a short drop to the floor.

My knees collapsed when I hit the planks at the bottom. I fell forward and lay on the dank, manure-smelling wood. I closed my eyes and rested like a child drifting on a raft down the lazy Milk River all the way to Havre.

Then tears came with great rasping sobs. My poor deranged sister had been sleeping on a wooden box built to hold snakes instead of her mother and her brother. She even called it home.

My tears finally dried. There was no hurry, none at all. I would bury my *Maman*, then confront Didier. I shut the side door quietly as if the slightest noise might disturb her or *Bébé* Larry.

Chapter 20

And so, my longest day continued.

~~~~~

The desire to build a house in the west field was gone. The prairies meant nothing, desolate as the inside of my heart. Unable to take a single step I leaned against the closed door of the old barn and looked up at the slice of first quarter moon. This morning, May 3, 1943, I listened to the High-line weather report on KOJM radio and learned about scattered showers, and that on the nineteenth the new moon would be a blue one. Then I learned of Alice's scheme to see Hyatt's father, drank tea in a playhouse with Lydia, searched three cemeteries and found *Maman* in the box in the hay loft. My life altered unimaginably in the span of one day. I ached over losses which could never be regained.

Didier proved the hardness in him when he sent Odette and me on the train. I tried to excuse him because of his inability to care for two small girls. I pardoned him no more. He discarded us because of his rotten guilt, and right after I buried *Maman* and *Bébé* Larry, he would explain to me just exactly what had happened. Had he even taken *Maman* to the hospital? Why not? Where had she died?

But now *Maman* needed her box placed under ground at the only spot in the prairies she loved.

The weathered side-door groaned as though relieved when I stepped away into a deepening night. I jammed my hands into my trouser pockets and slipped stealthily across the dark, uneven ground of the barnyard.

Night breezes seeped through Uncle Lanny's sweater. I hunched against the chill and angled toward a tool shed attached to the south side of the new barn. Didier had taken time to build an enormous barn with attached sheds like the Bromwell's. I had been amazed at the size and wondered why he had built it in front of the homestead barn. Now I knew why.

A horse in the corral nickered when I opened a hinged slat door. I stepped back, looked through the shadows and made out the milk cows wandering back to pasture. A knot in my stomach eased. Didier had finished milking and was no longer in the barn. He could not hear me.

I couldn't bear to see him now. He'd have no say about where to bury *Maman* and *Bébé* Larry; he'd left her in a box in a barn. Bile ran up my throat. I choked it back down.

I hauled a spade, a pick, and a rope to the Ford truck Didier bought after last year's harvest and piled them into the bed of the truck. The barnyard lay quiet in the first hour past nightfall. Rodents and owls waited to dash or dive, to hunger or feed, to live or die. A cricket chirped, breaking the oppressive silence. I hurried back for two kerosene lanterns and a hatchet to chop away enough of the spreading roots of the willow to allow room for the box at the base of the tree *Maman* loved.

"Blinny," Didier said. "What are you doing?" He was a shadow by the truck, a dark figure I didn't want to see. I walked right past him as though he hadn't spoken. I set the lanterns and the hatchet on the front seat, climbed into the cab, slammed the door in his face and fired the engine.

He yanked at the handle.

I shoved the gear into low and popped the clutch. He hung onto the jerking truck for a few running steps then let go, but he would follow on foot. I spun the steering wheel, drove hard to the old barn and waited at the side door for him to catch up, holding in my anger.

"Why didn't you bury them?" My words fell between us cold as the night wind.

He stopped a few feet away. "I meant to."

"I'm doing it now."

"Where?"

"*Maman* loved that willow on the ledge down by the river."

"Let's get to it then."

"I don't want your help," I said, my tone like ice needles during a storm. "You claim Platts take care of Platts. You *dang* sure don't."

"No, but you can't dig a hole deep enough without me."

I accepted only for *Maman*.

I kept from gagging as I ascended the ladder to the loft. Didier so close behind me, his breath hot on my ankles. I fumbled around in the dark until I found the candle in the can. He struck a wooden match with his thumbnail. In the flickering we silently carried the snake box to the loft door. He pried one side of the heavy double doors open. The rotten wood gave way, and the door fell from its hinges, thudding down to where the manure pile used to be. The noise of it faded into the prairie as if soaked into the ground like raindrops, splat and gone; an old door falling twelve feet should make more of a crash – something needed to protest the outrage of *Maman* put in a box.

We tied rope to the leather handles on either end of the box and lowered *Maman* and *Bébé* Larry to the ground. The box rested on the old door, that rested on an old manure pile, that rested on the Platt ranch, that rested on the prairie. None of it made sense to me. I would never sleep in innocence again.

I was down the ladder first. Through the side door first. Grabbed the handle on one side of the box first, then waited, glaring at Didier as he grabbed the other end. Together we hefted the box onto the truck bed and slid it forward so the vibration of the rough ride wouldn't walk the box to the end. My stomach knotted at the thought of *Maman* rolling out of the box and down the side of the coulee.

I slid behind the steering wheel before Didier could come around the end of the truck. This time my choices counted for something besides dry weeds in the prairie wind.

Didier one-armed onto the truck bed to brace the box. His boot clanked against the spade. Hopefully he would suffer the pangs of purgatory and Hades, riding beside the snake box filled with his wife and son. What punishment could fit his uncaring? How could he not put my mother to rest?

I jabbed the choke a couple of times. The engine spluttered like I had flooded it. I licked my lips and tasted dryness in my mouth. I needed a drink of water more than anything I ever wanted. The engine caught on the second try.

I rolled the window down, drove past the well and headed for the two-rut road that was gouged out of the side of the coulee. We plunged down the steep switchback, headlights bouncing off sandstone boulders on one side and disappearing into a black vacuum on the other. The steering wheel vibrated and my hands slipped. One of the tires caught in the berm. I pulled the wheel hard. The tire freed from the edge and I centered the truck on the road. My foot rode the brake pedal the rest of the way down.

Ebony limbs on cottonwood and willow trees along the river bottom appeared satin, their twigs like fingers grasping at the night. The sliver of moon hung above them.

I guided the truck along rough terrain near the river bank until the ground gradually rose into a high flat ledge where saplings formed a windbreak and created a place that was guarded from the prairie sun by green leaves. *Maman* had brought us here at least once a week to weave willow baskets, eat jelly sandwiches and pretend we were highborn ladies in royal courts.

I would bury *Maman* and *Bébé* Larry in the spot she loved, come hell or rough ground or Didier.

The right front tire hit a boulder and the truck shuddered and coughed to a stop before I could engage the clutch. I stamped on the clutch, pumped the choke and fired the starter.

"Stop it, Blinny," Didier yelled. "We'll carry the box the rest of the way up."

He couldn't even say coffin. I slammed out of the cab.

Didier slid the box to the end and jumped out. He put the pick over his shoulder and grabbed the box handle. I did the same with the shovel. We lifted the box down between us and walked silently, picking our way more by feel than sight, until we reached the huge cottonwood in the center of the saplings. We set the box down near its trunk.

"Where?" asked Didier as he shook his arm to force feeling back into his hand.

Mine stung with numbness as I pointed to a spot below a gnarled limb. "I want the tree to guard *Maman*."

"You never did learn to call her Mom."

"She preferred French. But you should know that."

He turned his back and sank the pick into the ground.

The thwack, thwack, thwack sounds reassured that the ground would yield and finally accept the remains of my mother.

I scraped away the loose soil with the shovel, and Didier broke more earth with the pick. We worked together without words the same way we did farm work, each knowing what the other would do. Why couldn't we live like that?

I broke out in a sweat, my back ached, my hands blistered, but I kept digging. I hit a root.

Voice rasping, chest heaving, Didier said. "Go back and get the hatchet and lanterns."

I did as I was told only for *Maman*. I handed him the hatchet, lit the wicks and jumped down into the hole.

"Girl! Make room."

I scrambled back out and sat on the mound of dirt, feet dangling over, wind freezing the sweat of my exertion.

He cut roots as thick as an arm bone and tossed them to me. Something rustled in bushes off to the left. An owl hooted. Didier stopped chopping. The shovel scraped against dirt. He tossed shovelfuls out, scraped around to level the bottom, and said, "It's ready." He hoisted himself out of the shoulder-high hole.

We lowered the box inside and dropped the rope on top.

The drum of the rope landing on the cottonwood box would vibrate in me forever − in the same way the feel of, what I believed was, Larry's bone stayed. I swore I tasted acid tar smoke.

We threw dirt into the hole, shovel by labored shovelful. The falling dirt pulsed into the night. A coyote wailed deep in the coulee. As the mournful, lonesome sound carried, my heart broke and soundless tears fell without end.

"It's done," Didier said.

I grabbed a dead branch, fell to my knees and poked it into the ground to mark the head. I rose in one motion and faced my father. "You'll part with some of that crop money you hoard and buy a headstone for Essie Faye and Larry." The low menace in my voice scared me.

"Blinny–"

"Did you kill her?" I spat on the ground by his feet. My hands froze into claws to rake the answer from him.

"Your mother died and that's all you'll learn from me." Didier spun and walked away into the night, his boots striking rocks and slipping in sand.

Forces inside me pulled every which way. I needed to force him to confess. I needed to never see him again. I needed to know how my mother died. I needed not to know. I dropped to my knees beside the branch jabbed into the ground and pressed my palms into the loosened soil.

"Goodbye *Bébé* Larry. Goodbye *Maman*. I'm glad you have each other." I was jealous. They were together and I had no one. Not my father, not my sister, not even Monty.

The emptiness of the prairie encompassed me as I huddled on the rough ground. I tried to concentrate on the night sounds to prove I wasn't the only living, breathing thing left. I pressed my ear to the dirt and felt more than heard the Milk River flowing below the ledge. That little bit of flowing brought my heart some ease.

Maman's spot in the ground was far enough above the flood plain to be safe, not that she would mind a little water. She loved the river and the promised escape of currents ever seeking a bigger river that, in turn, sought the ocean. I knew her dreams never ended at the sand where God bound the sea, but rested in her homeland.

"I hope you're at peace, *Maman*. I'm so sorry I asked for a gift that cost you the life of your baby and yourself."

I stumbled to the truck and drove hell-bent up the coulee road. I would leave this place of isolation and destruction, leave Didier to his hermit ways, leave Odette to her craziness, and try to leave my bruised soul behind.

Chapter 21

Junior's party was well under way by the time I parked at the far end of the ranch buildings. I walked with my down jacket snuggled close to my ears and hands deep into the pockets. Crickets chirped beneath the cold velvet sky. A barn owl fluttered up from the peak of the weather vane and was outlined for a moment in the October moonlight. The moon hung low to the east, large and silver. I could picture witches on broomsticks flying in front of it and the headless horseman riding across the moonlit prairies. I chuckled, more in tune with these imaginary stories than with the family and friends Alice had invited to celebrate my brother's birthday.

Alice loved huge family gatherings. I preferred small ones, relating better to a few close friends. Crowds made me nervous, probably a leftover from childhood. It was hard not to be shy when *Maman*, Didier, Odette and the baby, plus a few classmates, the teacher and Mr. Galloway at the mercantile were the only people I saw.

Near the corral a mare nickered. Maybe I should just hop up onto her back and let her wander in the pasture. The two of us could commune with the forces of the earth, sky and wind; all three were crisp, but gentle. A time to share the space with a trusted friend. The mare might not consider me a friend, but she would with a few rubs and soft spoken words. If only people were as easy.

I bypassed the temptation and walked toward the vehicles parked in a semicircle in front of Didier's tall house. Laughter came from behind. I walked alongside a row of caragana toward the back. A hand grabbed my arm.

"Where have you been?" Fran whispered. Before I could answer, she pulled me around and marched me back to the front door. She put a finger to her lips.

I didn't dare make a sound and followed her through the living room, through the dining room, down the hall and into Alice's bedroom. Muted tones from a Tiffany lamp softened the room. Gardenia perfume. Didier's picture was shadowed by the wardrobe.

Fran shut the door and pulled me over to the side by the bathroom. "I found something you have to see," she whispered.

"You're scaring me half to death."

"Quiet." She opened the bottom drawer in a Renaissance bureau. "Look at this."

"Are you snooping on Alice?"

"Somebody has to find out what's the matter with her. Just look."

One side of the deep drawer was lined with brown bottles. I picked one up. Drumguish Scotch Whisky. "So she likes a night cap. What's the big deal?"

"Look in the other corner." A plastic bowl was filled with brown prescription bottles. "It's sleeping pills," Fran hissed. "She's mixing drugs. She's gonna kill herself."

"I can't believe she's doing that."

Fran's eyebrows arched. "Why else would these be in here?"

"There could be any number of reasons."

"Name one."

I couldn't. "She never seems hung over when she shows up at my place."

"Would you even know?"

Would I? Mostly we argued or I ignored her. "Maybe not, but I know we shouldn't be searching her drawers."

"We didn't. I did. Was she doing this before you moved out?"

"How do I know? My room's on the top floor. We might as well have been in separate houses."

"We have to confront her. I'll meet you here tomorrow at noon and we'll make her understand she needs help." Fran blinked a couple of times. "Oh for crying out loud quit gawking at me like I'm nuts."

"If you want to have a high-noon shootout with her, you are completely nuts. We don't even know if she's drinking this stuff. Maybe it was Didier's and she just has never thrown it away."

"Label says it was bottled in 1980. Twenty years after your father was gone."

"Fran, I'm getting out of here and you should too."

Footfalls sounded on the hallway's hardwood floors. Fran quickly shut the drawer and grabbed my arm. We rushed into the bathroom, leaving the door open and hiding behind it.

Alice's voice carried. "Hyatt, I want to give you something without your brothers knowing about it."

"Ma, I don't keep secrets from them."

"I know, but I've never felt right about their inheriting the ranch instead of you. Didier fixed it so I couldn't change the will after he died. Wasn't right. I should've had my say in it."

"Ma, it's water under the bridge. I'm happy. I like practicing law."

"Well, I don't like you so far away."

"Denver is my home now and I'm doing great. Sara and the boys love living there as much as I do."

"I know, but I still wish I saw more of you."

A drawer squealed open. Fran pressed her fingertips to her lips. Her eyes pleaded for me to be quiet.

Alice spoke, "This key is to Didier's safety deposit box in the Cattlemen's Bank in Havre. He bought God knows how many corporate and municipal bonds. They're worth a small fortune now. I don't need the money and neither do your brothers. The ranch takes care of us.

"Mom, I can't steal from them and Blinny. And think of Odette. She doesn't have anything. She's just stuck in a house for crazy people."

That was enough. Fran's grip slipped from my arm as I stepped into the room and moved into the light. "Good for you, Hyatt. From the first time I saw you as a tiny baby I knew you had a good heart, not anything like your mother."

Alice's jaw dropped then her face flushed. "What are you doing in my bedroom?"

Fran stepped into the light. "I dragged her inside to show her what you have in that drawer." She pointed at the bureau.

"What makes the insides of my drawers your concern? I shoulda put a snake in it, a big fat rattler. You deserve to be poisoned. Snake bite is too good for you, maybe I'll force feed you some strychnine."

Fran jabbed her fists into her waistline, elbows askew. "Go ahead, be the drama queen. I don't care how much you holler at me. I want to know about this." She yanked the drawer open, bottles clanking together. "Look, Hyatt. Alice is mixing booze and pills.

Hyatt gaped at his Aunt Fran and then his mother. He was in his prime, a scholarly yet a physical man. Handsome and confidant, he was his mother's son. He stared down at the bottles, then pulled his mother into his arms. "What's going on, Mom?"

Alice hugged him and stepped from his arms. "I don't answer to any of you. But we have guests and shouldn't stand here picking at one another." She walked out, leaving Hyatt, Fran and me staring after her.

Hyatt broke the silence. "Don't worry, Aunt Fran. I'll take care of it. Might be she's just lonesome. I'll take her home with me and show her fun in the city. Could be we'll hire her a companion, maybe a butler. She'd like that.

"Hyatt," I said "you're missing the point. She doesn't socialize with anyone except family. We're her whole life."

Hyatt thought for a moment. "I'll send her on a singles cruise. Spice up her life."

Fran giggled. "I'll pray for an old codger to sweep her off her feet."

"It'll take something more than a cruise or an old codger to fix up your mother. I am sick of Alice running away every time she doesn't like what's going on. She's been doing it all summer."

"She has been doing that since we were kids," Fran said. "My brothers spoiled her rotten and gave in any time she left in a huff. Apparently she's trying to be in control again."

"Alice will be even more upset, if we don't make our entrance." I stepped outside through the French doors and cuddled into my jacket. Japanese lanterns swayed in a westerly breeze. Tangy pork barbeque flavored the smoke rising from a fire pit. Conversation and the laughter of many people covered my entrance, then Junior raised his glass to me and waved me over. I shook my head and sat down on the edge of a bench.

Alice stood by two of her gangly grandsons. Our eyes met and held for a long moment. She relayed with the slant of her head and the set of her mouth that she wasn't drinking and popping pills. I nodded so she'd know I understood. So many times I had misunderstood her, like the time she threw the most clarifying thing I ever read into my lap and walked off without a word.

~~~~~

After my mother lay safely buried beneath the branches of the tree by the river and after ramming the truck up the side of the coulee and sliding to a stop just shy of the bent willow fence, I stomped into the house and through the parlor without a word to Odette or Alice or Fran. Eyes wide and mouths hanging open, they watched from the sofa as if I was Lucifer himself striding through the house.

Sleep eluded me. For hours, I stewed that Alice, Fran and Odette had let me climb the stairs without any word of sympathy for *Maman*. I shouldn't have wasted time fretting over an unhinged sister and an aloof stepmother. Why hadn't I just packed and left?

Before the rooster atop the hen house crowed, I finally brushed the quilt back and climbed from my bed. I hesitated to turn on the bedside lamp. The light would force me to see what I simply couldn't face – no one wanted me to stay. Odette loathed me, Alice would be glad to see the last of me, Hyatt was too young to understand, and Didier didn't count.

And Monty was at war, and I hadn't heard from him. I was going to leave all of them and run for my sanity.

The pillowcases bordered with Aunt Elaine's cross-stitched blue hens lay on the oak bureau, ready for me to decide what to take. I fingered the stitches, wondering if my aunt had gone to the Holy Land, walked on those holy streets, and seen the holy shrines she longed for. I hoped so. She must have felt the same desperate urge to flee as I did now – any place with less burden. I didn't know how unburdened Jerusalem streets were, but I knew the Platt ranch was a place so weighted down, it broke the spirit. I needed my own house, but somewhere without the torment of a family broken beyond repair.

I picked up a blouse to fold and smelled the freshness of the wind-dried cotton. I buried my face into the cloth and breathed in prairie air so sweet the spoilage of my family couldn't foul it.

Could I really leave and forget building my house in the west field?

I sat down on the edge of my bed. Uncle Lanny had let his house go for debt owed by a wife's gambling. Could I let go? I needed Uncle Lanny now and would take the train to him if only I knew where. It was a silly thought. He must be dead or he would have written.

I'd go to Havre instead and ask Lydia if she would help me find a job and a place to live. Or maybe I'd wire Mrs. Tiffany in Kalispell and become her companion. Then I'd write Monty and tell him where to find me. I'd also write to Marvel in case my letter to Monty became lost in some battle somewhere in Europe. I ached for Monty's arms to hold me.

I tapped my forehead with my index finger. "What kind of idiot am I?" Again my thoughts had wandered from a painful task, ranging from a ranch spoiled, yet smelling fresh, to Aunt Elaine and wishing her well – and Monty. Maybe Odette wasn't the crazy one.

Well, I might be looney, but I wasn't going to be bonkers on the Didier Platt ranch. I stiffened my backbone, stuffed the blouse into the case and crossed to the closet, but then my posture sagged. How could I leave my marked-off house where I had lain in Monty's arms? I had to say goodbye.

I glided my fingers along the dark stairwell and hurried down the steep stairs to the second floor landing. I slipped by the closed bedroom doors in the hallway, and ran the open staircase to the main level. Fran was snuggled under a down quilt on the living room couch. I slipped into the kitchen, broke free through the back door and fled across a farmyard fresh with dew.

The rooster crowed.

I clipped along, breeze in my face, pink-blushed clouds sailing above me. A couple of times I glanced up to check the colors of the coming sunrise. The shades of rose and yellow invading the watery slate sky always satisfied me like a drink from a cool well.

I walked beside a field of ankle-deep winter wheat. The plants, thick and lush from spring moisture, promised a bumper crop in July when the stalks would stand up past my knees – as long as the rains continued. Last year's wheat berries had shriveled from drought and our yield had been low. I felt a pang of sadness. How would Didier harvest without me? Who would drive the tractor? I let the sorrow build. My sadness came from my inborn need to bring the golden grains in from the field.

Prairie crocuses slept nestled in the buffalo-grass on the knoll where I hoped to build a home. I trod carefully, trying not to damage any of the sleeping blossoms. Enough on the Platt ranch had been ruined, and the blooms should shine forth when the warmth of the sun awoke them.

My stakes in the ground appeared as gray and weathered as my plans to build. I walked the perimeter of the markers, checking, deciding, grieving that the size of my planned house still suited me.

I pulled up each half-rotten stake and piled them square like a stick house. Then I laid down in the same place I had when Monty came to tell me he was leaving. I needed his hugging. "Monty, where are you?"

I closed my eyes and concentrated on the ground beneath me – firm and rough, trying to poke and scratch through my clothes. I should undress and let the surface of the prairie mark my skin the same as my soul was scarred.

With my senses zeroed on the ground I felt more than heard someone approaching, although I did detect a swatting of paper.

I sat up, praying it wasn't Didier. I held no desire to see him or talk to him. Please let me leave unseen and unheard.

Alice walked toward me, flapping several sheets of paper against her leg as she stepped. She said without any sort of greeting when she drew close enough, "Read this and then decide whether or not to leave." She held the papers out.

I sat still, hands flat on the ground and studied her proud, pouty face outlined by flyaway hair, and I couldn't see any sign she wanted me to stay. "What is it?"

"Another one of your father's poems."

"He killed my mother."

She tossed the pages on my lap and walked back toward the house, wind blowing her muslin dress against the sway of her hips. Her beauty seemed lost in the vastness of the land.

The papers on my lap fluttered. I brushed them aside. One caught a current and drifted a few feet away. I couldn't see the writing, didn't want to see.

I picked up the top page.

How could my blond boy be?

My daughters curls are ebony.

Essie Faye is far from fair,

Matching me with darkest hair.

This was my secret question,

Until my wife's confession.

Forgive she cried and pled,

Over the son who was dead.

She blamed her homesick ways,

That ended with our home ablaze.

Confess whose son, I did demand,

A stern, unforgiving reprimand.

My wife grew wild and crazed,

Blurted out whose son I raised.

Now grocer's seed and Essie Faye

Share a box behind the lofted hay.

My farm, my life, my soul, empty.

How could my perfect blond boy be?

I crushed the page to my chest. He's blaming *Maman*? How dare he blame *Maman*? I read the heartbreaking rhythm again. *Maman* to blame? *Maman* to blame? Grocer's seed? Mr. Galloway? Mr. Galloway had sandy hair. I gasped, then grappled with the thought. He would have been a blond boy. *Bébé* Larry belonged to Mr. Galloway? Not Didier?

"No," I screamed at the fully awake morning sun. Brazen spears pierced my eyes and I hung my head.

Then sharp as the sun rays, a kaleidoscope of prairie prisms flashed through my mind, moments I hadn't understood before this instant. I grabbed my temples, trying to hold the memories back. They surfaced, forced by painful knowledge.

I closed my eyes. In the darkness behind my lids, *Maman* washed under her arms, put on a clean dress, brushed her hair until it lay in soft shiny waves around her head. She hurried Odette and me to do the same for the trip to the mercantile. We had better be ready by the time she packed extra food in case Mr. Galloway was hungry and could join us for a picnic.

That day when Mr. Galloway teased *Maman* about her French accent, her normally pale cheeks warmed with color, and she laughed behind her hand. Her sable hair shone as she tipped her head, listening to him explain about the variety of wild flowers we brought in our basket, her violet eyes shining deepest lilac. *Maman* resembled a patchwork of color – a prairie prism I hadn't recognized. I had only been happy to see my melancholy mother interested and alert, instead of gloomy because a letter from *Grandmaman* had not arrived.

And then there was the mail trip where *Maman* touched Mr. Galloway's arm with trembling fingers, and he rested his palm on her back where her skirt joined the bodice. He walked us to the door, talking all the way as though trying to keep her with him.

Was it the next mail trip that Mr. Galloway gave Odette and me penny candy to eat on the porch while *Maman* looked at new bolts of cloth?

Mr. Galloway had pulled *Maman*'s hand, softly saying, "I ordered a rose-colored linen you must have. I need to see the hue of it against your cheek. I'm sure it'll match."

"I mustn't," she replied, but let him lead her away, his hand again on her lower back, below the gathers of waistline. His long delicate fingers holding, guiding, petting.

That day *Maman* cried as we rode home on the mare – Odette astride in front, *Maman* in the middle, and me straddled behind.

"*Maman*, what's wrong?" I asked, tears running down my cheeks, too. Odette snuffled. We cried because our mother cried.

"Nothing, Blinny. I'm just sad, oh so very sad."

I hadn't understood then, but the full knowledge bloomed now. *Maman* had fallen in love with Mr. Galloway's stories of the flora and fauna, fallen in love with his interest in something besides crops and animals. He lived on the flat lands, but like her, his mind wandered to green valleys. She had followed his fantasy, even when he came to visit on the day Didier went to Rudyard with a load of wheat to sell. I could see my mother and the grocer walking toward the barn, whispering together, his sandy head leaning next to her raven locks.

No! I crushed the poem against my chest. I should have known something was amiss the moment I looked at *Bébé* Larry all pink and blond and *Maman* so protective of him. Didier should have known. He was the father, and I just a child.

I remembered how Didier loved the baby boy, going to look at him after a day in the fields, holding him and talking as if the baby could understand. My father had not guessed. I was sure of it. The poem proved it.

When did he find out? And how?

I sat under the dome of God's sky and watched a pair of yellow-headed blackbirds pester each other over some morsel near the west field fence. Beside my foot, an ant scout wiggled his feelers in his frantic search. A buckeye butterfly flitted over the fresh faces of the sun-warmed flowers. None of the life in the prairie mattered as I tried to comprehend what had happened between my parents. Didier sent Odette and me away on the train, claiming he couldn't care for us and work the homestead, too. Or had he sent us away because he couldn't bear to look at the daughters of a wanton wife? Had my mother died because she couldn't bear losing Mr. Galloway's son? Or was it the guilt over betrayal of her family?

Both *Maman* and *Papa* destroyed the Platt family.

I would never understand.

The morning breeze again fluttered the pages in my lap. I gathered them up and carefully folded them with the Blond Boy poem into a square small enough to fit into my pocket. I left the one that drifted away lying near my pile of markers. Let the prairie tear it apart, too. I refused to read any more of Didier's words. But I would hear his explanation.

And he would give one.

Chapter 22

My heart ached from the destructive power in secrets.

~~~~~

Alice had simply thrown Didier's poems in my lap and walked off. She knew all along about *Maman*'s affair. In fact, he probably told her everything. I controlled the urge to scream, and locked the pain of this family behind a good amount of justified anger. I slapped my pocket to sting the words of the poem that hurt so much. How could my parents be so dishonest? They were the ones who should shoulder the blame; instead they escaped into places I could never enter – *Maman* into her mind and Didier into his land, leaving me to blame a chicken and myself. And furthermore, if my father had killed my mother, he would spend eternity behind bars, and I'd help lock the door on him.

I trotted from the west field to the house and barged through the kitchen door, figuring he'd be eating breakfast. The room hadn't been used, no lingering smells of bacon or eggs or oatmeal mush. The dining room was also empty. Alice's spot on the living room sofa was bare, and the main floor was quiet and vacant.

The bedroom doors on the second floor stood open, no one anywhere in sight. Surely Alice and Hyatt were in Odette's room. I ran up the attic stairs and checked her room. Messy and empty.

My room?

Odette sat alone in the middle of my bed, cutting buttons off my gabardine shirts. She raised her *faëry* face. Dark smudges marred the tender skin below her eyes, her pinched cheeks the color of parchment. The depths in her shadowed pupils showed an effort at trying to figure out a great problem. "Why did you ruin my house in the barn?" She spoke as if the question were the most natural a girl could ask.

I eased down on the foot of the bed not wanting her to think I was standing over her. "Do you remember weaving baskets with *Maman* under the tall cottonwood down by the river?" Her eyes remained troubled, like crosswind ripples on a stock pond. I wanted to pat her leg, try to calm those eyes. "You were so small, I don't know how you could remember." I kept my hands in my lap, knowing one touch and she would bolt.

"Anyway," I continued, "under the tree was one of *Maman*'s favorite places because the saplings suckled around it and their summer leaves reminded her of all the green and nurturing things in her parents' vineyard. Didier and I buried her and *Bébé* Larry in the midst of the saplings last night. Your mother is at peace now."

"She isn't dead."

"Yes, Odette, she is." I picked up a few of the pearl buttons laying on the quilt. "Why are you cutting the buttons off my shirts?"

"Go ahead and snake twist my arm. I don't care."

"I never have."

"But you've threatened to ever since I can remember."

She was right, I had promised pain over her bratty actions. "I'm sorry." She wouldn't forgive me, but I needed to apologize anyway.

"You wrecked my house," she whispered. "Destroyed the one place I was happy."

Sorrow rose from my heart for the sweet innocent child she used to be. Too much had happened in her short twelve years. "When we went to the uncles, I promised I'd take care of you. I have and always will."

"I don't want *you*. I'm staying with Alice."

It hurt, even though I expected her rejection. Nothing would ever make things right between us. I gathered up the rest of my buttons and set them in a row on the vanity.

Scissors gripped in her fist, Odette watched my every move.

"Where is Alice?" I asked.

"She took the truck to look for *Papa*."

Odette had called our father by the long-ago French. It sounded strange. Neither of us had called him that after the day we boarded the train eight years ago. I couldn't think of a time she'd called him by name since we had come back to the ranch, or a time when I'd seen her talking just to him.

"Did you bury *Papa*, too?" Odette asked.

"He walked away in the night. Wanted to be alone, like he always does. Maybe to grieve." I was unsure whether he had any grief for *Maman* and felt like I lied. I slid the scissors from Odette's fingers, took her hand and led her downstairs. She came easily, but as soon as our feet touched the main floor, she broke free from my grip and bolted out the front door. I let her go, but followed outside.

She flitted across the farmyard and angled past the big barn. Chester ran to her, but she swatted him on the nose. The calf kicked up his heels and ran in the other direction. Odette disappeared behind the building. The side door in the old barn slammed.

She would stay in the hayloft for hours. At least I knew where she was, no need for her to overhear me confront Didier about the poem, or for her to know about *Maman*'s infidelity yet. I'd tell her though, not let her find out like I had.

My thoughts jumbled and twisted every which way, worse than a snarl of barbed wire. The more I tried to straighten them out, the deeper the barbs of confusion cut. Had our mother's loneliness set in motion the breakdown of our family? Or was it broken before she set foot on the desolate homestead Didier brought her to? I'd probably never know, but I swore to find out what Didier had done.

The privy door opened and Fran stepped out. She spied me and called. "Where is everybody?"

The faint sound of the truck speeding up the coulee road grew louder. My chest tightened. Was I more frightened of what he would tell me, or more worried that he wouldn't answer at all? I felt Fran beside me. She was listening too.

The wind kicked up and lashed at us. Dark clouds scudded in from the west, shading the prairie gray. My hair whipped into my face and I held it back. Lightning flashed in the distance. My muscles tightened, my breathing deepened, my senses spiked. I thundered in my soul. The elements and I knew each other. I was glad they would witness what was about to pass between my father and me. Whether it would be a violent shouting or a dead calm, I faced it knowing I'd come out the other side with the knowledge of what happened to my mother.

The cab broke into view.

Didier parked beside the tool shed and helped Alice and Hyatt to the ground. They walked toward me shoulder to shoulder, at peace like they'd shared an open-air tryst like Uncle Lanny told Aunt Elaine everyone needed. Alice's wind-tossed hair looked like fine strands of spun gold even in the cloud cover; her blue dress clung to her legs and revealed her perfect shape. Didier looking tired and rumpled. Hyatt clutched onto Didier's hand. A perfectly nice looking family. One that I was about to rend. And Hyatt isn't his child either.

I stepped forward and flung the poems at his feet. Pages fluttered and scattered. "When did you learn *Bébé* Larry was Mr. Galloway's son?"

Chester's cowbell clinked on the far side of the barn in the quiet after my question, and Hyatt pulled free from Didier's grip to latch onto Alice's leg.

My father sighed. "Girl, there are things better left unsaid. Keep the memories of your mother the way a child sees."

I was better off not knowing? How could he say that? I stepped closer. "What did you do to my mother?"

"It's none of your business what happened between Essie Faye and me. You are only sixteen. What do you know of life? Nothing."

Alice threw up her hands. "For cryin' out loud, Didier. Tell her the truth. She's a right to know." Didier gritted his teeth and glared at Alice. She eyed him back.

He faced me under the roiling clouds. He wet his mouth and swallowed, but said nothing.

Alice groaned. "I'm not doing your talking for you."

Fran scooted closer to me.

He struggled with what needed to be said. The words finally broke free and he spoke, "I walked along the river in the dark for hours, trying to forgive. I couldn't until I returned to the grave and leaned against the cottonwood. It seemed as though the tree covered my hurt and made it possible to see Essie Faye clearly for the first time."

Hearing Didier use *Maman*'s given name sounded so familiar. He spoke as though they were talking. I tucked my fingers in my armpits, waiting for him to get to what I wanted to know, willing him to hurry, but he didn't.

His voice strengthened. "She was my bride, willing to leave France and seek a new life. I still can't understand why she changed. During each spring planting she was full of dancing and laughter, but by harvest her moods sank, by winter her tears couldn't stop. You jammed a stick into the ground to mark her place, but I can't believe buried under that tree is stopping her tears any better than resting beneath a pile of sweet-clover hay in the homestead barn. The place where she'd conceived her blond boy. Yes, I know that, too. I left her to him."

Didier paused like he wanted me to say something. I just chewed on my lip.

"Blinny, that pitiful, twisted, dried-out willow stick is a true metaphor of what it marks. What kind of tombstone could ever convey the sorrow that lays below?"

There was no answer for his question and he knew that.

"Just tell me why *Maman* died."

Didier was groggy from lack of sleep and emotion, yet he asked another insane question. "Do you remember me running from the Bromwells' house carrying Essie Faye?

"How can I forget? That crazy, tap-dancing Clarence was scaring *Maman*. You had to get her away, but why didn't you take me and Odette?"

"Are you going to listen or just accuse me?"

"I don't need to. Her dying did that."

Alice spoke, "Blinny, he's finally telling and you need to hear him."

"Don't tell me what I need. This is between him and me."

Didier snorted. "Maybe I'm done talking to someone who doesn't respect me or my wife."

"I'm sorry." I apologized only to keep him talking.

Didier kicked the toe of his boot against a dirt clod, smoothed it out and tapped it flat. He sighed, the sound filled with the inevitable hurt he was passing to me. "Essie Faye already had the look of death about her. I knew it and Marvel knew it. Taking your mother to the hospital was a fool's errand, but I had to try. She was my vineyard girl, running down rows of vines, skirt held high, showing legs strong enough to stomp grapes into wine. Maybe the hospital could bring her back. I drove too fast. The right tire hit a hole and we skidded into the ditch. Then suddenly I heard, *'Watch the road.'* Essie Faye had said it."

Tears leaked from the corners of my eyes as I watched Didier for any signs of lying.

He cleared his throat. "I almost jumped out of my skin. I hit the brakes and the truck shuddered to a stop, half in the ditch, half out. Your mother hadn't moved, but her eyes were open and she asked, *'Where are we going so fast?'* I told her to the hospital. She closed her eyes and rested against the seat, peaceful as a sleeping child. I couldn't let her slip away again and shook her arm. She opened her eyes and said clear as day, *'Take me to the shanty.'*"

"*Maman* asked to go?"

Didier nodded. "My wife had come back. I felt like a fresh-dug well filling with water. I reached over and tucked the quilt tighter under Essie's wan, thin chin. She needed food and I had some at the homestead. The truck came right out of the ditch, but even with the noise and vibration of driving on the gravel road, she might slip away again. Twice I touched her cheek, and she cracked her eyelids long enough to let me know she lay quiet to conserve strength. Living on the homestead without a house would be hard, but the barn was tight. I figured we'd manage. Essie Faye had returned from the brink of death. That was all that mattered. We'd rebuild plant again, and create another son. Blinny, can you understand how I felt?"

Didier had never spoken to me with much emotion, and I wasn't sure how to deal with it. I wiped away the leaking tears, only to have them well again.

When I didn't answer, he said, "I drove us onto our land in the heat of the late afternoon. Essie Faye stirred and straightened enough to look out. She gasped at the first sight of the burned house and stared through the window at the ruins for the longest time. I finally asked her what she was seeing and she answered, *'Us when we first arrived.'"*

Didier swallowed like he was dry to the bone. "I fetched her some water from the well and heard the cows coming up the coulee road, bawling, wanting their evening grain and their full bags relieved. Thank God the pigs were napping and the chickens were perched on the corral next to the barn. They could wait, but the cows couldn't."

Didier wasn't even aware that he had admitted to caring more for his livestock than my mother. It was no wonder Odette was messed up with a father like that. I didn't bother to interrupt him with that fact. I just added it to his long list of uncaring and listened to him explain hurrying water to my mother so he could go milk.

He got my attention when he said, "She pushed the cup away and asked, *'Where did you bury my baby boy?'* How could I tell her? She accused me of leaving him in the barn. How could she have known? How could I explain that I'd been too busy to pick a place for the cemetery? That I needed time to decide where we'd be buried?"

That did it. My knees locked and my cheeks grew hot. "You're asking me to explain why you didn't even bury the baby you believed was yours? You're one crazy sorry-excuse of a father."

Didier flared back. "I'll admit to that. Now are you going to cuss at me or hear the rest?"

I nodded once with a jerk of my head.

"Essie Faye tried to walk, but stumbled. I caught her up and carried her down the rise. She clung to me, arms so thin, so white, skin so loose. She was little more than bones. She needed milk and meat. I carried her into the barn and to the ladder. She grabbed hold of a rung and climbed upwards. It seemed as though a spirit carried her upward. She swayed at the top, then disappeared into the opening. I scrambled up in time to keep her from falling in the murky loft. She demanded to know where the box was. I held her tighter and begged her to come away. *'Where,'* she cried again and again until I told her in the back corner under the hay.

"She rushed forward, her white nightshirt just a spot in the shadows. I hurried after her and brushed the hay from the box. She dropped to the floor beside it, gasping for breath. Her eyes flashed. *'Open it.'*"

I cringed at Didier repeating *Maman*'s words. How desperate they must have been.

He cleared his throat like clearing away a thing not wanted. "You want me to quit?"

"Tell all."

"Your mother fought me when I told her it did no good to see. Told her she needed to eat, regain strength, then deal with the loss of our son, but she had to make sure he was dead. Her plaintive cry hit me like nothing I've ever heard, but I refused to open the lid. She shook her head like a wild thing. Pity. I felt it for the pitiful way she clutched the box, and I lifted the lid. Essie grabbed the side and pulled herself up to peer inside. A low moan rose from her until it grew into an eerie whine that grated against the rafters. I couldn't bear to see her so needy, as if the baby was all she had.

"Your mother grew so silent; I couldn't even hear her breathe. I had to touch her. She jerked away and slapped at me over and over. He was my boy, too. I told her that, but she recoiled. *'The boy is not yours.'* She sank beside the box, staring up like a wounded animal. She told me that he belonged to a green place, a place in her heart that I had forgotten about in this never-ending dried out prairie. Said her baby belonged to a man that knew her longings.

"My body drained, unplugged by understanding. I asked what she'd done. She told me she'd found a love so pure it was like wine in a desert and I demanded to know who it was. She asked if it mattered, said her baby was gone, that I left her and her lover left her. Essie sobbed. I thought her wasted body would break.

"She'd betrayed me, given away what was mine. She not only gave birth to another man's son, but she told me as though the fault belonged to me. Why didn't she just let me believe the blond boy was mine? I raised my fists to her, demanding the name again. *'Mr. Galloway.'* She collapsed and curled around the box as if she held a baby. I scrambled down the ladder and made it as far as the door before I slumped against the doorjamb, drained, not even enough fluid left in me to urinate."

Didier was so much into himself that he told me, his daughter, he couldn't pee. Unbelievable. I wanted to lash out at him with something hurtful. Nothing bad enough surfaced and I clamped my mouth shut.

"Night settled," he continued, "and the bawling of milk cows grew urgent. I left her in the loft, tended the livestock, drank at the well, and peed, not seeing anything but the blackness in my heart. Come morning, Essie Faye was dead. I knew she would be. I lifted her, put her in the snake box and lowered the lid, squaring it to the sides. I pulled hay around it, burying it from sight and from mind." Didier swallowed and said, "Then last night, Essie Faye was finally planted with her grocer's seed. And I have no more to tell you."

His explanation sounded true, but I was by no means satisfied. He held something back. The guilty look of withholding in his eyes said as much.

How would *Maman* explain why she had wilted like the prairie wild flowers? She died from a thirst that Didier could not quench?

I asked my father, "Did you send Odette and me away because of what she did?"

His eyes reflected torment. "You girls look so much like Essie. I needed time."

"And what about our needs?" I realized I was yelling at him. "We lost our brother, our mother, and then you."

He cast his look to the ground, avoiding the wrath caused by his own doing. When he could look me in the eye again all he said was, "I came for you."

"Because you needed us to work this land. You couldn't even take enough time away from it to be with *Maman*, not even for the birth of a baby." I jabbed my thumb at my chest. "I had to do it. And I was just a little girl."

His jaw tightened, facing my anger without an excuse. "I want you to live here," he said as if that made everything all right.

He was trying to guide me away from the bitter past. I didn't like it, but I couldn't keep from asking, "Then why won't you deed me the west field and let me build?"

Alice broke in. "Because he can't. It's mine."

Hers? The west field was Alice's? I looked from her to Didier and back again. I wanted to shake the sly look from her face, and I wanted the sheriff to arrest both of them: a killer and a thief.

Didier turned on Alice. "You stay out of this. Take your boy and go inside."

Alice bent over and said to Hyatt, "Run along and play. Better yet, go find Odette. She's probably in the old barn. Fran will go with you."

Fran grabbed my hand. "I'm staying with Blinny."

"Maybe you should," I said. Fran dropped my hand, but stayed rooted by my side.

Alice nudged Hyatt. "Go along," she said. As soon as he scooted away, she faced Didier square, shoulders back, feet slightly apart, chin jutted with determination. "It's high time you told Blanche that you signed a marriage agreement. She should've known long before now that this place will be mine. But oh no, you've let her plan that stupid dream house on my land."

Didier cursed. "Alice, shut up. I'm trying to explain."

My stomach knotted, my hands clenched. "What did you do?" I shouted.

Didier's face reddened. A vein in his temple pumped. "Your mother died. I didn't do anything to stop it. If that makes me at fault, then I am. But I did make provision for you and Odette in the will."

Alice drew back like a cat touching water, then leaned forward, eyes wide, glaring at him. "You signed the paper. I watched you standing over your fancy cherry table struggling with the words, demanding the paper be changed to suit you, as if you were afraid my mother would cheat or steal. All they wanted was a name for my baby. And she did it, wrote down that you agreed this ranch would belong to me." Alice shook her finger. "But, Mr. Platt, she didn't have to, I knew you'd agree to anything by the way you kept looking at my chest."

"So that's why you came down in the coulee to find me this morning, unbuttoning your blouse and ready like a bitch in heat. You wanted to make sure this land is yours."

"No, Didier. You're wrong again. I was worried about you and wanted you to understand that I'm ready to complete our marriage. I want us to share life, birth sons together, work my land."

"It is not your land until I die. It's *my* land, always been *my* land, and will always be *my* land, because only *my* sons will inherit. You can't pass it to anyone but sons by me. And just so you know it. You won't get all of it," Didier said evenly, as if he was past caring how angry Alice got. "Odette's son will have half of any new land I buy. I owe Essie Faye that much."

"Odette's son?" I blurted. "Why not my sons?"

Didier cleared his throat. "You're to build the house in the west field like I said. The paper says you and Odette can live here as long as you want. I've already made a deal on the McFeatter place, and it'll go to my grandsons through Essie Faye."

Alice sucked in air. "Over my dead body," she said, then burst out laughing. "That was certainly a poor choice of words."

I spluttered, "That isn't funny, Alice."

"No and neither was the night I came with my folks for his answer. He met us in the yard with a loaded rifle by the door, like we were out to rob him, he said he'd give me and my bastard a home. Said we'd learn to get along." Alice turned to Didier like I wasn't there. "It hurt when you made my mother write down that the bastard would not inherit. That hurt like hell, Didier."

I rubbed my forehead. "I'm wanting to know about my mother's death and you two are arguing about this ranch. What is important anyway? Certainly doesn't seem to be Odette or me."

Alice scoffed. "That isn't the worse of it. Didier haggled with my father over Monty working for him. Wanted my brother to work for nothing, but my father wouldn't let Monty come over unless he got wages."

Didier leaned near Alice's face. "You got a name for Hyatt and an inheritance. What did I get? Mouths to feed, that's what."

She studied him for a long moment, then the tip of her tongue ran across her bottom lip and a smirk of pleasure touched her pouty face. She laughed again, sounding even more delighted. "Unless they marry my brothers. I have lots of them to pick from."

Didier grabbed her arm. "What was that this morning? Playacting? Pretending you want to be with me? Now the truth comes out? You married me only for the land?"

"Of course. And you knew it." She broke his grip. "You married me for my brothers' work and because I was pregnant. You knew I could give you sons for this land. And I knew that. Wasn't any secrets between us? But I sure as hell figure we can build a ranch together. We will produce something fine."

"Then why the visit to Hyatt's daddy?"

"If you'd ever quit acting like an ass we could have a family and a working ranch that would make us both happy."

"Hard to be happy when your wife wants only your land."

"Is it so hard to understand that I'll have what you promised by signing the agreement?"

Didier and Alice sizzled at each other so much that I wanted to throw a bucket of water on them. I no longer looked at Didier and Alice as anything but scrappers. They had stooped as low as they could go. No wonder *Maman* looked for a way to escape.

Didier straightened and cocked his head to hear something.

I heard it too.

A faint scream. Coming from the old barn? Hyatt?

We spun to the direction of his yell. A spiral of dark-gray smoke rose above the barn, met the wind, and broke apart.

There is a speck of time that is measured only in disbelief, then fear sets in and then reaction.

I gasped and bolted forward. Didier sprinted past me and raced across the barnyard, and along the side of the new barn. He rounded the end and disappeared behind it. I out ran Alice and broke around the corner in time to see *Papa* charge through the side door of the old barn. A motion up in the loft opening caught my eye. Hyatt appeared in the smoke pouring from the opening some twelve feet above us. I skidded to a stop. Fran did too. Alice beside us.

Hyatt clung to the frame, staring down at us. Dense smoke swirled around him, and fire glowed behind. Sparks flew.

Broken boards from the old loft door that fell when *Papa* and I lowered the snake box lay on the ground below Hyatt. I scrambled up onto them. "Hold tight. Didier will get you in a minute," I called.

Hyatt wobbled and clutched the weathered frame, his pudgy fingers dug in like claws on a cat. Fran gasped. "Hang on," Alice cried.

Odette suddenly stepped from out of the smoke and stood beside Hyatt. Scrawny, hair wild, face calm, she stared down at me. "He knocked over the candle and started the fire. I told him to leave it alone."

"Take Hyatt to the ladder," I yelled. "*Papa*'s coming."

"Do it now!" Alice bellowed as she crowded up on the boards behind me.

"You don't want him dead, do you? Catch." Odette shoved Hyatt. His grip on the frame broke and he tumbled down. Alice screamed. I stretched out my arms. Hyatt hit them. I fell backward, clutching him to my chest. Alice tried to brace me, but we all crashed. The pile of boards held us. It was as if the old barn cradled us like it had *Maman* for so many years. I squeezed the squirming boy; his terrified squalling was a hymn of pure relief.

Alice pulled her legs from under me, grabbed Hyatt, and ran for the house. Fran ran after her. Bromwells taking care of Bromwells.

I glanced up and met Odette's eyes. In that instant I understood she was glad Hyatt was safe. She disappeared back inside the loft.

I scrabbled to my feet, jumped from the boards, and dashed through the side door. The air inside the barn was clean. A fire burned above, but down here the smells of cow, old fodder, and dust were pure.

A roof beam crashed. The barn trembled. The fire roared. How long before it all collapsed? I ran to the ladder, praying the roof held until *Papa* got to Odette.

They should be down by now. He'd had plenty of time. Where were they? I scrambled up the ladder. Suffocating smoke hit me worse than a dust storm. I covered my nose and mouth with my shirt. I could see nothing. "*Papa!*" I cried. "Where are you?"

"Stay there," he yelled back. "I couldn't find her in the smoke but I've got her now."

Flames licked the thick slab walls. Wood crackled. A support beam toppled at the back and crashed to the floor. Embers shot upwards and spread.

Papa appeared out of the inferno, carrying Odette. "Get down the ladder. I'll hand her to you."

I descended six rungs, braced my knees against the studs, and reached up. Didier lowered Odette, feet first, through the opening. I grabbed her around the waist. She was limp and floppy. I teetered, grabbed a rung and hung on until I balanced her between my chest and the ladder. We backed down one rung at a time.

Papa jumped from the loft, landed in a roll, and came up on all fours, coughing and choking, his back wracking from it. His face was black from soot, his eyes bugged from coughing, cheeks indented from gasping for air, but he appeared satisfied. I was too. This time he had saved the child.

"Run," he gasped.

I ran for the door with Odette in my arms. A rattlesnake crawled out of a crack in the wall. I skidded to a stop. The snake ignored me, wriggled to the door, and out. Mice darted, searching for a way out. Honey bees poured from a hole above a window and got lost in the smoke now pouring down from the loft.

I burst forth into fresh air. The roof caved inward. Flames swirled and a whirlwind of embers shot skyward.

Papa stumbled out of the barn, grabbed my arm and hurried us up the rise. "We're safe now." He lifted Odette from my arms and sank to the ground holding her as though he truly cared.

He loved her enough to risk his life, yet would leave his land only to our sons? Made no kinda sense. In the urgency of the rescue, I thought of him as *Papa*, but I no longer could. He just didn't deserve it.

Odette lay across his legs like *Maman* had. Eyes closed, breath shallow, unflinching, death-like.

Except I knew her playacting. "Stop it, Odette."

She burst out laughing. "Don't worry. I'm not going to die like *Maman*. I'm going to stay here and torture you."

I grabbed my father's shoulder and shook it. "Now do you finally see?"

He sat Odette up, searching deep into her eyes for the longest time. "I don't know what to do," he said as though I should understand that.

"Of course you don't." Sarcasm laced my tone. "You never know what to do. Just like you didn't after our place burned down. But I'll tell you. Odette needs to be away from us. She needs a woman who will love her and I know just the one. I'm taking her there tomorrow."

He kept his grip tight on Odette and shook his head. "Platts take care of Platts."

"Not this time."

Odette wiggled out of *Papa*'s grip. She stamped her feet in the powdery dust, defiant and hateful as always. "I'm not going anywhere you say," she said as though she really had a choice.

Why did I care? "Do you remember Lydia? The lady on the train?"

That was the last thing she expected me to say. Her violet eyes clouded over and grew faraway. "A little. She was soft and smelled good."

"She wanted you then, and she still does. I visited her in Havre. She said as much."

"You should've let me go with her back then. You ruined my life because you were too selfish to let me go."

"It isn't too late."

"How long do I get to stay?"

"Until you want to leave."

The barn crashed down, hot and noisy, same as the homestead house had caved in on itself. The timbers glowed orange so hot it looked as if the wood would melt and run into the prairie soil. The last evidence of the family we once had was gone.

We all silently, reverently watched until Odette said, "I'll pack."

Didier stood all in one motion. "No you won't. I've had enough of this. You aren't going anywhere. Not now, not ever. This ranch is mine and so are you. You are blood of my blood and will stay here."

I felt no pity at his distraught manner. He had earned our disobedience, lost the last of our respect. "Come on, Odette." I reached for her hand.

She stepped back as if I were Satan himself and faced our father. "I loved you best. But you never cared. You chose your land, *Maman* and *Bébé* Larry over me. You put them in a box for me to sleep on. I talk to dead people. They're all I have."

Odette reached out and clasped my hand. We walked toward the house with as much courage as Uncle Lanny had to sell his house to pay off debt. Odette and I would not look back. I experienced a oneness with her, but felt no response on her part. She was only using me to get away. So be it.

Didier's words behind us were a blizzard wind. "If you leave, you'll walk. Not one thing on this ranch belongs to you."

"I'll drive you," Alice said from where she stood on the porch. She eyeballed Didier. "You may or may not see me again."

I left the dry land prairies on the train going to the Flathead Valley to work for Mrs. Tiffany. She had answered my letter within a week. Yes, she wanted me and I accepted. I'd be her companion and go to school.

I couldn't stay with Lydia even though she issued the invitation. Odette needed her full attention and I needed to be back where my uncles had so kindly mothered me. Who would ever think of Uncle Lanny as a mother, but he was. He taught so many lessons. I needed now to remember them and be restored. Mrs. Tiffany's house offered a place of refuge – a sojourn while I learned to accept *Maman*'s *affaire* and Didier's inadequacies.

Odette and Lydia waved to me as the engine gathered steam. They stood arm in arm, appearing rather sad. Neither had voiced relief at my going, but I knew they were. My sister was finally living in a house where she belonged. Didier had been hard pressed to give Lydia his okay about Odette living with her, but finally agreed. I think he gave in because somewhere deep inside he saw Odette's need in a way he never saw *Maman*'s.

Then the train picked up speed and Havre disappeared, replaced by the windblown prairie. I would miss the tug of that wind on my shoulders and the pull on my hat for a time, but someday I would come back and make peace with my father. I needed to forgive him, and I needed to forgive *Maman*, and I needed to forgive myself – but not yet.

I slipped an envelope from my purse. I drew it to my face and inhaled. Monty's hands had sealed it. His words had been short and to the point. Monty through and through.

Only a couple more weeks
of basic. Not too bad. I miss you
and the ranches. Don't know yet
where I'll be fighting. Don't
worry.

I couldn't believe the letter had arrived on the day I left the ranch. Alice had pulled in at Goldstone Mercantile and I checked one last time.

I wondered if Alice had returned to the ranch from her parents yet. If she hadn't, I figured she would. I hoped so.

A flock of swallows banked on the currents and sailed away, much the same way I was traveling to a lush valley with green meadows and forests. To the valley my Platt uncles had loved. I would wait for Monty there.

Chapter 23

Halloween 1982, I carried my breakfast coffee out onto the deck. My breath clouded before me as I stood wrapped in an old fleece robe looking toward the east. The sun was fully awake, no brazen spears. I had slept in, enjoying Sunday, my usual day to rest and catch up with myself. I wanted to just sit, but I had promised to drive all the way to Great Falls to see a sister who thought I'd ruined her life. Every time I visited she would accuse me again. She had done so since she was old enough to lay blame. No matter how many times she recited her ridiculous litany of spite, the words hurt. I couldn't brush them off, however untrue.

I sure didn't want to talk to her therapist about our screwed-up family. In fact, I didn't really want to see my sister. No, that wasn't quite true. I did want to see Odette - but every visit to the group home left me in a muddle, torn between the bond of sisterly love and self-defense.

The only solid thing in my life was building this house, and I just wanted to sit back and visualize the cupboards I planned to start next week. Didn't matter that I had all winter to finish the interior. I was selfish and knew it. Missing one day shouldn't matter, but it did.

I held high pride in the solid red brick, clean white trim, and tight roof; I yearned to make the inside as warm and inviting as the outside. I had moved in a few days ago even though it was unfinished. A bed was in the partially done bedroom, a few clothes hung in the door-less closet, dishes were stacked in boxes along a kitchen wall, and towels were piled beside the bathroom sink. Food and meat still filled the refrigerator in the trailer, but I was under my roof, inside my walls, standing on my floor.

I was set.

And I had to leave. *Dang* disgusting but I sucked up my irritation, bucking up like Marvel used to say and went inside to dress. I missed her. She had lived on the Bromwell spread until she was eighty-four, then passed on like she had lived. No bother to anyone. Just did it.

Unlike Didier, who had lain on a bed full of pain and remorse, cursing the unfairness of cancer until it took him away. I'd agreed about the awfulness of cancer as I helped Alice care for him, her sons, and the ranch. Terrible way for a vital man in his fifties to pass, and I was glad I came when Alice called in July of '62. My father was sick. She needed me to come back and bring in the harvest, so I did.

I thought it would be hard to leave the Flathead Valley and the law firm where I worked as a paralegal, but I was elated after saying goodbye and walking out the leaded-glass door of the law firm. The prairies and my past were calling.

Forgiveness had slowly seeped from my unconscious mind to awareness during the twenty years I lived in the valley. Bitter thoughts were replaced by acceptance. My mother and father had been imperfect and unable to respond to the needs of their daughters. They couldn't help it any more than I could help staying away, keeping distance between me and those painful days.

I felt ready. I could leave Mrs. Tiffany now, although there was a time I couldn't have. She cared for me when Monty disappeared into a war zone, never to return. She insisted I set aside the hurt that had become part of my fiber, get an education and work. The years slid by and now I was ready to return.

Mrs. Tiffany was ready for me to go when I received Alice's call. She wanted to move to Florida and join her sister in a retirement community. Mrs. T was looking for a man, hopefully a rich widower. We hugged, and then she pushed me out the door. "Go home, child," she said. "Make peace and write to me about it."

I never did, choosing instead to imagine her a happy bride at age ninety living under palm trees. Deep down I recognized I'd never made peace within myself.

Didier was glad I returned. As he waited to die, he trusted the ranch to me and his care to Alice. It took seven months for him to wither away. I stayed on for the next nineteen years, working the ranch and living on land where I was grounded.

Sheesh. I thumped the side of my head. Quit thinking about death and dying. Past and gone. You're only going to see your sister.

I grabbed my purse and keys. A night frost crunched underfoot. Time to plant the maple tree on the west side and a row of American elms on the north.

Maybe Lem could make time to help next week. I hated to ask him. It'd probably seem like I was encouraging him to spend time at my place. He'd been giving me signals that he'd like to come calling more, maybe to share something besides work. I didn't feel anything for him, even though I was now able to look past the outward appearance and see his good heart.

A suitor was the last thing I wanted. Monty still lay at the core of my heart. Hope for a miraculous return had ebbed year after year until it finally receded to a place where I could find joy in sun rises again. No one else could still my loneliness. The first time he drew me into the shelter of his arms was like nothing I'd ever known, his touch cradling, like holding a shy child. We lay entwined as a different need budded and bloomed between us. I still felt the warmth of my cheek as it nestled against the safety of his chest. That's why I wanted a maple with strong branches spreading shade over my house. It would be my Monty tree.

Who else could I ask to help with the planting? Alice wouldn't. She was done with me now that I was finally on my way to Great Falls. I didn't know what she expected from this trip, but I was sure a miracle wasn't on the agenda.

I scanned the horizon. Yes, the wild dog sat there, off in the distance to the south. First time he'd been near the road. We hadn't faced off again but I'd caught sight of him more often. A wary friendship was budding. I waved goodbye to him. He would probably have to have a name soon. Couldn't just keep calling him *He*. He loped away when I started the pickup.

The two-and-a-half hour trip to Mrs. Henley's house dragged by until I turned onto Highway 223. Who could possibly stay in a bad mood driving through the vast brown grasslands and harvested fields? All spoke of fertile soil, feeding endless numbers of bovines and humans. I loved how the blue sky met the earthy land, how the wind fussed with it, how the seasons repeated.

I was turning onto Highway 87 at Fort Benton before I realized the miles had slipped away. Only forty more miles. The relaxed mood of the drive ended, replaced by dread. Which of Odette's moods would I have to deal with?

I entered Great Falls from the north, crossed the Missouri on the Fifteenth Street Bridge, turned onto Eighth Avenue North and drove about a mile to Mrs. Henley's ranch-style house tucked to the back of a large city lot. Why they had built almost on the alley made no sense, but then who asked me? I built the way I wanted, and why was I even thinking of it? To place my disconcerted feelings on something other than the expected clash of wills? Of course.

Odette had entered Mrs. Henley's group home for people who needed a secure place at Lydia's urging. If anyone needed watching over, Odette did. She had been diagnosed as schizophrenic; a tormented soul who was unable to cope with her past. She agreed to live there only because Lydia suffered from crippling arthritis and could barely care for herself. For once Odette wasn't selfish and went without a scene.

I parked on the street and unlatched the wrought-iron gate and walked up the pathway.

Then I saw her.

Odette watched from a garden bench hidden beneath the swaying tendrils of a weeping willow. She wore a woolen cape and gloves, both the same violet as our eyes. She looked radiant in her fiftieth year. White streaks at the temples of her raven curls gentled any wrinkles. Her petite shoulders were thrust back, chin tipped up. It could have been *Maman* watching me walk toward her.

Then I noticed something very rare. She smiled as though she was glad to see me, the expression fetching and shy.

My return smile came easily. I was glad to see her.

"Come sit by me," she said. "I know you didn't want to come. Thank you for always doing what is right."

She could have knocked me over with a piece of straw. "I'm glad to see you." I smiled again. "Surprising thing is that I mean it."

Odette laughed. She sounded merry, light, and at ease. "I've been the thorn in your side for as long as I can remember." Her voice echoed *Maman*'s.

I searched her eyes. They were clear of the confusion I so often saw. I sat beside her. Each of us kept to our own space. We had lost any kind of touching years ago. We were silent, each thinking of what to say.

She broke free with, "I wanted to see you today because it is Sunday, not because it is Halloween."

"I thought maybe it was something about Didier taking us from the uncles at the end of October."

Odette blinked. "I hadn't thought of that. I was simply trying to avoid the therapist. She isn't here on Sundays."

"I wasn't looking forward to speaking to one. But there have been lots of Sundays. Why now?"

"I wanted to give you time to work on your house."

Who was this considerate Odette? "You approve of my project?"

"You have to take me to this new house so I can live in peace. I cannot continue dredging up our past to entertain nosy so-called doctors." A hint of the old Odette came through.

Now that she had brought it out into the open, how did I feel about sharing my house? She watched me like a cat staring at a hole in a wall. She licked her lips, actually looking hungry.

"I've built a room for you," I said. "Was going to put a brass name plate above the door to shut Alice up."

Odette clapped her hands together once – a small sound muffled by her gloves. "Okay then, we need to clear up some things before we can live together." Her voice turned eager, almost joyful.

This was not the Odette I knew. What had happened?

As if she read my mind, she said, softly, "The new therapist changed my medication and I am so much steadier. It has changed my thinking."

Was this the miracle I'd waited for?

Odette fumbled inside her cape and withdrew an envelope. "What is written in this letter will hurt. But after you read it you will forgive Didier, me, and yourself."

I scratched my ear. She wanted me to forgive? "I know you think I'm hard but I've learned to be that way from the hardest, most unforgiving person I know."

"Me?"

"I was thinking of our father but you're a close second."

Her violet eyes held mine before she cleared her throat. "I wrote to *Maman*'s sister in France. Several cousins wrote back to say Aunt Remy had passed away. I've been writing back and forth with them for a few months."

Speechless, I finally blurted, "Whatever made you write?"

"Alice gave me the address and said I should."

Alice? Now what? "Has she been bugging you, too?"

Head bent, Odette played with her gloved fingers. She was gathering words. Never before had she been careful of what she said to me. Mostly she accused or said hateful things. The last time we had any kind of a talk was decades ago when I took her to Lydia's. After that, she just shunned me when I came to check on her.

"I wouldn't call it bugging," Odette finally said. "But Alice feels guilty. Seems she knows things we weren't told."

"I knew it!" In my glee at being right, I didn't question what the something was. Odette's sudden frown dampened my smugness, and I asked in complete seriousness, "What have you found out?"

"Our cousins cleared up a lot of questions. Did you ever write to them and not tell me?"

This totally baffled me. "I never wrote. Couldn't see the need."

Odette sighed. "Could you love half of me? The *Maman* half?"

My breath caught. The edge of a prairie prism was about to shatter, and I had no control over it. "You weren't Didier's?" My question was a shocked whisper.

True sadness softened Odette's eyes and mouth. It was the first time I'd seen it in her. "He was my father. Not yours. We are sisters only through *Maman*."

I reeled. "I'm a Platt."

Papa and *Maman*'s harbored secrets gushed forth from my sister. "A German wine merchant lured *Maman* into bed. He left her pregnant. *Grand-Papa* bargained with Didier to marry our mother. You're a bastard."

I couldn't get around the meaning of her words. "Didier did that with Alice, not *Maman*."

Odette shook her head in barely perceptible moves. They spoke louder than if she yelled at me. "He married *Maman* for the same reason." Her tone was devoid of any pleasure. She hated what she told me, but I denied what she said.

"No. He loved *Maman*."

"He loved Alice too. You know that."

Was Odette punishing me? Saying untruths just to hurt? "I'm a Platt," I repeated. The central part of me severed, the part that knew how to live, to work, to be. I was a French Platt. I didn't know how to be a German. Was that why I was taller and big boned? My mind slipped a notch to understanding.

No wonder. No wonder. The feeling of being different had a source.

Odette reached out and took my hand. The touching made me tighten, then, I relaxed. We sat hand-in-hand like normal sisters as she continued, "When I learned this I was as outraged as you are. But it makes perfect sense. That's why he sent us away. He couldn't live with the thought of *Maman*'s unfaithfulness."

"I don't believe it. The cousins are lying."

"For what reason? *Papa* worked in *Grand-Papa's* vineyard for eight years. He watched *Maman* grow into a beauty. Remember how he always called her his beautiful bride?"

Anger flowed into my veins. "Did this wine merchant rape *Maman*?"

Odette gasped. "Oh no-no. The cousins described her as a free spirit who lived life with a passion. She fell easily into and out of love. Our mother loved men. It's probably shocking to you but I don't think she was wrong to have lovers. Her life was a darn sight more exciting than either yours or mine."

"Didier must have known."

"The cousins claim Didier moved her to the prairies to have her all to himself. They thought it all very romantic until they read in *Maman*'s letters about the loneliness."

"Letters from France always made her happy," I said. "But she became depressed when one didn't come. They should've written more."

Odette bowed her head. "I can't remember that."

"You were only three, such a tiny girl." I felt again her small sobbing body against me on the train.

Odette looked at me. She was trying to be clear. Help me to understand. "From what they wrote, I don't believe *Maman*'s family understood our father's obsession with the land and her."

"Maybe I'm glad that he finally had two sons of his own with Alice."

"Are you so sure that they're his?"

Suddenly I felt like I was being lectured by my sister. "That's ridiculous. Of course, Junior and Steven are his."

Odette's nose flared. She took a quick breath. "Don't get mad at me. I don't care whose sons they are."

"Why would you even think that?"

"They don't look anything like *Papa*."

They didn't, but they worked the ranch like Platts. "Odette, that's crazy."

"Maybe and maybe not. But we're talking about Didier sending us away. Not Alice and her flings."

"Alice didn't have flings."

Odette's eyes clouded. "Whatever you say."

I didn't want her slipping away. "I'm sorry. I don't mean to argue. I'm just trying to understand."

She sighed. "We can't seem to stop spatting, but I do want you to understand that every time Didier looked at you, he saw *Bébé* Larry."

I sucked in air, trying to dislodge the feeling of suffocation.

Odette squeezed my hand. "Don't you see? What *Maman* did before they were married didn't concern our father, but afterward was different."

I reeled from the shock.

Her voice droned on. "You can't take blame unto yourself anymore. He sent us away not because of *Maman*'s dying but because he couldn't get past her betrayal of his marriage bed. *Maman* was the one who was really to blame. She entered into a marriage of convenience and couldn't find happiness within it. Worse yet, she couldn't control her heart, not even for you and me. She broke Didier's heart worse than hers broke in the prairies." Odette inhaled a jagged breath, then pointed at me. "We were tarred with their sin. I'm sorry I blamed you."

I sat there like a fool. It was as if the kaleidoscope of our life had turned and the edges no longer matched. Bright colors burst behind my closed eyelids. Colors of violet, green and brown. The colors of the lilacs: green in bud, brilliant violet in bloom, dried brown in wilt. Contentment existed somewhere past those colors. I needed time to find it. Didier might not be my father but I was his daughter. I obsessed to build a house in the same way as he did the ranch. How could I let go?

Suddenly a thought surfaced. Alice had been afraid to tell about my real father. Why? My mind wormed around, discarded one thought for another, then another.

"What are you thinking?" Odette asked. The demand in her tone differed from the usual accusing demands. She really wanted to know what I was pondering.

"Maybe Alice was afraid to tell me the truth, but I can't figure out why."

Odette looked at me as if she couldn't believe I didn't know. It was an expression I'd seen since she was a child. She believed she lived in a realm of wisdom that I never reached.

She shrugged her shoulders and said simply, "You would've left the ranch before she finished explaining and she needed you to work the place."

"That conniving witch!" Alice had played me and I fell for it. In the quiet moments after my outburst, I sorted out my anger. Odette sat still beside me. It felt foreign but good to have a common bond with her as we tried to figure out the most complicated woman who ever lived on the flat lands.

Odette spoke first. "Therapists have probed around in my brain enough for me to recognize when another brain is screwed. Alice is scared. She used up your life in hard work and loneliness. She's afraid to admit it. It's guilt pure and simple."

That made sense. "After I decided to leave she figured I should know, but couldn't bring herself to tell me what she's done. Confession is supposed to be good for the soul but this isn't going to do Alice any good. She will have to face me and explain."

"What will that change?" Odette loosened her grip on my hand and released it. "You didn't start the fire. I did."

What was she saying? "How could you possibly know that? You were just a tiny girl."

"I remembered through hypnosis. I saw myself peeking into the pot of dumplings. It tipped a little. That Sadie Chicken was so fat that her grease splattered onto the flames. They flared up and the curtains caught fire. I ran away, probably hoping that *Papa* would blame our mother. She was all he ever loved, her and that piece of dried out prairie we call home."

I gaped at her. She couldn't believe that. "You were too small to reach that high."

"I stood on a chair and had the long-handled spoon. It spilled." Her words sounded so accepting. She didn't mind the truth even if it lay at her feet.

I was appalled. "It was an accident." I wanted to reach for her, instead I sat like an unfeeling dope. What an awful memory for her to live with. I searched her eyes for signs of confusion. "You must be hallucinating again."

"I'm taking my meds. Why can't you, just for once, believe me? I loved our mother and it's my fault she's dead. I took her away from *Papa*." Odette stood too quickly and swayed, the cloak wrapped around her slender body: so thin, so frail, so like *Maman*. "This is a shock you need to come to terms with. Come for me when you do."

Odette had opened up to me for the first time ever, until now she had withdrawn into a realm of insanity. But she wasn't the only one to hide. I withdrew to the land of my father. After he died, I felt safe working his land. I didn't have to form relationships. I communed with the elements and the prairie. And that had been enough until this last spring. It wasn't a house that I wanted, but someone to love.

Odette also desired a kinship, one dependent on family ties. I had promised her long ago that we would find a house. We had one now. She was halfway across the yard before I called, "You have to paint the insides of the kitchen cupboards."

She turned toward me. "May we have Alice for Sunday dinner?"

I groaned, but nodded.

No matter what, Platts take care of Platts.

~~~~~~

The prairie labored in the throes of late spring, bursting with the need to bloom and paint the land. The solitude I sought was filled with bees droning, birds calling, sage brush rustling, and rabbits sprinting away. How could anyone be lonely in a place so busy?

I wandered the land, the wild dog beside me or running ahead. Beau never trailed behind. A year to the day had sped by since I drove the corner stake into the ground, and now the pictures were hung, rugs scattered on hardwood floors, trees planted, garden spot tilled, and root cellar dug.

Beau turned and perked his ears. Behind us Alice waved. Odette had invited her and Fran to dinner, a small party of sorts to celebrate the anniversary of my project. We would crack a bottle of Dom Perigon and toast each other. We had completed more than the house.

Alice drew closer. She was actually dressed for a walk on the prairie. Denims, suede jacket, and knee-high boots. She knew I'd be out on the grasslands. I had been waiting for this, our talk; the one that had simmered throughout the winter while she was in Denver with Hyatt.

"Dog got a name yet?"

"Beau. He's my fella."

Alice had the good sense not to reach out to pet him. "Odette, told me to go see her place whatever that means."

We ambled across the pasture to Sage Creek and followed upstream until we came to a newly planted maple tree. An open-wall gazebo sat between it and the creek bank. I had built the small eight-sided summerhouse from tongue and groove pine. The triangles of the shiplap roof joined at the peak under a tall spire. Odette had me hang a bright yellow windsock from it. Today was one of the rare days it hung limp.

We didn't enter even though it was screened against horse flies. Alice sat down on the bank, and I leaned against the railing careful not to step on the tender creeper vines I was training to climb the sides. Beau sat on the toe of my boot.

"Odette's spot is nice," she said.

"She needed a place to call her own. She needs goals. A walk to her place by the creek seems to satisfy as one."

"She seems better."

"She is on her lucid days. On the days her mind slips, I protect her. It isn't a burden."

"Too bad her new meds make her so drowsy." Alice hugged her knees. "By the way, I cleaned out the drawer. Dumped the booze and pills in the river. Some fish are gonna have a party."

My lips turned up in a half-smile. "Those pills were just insurance in case you couldn't stand the empty house one more night."

"Didier gone, the boys married. It was hard after you left, but not hard enough to end it all."

"Easier now?"

"Hyatt wants me to move to Denver so I can bug them, but I'm not going to. This is where I belong. However, frequent trips are planned."

"Are you going to walk on the streets Jesus walked like Aunt Elaine?"

Alice's laugh was something to hear, deep and loud. "I haven't thought of that in years. Your aunt was completely nuts that day we found poor Tyson dead in his chair." She sat quiet for a long moment. "You and I have buried a lot of people."

Sage Creek flowed like sand slowly shifting from a clenched fist. I reached down, picked up a pebble, and chucked it into the water to make some ripples. "You've come to grips with living alone?" I hoped it was so. Alice was a pain, but one that I'd grown accustomed to.

"I'm not."

I gaped. "You devil. Why didn't you tell me?"

"You don't need to know everything. But I found an old codger in Denver and I'm gonna stuff him between my sheets. We're eloping to Vegas, then flying to Paris. He has a big family, plenty of people for me to boss around."

"I'm happy for you."

Alice patted the ground beside her. "Come sit."

I sat down on the soil. She crunched over, pulled two cigars from her jacket pocket. "Uncle Lanny would want us to smoke one in honor of peace between us."

I bit off the end, smelled it deeply and clenched in my lips. I struck the match Alice handed me. I let the smoke roll on my tongue and then exhaled.

Alice did, too. She studied the charring end of the cigar. "You're giving Odette a calm life beside a creek running through a prairie."

"A spot of lush green. *Maman* would be happy."

Alice took one more drag. "Oh piss and vinegar. I'd rather fight with you." She pitched the cigar into the creek, jumped up and stomped away toward my house.

"You wanna argue?" I tossed my cigar into the water and hustled after her. Beau *dang* near tripped me. We untangled and he ran ahead.

I yelled after Alice, "How dare you just up and get married? What is your family going to say?"

She walked faster.

I broke into a run and passed her by, Beau beside me. "Last one to the table washes dishes."

We both ran, and neither had enough air left to argue.

The End

About the Author

 Marie Martin lives in a fertile valley at the base of the Rocky Mountains. She enjoys a quiet life where laughter comes easy, love easier. Marie and her four siblings were raised on ten acres of clump grass and bull pine trees. They roamed nearby creeks, woods, and the cemetery. All places for good fun. Her father worked in a sawmill, and her mother was a librarian; an upbringing that fostered love for people and books. In her blog, *Shady Nook*, you may read stories of her exceptional childhood growing up in a rich, rural area filled with unique people and a magnanimous landscape known as the Big Sky County.

Marie is the mother of four grown children and shares her life with a side-kick cocker spaniel by the name of Katie Lou. Links to her two blogs are available at www.mariefmartin.com